BLOOD AND SILVER

A GUNN BROTHERS' THRILLER

James Hilton

Ukiyoto Publishing

All global publishing rights are held by

Ukiyoto Publishing

Published in 2020

Content Copyright © **James Hilton**
ISBN 9789357873703

All rights reserved.
No part of this publication may be reproduced, transmitted, or stored in a retrieval system, in any form by any means, electronic, mechanical, photocopying, recording or otherwise, without the prior permission of the publisher.

The moral rights of the author have been asserted.

This is a work of fiction. Names, characters, businesses, places, events, locales, and incidents are either the products of the author's imagination or used in a fictitious manner. Any resemblance to actual persons, living or dead, or actual events is purely coincidental.

This book is sold subject to the condition that it shall not by way of trade or otherwise, be lent, resold, hired out or otherwise circulated, without the publisher's prior consent, in any form of binding or cover other than that in which it is published.

For Wendy

CONTENTS

Chapter 1 1
Chapter 2 5
Chapter 3 12
Chapter 4 17
Chapter 5 21
Chapter 6 25
Chapter 7 33
Chapter 8 39
Chapter 9 45
Chapter 10 49
Chapter 11 53
Chapter 12 58
Chapter 13 64
Chapter 14 69
Chapter 15 75
Chapter 16 80
Chapter 17 87
Chapter 18 92
Chapter 19 98
Chapter 20 104
Chapter 21 108
Chapter 22 113
Chapter 23 117
Chapter 24 121

Chapter 25	125
Chapter 26	130
Chapter 27	134
Chapter 28	139
Chapter 29	143
Chapter 30	147
Chapter 31	153
Chapter 32	160
Chapter 33	165
Chapter 34	170
Chapter 35	176
Chapter 36	180
Chapter 37	185
Chapter 38	189
Chapter 39	193
Chapter 40	197
Chapter 41	202
Chapter 42	206
Chapter 43	210
Chapter 44	215
Chapter 45	220
Chapter 46	225
Chapter 47	232
Chapter 48	237
Chapter 49	241
Chapter 50	246

Chapter 51	249
Chapter 52	253
Chapter 53	257
Chapter 54	262
Chapter 55	265
Chapter 56	272
Chapter 57	276
Chapter 58	281
Chapter 59	285
Chapter 60	289
Chapter 61	294
Chapter 62	299
Chapter 63	306
Chapter 64	312
Chapter 65	317
Chapter 66	323
Chapter 67	328
Chapter 68	333
Chapter 69	340
Chapter 70	347
Chapter 71	352
Chapter 72	356
Chapter 73	360
Chapter 74	365
Chapter 75	368
Chapter 76	372

Chapter 77	377
Chapter 78	381
Chapter 79	386
Chapter 80	391
Chapter 81	394
Chapter 82	399
Chapter 83	402
Chapter 84	405
Chapter 85	409
Chapter 86	412
Chapter 87	416
Chapter 88	420
Chapter 89	424
Chapter 90	427
Chapter 91	431
Chapter 92	435
Chapter 93	440
Chapter 94	443
Chapter 95	446
Chapter 96	450
Chapter 97	454
Chapter 98	458
Chapter 99	462
Chapter 100	466
Chapter 101	469
Chapter 102	473

Chapter 103	476
Chapter 104	480
Chapter 105	484
Chapter 106	489
Chapter 107	493
Chapter 108	496
Chapter 109	500
Chapter 110	503
Chapter 111	508
Chapter 112	512
Chapter 113	517
Chapter 114	521
Chapter 115	525
Chapter 116	529
Chapter 117	534
Chapter 118	538
Chapter 119	542
Chapter 120	547
Chapter 121	552
Chapter 122	558
Chapter 123	564
About the Author	*567*

Chapter 1

As Danny Gunn regained consciousness, sour acid rose, burning the back of his throat. With no option of vomiting, it out, he swallowed the bitter fluid. Liquid spilt through his nose. A sickening heat scoured his nasal passage with each desperate breath. The thick duct tape that held his mouth closed felt like the same tape that secured both his arms and legs to the metal chair. Blood trickled from a recent laceration at the corner of his left eye. A layer of grimy sweat coated his skin, the smell sour but hardly noticeable against the heady fumes in the room. Glancing down, he remembered he was naked.

The barrels that surrounded him filled him with dismay, the pain from countless aching bruises slipping away in comparison. The contents of any one of the fifty-gallon drums, if ignited, were more than enough to kill him. He could see at least ten barrels. A low rumbling sent a constant vibration through the steel panels of the floor and walls. Rounded rivets, layers of flaking paint and exposed patches of rust decorated the steel walls in abstract patterns. A single wire enclosed bulb silently flickered overhead. Danny tried pulling against the tape on his limbs to little effect. Tensing every muscle in his body, he then attempted to stand up. The pressure behind his eyes was almost unbearable as he strained. A gnawing pain spread across his ribs; they had worked him over pretty damn well. Succeeding in lifting his hips only an inch or so from the seat, he flopped back in place. The chair felt welded to the floor. The men that had secured him had done a thorough job. The tape covered his forearms from his elbows to the back of his hands, leaving only his dirt-encrusted fingers free. He felt sure his lower legs had received the same level of attention.

At the opposite side of the room, a simple yet ominous mechanism had been rigged to one of the fuel barrels. A fist-sized block of what looked at first glance to be putty sat at the centre of a clear plastic tub. Danny felt confident that this putty was not the kind used to secure window panes. Fixed to the side of the explosive block was a basic model cell phone, its display screen unlit. Danny forced himself to breath, his racing heart pounding inside his chest. He had made a serious error in underestimating the men that had done this to him.

As he looked around the room, he realised that his feet were wet. The cold steel plate of the floor too was covered in a viscous layer of what he presumed to be gasoline or its maritime equivalent. The smell of the fuel did little to ease the cold spider of dread that traced a path down his spine.

A single door faced him. A spine work of pitted metal divided the door into six equal sections. A rusted metal lever formed a handle; locked he was sure.

For the first time in his life, Danny felt completely helpless.

Where the hell was Clay?

Knowing that simply straining against his taped bonds would do little but bring further fatigue, Danny instead began to concentrate only on his right arm; first tensing the muscles of his forearm and pulling against the tape, then relaxing and pushing the opposite direction. He began to count his exertions. At first, he could feel little in way of results, his skin pulling back and forth over his muscles, then after his twenty-seventh motion, he felt the edge of the tape pull away from the skin of his arm. A gap of a quarter-inch or so now showed between the duct tape and the crease of his elbow. Sweat trickled down his face, stinging his eyes. A shake of his head sent a spattering of sweat and semi-congealed blood onto his thighs.

'I will not die in the hold of a rust bucket ship,' thought Danny. He started to work at the tape again.

After another ten minutes of arduous repetition he could roll his lower arm in a circle, the gap between skin and tape slowly widening. The grim smile beneath the tape on Danny Gunn's face evaporated as the cell phone illuminated. A second later the lyrics *'Boom, shake, shake, shake the room,'* filled the air.

Danny winced as he waited for the explosion.

Seconds ticked by.

No explosion came. No: *'tick, tick, tick, tick, boom.'*

Was this some elaborate ruse, designed to scare him? No, that wasn't how this crew operated.

The ringtone sounded again. *'Boom, shake, shake, shake the room.'*

A groan escaped Danny's throat.

A digital display next to the cell phone sprang to life, its numerals glowing a demonic red.

A countdown had begun.

'Tick, tick, tick, tick, BOOM …'

Sixty seconds….

Fifty-nine.

Fifty-eight.

Fifty-seven.

Fifty-six.

Chapter 2

Three days earlier

Clay Gunn stood sombre and quiet. The funeral service had been held graveside. He had never met Chrissie Haims, knowing her only through the saddened words of his younger brother. Both he and Danny still respectfully wore the yarmulke provided by the family synagogue. The Rabbi, a surprisingly athletic-looking young man, had delivered the service, first cutting a length of black ribbon to symbolise the breaking away from the family. Clay had no grasp of Hebrew that the square-jawed Rabbi spoke but his solemn intonation transcended language. Clay had no personal connection to Chrissie other than that she had been a friend of Danny's, *no*, a lot more than friends. The service seemed to be drawing to a close. Chrissie's parents were helped back to a waiting funeral car.

Danny too stood in silence. The look in his eye was one Clay was all too familiar with; a cold yet burning promise of retribution. Reaching out, Clay placed a hand on Danny's shoulder. He then took a step back. The closer family and friends of Chrissie moved like automatons, the grief on their faces forming tormented masks, no one in the crowd knew who Clay or Danny were. They received a few polite smiles and nods, the kind that are exchanged at funerals everywhere. The cloying Miami heat caused the suit Clay wore to cling to his skin. He slowly shifted from foot to foot. His hand crept to his left pectoral; the sutured muscle still stiff and sore. Clay clenched his teeth. Getting shot by a crossbow was no fun. A dark memento of their recent trip to Mexico. At least he was still able to feel pain. He hoped that the dead indeed felt no pain and Chrissie Haims was truly at rest.

Danny cleared his throat and Clay looked up to see an older man walking purposefully towards them. The brothers had stood well back from the graveside service. The immediate family, of which there were few, had sat on simple folding wooden chairs. A larger group stood behind them.

Clay nodded at the man as he approached.

'Hi there. Were you friends of Christine?'

Danny lifted his chin. 'I was. I only knew her for a little while, but I liked her, a lot.'

'Christine was my niece. I'm Gabriel Falk. Christine's mother, Sarah, is my younger sister.'

Clay towered over Gabriel. 'Clay Gunn. This is my brother Danny.'

Gabriel's bushy eyebrows moved like a

sluggish caterpillar as he eyed the brothers. His dark suit was immaculate and looked newly tailored. His olive skin was blemish-free despite his apparent age. Wisps of black hair decorated the sides of his head. Gabriel too wore the yarmulke. He shook hands with the brothers in turn. His grip was firm.

'Brothers?'

The corner of Clay's mouth twitched into a small smile. 'We're twins. Only our mother can tell us apart.'

Gabriel laughed a hiccup. 'Brothers eh? Never would have pegged that.'

'We get that a lot,' said Clay. 'We're not twins by the way.'

'I figured that for myself, thank you.' Gabriel alternated his gaze between the brothers. 'How did you know Christine?'

Danny rubbed the back of his hand across his face. 'Chrissie and I were friends. I met her a little while ago at the gym she worked in.'

'Friends or *friends*?' asked Gabriel. His voice carried no disapproving tone.

Clay watched as more of the family left the graveside. It was the first Jewish funeral he had attended. Chrissie's family and friends carried themselves with a quiet dignity that he respected.

'A little more than friends, but I'd only just met her. Chrissie was a lovely lady. I was in her company for less than three weeks though.' Danny nodded at Clay. 'We had to leave for a job.'

Gabriel again looked at both brothers, in turn, his head cocked to one side. 'What kind of job? You don't look like insurance salesmen.'

'No. We're not in insurance,' said Danny.

'More like demolition,' added Clay.

'And have the scars to prove it,' said Gabriel. 'You serve in the military?'

Clay gave a curt nod. 'We both did. Opposite sides of the Atlantic though.'

'Nu?'

Danny recounted the potted family explanation. 'Clay and I are brothers but we grew up apart. Our parents split and I lived with my mother in Scotland. Clay followed dad to Texas.'

Gabriel smiled. 'Family, what ya gonna do, huh?'

Danny continued. 'Clay joined the Rangers and I served as a green jacket in the British army.'

'Green jacket? Is that like a green beret?'

'No, the Royal Green Jackets are shock troops, skirmishers but top-class soldiers, riflemen,' said Danny.

Nodding, Gabriel reached out and tapped Clay on the upper arm. 'One of my oldest friends was a Ranger too. He was a trainer out of Fort Benning. You been there?'

'Yeah, I've been through the grinder,' said Clay.

'What about you Gabriel, you serve?' asked Danny.

Gabriel turned and gave a slow wave to several couples who had now moved away from the graveside. They headed for a row of parked cars. He spoke a few words to a white-haired man who ambled past on a cane before turning back to the brothers. 'Yes, I served. I spent seven years in Israel.'

'IDF?' asked Danny.

'Yes.' The old man seemed to straighten a little more.

'I trained with some of your guys a while back. I studied Israeli martial arts for a little while,' said Danny.

Gabriel gave a knowing smile. 'Krav Maga, right? It's all over the place now. Back in my day, it was just for the soldiers.'

'I liked it, very practical.'

'Oy, it certainly gets the job done.'

Clay nodded respectfully as the last of the family members passed by. The three men watched as they climbed into waiting cars. When Gabriel again turned back to the brothers a very different expression passed over his features. 'My niece was beautiful and some evil bastard took her from us. I feel partly responsible. I helped her find the house in Coral Gables. The man that owns it is a friend of a friend. Maybe if she had stayed with her family, she would still be with us. I'm an old man and I know I'm too old to pick up the knife, but I would kill the man who did this if it took my dying breath.'

Danny stepped closer to Gabriel. 'I only got back to Miami two days ago, but I know the cops want to speak to me. My prints and DNA will be all over Chrissie's house. I'm going to the police station tomorrow morning.'

'So that they can eliminate you from the suspect list?'

'Aye, exactly. My alibi is cast iron, but I'll still be on their list. While I'm there I'll see if I can find out any information, see what they know so far. Then Clay and I will do a little digging of our own.'

Nodding, Gabriel fished around in his pocket and produced a small notebook. The stub of a pencil was pushed into the spiral binding at the top of the pad. Gabriel removed the pencil then touched the point to the tip of his tongue. 'Here, this is my home number and my cell number. You need anything, you call. Day or night. Do you live in Miami or do you need a place to stay?'

Danny took the paper from Gabriel and carefully folded it into his wallet. 'We don't live here but we're okay for digs, we're staying at the Sunset Inn near the airport.'

'This *beheima* that took little Christine needs to pay. No long court case, maybe just a trip out to the glades and a bullet in the back of the head.'

Danny lowered his head, his teeth clenched. 'Watch this space Gabriel, watch this space.'

Clay kept his face stoic as a nipping pain tugged at his injured chest.

Chapter 3

'Was it all puppies and rainbows?' asked Clay.

'If by puppies and rainbows you mean a cop big enough to play the incredible hulk and the worst coffee known to man, then yes.' Danny wasted no time moving back to the rental Clay had parked one block over from the police station. The sun was threatening to crack the sidewalk and it wasn't even midday yet. Miami City Police Department occupied a modern building, the white exterior walls and tinted glass lending a sleek and contemporary look. The interior had been deliciously cool, even the interview room. The popular Bayside Marketplace was located only a few blocks east, but where Bayside welcomed sun-kissed tourists and smiling shopaholics, the police station routinely dealt with the opposite end of society.

Less than twenty-four hours had passed since he had stood at Chrissie's graveside, but Danny had known there was no point in delaying his interview. The two homicide detectives, Anderson and Brockovich, assigned to the case had been courteous to the point of tiresome but had conducted the interview methodically.

'They had already checked out my alibi but I'll give them their due, they certainly are thorough. They knew the flight number back from Mexico to Texas that we took, and also had printed confirmation that I boarded the plane. They even had a picture of me at Austin airport coming back through immigration.'

Clay pressed the key fob and the lights on the rental blinked twice. The Dodge Nitro listed slightly to one side as Clay climbed into the driver's seat.

'I can do the honours if your shoulder is still hurting,' said Danny as he too entered the vehicle.

'Nah, I'll manage.' Clay rolled his shoulder as if to illustrate his capability.

Danny gave a wan smile. 'I can drive over here just fine you know, got a licence and everything.'

'I'll drive.' Clay gave Danny the flat eye then added, 'Just think of it as a big brother thing.'

'Uh-huh,' said Danny. He knew that regardless of Clay's protestations he was still in a fair amount of pain. Less than two weeks earlier he had been speared by a crossbow bolt, the cost of bringing home a busload of abducted tourists from Mexico. Celine Chavez, the daughter of his live-in housekeeper had been among them. Getting her back had not been achieved without a heavy toll.

'Did they tell you anything about Chrissie?' asked Clay.

'Very little that I didn't already know. They confirmed that she was strangled. Her body was found in her sitting room.' The muscles in Danny's jaw bunched before he continued. 'She hadn't been raped. The house had been ransacked to the point of big holes knocked in the walls, and the floors had been lifted with crowbars.'

'Did they venture an opinion as to who or why?'

'They were a bit tight-lipped on that score. Cops being cops, I guess.'

Clay started the engine and nosed the Dodge into the traffic. 'I can't believe that the house got ripped up and none of the neighbours heard anything.'

'The cops did say that there was a truck parked outside her house on the day she was murdered. The sign on the side of the truck was Jones and Drake Renovations. The business doesn't exist. No surprise that it turned out to be bogus. The signs were probably one of those magnetic jobs that you can buy on the internet for peanuts. With a truck parked outside, no one would give the noise a second thought.'

Clay stopped at a red light near Henry Reeves park. 'Did they get the plates on the truck?'

'Only a partial number from one of Chrissie's neighbours, but I'm sure that'll turn out to be a false plate anyway.'

'Any suspects?' asked Clay.

'The cops weren't in the mood for sharing but they did mention a big guy that was seen by the truck. White. Big, like your size big, with a bald head.'

'Do they need to see you again?'

'No. I've been eliminated from their list,' answered Danny.

'And how do you feel about leaving it to the cops to find Chrissie's killer?'

Danny huffed air through his nose. 'The cops seemed as sharp as they come, but are thinking this was a home invasion gone wrong.'

'And?'

'Just a few weeks ago Chrissie attracted a stalker, a real piece of work, and then house breakers invade, kill her, and wreck her house. No. No one could attract that much bad luck. There's something else going on here.'

Clay slowed and waved a delivery truck out from a side street. The truck driver gave him a thumbs-up in return. 'Is the stalker still in commission? Could he have anything to do with it?'

Danny shook his head in the negative. 'No, I put him away for good. The only thing he's doing is lining the stomach of an alligator or two.'

'One of the bad ones?' asked Clay.

'Aye, he broke into Chrissie's house with a full murder kit. Even if he hadn't have killed her, what he had planned would have ruined her life.'

'So, no great loss to society then?'

'None whatsoever.'

'Did the cops know about the stalker?'

'No, I don't think so. This guy was operating under the radar. I only spotted him because I was using the gym every day where Chrissie worked. He would show up minutes after Chrissie arrived. He passed the front windows of the gym like clockwork, pretending not to be watching. It was his eyes that gave him away, like a cat watching a canary.'

'Okay, so that rules him out, so what else do we know?'

'Not a lot at this point. I think we need to take a proper look inside Chrissie's house, that might give us something to go on.'

'Now?' asked Clay.

'Aye. Now.'

Chapter 4

Danny felt something coil in his stomach as he moved slowly from room to room. The last time he had been in these rooms they had been pristine, every item arranged neatly, each with a place of its own. Chrissie had been beyond diligent in keeping her home neat and presentable. The smell of sandalwood was now a faint memory, one which Chrissie had used in a diffuser. The wooden floors in each room were now ripped up, a gaping hole in the centre. The wooden planking, stacked in untidy heaps like fuel for a bonfire, added to the disarray. Holes big enough to lean inside had been knocked into the pale-yellow walls, chunks of ruined plasterboard left strewn on the floor below. Picture frames now lay face down on the floor, shards of broken glass like fallen tears beside them. In one corner, a three-drawer unit had been overturned. A small wooden stand lay like a miniature tree felled and forgotten, the assortment of costume jewellery it once held now scattered across the floor.

As he moved fully into the master bedroom Danny felt a pang of anguish. He had spent several nights here with Chrissie. She had been a gentle, loving young woman. A woman that Danny had felt the first and definite stirrings of love for. The first woman that Danny could have thought of as *'the one'*. Now she was gone; stolen from him, her life cut short by an unwarranted act of evil. Danny lowered his head as he sat on the edge of the bed, a bed he had willingly shared. *Her soft hands on him…*

'I'll check out the kitchen,' said Clay.

Fighting an unaccustomed lump in his throat, Danny's gaze fell upon a framed picture on the wall. The picture dangled at an angle, upset from its moorings. Chrissie stared back at him; her smile immortalised. To the left of her stood one of the Hollywood elite. Chrissie had told him that actors often used the BodyTrick Gym while filming in and around Miami. The actor known to millions as Rocky was giving a double thumbs up in the picture. But for Danny, it was Chrissie's smile that made the picture. She could have been standing next to the rear end of a horse and the picture would still have been great.

'I love you, Chrissie Haims.' Danny's voice was little more than a whisper. Was this one of life's big chances he had been cruelly denied? He silently feared so. He had felt a burgeoning closeness with Chrissie that he never had before. He swallowed with difficulty. If he had only returned to Miami immediately after getting back from Mexico, she might still be alive. 'I'm sorry I never told you that I loved you, but I will find who did this to you and make him pay.'

The cops had already been through the house, collecting what scant evidence there was to be found and taking numerous crime scene photographs, so Danny wasn't overly concerned about moving any items or handling them. The damage had already been done. He forced himself up from the bed. Pulling his phone from his pocket he activated the torch function. Dropping first to his knees, he then flattened himself on the floor. Leaning into the hole that now desecrated her bedroom, Danny slowly played the light into space below. A crawlspace of about two feet showed a hard packed earthen floor. Several scuffs in the dirt surrounded what was a footprint. Another partial print was cut into the dirt about eighteen inches to the right. Danny pictured the man dropping first through the hole, then squatting onto all fours to peer around under the house.

Without a second thought, Danny dropped into the gap and lowered himself into the assumed position. The air below the floorboards was musty, dust motes turning lazily like cigar smoke in the narrow cone of light. Danny held the phone in his extended right arm. He inched away from the hole in the floor, frowning as he noted more imprints in the dirt. Not full imprints, these were shallow indentations like half-moons. Whoever had done this had crawled all over the length and breadth of the cavity. Danny too worked his way around the space in an expanding spiral. Several more holes, each one leading from a different room in the house allowed a shaft of pale light into the musty space. In a far corner, a hole had been dug, the dirt piled like a small anthill to one side. An exposed water pipe lay at the bottom of the excavation.

Turning in a slow circle, Danny began to crawl back to the opening. He grunted as the back of his head met one of the thick wooden joists. Ducking lower, the light played out at a new angle.

Danny stared as he took in the details. Turning in a circle once more, he noted the same marks spread around the crawlspace. Straight lines an inch or so wide, one every twelve inches or so apart.

Careful not to knock his head again, Danny climbed back into the bedroom. Bending at the knee, he brushed the loose dirt from his trousers back into the hole. He turned off the phone's light and passed a hand over the back of his head. His hand came away unstained with blood. The side of his mouth twitched as he gave begrudging thanks for that small mercy.

Chapter 5

Clay heard a muttered curse. Even though muted, he recognised the distinct Scottish tone. He raised an eyebrow but left his brother be. From Danny's sombre demeanour, he knew it best to give him space.

As Clay moved around the kitchen he stopped to peer behind the large refrigerator. A square of floor tile had been ripped up. The refrigerator stood at an angle, pulled from its original position. Grasping the humming appliance in an open bear hug, he tested its weight. The sound of bottles clinking together came from the inside as he tilted the fridge onto one corner. A sharp pain tugged at the joint of his left shoulder. 'Son of a bitch, you're heavy.'

'Who're you talking to?'

Clay turned to see his brother now framed in the kitchen doorway. 'I don't think one man did this on his own. This refrigerator would have taken a lot of effort to get it out from its place between the kitchen units.'

'I know, I was thinking the same thing. The floorboards have been prised up in each room. At least six boards, wide. That takes time and effort. Someone was under the house, crawled around every inch under there. As he went, he was testing the ground with a knife.'

'What do you mean testing?'

Danny mimicked a series of short stabbing motions. 'On his hands and knees, stabbing the dirt like he was checking for landmines.'

'Did you find anything down there?'

'There was a hole dug in the dirt. I reckon he tapped a water pipe with his knife and dug down to investigate.'

Clay leaned his bulk against the fridge. 'So at least two men were in the house. Ripping up floors and cutting holes into the walls. It's pretty damn obvious they were looking for something, but what? Could Chrissie have had a big stash of jewellery or something in the house.'

Danny gave a small shrug. 'I don't think so, but the truth is I couldn't say yes or no. I never heard her talk about money, other than to go Dutch on our dinner at a restaurant or buy cinema tickets. She was just a regular working-class girl; I don't think she was sitting on a pot of gold. She was kinda careful when she went grocery shopping. We drove miles over to the Publix supermarket because it was cheaper than the others.'

'So maybe it wasn't money or jewellery they

were looking for.'

'What else then? What the hell could be worth ripping a house apart and strangling a woman to death for?'

Clay moved to his brother and rested a hand on his shoulder. He recognised the look in Danny's eyes all too well. It was a look he had seen many times before.

'And you're sure this couldn't be tied to the stalker you made disappear? Maybe his family looking for payback?'

Danny paced as if looking for something to lash out against, his knuckles white. 'That doesn't feel right. The arsehole I capped was a sexual predator, he's gone, this is something else.'

'Do you want to look around anymore?'

'No. I think I'm done in here,' said Danny. 'I want to have a look in the backyard and around the outside of the house, just to be thorough.'

'I can give you a minute to yourself if you want.' Clay knew how much Danny was hurting despite his lack of admission.

'No, I'm fine. The best thing I can do for Chrissie is to find whoever did this and pour battery acid down their throats.'

'We need to be careful with this little brother,

the cops will be all over it as well. We need to stay under the radar as much as possible.'

Danny gave a curt nod. 'Aye, same shit different day.'

'So, what's our next move? Talk to the neighbours?'

'No, the cops did that already. I want to talk to the people that don't speak to cops. See what they've heard on the jungle drums.'

Clay rolled his shoulders. 'There might be quite a lot of those bad boys to choose from.'

'Good. Are you ready to shake some trees? See what falls out?'

'Ready to pull the damn tree up by its roots,' said Clay. His left pectoral muscle twitched as if in a warning. Clay ignored the nipping pain in his shoulder. It wasn't the worst injury he'd suffered by far. The surgeon in Mexico had performed a top-notch operation and had removed the offending crossbow bolt without any resulting nerve damage to his arm. 'I'll wait in the car while you scout the yard.'

'Then we go and have a wee chit chat with the natives.'

Chapter 6

Hector Alvarez took a long pull on the can of grape soda as he watched the two men climb from the Dodge Nitro. He didn't recognise them and he knew most of the local faces if only to nod at. He had lived in the same house from childhood and now at age twenty-seven had a regular day job and could turn his hand readily to move off the books business transactions. The two men didn't look like cops. They looked like something else. His hand slipped under his open shirt, fingers brushing the grip of his Glock 42. The smaller of the two men held up a hand in greeting.

'Hey, how ya doing?' said the smaller guy. His accent sounded funny, Irish maybe?

Alvarez lifted his chin but remained silent. He scanned the two white men for weapons as they approached. Nothing visible, but that meant little, they could have anything tucked under their loose shirts as he did. The two men looked an odd pair, the smaller of the two men stood about three inches taller than Alvarez, maybe five-nine. The man's hair was cut short and he moved with athletic grace. He looked like a boxer, lean and toned, the shape of his eyebrows and cheekbones too looked like a boxer's. The man behind him looked more like a pro-wrestler. There were more scars on his face than on a junkyard dog. Alvarez secured his grip on his pistol.

The smaller man again raised his hand in greeting as he drew closer. Alvarez pushed himself away from the hood of his car. His finger slipped lightly onto the trigger. He pulled the Glock an inch, loosening it from his waistband. If shit went down the big guy would get two in the face first.

'Hey man, how ya doin'?' The smaller man stopped three feet away. He kept both hands in sight. The monster behind him crossed his arms and offered something that may have been a smile.

'Whassup? asked Alvarez. He looked past the two men and allowed himself a secret smile. Paco was now in his front yard across the street, talking into his cell phone. Paco never missed anything.

'I wonder if you can help me?' The smaller man took a step closer.

'With what?' Alvarez, pulled his Glock another inch.

'Did you hear what happened to that woman the other day, Chrissie Haims, just a couple of streets over?'

'Yeah, I heard. What about it? You two cops?' asked Alvarez.

'Nah man, we're not cops. You think they'd let someone on the force that looked like him?' The smaller man hooked a thumb at the big dude with the scars. The big man didn't seem impressed by the barb. 'No, Chrissie was a close friend of mine. What happened to her doesn't sit well with me at all.'

Alvarez bristled. 'You think I had something to do with that shit?'

'No, not at all.' The smaller man held up both palms. 'Let's start over. My name's Danny Gunn, Chrissie and I were seeing each other. This is my brother Clay.'

'Brothers? I wouldn't have pegged that.'

Clay pursed his lips. 'We get that a lot.'

'You speak differently, too.'

'Scottish,' said Danny.

'Texan,' said Clay.

'Scottish, right, that's it.'

Danny slowly lowered his hands. 'I was wondering if you saw anything unusual on the day it happened? The cops told me there was a truck parked outside her house on the day she was murdered. You hear anything about that?'

'Nah, I was down in Key West when it happened.' Alvarez relaxed his grip on his pistol. 'You talked to the cops?'

'They talked to me. They had me down as a person of interest. I had to go in to clear my name. You know how it is.'

Alvarez looked into Danny's eyes. He recognised a sadness there, barely concealed by the icy façade. 'You and Chrissie were tight?'

'We were,' said Danny. 'The cops told me that a big guy was spotted outside of her house. A big guy about the size of Clay. White. Baldhead. That ring any bells?'

Alvarez shook his head. 'Man, you just described half of Miami.'

'I know you don't know me from Adam, but if you know anybody else that might have seen or heard something, I'd appreciate it. I'd make it worth your while.'

Alvarez took his hand from his pistol and leaned back against his car. 'So, you're not cops.'

'No, definitely not cops.'

'And what will you do if you catch up with the hijo de puta that did this?'

A new expression passed over Danny's face like drifting smoke. 'What would you do if some arsehole strangled your woman and left her house looking like Nagasaki?'

'I would find him and cut out his heart.'

Danny gave a single nod.

Looking past the brothers, Alvarez tilted his head. Within seconds Paco was at his side. 'This is Paco. He knows everything on the coconut telegraph.'

Danny repeated his query.

Alvarez gave a nod of encouragement to his younger friend. There was little that passed Paco by. The kid struggled with reading and writing but was a math genius and could recite every state in America, their capital cities and population numbers.

'I passed Chrissie's house that day. There was a truck parked outside for a minimum of two and a half hours.' Paco talked with a slight lisp. He held up his hands in front of his face as if framing a camera shot. 'A panel truck, white, signs on the doors. Jones and Drake renovations. The signs were in red block lettering. A big guy was standing in her front yard. Big. He had ink on his face. Left side. Tribal; like Tyson.'

Paco lapsed into silence for a moment. 'You know the signs on the van are bogus right?'

'I figured they might be,' said Danny. 'Why do you think they were?'

'Jones and Drake's ...you're kidding right?'

'You've lost me,' said Danny.

Paco shook his head. 'Indiana Jones and Nathan Drake. They could have added Lara Croft in just for good measure.'

'Aye, I see it now.'

'Some dickwad probably thinks that they're being clever.'

'Not clever enough it seems, my wee friend.'

'*Wee friend*,' repeated Paco, flashing an amused smile.

'Did you know Chrissie?' asked Danny. 'How do you know it was her house?'

Paco's gaze twitched back to Danny. 'I didn't know her. But I knew who she was. She worked down at the BodyTrick. My older brother does weights down there. She was hot.'

Alvarez rested his arm across Paco's shoulders. 'You remember anything else about the big guy?'

'He was sweating. Big, like Hulk big. I could draw you the tattoo.'

Alvarez gave Paco a gentle nudge. 'You go do that. Be quick.'

Paco scooted back to his house on the opposite side of the street.

'Thanks, man. I appreciate this,' said Danny.

'Promise me one thing. If you catch up with this asshole, come back and tell me what you did to him.'

'Deal,' said Danny.

Alvarez leaned back against the hood of his car; hands flat on the warm metal. 'Why did you stop to talk to me?'

'You've got the look.'

Alvarez raised his eyebrows.

'I can tell you've got street smarts, but you look like you're a stand-up guy as well. I bet you wouldn't let any shit slide on your doorstep.'

'You've got to look out for your own,' said Alvarez. He felt himself warming to Danny, his Scottish accent was cool.

'Chrissie was my own.'

Alvarez reciprocated the slow nod. 'I get that, man.'

Moments later Paco was back with a detailed drawing. The picture showed a wide face, bald head with a thick sloping brow. The left side of the man's face was decorated with a curving tattoo. The uppermost curves resembled talons of some mythical beast, each one ending in a wicked point. The lower portion of the ink work looked more like a dragon's tail, the forked tip level with his ear lobe.

Danny held out his hand. Paco handed over the drawing. 'This is what you remember?'

Paco nodded. Alvarez pointed to the picture. 'If Paco draws it, it's as good as a photograph.'

'Thank you, both of you,' said Danny. 'Any idea who this might be?'

Paco shrugged. 'Sorry man.'

Alvarez looked both ways up and down the street before he answered. 'He looks like one of those Aryan assholes, the Southern Unification. A few of those dickheads have ink on their faces. Looks like he would fit right in.'

Clay took a step closer. 'Southern Unification? Never heard of them.'

Alvarez clicked his tongue. 'A real bunch of cock knockers. They hang out over in Kendall, South Miami. They've got some kind of Klan clubhouse down there. I hear it used to be a church. It's painted bright red now, something to do with their willingness to die for white rights.'

Danny talked through clenched teeth. 'Well now, I might just go and introduce myself to the whiter than white boys.'

'Chrissie was Jewish, right?' asked Alvarez.

'She was.'

'Then she qualified to get on their shit list.'

Chapter 7

'So, what's the plan?'

Danny glanced at Clay. 'As I said back there, I'm going to introduce myself to the glee club. Let me get Kendall up on the sat-nav.'

Clay steered the Dodge south, driving slow and careful through the narrow tree-lined streets. An older lady wearing orange spandex jogged along the sidewalk, a Pomeranian on a leash trotting beside her at the same pace. The woman's skin was the colour of tan leather. Clay gently braked as she crossed the street twenty feet ahead. She raised a hand to Clay. Her smile showed the whitest teeth he had ever seen.

'Got it,' said Danny. 'Follow this road until we get to South Dixie Highway. That leads us straight to Kendall. We'll find the church when we get there.'

'These boys, the Aryans, they're not all yahoos. Some of them are hardcore, not something we can underestimate,' said Clay.

'Didn't plan on it.'

'And what were you thinking in the way of a plan?'

Danny stared at the drawing. A brief image of

the man with his hands around Chrissie's throat caused a flash of red behind his eyes. 'I figure we swing by the church, pick up one of the faithful, then maybe head out into the glades and ask him some pressing questions.'

'Hardly the most detailed plan you ever came up with, but I guess it'll do to get us going.' Clay had adopted his normal driving position, his bulk leaning over the steering wheel as if he was about to rip it free from the rest of the vehicle. 'You carrying?'

'All I've got is my knife.' Danny produced his Fox ERT. The hilt of the folder was matt black and fitted his hand as if custom made. He tucked the blade back into a pocket.

'You still using that toothpick?'

Danny tapped his pocket. 'The Fox has never let me down so far. If it's not broke…'

'I've got nothing with me.'

'Pull into there, that strip mall.' Danny pointed to a row of squat storefronts, each with the same plate glass window and brown roof. 'Third store along.'

Clay parked the Dodge in front of a sporting goods store. They climbed from the car in unison. The main windows, one each side of the entrance, displayed a variety of sports shirts, each with its distinctive logo. Miami Heat, Marlins, Dolphins, and several UFC jerseys were draped over posed mannequins.

Danny held open the door. 'Age before beauty.'

Clay shook his head but entered the store anyway. 'Who's Nathan Drake?'

'He's a video game character. Uncharted.'

Clay gave a slow nod but said nothing more.

Danny had become a fan of the big sports stores over the last few years. Many of them carried high quality outdoors ranges, items designed for climbers, ramblers, and shooters. Much of the kit was equal or better quality than army issue but available for a fraction of the price. Danny picked up a baseball cap and a pouch containing a green paracord. A glance at the packaging told that it contained a hundred feet of 550 cord. After taking another look at the range of goods on offer he walked back to the entrance and pulled a shopping cart from its parking bay. Deeper in the store he could see Clay talking to one of the store staff. Danny slowly made his way through the shop adding various items as he passed each display. Minutes later he bumped the cart into the back of Clay's legs.

Clay turned with a non-amused look on his face. 'Oh, it's you. Watch it, doofus.'

Danny thumbed his nose in mock annoyance. 'What you got so far?'

'Just a couple of old favourites. Bernice is in the back getting a few things from the stockroom.'

Danny looked at the items sitting on the countertop. 'Big-assed Bowie knife, there's a surprise.'

'I'm a Texan, it's the law.'

'There are more practical knives to be had than a machete sized pig sticker you know,' said Danny. It was a conversation they had enacted on more than one prior occasion.

'I know, but a decent Bowie always gets the job done. I've picked up a multi-tool for domestics, but when it comes down to putting the fear of God into some asshole there's nothing quite like twelve inches of American steel.'

Bernice emerged from a door behind the counter cradling three baseball bats. Danny's smile was returned. Bernice looked to be no more than seventeen or eighteen years old. The yellow polo shirt she wore contrasted nicely with her ebony skin. Her hair was coloured a deep red. 'These were the three longest bats I could find. All three bats are solid, those two are Birch, perfect for Sunday league games. That one's Aluminium. All three are of top quality. We can even have your name engraved into the wooden ones if you'd like.'

Danny watched Clay heft the first bat. Stepping back from the counter he took a couple of slow swings through the air.

'Feel good in the hand, right?' asked Bernice.

'Uh-huh,' said Clay as he tried the second wooden bat. 'I'll take this one.'

'You want to try the Aluminium?'

'Nah, wood is good,' said Clay.

Danny picked up the third bat. The metallic bat felt cool in his grip. As he rolled the bat around in a loose arc he smiled. The Mizuno bat was perfectly balanced. The grip felt good too, wrapped tightly with an anti-slip material. 'I'll take this one too.'

'You need any balls?' asked Bernice.

'No, I think we're good,' said Danny.

Bernice leaned forward, resting her elbows on the countertop. 'It's just that if you get stopped by the police and you have a bat in your car, it looks better for you if you have a few balls there too. You can say it's for batting practice.'

'What makes you think they aren't?' asked Danny.

'You know how many bats I sell every week? I sell them to housewives, truck drivers and to guys that wouldn't know how to find the batting plate if I drew them a map. I have one behind my front door at home and one in my car. And then there's that.' Bernice nodded at the Bowie. 'No offence, but you don't look like you coach little league on weekends.'

    Danny nodded. 'We'll take a pack of balls.'

Chapter 8

It had taken less than half an hour to find the building. Clay had driven in a winding snake pattern, moving east to west for a couple of miles then reversing the direction every two blocks south. Danny spotted the red building on their fifth zig-zag sweep. The church was a drab affair, the only indication of its religious background being a modest steeple. An empty rectangular gap displayed the remnants of where a bell, once probably hung. The roof of the building looked to be made from overlapped tin sheets painted a dull grey. The exterior walls were a deep red. A wooden sign, embossed with gold lettering left no ambiguity as to who now operated the building. Clay parked a half-block away. The streets were residential with neat houses spaced like oversized Lego blocks as far as the eye could see.

'Doesn't look like the clubhouse is open,' said Clay.

Danny drummed his fingers on the aluminium bat. 'Just because the front door isn't wide open doesn't mean there isn't someone inside.'

'True,' said Clay. 'I could just walk in and put the hurt on the first cross-burner I see. People tend to want to share when I have them in a chokehold.'

'Hold that thought.' Danny pointed to two men that were stopped at the front door of the old church building. Both men were white. One man had close-cropped black hair, the other was shaven bald. The back of the bald man's head sported an intricate tattoo. 'Looks like kindergarten is open.'

Clay opened his door and began to haul his bulk out of the Dodge. The heat washed into the car like a thermal wave.

'Hang on a minute,' said Danny. A third man had emerged from inside the building and after a brief conversation began to walk away from the converted church. The first two men went inside, closing the door behind them. 'Plan B. That's our fish. I'll head him off. You follow in case he gets into a car. Stay well back. If we lose him, we'll come back here and try it your way.'

Clay slipped back into the Dodge and started the engine. Danny started briskly after the man on foot. The man wore dark jeans, combat boots and a light blue shirt with short sleeves. The shirt was tucked tight into his jeans. The corners of Danny's mouth twitched in an inverted smile. It would be hard to carry a concealed pistol under a shirt that was tucked into his belt. As Danny drew closer, he could see a series of tattoos on the man's forearms. His hair, once brown, now mostly grey was cut close to his bullet-shaped skull.

The street held only four other pedestrians,

all looked to be kids in their mid-teens. They were on the opposite side of the street, three girls and one boy. All four were staring at their phones as they walked. Danny quickened his pace as his target stopped alongside a Ford Transit van. Plain black lettering on the back doors read; *Harriet's Produce and Groceries. Freshness delivered to your front door.* A graphic showing an old-style shopping basket with a baguette and a wine bottle poking from the top finished the sign.

A brief blinking of lights and one of the two rear doors swung open. The man was leaning inside as Danny stepped off the curb.

'Hey man, can you help a brother out?' asked Danny, his voice slipping into a perfect parody of Clay's Texan accent.

The man turned, straightening, and looking Danny up and down. 'Help how?'

'I was up in Fort Lauderdale the other week and got talking to a big guy, can't remember his name, John maybe?' Danny leaned in a little closer to the man. In the hollow of his throat, Danny could now see a pair of letters inked in a runic style. *88.* Danny had seen this before, on the opposite side of the Atlantic. He had tangled with a Skinhead gang in England many years earlier. They had cornered Danny in a warehouse on the outskirts of London. A dozen men armed with police issue ASP batons. That had been a rough night. Several of the London gang had worn the same symbol. 88. It represented the eighth letter in the English alphabet. Double H: *Heil Hitler*. It was just one of the many coded tattoos worn by gangs the world over.

'John?'

'Yeah man, a really big guy, like six-six or something. Had this great ink on the side of his face. He was there with a blonde chick, a real looker. We got talking and he said if I was ever down in Miami proper, I should give him a call. I was looking to get some ink done and he said he would take me to the best parlour in the state, the same guy that had done his.'

'I don't know, no John,' replied the man. 'I'm kinda busy. I gotta go.'

'His chick drew me a picture. Love his ink work.' Danny pulled Paco's sketch from his back pocket and unfolded it. The skinhead took the picture from Danny.

The man's gaze flicked from the picture to Danny a little too quickly. 'I don't recognise him.'

'You sure man? Take another look.'

The man shoved the drawing back at Danny. 'I don't know him.'

As the skinhead turned, he reached into the back of the van. Danny closed on him, his right-hand snaking between his legs. A sharp but strangled squeal rang out as Danny tightened his grip on the man's testicles. A hard yank brought the man onto his tiptoes. As the man pitched into the van, his hands outstretched to prevent his face slamming into the floor, Danny drove the tip of his left elbow deep into the nerve cluster between his shoulder blades. While the skinhead emitted another squeal, his feet were hoisted from the pavement and he was thrust bodily inside the vehicle. Danny retained the grip on his captured genitals as he followed inside the van. Reaching back with his free hand, Danny pulled the door closed behind him. The inside of the van smelled of onions.

Danny gave another pull on the skinhead's undercarriage, then pivoting, dropped his knee into the exact spot he had struck with his elbow. As he shuddered from the shock of the pinion hold, Danny pulled the man's wallet free from his back pocket. The skinhead mewled as Danny angled himself to hold the wallet open in the direction of the front windscreen.

'Well now Adolf, let's see what your real name is. Cedric Joseph Applewhite. I bet that just strikes terror into the hearts of the inferior races. Let me guess; the guys call you CJ?' Danny pulled the drivers' licence free then tossed the wallet to the floor. He then slipped the licence card into his back pocket.

'Who's the arsehole in the picture?' The picture was again thrust in front of his face. Applewhite gave out a protracted yowl as his spine compressed under Danny's knee.

'He's not one of us.'

'But you recognise him, don't you? I saw it in your eyes.'

'You better let me go. You don't know who you're messing…'

Danny slammed the side of his fist into Applewhite's face three times in as many seconds. The blade of Danny's Fox ERT then snapped open in front of Applewhite's face. He went rigid as the tip of the blade entered his flesh just below his jawline. 'You're going to tell me everything you know or you are never setting foot out of this van again. By the time they find you, you'll look like a gator got to you first.'

Chapter 9

Clay watched Danny grab the skinhead and hoist him into the back of the van. The door closed behind them. Moments later the Transit began slightly rocking on its suspension. With a half-smile, Clay looked both ways up and down the street. As far as he could tell no one was paying the van any heed. Reaching into the glovebox, he retrieved a Butterfinger candy bar. Three bites and it was gone. He was mid-action of reaching for a second bar when another man stepped from the old church into the sunlight. Clay studied him in the rearview. The skinhead wore wrap-around shades. Bending forward, Clay watched him cup his hands in front of his face. Cigarette break. Maybe the concerned constituents of the Southern Unification had a no smoking indoors rule? It looked to be the same bald guy that Danny had spotted, same elaborate inkwork on the back of his bald head. Clay flicked his attention from the skinhead to the parked van and back again. The man's cigarette briefly glowed, then a cloud of blue smoke filled the air around him. After taking several more drags on the cigarette, he flicked the stub unceremoniously into the street.

Clay took another quick look at the van. It

was now still. From his parked position Clay slipped the Dodge into drive. The skinhead from the old church was now walking towards the Transit. Had he expected the other man to return?

Watching his approach, Clay guided the Dodge on a parallel course and parked two car lengths from the rear of the van. Keeping his head turned away, Clay climbed from the vehicle and bent as if inspecting the front passenger tyre. Using his peripheral vision, he let the skinhead pass by, paying no overt attention. Clay could smell the cigarette smoke on the man as he stepped past, closing on the van. Clay moved like a shadow, a *Ranger* still; close enough to reach out and touch. The skinhead strolled to the front of the van, peering inside. Clay stepped to the rear doors as the skinhead turned and plucked his phone from his hip pocket. A second later a ringtone sounded from inside the van. The skinhead approached the back doors; the phone still pressed to his ear. Clay relaxed, aiming for centre mass. He knew one of the body's major weak points is the solar plexus; the diaphragm especially vulnerable to a blow on an upward trajectory. The man looked up a split second before Clay's fist slammed into the sweet spot, exploding the breath from his lungs. Taking half a step back, Clay timed his next action. The man's head bowed down as he folded around the pain in his torso, giving a clear view of the tattoo. A stylised combination of a swastika and a Celtic cross covered the back of the man's head. The ink was a dark blue not black. Clay slapped down hard onto the inkwork with both hands as his knee drove up from the pavement. The skinhead went down, his head bouncing from the rear fender.

Clay rolled his shoulders as he looked up and down the street. Satisfied nobody was paying him any attention he rapped on the van door.

'Ding dong, Avon calling.'

Moments later the door opened and Danny stared back at him through the gap.

'Asshole delivery, I need a signature.' The door swung open. Clay raised an eyebrow, 'Room for one more?'

Danny gave a curt nod. Grasping the barely conscious skinhead by the belt and the back of his neck, Clay hoisted him inside the Transit van. The man Danny had followed lay on his side. Plastic grocery bags twisted into ropes secured his hands and feet, arms bound behind his back. Another bag was tight around the lower half of his face, acting as a gag. The skin below his nose was painted red.

'I'll stay on watch,' said Clay. Danny offered no dispute. Moments after the van door closed Clay heard the interrogation begin. A brief curse, not Danny's voice. Clay gave a tight smile as he heard a familiar sound, a hand striking flesh. After walking back to the Dodge, Clay took a long look at the old church building. All was quiet. He climbed back into the vehicle. He reached for another Butterfinger. Using his mirrors, he continued to monitor the street. *Dinner and a show.*

Chapter 10

Danny discarded the red-stained tissue after wiping clean the knuckles of his right hand. The tissue dropped into the waste bin was lost among the remnants of old food wrappers and half-eaten tacos.

'You left those fools still breathing?'

'Aye,' grunted Danny. He looked down at his own grilled veggie tortilla and placed it on the table. The heat of the afternoon sun was only slightly lessened by the wide canopy that stretched from Rico's Tasty Tacos over the sidewalk. 'I know they're class-A cretins, but I think what they got was enough for them at least until they prove me wrong.'

'I'm sure someone will find them sooner or later,' said Clay.

Danny shrugged. 'They'll work their way out of their ties soon enough.'

'Did they tell you anything of worth?'

'The second guy, the one you dumped on me, was pretty senseless, but my guy swore that the man in the drawing wasn't one of their crew. What he did tell me was that he had seen the tattoo before. He didn't know his name but thought that he had seen him a couple of times, kind of a local tough guy, he thought he had something to do with a marina.'

'Which marina? There's about thirty of them that I know about in Miami alone.'

'He couldn't say, just that the guy was big and maybe worked at a marina or maybe worked on a boat.'

'Well, that narrows it down to about a quarter of the city,' said Clay.

'Aye, he should have just told me that in the first place and saved himself a beating.'

'Bullshit and bravado,' offered Clay. 'The SU boys don't look in short supply of either.'

'Hmmn.' Danny took a sip of soda. Drops of condensation trickled down the takeout cup-like slow-moving art. He moved a sliver of red pepper around the inside of his mouth. Despite the delicious spiciness, the food tasted like wet cardboard to his palate. A conjured image of Chrissie slunk into his mind like a sneak-thief, her body lying cold and alone on a mortician's table. He had not seen her body before the burial. The family did not have an open casket. His memories were all he had; fragile thoughts that slipped away from him like smoke. 'Going from marina to marina will take a lot of time.'

'It will.'

'And we may or may not strike lucky with someone that recognises him. I was thinking about Chrissie's house again.'

'Go on,' said Clay.

'The men that did this went to a lot of trouble to search her house and we both know that this doesn't seem like a random attack, it's way too focused. Chrissie told me she'd lived there for about three years when I first met her.'

'Okay.'

'I think we need to speak to her landlord to find out more about the house.'

Clay gave a nod. 'Sounds like a plan. Do you know who owns it?'

'No, but her uncle Gabriel said he did.' Danny removed a slip of paper from his wallet and typed the two sets of numbers, home, and cell into his phone contacts list. 'I'll call him and see if he can put us in touch with the owner.'

While Danny talked to Gabriel, he changed screen options on his phone, adding the supplied details into his contact list. Clay looked up between the three beef tacos he devoured in sequence.

Danny ended the call. 'Got it, a guy called Saul Rubnik. Got his address too.'

'Is it far?' asked Clay as he used the corner of

the last taco to scoop up a splodge of runaway guacamole. He wiped the corners of his mouth clean with a paper napkin. He scrunched the napkin into a ball and dropped the remains in the trash can.

'He lives in a big house in South Miami Heights. Gabriel said he spends most of his time on the greens. I'll call him first, save a pointless drive if he's out golfing or sozzled in the clubhouse.'

'Sounds like a plan,' said Clay. 'While you're doing that, I'll get another couple of tacos. You want anything?'

Danny shook his head in the negative and called Rubnik.

Chapter 11

Carl Anderson adjusted his service pistol as he slid his body from the cool interior of the unmarked car.

'You want to take the sunny side of the street?'

Anderson looked first both ways along the street, then back at his partner. There were several more cars parked than last time they had worked the doors. He plucked a notepad from inside his suit jacket. Flipping it open, he scanned the list of addresses that they still needed to canvass. Seven numbers remained without a tick beside them. 'I left my Ray-Bans at the precinct, I'll take the walk in the shade, besides you guys never seem to sweat, must be in your genes.'

Gina Brockovich raised a perfectly shaped eyebrow. 'Which genes are you referring to?'

Anderson shrugged.

'If you mean my Anglo-Saxon blood, I believe my ancestors came from Poland and the midlands of England, I don't think the sun shines over there more than a half-dozen times a year.'

'Let's go with the other ones then.'

'So, you think because my grandfather came from Hanoi that I'm somehow impervious to this?' Brockovich pointed a finger into the sky.

'I have to wring out my shirts at the end of watch, you always look as fresh as a daisy, so I've decided that it's down to your genes.'

Brockovich drummed her short but perfectly manicured nails on the roof of the car. 'You sure it's not down to the fact that the last time that you ate a green vegetable, Reagan was still in office? I've told you, you got to lay off that deep-fried chicken, eat some leafy greens, some fresh fruit.'

Anderson pulled a face.

'Just remember that when you drop face down in the street with a damned heart attack, that I told you so.'

'Duly noted and ignored, *mom*,' said Anderson. Despite his size, Anderson still moved with the grace and power of a linebacker. Carl had been a rising star some twenty years and fifty pounds earlier, trying out for several of the state teams. A dislocated hip had ended those dreams in one fateful game. The police force had been his second choice but ultimately the one that had served him best. He had tried out for the shirt and ties several times before making the grade but had settled into the life of a homicide detective as if it had meant to be.

Brockovich locked the car and slipped on her shades. The lenses of the glasses were the same raven black as her hair. 'Have it your way. You stay in the shade in case you begin to melt into a big ol' pool of grease.'

Anderson wiped his forehead with the back of his hand, a strand of dark blond hair bouncing at his touch. 'Buzz if you need me.'

Brockovich gave a perfunctory nod then moved to the opposite side of the road. Anderson watched her knock on the first door before he moved to the closest on his list. He rapped on the door. After waiting ten seconds; a reasonable response time he thought, he knocked again. The house remained silent. After checking the next house number in his pad, he headed for the address. A glance across the street showed Brockovich in conversation with an elderly couple. The two aged residents were shaking their heads in the negative. Anderson squinted despite being beneath one of the many hundreds of trees in Coral Gables. A dog was barking further down the street. Another glance at Brockovich, *all good*, then he moved to the next door. The door was fitted with an ornate knocker in brass. The metal was warm to his touch.

Clack-clack-clack. He began to count. He reached seven when the door opened. The man that stood in the doorway was dressed in pale denim jeans and an old-style cap sleeve T-shirt. His black hair was shot through with silver and slicked up into a neat quiff.

Anderson held out his badge as he introduced himself.

The ageing rocker offered a wan smile but opened the door wide. 'You wanna come inside? I've got coffee on the stove.'

The unmistakable aroma of coffee tempted him greatly. 'No, thank you just the same. I won't take up much of your time, mister…?'

'Collins, Jared Collins. My friends call me Corky.'

Carl Anderson added the name to the line below his address.

'You here because of what happened to Chrissie Haims?' asked Collins.

'We are. Were you at home on the seventeenth, Mister Collins?'

'*Corky*, Mister Collins is my father.'

'Corky.'

'Is that your partner over there?'

Anderson said yes without looking over his shoulder.

Corky smiled. 'Call her over, you can both have a coffee. I've got stuff to tell you.'

Anderson plucked his cell phone from his belt and tapped in the first three letters of his partners' surname. Seconds later he heard Brockovich answer.

'Seven doors up on the right.'

'I see you.'

'Come on up. We may have something.'

Anderson watched his partner finish her conversation on the doorstep then make her way towards him. 'This is Detective Brockovich.'

'Corky Collins. Come on in.'

The smell of the brew was even more promising as they stepped into the house.

Chapter 12

Clay stood more than a foot taller than Saul Rubnik. The landlord had agreed to meet them at Kellerman's Diner near Eureka Park. The diner was a corner building with a fully-chromed exterior, one of the few in south Miami.

'Gabriel told me you may call,' said Rubnik as he moved to a vacant booth.

Clay glanced at the service counter as Danny slipped into the booth next to Saul. Danny sat with his right leg slightly to the outside of the booth. Clay allowed himself the briefest of smiles at his younger sibling's poise. He knew what would follow. Danny's eyes flicked across the entire diner. Clay knew he would be checking for any perceived threats, potential trouble, defensive and exit points. It was a habit Clay carried too.

Saul Rubnik plucked a laminated menu from the wire rack on the wall above the table. 'The pastrami sandwich is really good here, comes with potato salad and a side of pickles.'

Clay inhaled the mixed aromas of the diner. Everything smelled good. A waitress hustled past with two plates, what looked like meatloaf, mashed potatoes and gravy and a huge burger and fries. After tending her table, the waitress returned. Her hair was tied back with a red polka dot ribbon. Maybe in her late fifties, she looked healthy and trim. Clay had heard a woman recently described on the news as *svelte*. That seemed to fit. Svelte. She smiled what looked to be a genuine smile, obviously recognising Rubnik.

'Hey sweet cheeks, if it's loving you're after...'

'Better, call Saul,' said the waitress.

'Guys, this is Barbara. The damn best server in all of Miami,' said Rubnik. The older man smiled, his eyes sparkling.

'Miami?' Barbara shrugged. 'Best in the whole damn state.'

Rubnik dropped his voice a tone deeper. 'Oh, my mistake.'

Barbara clicked her fingers, then pointed. 'Don't let it happen again or there'll be no more bagels and lox before you hit the fairways.'

'Oy vey, I can't get them at home these days. Everything is cholesterol this and calories that.' For a moment Saul looked like a berated schoolboy.

Clay watched Barbara's smile waver ever so slightly as she took in the scars on his face. It was a familiar reaction, one that he had encountered countless times.

'Y'all want coffee while you decide?'

'Yes please,' said Clay.

Barbara returned with three large mugs of steaming java. She pushed the plain white mug to Rubnik then looked at the Gunn brothers. 'Do you need cream or sugar?'

'No thanks. It's fine as it is,' said Danny. Clay looked at his brother, the dour frown that had taken up residence on his face. He knew that Chrissie's death had hit him hard. He also recognised the subtle change in his brother's eyes. He knew what was bubbling beneath the surface. The skinheads at the old church had tasted some of it.

'D'you want your regular, Saul?' asked Barbara. Saul said yes. 'Extra pickles with your sandwich?'

'Always,' said Saul.

Clay tapped the menu. 'I'll try the pastrami sandwich as well?'

'Extra pickles too?'

'Extra everything, if that's okay?' asked Clay.

'Sure, I can make that work,' said Barbara. 'And for you, honey?'

'Just the coffee thanks,' replied Danny.

Barbara smiled and moved to the counter. Another woman took her order, calling it through the kitchen.

Saul took a sip of his coffee after blowing on the dark liquid. 'It's a crying shame what happened to Chrissie.'

Clay too took a sip. The coffee was good and strong. 'We're looking into what happened to her. Danny thought you might be able to help us with that.'

'If I can,' said Saul with a despondent shrug. 'I only saw Chrissie a couple of times a year, if I was doing repairs around the house. I didn't know her so well. She seemed like she was a sweet girl though. Good to her parents too.'

Danny pushed his mug away. 'I wanted to ask about the house rather than Chrissie. I think maybe whoever did this was looking for something inside the house and Chrissie got caught in the crossfire.'

'The house? It's just a normal house. I can't see that the house could have been the target, although the *beheima* that did this certainly did enough damage. Every wall in the house had a hole knocked in it and the floor's all ripped up.'

Clay took another gulp of coffee. 'We saw.'

'You've been inside the house?' asked Rubnik.

'We have. I hope you don't mind,' said

Danny.

Saul waved a dismissive hand. 'Forget it. It's not a problem.'

'Did anyone else live in the house with Chrissie at any time? A boyfriend? A lodger?' asked Danny.

Saul pulled at the thinning hair just above his right ear. 'I don't think so. She was a quiet girl. I don't remember ever seeing anyone else in the house.'

Clay finished his coffee. 'What about previous tenants? Who had the house before Chrissie took it on?'

Saul took his cell phone from his pocket. It looked to be the latest model iPhone. 'Give me a minute. I've got all of my records saved in the cloud.'

Clay cocked his head to one side.

'What? You think because I'm in my golden years I shouldn't keep up with the latest tech?'

'The thought never crossed my mind,' said Clay.

'These things are great. I can access my accounts from anywhere in the world. Gone are the days of schlepping ledgers from the house to the office; not with these babies. It's the same with banking, no more standing in line waiting for the teller to leave you standing like a fart in the wind, while off they go for their lunch.'

Barbara returned with the two plates of food. Seconds later she refilled the coffee without being asked.

Chapter 13

Cedric Applewhite wriggled free from his makeshift bonds with a curse. He worked his mouth, scowling as he removed his gag. His face hurt like a sonofabitch. The taste of blood was strong in his mouth. He spat out a wad of red saliva. The smell in the van was sour, *fear and flatulence*. Applewhite lurched to his knees, wiping at his sweat dappled face. The man that lay next to him in the van was in a bad way. Both of his eyes had swollen, the skin darkened to a livid red. His nose was surely broken the way it sat angled across his face. 'Jesus-H-Christ, are you okay man?'

Applewhite, known to his friends as his attacker had correctly surmised as CJ, gently shook the other man. CJ pulled at his friend's bound wrists. 'Teasle? Teasle, man, you okay?'

Marlon Teasle stirred, groaning, but didn't seem to know which part of his anatomy to hold first.

'Come on man, we gotta get back to the clubhouse, let the others know what happened.'

Teasle uttered something unintelligible. The guy had gone to work on them both, seeming to get angrier with every punch thrown. He'd talked funny.

Not American…Irish maybe?

'You stay here. I'll pull the van around back to the clubhouse. Sanderson will be out for blood when he hears about this.' CJ rested a hand on Teasle's shoulder then climbed through the gap between the front seats. His balls ached something terrible. The van roared to life. He swung the vehicle into a tight U-turn. The horn of a passing Honda blared as CJ missed it by mere inches. 'Yeah, yeah. Stick it, buddy!'

Moments later he steered the van to the side of the repurposed church building. CJ scurried from the van into the old church, wiping the blood from his nose. His hand flicked to the nick under his jaw where that asshole had used a blade. Thankfully the wound was little more than a shaving cut. If the fucker had wanted to, he could have left him with a Cuban necktie. After fumbling with the door, CJ yanked it open. Flecks of red paint drifted down like autumn leaves.

Twenty minutes later, after first blurting the story to the three men inside, their chapter leader arrived. Syrus Sanderson said little as CJ recounted the incident once more, instead making sure that both Applewhite and Teasle were tended to. Bags of crushed ice were pressed to their faces, the blood wiped away. CJ looked back at Sanderson, a mix of emotions vying for prominence in his mind. He felt a sense of both relief and comfort as Sanderson held his face, cupped gently between both his hands.

'Rest assured this will not go unavenged. We will not rest until your transgressors lie bleeding at your feet. You shall be the one to place your boot on their necks, my brother.'

'I feel like an idiot for getting suckered. I…I,' said CJ.

'It can happen to anyone, my friend. You know our creed.'

CJ stared back at Sanderson, at the tiny inverted cross at the corner of his left eye. 'Any harm done to a member of the Unification will be paid back tenfold, unto death.'

'What else?' asked Sanderson.

'Every brother stands for every brother. Your blood is my blood, my blood is yours.'

CJ looked behind his leader, surprised at the collection of men now present. He had not noticed them arrive. Nearly twenty men stood in four neat rows. Every man present wore the same burning expression. CJ felt a surge of pride in his chest. His brothers were here. His brothers were ready. His brothers were armed.

'The bastard that cold-cocked me was big, like pro-wrestler big. I only saw his face for a second but it was all scarred up like he'd been in an accident.' Teasle sat propped against a wall, his legs spread out in a wide V. He had a glass of a dark amber liquid in his hand. CJ could smell the whisky despite the congealed blood in his nose.

'Fresh scars?' asked Sanderson.

Teasle shook his head. 'Nah, old ones, white lines all down the left side of his face. You wouldn't miss him in a crowd.'

'Okay. Let's see if Lyle can find anything on the CCTV,' said Sanderson.

CJ had been instrumental in getting cameras installed in the old bell tower and at each of the building's three doorways. He hoped they would now pay dividends. A glass of whisky was offered and accepted. The first slug of bourbon CJ downed was tainted with his blood. The second was good. The third was better. The ache in his balls was easing ever so slightly.

Lyle's voice called from a side room. 'You'll want to look at this.'

Sanderson and several of the other men crowded into the room that housed the video screen. CJ's glass was refilled once more.

Minutes later Sanderson and the others emerged from the room. Their leader held three colour prints. 'Got them.'

CJ looked at the pictures, frozen images from the CCTV system. One showed the wiry bastard that had clobbered him, his face turned in a three-quarter profile. The second showed a Dodge Nitro, its plate visible in the hi-res image. The third showed the scarred man. He was every bit mean looking as Teasle had described.

Sanderson drummed his fingers against the pictures. 'And you're sure the guy he was looking for wasn't one of ours?'

'Sure. If it's who I think it is, I've seen him around, but no, he's not a brother. The guy was so angry I reckon he would have beat me whatever I had told him.' CJ stared at the first picture. That wiry little bastard. It was a face he would relish kicking in.

'Okay,' said Sanderson, turning back to Lyle. 'Does your sister still work over at the DMV?'

'She does.'

'Get her to run that plate. The more we know about these two the better,' said Sanderson. 'Then we find them, nail them to a cross and watch them burn.'

CJ emptied his glass and gave a pained smile as it was again refilled.

Chapter 14

Danny looked down at the screen as Saul tapped his fingers on various icons. Wrinkles, deep enough to wedge pennies in, framed the corners of the older man's eyes. His hair was thinning and his skin on the back of his hands was mottled with dark blemishes, marks Danny had heard called liver spots.

'May I?'

Saul handed the phone to Danny. 'Just scroll down.'

Danny looked at the page on the screen, scrolled to the bottom then back to the top. A series of names, six in total. Chrissie was the most recent. 'These were all tenants in the house?'

Saul had made a start on his pastrami. He swallowed down a mouthful before answering. 'Yeah, and the figure on the right is the length of term in months.'

Danny scrolled again down the page; this time much slower.

Christine Haims - 39.

Desmond Marlowe - 6.

Philip Jackson - 13.

Erik Delacroix - 32.

Herb Kellerman - 12.

Vivian Liebowitz – 3.

Something tightened in his throat as he read Chrissie's name again. A beautiful young woman reduced to a statistic. A tenant in the house for thirty-nine months. Just over three years living as an independent adult. Danny took a deep breath. 'What do you remember about these other names?'

Saul wiped his fingers on a napkin then pointed at the second name. 'Desmond Marlowe was an actor. He was down here filming some sitcom or another. I watched him once, just one episode, heh, that was enough. He acted by shouting every second line. The guy was never at the house.'

'Philip Jackson?'

'Yeah, he was a muscleman, you know mister universe and all that posing stuff. Big as a house he was.'

'Anything else about him?'

Saul took another bite from his sandwich. 'No, not really. I think the guy across the street was jealous because he walked around with no shirt on in the front yard. I think the wife had eyes for the beefcake if you know what I mean.'

'Uh-huh. What about this next guy, Erik Delacroix?'

'Oh yeah, that guy was a piece of work. He was down here for quite a spell. He looked kinda like Jack Nicholson, you know with those crazy eyebrows.'

'When you say he was a piece of work?' Danny scanned the diner again. A big guy eased away from one of the stools at the counter. He was six-three and carried himself well. Big arms and thick wrists. His blond hair was pulled back into a woven plait. The big guy dead-eyed Danny as he passed. A flash of violence passed through Danny's mind. *Step out of his powerline. Stamp kick to the knee. Snap kick to the groin. Elbow to the face. Chokehold.* But the man was past him and leaving the diner. No threat. *Relax.* Danny turned his focus back to Rubnik.

'Delacroix was one of those older guys who still thought he was twenty. Old style surfer dude from California. Had rock 'n' roll hair, like Jagger or something. He and his buddies were always out somewhere on a boat and when they got back, they raised the roof. The neighbours called the cops more than once. One time, one of his buddies was picked up, naked as the day he was born, just strolling through Coral Gables like it was perfectly normal. Take it from me, no one wants to see a schlong bouncing around outside like a puppet on a string while they're cutting their lawns.'

'What was his deal?'

'His deal?'

'Aye, what did this Delacroix do for a living?' asked Danny as he glanced up from the screen.

Saul Rubnik speared a dill pickle with his fork and crunched off a bite. 'Not so sure to tell the truth. This is six years gone, remember.'

'You said he was always out on a boat. Did he work the sea for a living?'

Rubnik shrugged. 'Maybe, but I couldn't swear on it in a court of law. He looked like he might though. He was weathered like old leather, covered in tattoos. He always wore a headband, tied like Rambo.'

'That doesn't qualify him for much,' said Danny.

'I remember he looked like you wouldn't mess with him, a bit of a tough guy I think.'

'Aren't they all,' said Clay as he fed the last of the sandwich into his mouth.

'What about the others that lived there? Herb Kellerman and Vivian Leibowitz?' Danny asked the question but his mind slowly circled Delacroix like a bird of prey.

'Herb was a cousin to Larry Kellerman that set up this place. Both dead and gone now, nice guys. I miss them, they both used to play at the same golf club as I do.'

'And Leibowitz?' asked Danny.

'She was a short term let. She worked as a hotel manager at Miami airport. She was foreign, can't remember where from, Poland maybe?'

'Did you get a forwarding address when Delacroix moved on?'

Saul shook his head. 'No. He just up and left. I had to empty some of his gear from the house. I kept it in storage for a couple of months then gave it to GoodWill. He never collected his security deposit either.'

'You still got anything of his laying around?'

'No, as I said, I gave it all to charity.'

'Okay. If you think of anything else, I would appreciate a call,' said Danny. He passed the handset back to Rubnik. 'Could you send this list to my phone?'

'Done.' Saul glanced at his watch then back at the brothers. 'I gotta get going. I said I would drop off my grand-daughter at Bayside. She's meeting her latest Romeo at the Hard Rock Cafe.'

'Thanks again, Saul,' said Danny.

Saul reached for his wallet but Clay stopped him. 'It's on us.'

Saul raised his eyebrows playfully. 'If I'd only

known, I would have ordered a to-go dessert box too.'

Danny eased from the booth and let the older man out.

'I hope you find the animal that did that to Chrissie. No one deserves to go like that.' Saul looked like he was going to add more but then turned and headed for the exit. His hand was on the door handle when he looked back. He turned and walked back to the table. 'I just remembered; Delacroix had a framed picture on the wall. Took up most of the fire breast wall. It was him and another couple of guys in front of a boat. The Mariana Meg. You know like the Mariana Trench, the deepest part of the ocean. I'm not sure if it was his boat or not though.'

'I'll look into it,' said Danny. 'Thanks again, Saul.'

Rubnik gave a nod then left the diner.

Chapter 15

The engines of the four stolen motorbikes idled as their riders waited for the expected signal. The wooden fishing pier had once been a popular attraction for day-trippers and sea anglers alike. Today the pier was empty of both tourists and fishermen. The thick wooden planking was uneven and showed obvious decay in many places. Patches of lighter coloured wood dotted the weathered structure.

'Is Fish gonna keep us waiting all day? All he needs to do is hook the ramp over the end of the rails. It's not rocket science.'

Curtis Quantrill looked at his friend and nodded in agreement. Fish was dragging his ass today. 'I'm sure it's nothing to do with the litre of mezcal he drank last night.'

The pier stretched before them like a miniature runway. Wooden benches dotted every twenty yards divided the boardwalk into two equal sides. Quantrill revved his bike, feeding the engine. He was dressed in lightweight cotton. Black shorts and vest with pair of old and battered hi-tops on his feet. His phone, water and shockproof model warbled in his pocket. He answered it on the second ring. 'We good to go?'

'Yeah, man.'

'You got the drone camera rolling?' asked Quantrill.

'Going up now.'

'Okay Fish, comin' atcha.'

Quantrill pocketed the phone and added to the revs of his bike. The Kawasaki was nothing special. An old 250, stolen a few days earlier specifically for this event. He looked over again at his friends. Blaine looked like he was gearing up for the apocalypse. His old-style flying goggles and butchered neoprene bodysuit looked ridiculous, but hell, that was Blaine, over the top in everything he did.

Junk and Gato too revved their bikes, dark grey smoke billowing behind. A bright flash from the end of the pier sent all four men surging as a single unit. Quantrill hunched low as he accelerated to full speed, the wind whipping through his long brown hair. Gato's bike pressed to the front of the pack, engine roaring. Quantrill grinned despite Gato taking the lead. He was a wiry little shit! The wooden planking shuddered beneath eight wheels as the bikes tore towards the pier end.

Twenty seconds.

Blaine drew level with Quantrill and opened

his mouth wide, his tongue wagging like a dog. The tribal tattoos on the side of his head looked like a bird of prey speeding forward. Blaine too hunched low, his chest brushing the fuel tank.

Ten seconds.

The man on the far side of the group, Junk, hopped up so both feet were on the bike seat. Quantrill turned his focus to the front. The end of the pier seemed to race toward him. *Crap!* The makeshift ramp looked way too narrow. The wooden board was four feet wide at most. Junk began to howl, his yells adding to the madness. All four riders were now perched upon the seats, tricked and ready.

Quantrill experienced a moment of euphoric weightlessness as his Kawasaki powered up and over the makeshift ramp. The roar of his engine seemed to fill his senses as the four bikes soared off the end of the pier with mere inches of air between them. Fish was hanging off the side rail. With a roar of jubilation, Quantrill pushed hard against the bike with his feet. Gravity seemed to snatch the machine away as he stretched out his body like a diver. He was vaguely aware of the other men doing the same.

Whoomph!

Then he was underwater. The cold of the Atlantic Ocean hit him like a slap from an angry lover. The bikes were already gone, rapidly falling to the silt of the seafloor. The water around his face seemed filled with millions of air bubbles, rolling over his skin as he tumbled beneath the surface. The saltwater stung his eyes as he fought to right himself. A foot grazed his jaw as he turned in the water, his hair swirling across his face. *Swim towards the light.* Seconds later he broke the surface and taking a deep breath emitted a loud whoop of his own. Overhead, the drone controlled by Fish buzzed with an insistent hum. Quantrill showed a thumbs-up to the hovering camera.

'You guys are losers. I take the crown.' Junk was giving the bird to the three other men. 'I was at least three feet in front.'

Quantrill returned the middle finger but grinned anyway. 'Let's watch the cam footage before we go awarding you a backstage pass to Hooters.'

'No need man,' yelled Junk. 'You're looking at the sorcerer supreme, man. Numero uno. The big kahuna!'

'The dickless kahuna more like,' offered Gato.

The four men swam rapidly to shore. The police were seldom seen this far south of Miami but all knew that contact with the uniforms was to be avoided at all costs.

Fish was now waiting at the shoreline, drone in hand as they waded from the water. The bright orange shirt he wore was emblazoned with the acronym WROL. A skull with the message, 'better get prepping' sat under the acronym. He hooked a thumb at the minivan. 'Taxi for the asshole association of America.'

'Watch it, wheelman or I'll kick your ass *'without rule of law'.*' Quantrill playfully raised a fist to Fish. 'Come on you guys, playtime's over. We've got grown-up shit to do.'

Chapter 16

Clay sat opposite Danny. The waitress again refilled their coffee without being asked. Clay spooned the last of the pudding into his mouth. 'Peach cobbler; who knew?'

'Good?' asked Danny without looking up from the screen of his phone.

'Very.' Clay picked the menu from its wire holder. 'Damn it, they've got key lime pie here. I missed that.'

'So, get one,' said Danny.

Clay leaned back in his seat and patted his middle. 'Better not. I'm watching my figure.'

'Aye, right.' Danny shook his head. 'What are you watching it for, eruptions?'

'Can it, mister lean and mean. Some of us like to support the local economy by eating in local establishments.'

'Aye, but not all of them in one day.'

'Whatever…' Clay took a mint from his pocket and popped it into his mouth with a flourish. 'So? This Delacroix feller got your spider senses a-tinglin'?'

'He has indeed. I know it's slim, but the bald asshole with the tattoos may work the boats and now this guy. It may be nothing, but at least it's a thread to follow.'

'So, what's our next move?' asked Clay as he replaced the menu.

'I've Googled the boat Saul mentioned; the Mariana Meg. It's still in service, moored up in Fort Lauderdale. Looks to be used as a tourist fishing boat now.'

'I hear Fort Lauderdale is real pretty,' said Clay.

'Let's go and find out.'

Clay gave the menu another glance then raised his hand. Smiling, Barbara hustled over with the check. Clay paid and left a tip almost as big as the bill.

'You come on back anytime y' hear,' offered Barbara.

'It's a date,' replied Clay.

'That wouldn't upset me any either, rugged feller.'

Clay tipped a non-existent hat as Barbara gave him the same wink and a smile routine; she'd used on Saul earlier.

As the brothers stepped out into the street Clay noticed the shadows had grown longer. He looked skyward. 'The sun will be down in an hour or two. D'you still want to head on up to Lauderdale or wait for first light?'

'No time like the present. Besides, other people come out at night, exactly the kind of people we're looking for.'

'Fine by me,' said Clay. After two steps Clay paused, laying his hand on Danny's shoulder. 'They don't look like they're from the Miami tourist bureau.'

'Shite, it's the two detectives that interviewed me.'

'Well, let's not keep Miami's finest waiting,' said Clay as he appraised both cops. The guy was big and wide, like a grizzly bear in a department store suit. The woman that stood next to him was long and lean but looked small in comparison. Both cops wore shades. Clay wondered briefly if they were issued by the department; Agents Rayban and Foster Grant.

'Daniel Gunn, you remember us? Detective Anderson and my partner Detective Brockovich.'

'Aye, of course, I remember you. Have they sentenced that coffee machine to death yet?'

Anderson tilted his head to one side, the faintest hint of a smile, then it was gone. 'No, I suspect Mister Coffee will be around long after I hang up my shield.'

Clay loosely crossed his arms over his lower chest. He knew cops like to see your hands at all times, he was happy to comply. He wanted no beef with the cops. Anderson turned his head an inch in his direction. Clay knew he was being appraised in return.

'And you are?' asked Anderson.

'Sunshine on a rainy day.'

'Funny.'

'That too on occasion.'

'Name?'

'Clay Gunn.'

Anderson gave another tilt of his head. 'Same last name?'

'We're brothers,' said Danny.

'We're twins, only our mother can tell us apart.' Clay's gambit was met with silence. Maybe they'd both traded their sense of humour for the shades.

'I'd like to think this was a coincidence, running into you like this but...' Danny spread his hands, palm up.

Anderson gave the briefest of smiles. 'I'm a cop. I don't do coincidences.'

Brockovich took a step and spoke for the first time. 'It's been reported that you entered the property of the deceased.'

'Do I need to call my lawyer?' asked Clay, only half-joking.

Brockovich continued as if she hadn't heard him. 'Your license plate was given by a witness. Funny thing, it was reported again in a separate incident. It seems like someone roughed up a couple of white boys, leaving them a different colour than they started.'

'Maybe it was another vehicle that looked like ours. It's easy to misread a plate,' offered Clay.

'It's a rental. They have GPS.' Brockovich inched her shades lower on her nose. The eyes that peered over the rims were a deep brown and all business.

'Look, I don't give a crap about those supremacist dick-wads, but I do care about not one, but now it seems two, roughnecks taking the law into their own hands-on our patch. Let me take a wild guess at what you're up to; you figure, what the hell with the dumb ass cops, we'll go out and find Miss Haims' killer ourselves?' Anderson stood to his full height, his chest stretching the material of his shirt. 'Stop me when I'm getting warm, and then what?'

The Gunn brothers said nothing.

'What are you planning to do, huh? An eye for an eye, is that it, huh?'

Clay monitored Danny without looking at him. His demeanour was still casual and relaxed.

'It ends here and it ends now,' continued Anderson, his voice could have frosted up glass. 'I don't want to hear either of your names again, you understand.'

Clay narrowed his eyes. 'What if I use an alias?'

Brockovich pointed a finger. 'Don't push it. I've put down much bigger guys than you in my time.'

Danny held up his hands. 'Don't worry, we heard you loud and clear.'

'Okay then.' Brockovich gave them both the dead eye then adjusted her shades back up on her nose. 'Last warning.'

The cops took their time walking back to their vehicle. The vehicle they entered was dark and utilitarian. As they slowly drove past, Clay gave them what he hoped looked like a sincere wave. The cops failed to return the gesture. Clay turned to Danny. 'We're still going to Lauderdale, right?'

'Of course, we are,' answered Danny. 'We just need to get some new wheels. We'll ditch your rental back at the hotel then head on up. I don't want Miami's finest tracking us another minute longer.'

Clay nodded. 'There was a used car lot about

five blocks over. Let's go see what a wad of cash will get us at this time of the day.'

'Who do you think reported us to the cops? You think those cross burners dropped a dime?' asked Danny.

Clay shrugged. 'Dunno, maybe. Maybe just a concerned citizen. There are a few left, you know.'

Danny huffed and moved towards their vehicle.

Chapter 17

The acquisition of another car had taken less than an hour. The salesman at Conroy's used autos had seemed more than happy to make a cash sale at the tail end of the day. The Chevrolet Cruze had seen better days to be sure but was assured to be roadworthy with a sound engine. Conroy's offered a thirty-day guarantee on all of its used specials. The salesman, a stick-thin man with a silver crew cut, had personally testified to the fact that it handled well on corners, accelerated strongly, and braked just fine. Clay had paid for the vehicle in cash after a quick stop at a Bank of America ATM. As soon as the vehicle was released, Danny followed Clay back to the Sunset Inn close to Miami international airport. Both parked well away from the main hotel entrance. Clay climbed out of the Cruze, adjusting the jib of his shirt.

'Give me a minute to move the kit over,' said Danny as he leaned out of the rented Chrysler's driver window. Danny moved the items they had bought earlier at the sports supply. The two baseball bats felt like old friends as he switched them from one trunk space to the other.

'You ready?' asked Clay. He rolled his shoulders then leaned on the roof of the Cruze.

'Aye. I want to get up there as soon as possible.' Danny glanced at the hotel. They had done little more than using it as a changing room, once to get cleaned up and ready for Chrissie's funeral and again afterwards to change back into street clothes. It looked like a million other hotels around the country; bland, safe, utilitarian architecture surrounded by other buildings born from the same concrete generation. 'We need to head onto the I-95. That'll take us straight there.'

'You mind if I drive?'

Danny knew better than to debate it again with Clay. Despite Danny being a perfectly competent driver, his older brother almost always wanted to drive. 'Have at it.'

'Where do you want to start once we get there?' asked Clay, as he took the keys from Danny, locking the rental. The Chevrolet creaked as Clay climbed back into the driver's seat.

'I think the harbour launch where the Mariana Meg is moored is a starter for ten. I don't expect that to lead us straight to the bald guy with tattoos but it's something to follow.'

'Yeah, better to be movin', see what we see,' said Clay.

Danny flicked a finger at Clay's shoulder. 'How's that feeling?'

'Stiff as a Brit politician's ass, but I've had worse.'

'Look, if we get into any rough stuff just let me take the front line.' Danny received a look that could curdle milk.

'Yeah, I'll hold your jacket.'

'You know what I mean Clay, you don't always have to be the first man into the room.'

'It's more stiff than painful now. I'll be careful.'

'Okay then. We're heading for a marina on Seabreeze Boulevard,' said Danny.

'God bless Google,' said Clay.

'Indeed,' added Danny. 'Other search engines are available.'

'I've heard that.'

'I told Chrissie about your Diana, how she invented a computer code that's still used in the big search engines.'

Clay gave a slow nod. 'You tell her that's where my money came from?'

'I hardly ever talk money with anyone, so no.'

'I don't mind. It's hardly a state secret. I just wish she was still here to reap the rewards.' Diana Gunn had been a rising star in the tech world. That rise had been brought to a catastrophic end when her car had been involved in a side-swipe collision. Her car had impacted a concrete stanchion killing her instantly. The driver of the other car had not stopped. *Hit and run.* Just another statistic.

Danny looked at his older brother. He had only been involved with Chrissie for a few short weeks but her death had gut-punched him. Clay and Diana had been together for seven years. 'Here's to lost loved ones. May the next life treat them better than this one.'

'Ay-men to that.'

'We need to get onto the I-95 north.'

Clay glanced at the map on Danny's phone then pulled away from the parking space. Taking a slight chance, he nipped the Chevy into a gap in the traffic between a boxy parcel delivery truck and a city bus.

The drive lasted little more than an hour, the sun sinking rapidly, turning the world a different shade. Danny had always thought of Miami and Fort Lauderdale as two distinctly separate places on the map, but there was little to differentiate them on the journey. One seemed to blend into the other with little in the way of unoccupied space between. He knew the locals would probably disagree.

Chapter 18

Clay climbed from the car, stretching his arms and legs out like the Vitruvian man. Cartilage popped in his left shoulder. The muscles just below his collar bone silently protested. Placing his palms on the roof of the Chevrolet he looked at the variety of boats and yachts moored up in neat rows. 'There's a boat for every occasion down here.'

'Aye, I'm sure you could pay off the UK national debt just by selling half of these.'

Clay looked on in admiration. He had a love of all things with an engine. Some called him a petrolhead. That tag didn't upset him. He drummed his fingers on the roof of the car. 'Do you know the difference between a ship and a boat?'

'I think I'm about to find out,' said Danny as he joined Clay at the side of the car.

'A ship can carry a boat, but a boat can't carry a ship.'

'Thanks for that, Captain Crapper.'

'Happy to oblige. It's not often I get to amaze you with trivia, seeing that you're a know-it-all bookworm.'

Danny snapped out a lightning-fast jab. Clay felt the puff of air as knuckles came within a fraction of an inch of his jaw. 'Watch it wee one, or I'll use you as live bait and toss you in the ocean.'

Clay slowly turned his head and was rewarded by the hint of a smile. It was a look, sadly, but understandably, lacking from his younger brother over the past few days. 'Do you know which berth the Mariana Meg is moored in?'

'I don't. We'll have to put in a little leg work until we find it.'

Clay shrugged. 'Nice night for a walk.'

'I just hope it's not out on night fishing or a party run.'

'Let's go and have a look, see,' said Clay.

The boards underfoot were weathered but in good repair. Seabreeze Boulevard stretched out before them; long straight piers split into individual moorings for the boats. 'You go left and I'll go right?'

'Aye, sounds like a plan. Buzz me if you find it.'

'Of course,' said Clay.

Clay walked the boulevard, his gaze flicking from boat to boat, large and small. He walked those piers where his view was obstructed by a larger boat, one that may hide the Mariana Meg. The moored boats on the first three jetties seemed mainly those that would be categorised as leisure craft. The boats on the fourth pier appeared more utilitarian; still impressive, but a clearly commercial craft, many displaying signage and banners advertising the various fishing and snorkelling day trips.

The next three piers again proved not to be the mooring space of the Mariana Meg. Clay struck up an easy conversation with a crew member from one of the stationary fishing boats. The blue polo shirt he wore was emblazoned with 'Blue Marlon Fishing Tours'. The man had only been working out of the marina for two months so couldn't offer Clay, Meg's location.

As Clay was thanking the deckhand for his time his cell phone warbled. 'I'm having no luck down here. Any tugs on the line at your end?'

'Guess what's tying up right in front of me,' said Danny.

'The Meg?'

'Correctamundo. Come on down, you'll see a big blue framework, looks like a bus shelter, that's the pier you want.'

'On my way.' By the time Clay reached Danny, the Mariana Meg had shut off its engines and a red-haired crew member was finishing tying off. The crew member looked over and gave an amiable nod.

'Hey buddy, how's it going?' asked Clay.

'All good, but ready for home,' replied the man. 'I do believe it's brewski time'

'I know just what you mean,' said Danny. 'How long have you worked on the boat?'

The man rubbed his fingers across a layer of red stubble on his chin. 'Just over two years now.'

'Looks like a sweet ride,' said Clay.

'It is.'

'We're looking for a guy, friend of a friend who may have worked the same boat a while back, a guy called Erik Delacroix,' said Danny.

The red-haired man shook his head in the negative. 'He died a couple of years back, just before I came aboard. The guy was a bit of a legend though. He was a treasure hunter, always out in the keys and the Bahamas. I heard he worked with Mel Fisher's crew for a little while, you know, way back in the day, but he was a bit too much of a loose cannon for Mel.'

'Okay, it was a long shot. Thanks anyway. Do you know how he died?' asked Clay.

'He was murdered. I heard he got dealt a crappy hand, real bad mojo. Came back home after a night on the town and walked in on some dude robbing his apartment, at least that's how the cops tell it.'

Clay watched Danny take a step closer to the

crew hand. Danny's Scottish accent became a little thicker, his R's a little sharper. 'He was murdered in a robbery? How did he die?'

'I just heard the stories man, not saying they're legal and binding,' the crew hand looked at the crew, on the deck of the Mariana Meg, busying themselves.

'What did you hear?' asked Clay.

'I thought you said he was a friend of a friend. How do you not know Delacroix was killed?'

Danny answered. 'I was told if I was ever down in Florida to look him up, that he would set us up on the party line, you know, girls and blow?'

The red-haired man smiled. 'Yeah man, I know the score.'

'So, what happened to Erik?' asked Clay.

Stepping closer, the crew hand spoke with a glint in his eye. 'I heard tell that he was beaten to a pulp, most of the bones in his body broken. I think he was choked to death. My friend Jimmy Shingles reckons that he was probably caught in a Lion Killer strangle or something, he's into all of that MMA shit, but he knows his stuff so who am I to argue?'

'That happens here in Fort Lauderdale?' asked Danny.

'Yeah man, Lauderdale ain't always sunshine

and mermaid's tits you know.'

Danny gave a perfunctory nod. He pulled the drawing from his pocket. 'You ever see this guy?'

The deckhand took a closer look at the paper. 'Don't think so. I don't think that's Delacroix, though.'

'Okay,' said Danny tucking the picture away.

'Hey man, look, we appreciate your time,' said Clay.

'You guys wanna book a day's fishing with us? We go to all the best spots.'

'You got a website?' asked Danny.

'Sure man.'

Clay glanced at the web address printed at the bottom of the charter sign at the front of the mooring. 'We'll check it out over dinner. See you later.'

'Sure thing. Don't eat any green lobsters.'

'Sounds like good advice,' said Clay. He turned to Danny as the crew hand stepped back aboard the Meg. 'Talking of lobsters, I see there's a place over there that sells take out claws. You want some?'

'Nah, I'm fine. I'll see you back at the car.' Danny's voice carried an air of obvious frustration.

'Won't be long,' said Clay as he passed Danny the keys to the Chevrolet.

Chapter 19

Danny spotted the four men as soon as he rounded the corner. Two of the four had their butts parked on the hood. The third was using the front fender as a footrest. Only the fourth man stood free of the vehicle. Danny blew air through his nose. There was a wooden bench less than twenty feet from the car. All four men were dressed in expensive sports gear. Two of the four had baseball caps turned sideways on their heads. Danny never slowed his casual pace. 'Hiya boys, thanks for keeping the car safe and well.'

One of the four laughed. 'This piece of crap belongs to you? Damn sheepdog, I wouldn't admit it out loud.'

'It's not the prettiest but it has a nice personality. There's a seat over there, can you park your arses on it so we can head off.'

'We?' asked one of the men perched on the hood. His blond hair was slicked into a neat triangular wedge. The black and yellow shirt he wore declared he was *'Too Hot to Handle'*.

'Aye, my little brother isn't far behind,' said Danny.

All four men were white and looked like they could all be the same family. Pale eyes, fair skin, and blond hair. The right hand of the guy with his foot on the fender was decked out with three wide and ornate rings. Danny knew from personal experience they would have the same effect as brass-knuckles. No other weapons on display. 'Come on guys, I asked nicely.'

'Go jump in the sea, dick hea...'

Danny's open palm, locked back at the wrist, slammed into wedge's face. The man pitched to one side; his face frozen in shock.

'Move!' ordered Danny.

The guy with the rings turned, cocking his fist back to his shoulder. Danny moved in like a shadow, the blade of his left-hand snapping into the nerve cluster just below the man's ear. When the punch came, it was weak and unfocused. Danny moved in a basic bob and weave and tore a right hook into the man's exposed ribs. Rings dropped to his knees.

Too hot to handle gathered his feet below him, cursing loudly, leapt bodily at Danny from the hood of the Chevrolet. With a look of contempt, Danny sidestepped and *Too hot to handle* landed in a belly flop on the sidewalk. The sound of his face hitting concrete made even Danny wince.

The last of the four dropped into a nervous

crouch, his eyes fleeting from side to side.

'If you're looking for a weapon, don't; I'm not in the mood,' warned Danny. 'Just take these idiots and go.'

'You're in big trouble mister. My cousin is a district attorney.'

'You should go now.'

'I'll sue you for everything you have.'

Danny shrugged. 'Too late.'

Clay grabbed the blond-haired man by the back of his neck then yanked him off his feet. Danny watched the pale eyes go wide for the briefest of moments before Clay's knuckles met his jaw; then the guy was lying next to *Too hot to handle*.

'I can't leave you alone for a minute,' said Clay. The bucket of take-out claws was tucked safe and secure under his left arm.

'What we had here was a failure to communicate,' said Danny. 'I asked nicely and then I asked again in a way they would understand.'

'Dey no speaklee da Queen's Engerlish?'

'I think they only speak *'idiota'*. What the hell is up with the world. I asked them nicely too.'

'I think they got the message.' Clay dug his hand into his bucket. 'Claw?'

'No thanks,' said Danny as he moved to the driver side.

'Hey, what're you doing?'

'Driving,' said Danny. 'You're eating, aren't you?'

Clay glanced at his bucket of claws then back at Danny. 'Okay, just this once.'

Danny barked, 'You numbnuts have about five seconds to move or I'm driving over the top of you.'

The four men moved like apes, supporting each other without further comment. As soon as the road was clear Danny eased out of the parking space. Clay buzzed down his window and waved at the four men with a pincered lobster claw. 'Don't be so shellfish in the future.'

One of the four spat red saliva onto the ground.

Danny shook his head at mock sadness. 'Really?'

'Don't be so selfish…shellfish, oh come on.'

'Explaining it doesn't make it any better,' said Danny. The corners of his mouth twitched despite his best efforts.

'Okay, squid, pro quo.'

'Clay, are you going to keep going with the crappy fish-puns?'

'I might do, just for the halibut.'

'Clay…'

'What's an eels favourite dance?'

'Please stop.'

'The conger.'

'Dear God, make it stop.'

'What's the difference between a fish and a piano?'

Danny groaned.

'You can't tuna fish.'

'Clay…'

'The last one I swear,' said Clay. 'What's the difference between a catfish and a lawyer?'

'Go on, have your moment.'

'One is a bottom-dwelling, scum-sucking scavenger and the other is a fish!'

'Can we get back on the clock?' asked Danny as he steered away from the waterfront.

'We're moving ain't we?'

'This whole deal is starting to smell like that lobster bucket,' said Danny. 'Both Chrissie and a wild-card that used to live in her house, both found dead after supposed robberies; both strangled to death. It's a hell of a coincidence don't you think?'

Clay sucked the meat from a claw before answering. 'Like that cop, Panda-boy said; I don't like coincidences.'

'I think you mean Anderson…'

'That's what I said, Panda-boy and Broke-her-switch.'

'Close enough.'

Chapter 20

The mood in the Southern Unification building was electric. Syrus Sanderson smiled, his neat white teeth showing. As he looked at the collection of brothers in front of him, he felt a sense of pride. These were his real family, not those middle-class hypocrites back in Tulsa, with their mollycoddling *'live and let live, we're all children under God'* bullshit. That was for losers, for those with no spiritual conviction. All he shared with those people was the same last name. The members of the Southern Unification were to a man, born with the same noble fire in their blood. CJ and Teasle had been tended to and after drinking their fill of bourbon were now fast asleep in a room at the back of the clubhouse. Sanderson glanced at his reflection in the mirror mounted to one of the interior doors. The face that stared back might be considered handsome by some, square jaw, close-cropped hair and distinctive green eyes. He looked past his reflection at the other men.

Lyle answered his cell phone on the second ring. 'Okay, thanks, sis. Yeah, ping me it all over. Yeah. Yeah. Great. Give my love to Jackie and Simon. Tell them uncle Lyle will be over next weekend and the ice cream is on me. Yeah, we'll all go bowlin' or sumpin'.'

Sanderson raised his eyebrows expectantly. The phone gave a double ping. He received a confident nod from Lyle.

'Thanks, sis, see you later.' Lyle held up the phone so Sanderson could see the screen. 'Got it. The vehicle in the picture is a rental.'

'Do we know who rented it?'

'We do now. Some shit-kicker called Clay Gunn. He took the rental on a two-week standard package. He's got a Texas state license.'

'Did you get an address for Mister Gunn?' Sanderson asked.

'Yep, Adrienne called the rental office. She spun her some sob story about her daughter hooking up with some dirty old dude twice her age. Adi can be very convincing when she wants to be. The woman at the rental company gave her an address and did a quick trace on the vehicle's GPS. They're over at the Sunset Inn at the airport, or at least their car is.'

'Okay then, let's saddle up,' said Sanderson. 'When we get there, I want every corner covered, these two yahoos aren't walking away from this. I want them kicked to within an inch of their lives.'

'What if they're strapped?' asked Lyle.

'If they're dumb enough to pull a gun on me, I want them to live the rest of their lives regretting it.'

'The icepick?' asked Lyle.

Sanderson nodded. It was a fate reserved for transgressors to the Southern Unification. The icepick would be jammed in between the fourth and fifth Cervical Vertebrae. Done correctly, it would leave the victim paralyzed from the neck down, incorrectly and the victim usually choked to death on his blood. 'We go in low key and quiet. I don't want them knowing we're there until my hand is shoved up their ass. Gear up.'

'We're all ready to go, Syrus,' said Lyle. The pistol tucked in his waistband was neat and businesslike. The CPX 9mm would get the job done. Most of the other men in the room carried simple black nightsticks. A few sported telescopic ASP batons, the nightstick's modern equivalent.

Syrus nodded to Lyle's pistol. 'Don't pull that unless you need to.' Many of the men owned guns but Syrus Sanderson liked to do things the old way.

Lyle gave a non-committal grunt.

'When you beat a man down with a stick or brass knuckles you have to look him in the eye. That way the message is delivered loud and clear. No spray and pray for the men of the Southern Unification. No innocents caught in the crossfire. We do our business right.'

'I know man, but look at what they did to the

guys.'

'No one moves on them until I give the say so. I want this cold and clinical, that last thing we need is cops getting up in our business, that understood?' Syrus Sanderson received no overt objections from the group. 'I need to drop some money off at the night bank, but I'll only be five minutes behind you. Wait for me at the hotel.'

Five vehicles departed in convoy. Cold fire burned in the pit of Sanderson's stomach. This was the first overt challenge to the SU in a long time. He had to look like the leader that the men deserved. Most of the time it was the SU who did the pushing. Who were these two assholes to come into his patch and lay the hammer down on his men? They would pay.

Chapter 21

Clay wiped his mouth clean with a paper napkin. The claws had been very tasty but not the ideal food to eat on the move. The act of opening them up, even with the supplied claw crackers was a messy business. He pushed the balled paper into the bucket, then added the metal cracker tool. Flakes of shell and meat decorated his shirt. He gave Danny a sideways glance. No smart-assed remark was issued. His younger brother, usually light-hearted and smiling was again sullen. Losing Chrissie had hit him hard. Clay had recognized the promise of violence in his brothers' eyes many times, yet this time it was different. Danny was usually cold and calculated; getting the job done with detached icy efficiency. A sense of simmering fury now seemed to emanate from his brother. Clay held no hope for Chrissie's killer being spared any agony, in his fate. That troubled him none. There was, of course, the pressing matter of first *finding* the murderer. No small task. Neither Danny nor he being detectives, old soldiers yes, cops; no. So far, they had upset the locals both in South Miami and now in Fort Lauderdale but were no closer to identifying the tattooed killer, if indeed he *was* the killer. Yes, he had been seen outside of Chrissie's house, but that a murderer did not make.

'What do you want to do next?' asked Clay.

Danny huffed. 'I suppose I better put my head down for the night, start fresh again in the morning. I don't think I've had more than three or four-hours proper sleep in as many days.'

'Fine by me, wee one. I think a couple of slugs of Jack Daniels and I'll be out too. You fancy a couple?'

'Not for me. I'm just gonna hit the hay. I'll drop you at the front door and then park up. I'll park away from the rental just in case Anderson and Brockovich decide to swing by again.'

'Why would they?' asked Clay.

'Cops being cops. You can tell by the looks on their faces that they weren't enamoured with us kicking up dust.'

'Speak for yourself, I think the hot one had a twinkle in her eye when she was laying down the law. She's maybe never had a Texan and knows what she's missing.' Clay waggled his eyebrows playfully.

'She maybe never had scarlet fever either, but probably isn't in any hurry to try it.'

Clay laughed. 'Are you comparing me to an infectious disease?'

'If the rash fits,' said Danny.

'My foot will fit in your ass if there's any more of your BS.' Clay bumped Danny with his forearm.

'Drop me here. I'll ditch this stuff in the trash before I go into the hotel. I'll try not to disturb your beauty sleep when I get back to the room, God knows you need it.'

'Says the guy with a face like King Kong's arse.' The brothers shared a brief smile before Clay climbed from the car.

'See you in a while. You sure you don't want anything?' asked Clay. Danny shook his head in the negative. 'Okay then. See you in a spell.'

Clay watched Danny steer the car around the corner of the hotel building then walked to the nearest trash can. He squashed the bucket flat, then pushed it into the receptacle. Striding to the front doors of the hotel his right hand strayed to his front pocket.

'Damn it.' He'd taken out his wallet and pushed it into a recess on the dashboard while riding in the car. Sure, he could charge drinks from the bar to his room, but like most men felt like he was only half-dressed without his wallet.

The air had cooled after the sun had dropped below the horizon, a fresher breeze now providing a welcome relief from the relentless humidity. Clay followed the narrow sidewalk that flanked the hotel. Neat rows of shrubs and wide leaved bushes helped alleviate that blandness of the parking lot. Clay turned the first corner. Danny was not in sight. As he walked the path that led to the rear of the hotel, he found himself humming an old tune he'd heard on the radio earlier. Roberta Flack's voice was beautiful, always sticking in his mind when he heard it. His hands slipped into his pockets as he ambled to the rear of the hotel. The Sunset Inn was by no means one of the best in Miami, but it served its purpose. It held none of the charms of the art deco hotels on Collins Avenue. The rooms, however, were clean, and the food served in the bar and restaurant looked more than passable.

As Clay rounded the corner, he became aware of hushed voices. Three men, two with shaven heads, huddled at the side of a parked SUV. All three were armed. The two with bald heads carried batons while the third man, his black hair cropped short, brandished a snub-nosed revolver, maybe a .38. Clay slowed and moved to stand behind one of the larger bushes. Dropping to one knee he followed the eyes of the three men. It took little deduction that they were here for both him and Danny. Clay ran his tongue under his upper lip. *This is what happens when you kick a hornet's nest.* Across the parking lot, Danny had reversed the Chevrolet into a vacant space. He was out of the car with the trunk open. From his point of cover, Clay could see only the top of Danny's head. The three men started toward his brother. Clay silently followed, a shadow in their wake.

Chapter 22

Danny felt a weariness setting into his bones. He hadn't slept well over the past few nights. His mind seemed determined to dredge an unfamiliar sense of failure every time his eyes were about to close. *Chrissie...* A few hours of solid sleep would help. Maybe he should have taken up Clay's offer of a couple of bourbons. He ran the back of his hand across his mouth. Maybe he would.

Danny's attention was ripped into focus as three men closed in on his position. He instinctively knew who they were. Two of the three had shaved heads. The SU had wasted no time in tracking him down. He would ruminate on the method later. Two of the men held nightsticks, the third; a revolver. It looked like a .38 five-shot. Five shots; but it only took one.

'Where's the other guy, the big one?' demanded the gunman.

Danny forced himself to relax as the three drew closer. The gunman held his weapon pointed at Danny's chest while the other two skirted the Chevrolet, forming a rough triangle. The corners of Danny's mouth twitched. The gunman hadn't shot him yet so that wasn't his prime objective. 'I think you've got the wrong guy. I'm down here at the annual pet insurance convention. You guys got any dogs or cats or llamas that need to be insured? We're also running a special on collision cover for billy goats this week.'

The gunman stepped closer. 'You can drop the bullshit. I know who you are, *Clay Gunn*.'

'Dude, you couldn't be more wrong. I hope you never meet Clay. He's so temperamental, he has a thunder cloud that follows him around. He's also prone to pulling arms out of sockets.' Danny arched one eyebrow. 'No, wait, maybe that's Wookies.'

'Cut the crap.' The gunman took another step closer, his face twisted into an aggressive mask.

Danny let the other two men take another step closer, all three now in a tight triangle.

Move!

Ducking his head left, Danny swiped the gunman's wrist hard in the opposite direction. Rotating the man's hand in a tight arc, Danny peeled the revolver from his grip with little trouble. As he stripped the weapon Danny wrenched down, snapping the man's finger inside the trigger guard. As the black-haired gunman went down on one knee, he caught the revolver across his teeth. Danny planted a boot in his chest, casting him to the sidewalk.

'Now what, dip-shits?' The two men armed

with batons stared at the revolver with wide eyes.

Across the parking lot, a young woman in a dark blue convertible swung into an empty bay. Paintwork sparkled as the headlights briefly illuminated the other parked cars. Within a second, a young girl no more than seven or eight years old bounded from the vehicle. She began turning in tight circles, a soft toy held at arms-length. 'Look, mom, Duffy Bear can fly.'

Danny swore under his breath. The last thing he wanted was bullets flying, especially when there were bystanders close at hand. The two men armed with nightsticks remained motionless but did not drop their weapons. Danny's lip curled as Clay burst from behind a wide bush in a shower of leaves, right arm cocked to his shoulder. The first of the stickmen snapped his head towards the blur of motion. The fist that slammed into his face, took him off his feet.

Danny stamped out with his right foot. The side of his boot buckled the other man's knee joint in a way it was never meant to bend. As the man tumbled to the ground a loud wail escaped his throat. Danny silenced the wail with another kick. The man's head snapped back, blood spraying from his nose.

'Don't tell me, making friends and influencing people?'

Danny nodded at his older brother. 'Something like that.'

Across the parking lot, what looked to be another mother and child approached the convertible. The two children, with wide smiles, immediately began some kind of intricate hand-clapping game. The mothers were looking away from the fracas, but for how long? Danny aimed the revolver at the three downed men for long seconds before tossing it into the trunk of the Chevrolet.

The man who Danny had dropped with two kicks had his hands clasped to his knee. His scowling face was dappled with blood. Danny fixed him with a stare. 'Any more of you brainiacs waiting in the shadows?'

In way of answer, another four men rounded the corner of the building at a run. All four carried the same black batons as the downed men.

Chapter 23

The sharp tugging at Clay's left shoulder felt like a sliver of glass inside the muscle. The adrenalin burst would keep the pain at bay for a while. There would be time later for a glass or three of Jack and some Tylenol.

Three men lay scattered on the ground, all clutching various body parts. All three he was sure hailed from the red church, the Southern Unification. Clay glared at the four new arrivals as they sprinted into view. The parking lot was well lit, tall lighting poles lining the sidewalk. The scars on the left side of Clay's face crinkled as he gave a cold smile. The men were carrying the same black nightsticks as their fallen comrades. Clay felt confident they weren't armed with anything more lethal. Men tended to brandish their primary weapon first and foremost. If they had guns, they would probably be aiming them by now. The men were only seconds away.

Clay dropped to one knee, his right-hand streaking to one of the discarded clubs. He paused mid-action as Danny thrust the wooden baseball bat at him. 'Upgrade, nice.'

Danny too now brandished a bat.

The four men closed on them. Clay positioned his left foot forward and timed his swing perfectly. The sound of the seasoned wood cracking the first man across the side of the head echoed like a pistol shot. The skinhead jack-knifed as if electrocuted then pitched face down next to his fallen friends.

Clay manoeuvred away from Danny, giving him enough room to swing. As the next SU man closed on Clay he first zigged left then quickly back to his right, trying to slash the bat from Clay's hands. The nightstick caught the bat handle inches above Clay's fingers. Without pause, the man tried a backhand aimed again at his hands. Clay avoided the second blow by raising the bat above his head. Scowling, the man dropped into a crouch and raised his weapon, ready to defend. Danny's bat slammed into the centre of his spine catching him unawares. Clay watched the skinhead buckle at the knees, then cut down with his slugger like a samurai of old. The man's feet seemed to be snatched from below as he was up-ended. A flicker of a smile, like lightning in a cloud, crossed Clay's face as the bat again struck home a resounding *'clonk'*.

The two remaining skinheads faltered; batons extended but neither seemed enthusiastic to advance. The closest of the two, sporting the *88* and a confederate flag tattoo on opposite sides of his neck, dropped his baton as his hand streaked to his belt. Clay leapt into him. The trajectory of his baseball bat was a tight loop. Clay both heard and felt the bones of the man's clavicle snap beneath the weight of the slugger. A small pistol clattered to the ground.

Clay heard the remaining skinhead yelp in surprise as Danny's bat cracked across his shins. Stooping to retrieve the fallen pistol, Clay caught the look of sheer panic, wide eyes, and open mouth, on the face of the man Danny had just dropped. A now-familiar nipping emanated from Clay's shoulder. The sutures had been removed but the deep muscle tissue still felt tight. Using the bat as support Clay snatched up the pistol. With casual ease, he tossed the bat to Danny. Dropping back to one knee he grabbed the man by the collar, hauling him onto his side. He pressed the pistol hard into the skinhead's face. 'Not much fun when they fight back is it?'

The skinhead said nothing. Clay could smell stale tobacco on his breath.

'Is there any more of the Miami Reich heading this way?' Clay ground the barrel into the nerve cluster just below the man's cheekbone. 'What's wrong dickhead, you need a break?'

The man howled as Clay slammed the pistol into his already shattered collarbone. 'Speak now or I'll leave you lyin' here colder than a witch's tit.'

'Stop! Stop. I'll tell you, man. There's more of us coming. They'll be here any second.'

'How many?' asked Clay.

'All of us.'

'Fuck-a-doodle-doo,' said Clay, locking eyes with Danny. 'Well, there goes my plans for a bourbon and a cheeseburger.'

Chapter 24

The seven men from the Southern Unification lay in various poses. None were fit to give chase as Danny moved rapidly to the driver's seat. After snatching the revolver back from the trunk, he passed Clay his baseball bat. Clay slipped the bat between his knees as he joined him in the car. He accepted the revolver without comment. He then wedged the other pistol under his thigh.

'I'm driving again, no time for any dispute,' said Danny.

'It would be a lot more fun riding shotgun if I had a shotgun.'

'Beggars can't be choosers. Let's shake these dip-shits off our tail then we can look at laying hands to some better kit.' Danny sped from the parking place, giving the women and children a wide berth. As he rounded the corner of the Sunset Inn, an incoming SUV was forced to rapidly swerve to avoid a head-on collision. The three faces that glared back at Danny from the vehicle looked ready to spit venom.

Danny made a sharp turn into the sparse evening traffic. The steering wheel felt hot in his grip. Swerving around a taxi cab, he took the next right turn.

Another two turns satisfied him that they had left the men from the Southern Unification behind. Slowing the car, he looked to Clay. His brother regarded him with a slight frown.

'What?' asked Danny.

'I thought you were gonna shoot them dead.'

Danny gave a noncommittal shrug. 'Can't say I wouldn't have if those civilians hadn't been there.'

'I know they're class-A assholes, but the Rebel Yell collective isn't our target on this.'

'I know that Clay' said Danny, his ire rising. 'But when the blood's up…'

'I dig that, little brother, but I don't want to be facing murder charges for some idiot hometown bigots.'

'Two of those bigots just pointed guns at us. You know how that sits with me.'

'Fine. Have it your way. Just shoot them. At least it'll keep my lawyer gainfully employed for the next twenty or so years.'

Danny steered the Chevrolet into the parking area of a small strip mall. 'I never killed anyone that didn't need killing. I think you've quoted that on more than one occasion.'

'I'm just trying to watch out for you, little brother.'

'I know that Clay.' Danny's voice softened, the overt aggression melting away. 'I just want…'

There was a brief flash of light; rapidly approaching headlamps, then the world was comprised of ear wrecking noise and flying broken glass.

The rear window of the Chevrolet shattered as a larger vehicle rear-ended them at high speed. The Chevrolet Cruze was blasted at an oblique angle, the car spinning into a diagonal trajectory. Danny felt himself slam into the seat then be catapulted into the dashboard. Only his hastily extended right arm prevented his face striking the console.

'Mother trucker.' Danny turned; his first concern was his brother. A gash over Clay's left eye trickled blood. 'You okay?'

'I take back everything I just said about not shooting these assholes. I'll fire the first shot!'

The roaring of engines sounded again as a second vehicle raced towards them. The minivan would crash into the passenger-side at any moment. Danny stamped down on the gas pedal and the crumpled Chevrolet lurched away at speed. The minivan caught the rear of the Chevy a glancing blow, again sending the car into a spin. The screeching of metal echoed through the night as the vehicle slewed to one side. As Danny kept his right foot pressed hard on the gas random patterns of sparks followed the now hanging fender. Danny gritted his teeth. There was definite damage back there. The fender was in all likelyhood made from plastic or fibreglass, that meant that something metal was also trailing on the ground. Whatever it was, he knew it wasn't good.

The Chevrolet powered on despite the damage it had taken. Danny forced the car in a tight arc to combat the spin and again sped from the parking lot. His eyes flicked from the road ahead to the rearview like a metronome.

'I don't suppose we've left them behind?' asked Clay. As he wiped at the new laceration on his face.

'No such luck. They're right behind us.'

Chapter 25

'Have you uploaded the jump yet?'

Andrew Wyszogrodski, known to his friends simply as 'Fish' due to the fact no one could correctly pronounce his surname, gave Curtis Quantrill the thumbs up. 'It was out there two minutes after you left the pier.'

'You get it all?'

Fish gave the unofficial group leader a quick but sour look. 'Of course, I got it all. Who do you think you're speaking to, man?'

'Okay Fish, take it easy. I know you're a whiz with the tech, but you looked like shit on a stick after all the drinks you put away last night.'

'Here.' Fish felt a smile creep across his face despite being doubted by the boss-man. It had been a heavy night and despite sleeping in past lunch, his breath still carried tell-tale smells of the alcohol consumed. The latest addition to his prepping stash was a pallet of mezcal. When the shit hit the fan, alcohol could be used as barter currency. He had liberally sampled the mezcal while stripping and cleaning his weapon collection. Fish played the video on his smartphone. The jump was greeted by enthusiastic whoops.

'Alright guys, simmer down.' Quantrill looked to the five men gathered around his kitchen table. 'We need to get our shit together.'

Fish too looked to the men; his friends, men who he had trusted with his life. Each man brought their unique talents to the outfit, each united in their insatiable appetite for adventure. Junk placed a box file on the tabletop.

'You all need to read this before we head out.' Curtis Quantrill's voice left little room for negotiation.

'Jeez, are we getting homework now. When did that happen?' The other men laughed at Gato's barb. Fish had been friends with Gato for many years, the longest of all the group. Pele Gato had the body of a gymnast, and with good reason. Apart from being an accomplished boat pilot and able scuba diver, the Brazilian born adventurer was a skilled exponent of Parkour. The skills of the free-runner were beyond Fish but Gato never failed to impress. A dynamic blend of gymnastics, martial arts and sheer madness, Parkour was not for the rank and file. It took years to develop any real skill and still have your spine intact. While Fish was a capable exponent of MMA, he was happy to remain a Parkour spectator.

'What's in the box?' asked Blaine. The big man adjusted his glasses, perching them on the end of his nose and peering over the lenses. 'Paltrow's head?'

'It's the floor plans for the warehouse, I've been casing. It's minimum security but we still need to be in and out, quick and quiet,' replied Quantrill.

'Quick and quiet. I can do that,' said Blaine.

'Your girlfriend tells me you've got the quick part down to a fine art.'

Blaine stood to his full height then grabbed Fish in a bear-hug. 'Watch it little man or I'll squish you 'til you're, paste.'

Fish felt Blaine's arms constrict a fraction. That fraction was enough to severely hamper his breathing. 'Get off me, you freak of nature.'

'If you break him, you bought him,' said Quantrill.

Fish took a deep breath as Blaine released his hold. His vision swam momentarily as if he had stood up too quickly. Fish looked over at Gato as his distinctive laugh cut across the room.

'Thanks for your help everybody.' Fish rubbed at his lower back.

'You should know better than to poke the bear,' said Junk.

Fish shook his head in mock sadness. 'What's this great country of ours coming to if you can't point out a friend's sexual inadequacies?'

Quantrill rapped his knuckles on the stained wood of the tabletop. 'Your attention gentlemen, please.'

The men shared another chuckle then gathered closer as Quantrill unrolled two schematic drawings. Empty beer bottles acted as paperweights at the corners of the paper. Handwritten notes were scrawled in the margins. 'The warehouse is in Aventura, just off Biscayne Boulevard. This should be, an easy, in, and out, no muss no fuss.'

Fish looked up from the building plans. 'Are we going in tonight?'

'What's wrong Fish, you got a hot date?' asked Blaine.

'With his right hand maybe,' added Gato, a wide grin spreading across his face. The smile exposed his chipped upper incisor, the result of an ill-timed landing during one of his more frenetic Parkour runs.

'Yeah, rosy palm and her five sisters. Fish is well acquainted.'

Not wanting to be on the receiving end of another of Blaine's rib-crushing bear hugs, Fish let the barbs go. 'So, what's the prize in the warehouse?'

Curtis Quantrill leaned both hands on the tabletop. 'At the back of the warehouse, there are five storage units. Any guesses who unit three belonged to?'

'Our old friend Delacroix?' asked Fish. 'You found it?'

'I found it.'

All eyes went to the floor plans.

Chapter 26

Clay wiped the back of his hand across his brow. It came away red. Turning in his seat he glowered at the vehicles behind, squinting against the brightness of the pursuant lights. The revolver proved a great temptation in his hand, but he knew better than to open fire in a residential area. Gunshots would bring out the cops on high alert and he also knew better than to upset Miami PD. Some of the troopers down here were hardcore, used to dealing with organised and armed gangs. He wanted no beef with the law. Lights from shop fronts seemed to blur as Danny continued to weave past slower moving traffic. Clay talked through clenched teeth. 'Can you lead these ass-pickers out to the boonies?'

'We might not get that far but I'll get us off the main strip. Hang on to your hot dog.'

Clay wedged the handle of the baseball bat against the car door. He was thankful that he had missed the wooden shaft as they had been rear-ended; a good way to receive a punctured lung. Bracing his legs at the corners of his foot well, he felt the shuddering vibrations of the car through his feet. A cascade of sparks fan-tailed from the rear of the car as Danny forced the vehicle to cross the central median.

The Chevy lurched into the air as it negotiated the strip of sparsely grassed verge. Clay looked from side to side. On one side, the faces of three skinheads glared back, on the other countless sets of headlights flashed directly towards them. Without another word, Danny hauled hard on the steering wheel. Clay felt his stomach lurch as the battered Chevrolet streaked across two lanes of oncoming traffic. A bright yellow Hummer came within inches of flattening Clay's door but passed with a frantic blaring of the horn. The Chevy fishtailed for another ass-clenching moment then streaked past a convertible full of wide-eyed occupants. Clay pressed back into his seat as Danny swerved onto a side street. 'Good to see all those hours playing Grand Theft Auto weren't completely wasted.'

Danny sported a manic grin. Not for the first time, Clay wondered if there wasn't a streak of genuine madness in the Gunn family genes. With a moment of respite as Danny evened out the car onto a straighter path, Clay checked the revolver. Opening the chamber, he gave brief scrutiny to the bullets. None of the cartridges had been fired. Tipping the weapon to one side he recognised it as a Rossi .38. It wasn't a model Clay had ever used but a double-action revolver was a relatively simple point and shoot affair. Five shots. It only took one in the right spot.

Danny looked over his shoulder. 'Are they still following?'

Clay ignored the nipping in the muscle of his left shoulder as he twisted in his seat. Danny's daredevil road crossing had put considerable distance between their pursuers. 'I think you might have…no, hold the phone…here comes the glee club.'

The SUV that had sideswiped them powered into the street. Another two vehicles were close behind. 'I thought your demonic lane changing would have bought us a bit more time. These dick-wads are determined, I'll give them that.'

Danny said nothing. The engine of the Chevy grew louder as it increased in speed. The Chevrolet wasn't the fastest thing on the road but Clay knew it could at least match the SUV, minivan and the pick-up truck that followed. The surrounding terrain changed as the Chevy continued to race forward. The shop fronts and restaurants were soon left behind and the road took on a more utilitarian aspect. Clay cradled the revolver keeping his finger off the trigger. The car dipped momentarily as Danny took a left curve, powering into the sweeping bend. An overpass loomed over them, its concrete underbelly, dark and ominous. The tone of the engine again changed as Danny gradually eased off the gas.

'Here they come,' said Clay.

Danny again coaxed speed from the vehicle. The road beneath the overpass was a stretch of unlighted two-lane blacktop. A chain-link fence provided a barrier on the left side of the vehicle. The metal fence posts seemed to produce a canine panting as they sped past each one. Clay could hear loose pieces of dirt and pebble rattle on the undercarriage as Danny manoeuvred the car closer to the fence. 'That SUV is only five seconds out,' warned Clay.

'I see him.'

Clay cast another look at their pursuers. 'The other two are about ten seconds behind, maybe less.'

'Aye, I see them. Just lining up the cue ball.'

The SUV was drawing level. Clay counted down. 'Three! Two! One!'

Clay exhaled as Danny pumped the brakes. In a flash of dark blue, the SUV was now side by side. Clay lifted the revolver into view.

Chapter 27

Danny's foot hovered over the brake pedal until the closest of the three vehicles was side by side to the Chevy. As he stamped down on the brakes, the dark blue SUV seemed to leap ahead on the road. Danny laid heavy on the gas. He aimed the Chevy for the rear corner of the SUV. The HIT manoeuvre was used by police and military all over the world. There was a brief screech of metal on metal as the Chevrolet impacted the SUV just behind the driver's rear wheel. The SUV began to spin in a tight arc, the faces at the windows showing teeth and wide eyes. Danny had timed the interception to the second. The SUV slammed without mercy into one of the wide concrete support stanchions. The vehicle rocked up onto two wheels as the windscreen and one of the side windows exploded. The hood sprang open and a jet of steam issued from the engine block. A second later the minivan ploughed into the ruined SUV. Both vehicles parted like repulsed magnets. The minivan veered off at a severe angle. The sound it made as it rolled from its wheels onto its roof was one of horror.

Danny watched the carnage unfold in the rearview. The pick-up truck swerved to avoid the two ruined vehicles then screeched to a halt. Several denim-clad men jumped from the truck and sprinted back to the two wrecks. With a low growl, Danny slowed the Chevy enough to turn in a wide arc. He powered back to the vehicles which were now little more than scrap. Someone was screaming that their legs were broken. Danny couldn't tell which vehicle the wails emanated from. 'Time to put a lid on these southern fried arseholes!'

Danny sprang from the Chevrolet and intercepted the closest of the men. Grabbing his jacket collar from behind, Danny hauled the man off balance and slapped the pistol hard across his face. The man went down with a pained yelp. Another three of the Southern Unification turned to face Danny. One of the three dropped to a half-crouch, his hand streaking to his hip. Danny knew nothing good would appear in his hand. The pistol Danny had taken earlier felt a little small for his hand but it would get the job done. The pistol was an S&W Shield. The pistol was a compact but felt well balanced and he knew the 9mm loads were enough to put lumps in anyone's custard. Racing forward, Danny trapped the man's hand against his hip even before he could draw his weapon. The skinhead tried to pull free but sagged, his knife falling to the ground as Danny chopped down with the butt of the S&W. The man's nose opened in a wash of red. As he bent at the waist with a pained groan Danny levered the S&W Shield into the man's open mouth.

'That's enough!' Danny's voice was angry and thick with his native Scottish brogue. Clay loomed beside him, revolver in hand. 'If anyone of your arseholes so much as twitches, then this guy gets an extra hole where he doesn't need one.'

Steam continued to push free from the wreckage of the SUV. Someone continued to scream and Danny realised that the noise was coming from the back of the SUV. A man, his blond hair matted with blood crawled from the side door of the wrecked vehicle. After a shaky start, he straightened up to his full height. The man raised his right hand in supplication. 'Take it easy, man.'

'Don't tell me, you're the grand poohbah?' Danny pushed the pistol deeper into his captive's mouth.

'You wanna take that shooter out of my man's mouth then we can talk?'

'Nah, I think I'll just leave it where it is for now,' replied Danny. Clay shifted away from Danny, his revolver roaming slowly from each of the Southern Unification.

Danny stared at the man with angry eyes. Danny rephrased his question. 'You the boss?'

'I'm proud to lead and stand beside them.'

'I'll take that as a yes,' said Danny. 'Clay, if any of these nuggets blinks too quick, put a hole in the big boss man.'

'My pleasure,' replied Clay.

Danny scrutinised the leader. He stood a few inches taller than the others and looked well-muscled. The man could be considered good looking despite the blood marring his face, with a square jaw, close-cropped hair, and distinctive, almost jade green eyes. 'There are two ways this can end. Option one; you walk away and I never see you or your boys again or option two; I execute every last one of you, so there *is* no one left to walk away.'

'Take it, easy man, were all white men here, no need for this to go any further. We're all brothers here.'

Danny felt a low growl building in his throat. 'The colour of our skin is the only thing we have in common. It's bigoted arseholes like you that ruin the countries we live in.'

The leader turned his gaze to Clay. 'You're Clay Gunn, right? From Texas?'

'You better tell me how you know that or this will be a real short conversation.' Clay took a step forward, his revolver pointed at the centre of the man's chest. 'You know my name so what's yours?'

The leader held up both hands. 'Syrus Sanderson. I'm sure you just see a stereotypical redneck bigot, but I'm not that at all. We believe that America needs to get back to old fashioned values like the first true Americans lived by. You're Texan, I thought you'd understand.'

'Fuck you,' replied Clay.

'First Americans? I take it you mean the white settlers, not the native Americans who lived here for thousands of years before it was invaded by Europeans?' Danny thrust his captive aside with disdain. 'Take your men and go. If our paths ever cross again it will be the final encounter, I promise you that.'

Syrus lowered his hands to his hips, feet shoulder-width apart. 'You started this ruckus. Marlon and CJ were a real mess. Why did you come on all heavy-handed?'

'I don't have to explain shit to you, Adolf, but if you must know, I'm looking for a bald fucker with tribal tattoos on the side of his face.'

'CJ said you had a picture?'

Danny pushed his anger back down and reached for the drawing in his pocket. His finger still brushed the trigger of the S&W pistol. 'Take a look.'

Chapter 28

'I knew there was more to those two.' Anderson flicked a finger at the screen of his PC. Brockovich pushed with one foot, her office chair rolling silently to the corner of the desk they shared. Around them, a buzz of activity provided a constant backdrop.

'Do tell.'

'Well, I don't think they were giving the whole truth and nothing but.'

'You do surprise me,' said Brockovich. 'And here's me thinking they were bona fide boy scouts.'

'Well, they're something. They are full brothers despite looking like Lennie and George,' said Anderson.

The corners of Brockovich's mouth curled into a smile. 'Nice, Of mice and men. Book or movie?'

Anderson pushed a pen with the tip of his index finger. 'I wish I could say book, but there's a vicious rumour going around that you're some kind of detective or something. I watched it on cable last night.'

'Chaney or Malkovich?'

'Malkovich.'

'Pretty good, but I prefer the older version and I prefer the book over both.'

'It's on my *'to-read list'.*'

'Since when did you ever read anything more than the Sports Illustrated swimsuit edition and Guns and Ammo?'

Anderson flicked at the screen once more. 'Anyhoo, it turns out that while the Gunn brothers were down in Mexico not too long ago, a whole bunch of dead bodies turned up. Some sort of cult down there, kidnapping tourists. The bodies were mostly cult members and cartel soldiers. The brothers brought back a busload of American kids. One of them, Celine Chavez, lives in the same house as the big brother.'

'They ended cartel soldiers? Holy crap. Are they mercs?'

'Maybe, maybe not. Both brothers served in the military. Danny served in the British army, as something called a Green Jacket, some kind of rifle regiment. The big one, Clay, served as an Army Ranger.'

'So, they could be real trouble?' Brockovich moved closer to the screen.

'Uh-huh, but that's not all. I went further back. They were also tied into another spate of killings.

They saved a British journalist from a rogue PMC outfit with a kill order on her. They wrecked a mansion down in Key West in the process.'

'I remember hearing about that,' said Brockovich. 'You sure that was the same two guys?'

'Checked and double-checked.'

'And now they're here and linked to the murder of Christine Haims. Do you like them for it?'

Anderson's head shook slowly on his bull neck. 'No, Danny's alibi stands up, I double-double checked, but I do think we need to pay them another visit. I think we've got a couple of gun-slingers on our hands. I don't want to see a trail of bodies showing up in our fine city.'

Brockovich retrieved her service pistol from her desk drawer. After checking the magazine, she pushed it into the paddle holster on her right hip. 'You want to go find them tonight?'

Anderson glanced at his watch, a retro digital Casio. 'No, let's call it a day. We can pick up the trail in the morning.'

'You got a hot date or something?'

'Cindy makes meatloaf on Thursdays. That and a bottle of French red is as close to a hot date as we get these days.'

'You and Cindy have been together forever.

Do you know how rare that is these days? And you a dim-witted ex-footballer turned flatfoot.'

'Wow, I feel like you captured the essence of my being in one sentence. You should write Hallmark cards.'

'Go home, eat your meatloaf and kiss Cindy, you big lummox.'

'Okay. See you tomorrow, Brockovich.'

'You know you will, Anderson.'

Chapter 29

The padlock that secured the rear double doors of the warehouse was thick and sturdy. The chain that secured the twin gates too was thick, its links difficult to cut or break. The doors were constructed of welded plate steel. None of these precautions troubled Curtis Quantrill. His eyes followed the lithe athlete as he sprinted straight towards the high chain-link fence. Pele Gato vaulted high into the air, his hands catching the top of the fence. With feline grace, Gato levered himself so he stood on top of the closest fence post. Quantrill huffed through his nose in admiration. Gato leapt from the post and caught the drainpipe with both hands, well above the anti-climb spikes. Using the pipe, he climbed hand over hand, moving at a rapid pace. Then Gato was up and standing atop the warehouse roof. Quantrill tapped the button of his mini-flashlight once. Gato held up his hand before disappearing from view.

A truck rumbled past the front of the warehouse, but Quantrill paid it little heed. His vehicle was parked far enough from the main road so as only a deliberate search would uncover them. The three other men in the vehicle talked in hushed tones.

'What's taking him so long?'

Quantrill looked at Blaine then leaned closer to the big man. 'We all have our skills, just give him time, that is unless you want to try your hand at running up walls and shit?' Blaine said nothing. Beads of perspiration dotted the bald dome of his head.

Junk leaned his head between the front seats. 'You sure Gato will be okay? That's still a hell of a drop, even for him.'

'I asked him if he needed a rope but you know what he's like. It's that Brazilian blood of his. They're all a bit crazy if you ask me,' said Curtis. Pele Gato had done little more than twitch his nose at the suggestion. 'As soon as he gets the door opened, we go in quick and quiet. The crates we're looking for should all be marked with a big red Q.'

'Not an X?' asked Jerome Taylor, known to his friends as 'Sticks'. 'I thought X marked the spot?'

'Dumb ass,' said Fish.

'I'm smart enough to get in your mother's pants and dumb enough to want to.' Sticks laughed as Fish slowly raised his middle finger.

As Junk chuckled at the jibes, Quantrill looked to each of the team in turn. They were good men. They were his men, loyal and brave.

A smaller single door at the side of the warehouse swung open and Gato held up one thumb.

'Let's move. Quick and quiet. You know the drill, Fish. Radio silence unless there's incoming.'

'Ja vol, mien Capitan,' answered Fish.

As the team exited the vehicle Sticks leaned back in to peer at Fish. 'Now who's being a dumb ass?'

'You are. You're so dumb, you sit on the TV and watch the couch.'

'Prick.'

'Dick.'

'Be careful.'

'I will.' Sticks bumped fists with Fish.

'Move.' Quantrill's voice told them recess was over.

The interior of the warehouse was cloaked in shadow; the only light that of the moon, bleeding in through the skylight Gato had levered open. The majority of the building was subdivided into storage units, each with its roller-door. The doors were evenly spaced, a padlock at the base of each. Quantrill pulled the door closed behind him. With a flick of his thumb the flashlight he held cast a narrow beam across the room. He walked quickly to the right of the storage units. A second area held his attention. A chain-link fence bolted to metal poles formed a series of cages. The cages were filled with crates and boxes of every size and shape. Gato was already at work on the padlock of the first enclosure. His lithe form gently swayed in the darkness. Quantrill knew he would be mentally humming a tune as he picked the lock. He loved his music. In seconds, the cage gate swung open and Gato hung, the open lock, on one of the chain links. Soundlessly, he moved to the next cage. One open, four to go. Dust motes swirled as the team began searching the stacks for the marked crates. Gato continued to open the cage doors.

Sticks looked up from the crate he was manhandling. 'Did Gato take care of the alarms and cameras?'

Quantrill held the flashlight below his chin. The angled shadows that decorated his face looked like a vintage horror movie effect. 'Yeah he did, the alarm system was older than half the buildings in this city.'

Gato poked his head over Stick's shoulder, whispering; 'And as easy to get into as your girlfriend's pants.'

Sticks shouldered his friend away. 'Bite me.'

'Got one.' Blaine's baritone voice cut through the sound of suppressed laughter. 'One crate, marked with a Q.'

'There should be five crates. Keep looking until we've got them all.'

Chapter 30

Clay's boots fell with a clunk from the end of the bed. The weapons they had procured sat atop the drink-stained table. One leg of the table had a pizza menu folded into a wedge under it. 'You think that's the last we'll see of the Southern Unification?'

Danny offered him little more than a shrug. 'If they have any sense.'

'Yeah, because that's just what bigots and zealots are known for.'

'They're lucky they got to walk away at all.'

'I think there's a few that won't be walking anywhere for a while.' Clay stretched out on his bed. The wooden frame creaked as he adjusted his position in an attempt to get comfortable. 'I think half of them will be calling at the ER before sunrise. I'm pretty sure I heard more than a few bones breaking during the festivities.'

'They had it coming.'

Clay looked across at his younger brother. His mood had not lightened. Ignoring the nipping pain in his shoulder, Clay sat upright. 'We've changed hotels and I don't think they were in any state to follow us again, so we should be okay until morning. Handy that this flea pit takes cash, no credit card details to snoop on, just in case they have those kinds of connections. Not many motels still do that. At least we can get some shut-eye now.'

'You go ahead,' said Danny. 'I won't be far behind you.'

'Just remember that you need to sleep too. A solid eight hours and a decent breakfast and we'll get back in the saddle.'

'Okay Clay.'

***

When Clay next opened his eyes, bright sunlight illuminated the room through a gap in the curtains. The dagger of light had reached the toes of his left foot, warming them. He looked at the other single bed in the room. There was little more than a faint impression on the top sheet. 'Danny?'

There was no answer. Clay paused mid-action of pulling on his boots when he spotted a hand-written note folded into a standing V. The immediate urgency abated. He picked up the note. It was written on the hotel's own notepaper. A pair of leaning palms in green adorned the top left of the page.

Gone for a run.
Won't be long.
Needed to clear my head.
Danny.

'Who else would it be from?' said Clay replacing the note on the bedside cabinet. He moved to the bathroom. The face that stared back at him was thick with stubble. Clay looked at his features, his wide sloping forehead lined with distinctive scars. The left side was the worst. He had tried growing his hair longer a few years back but had not liked the look. Running the water until it was piping hot, he used the small bar of soap to produce a lather. The disposable razor did an adequate job and he was rubbing his face dry with the towel when Danny re-entered the room.

'Hey, you should have given me a nudge,' said Clay. 'I would have come for a run with you.'

Danny dead-eyed him. 'Really? The last time you ran there was a closing down sale at the burrito shop.'

'Ooh, low blow. Besides, it was a chicken shack.' Clay tossed the towel into the bathtub. 'I could have cheered you on while you ran. You know, for moral support.'

'More like moron support.' Danny pulled off the sweat-stained t-shirt as he too headed for the bathroom.

Clay looked at his younger brother. Danny too had his scars. A light patch mottled the skin of his left ribs. Getting set on fire was no fun. Despite being the wrong side of forty, Danny's muscles were tight and well defined. 'I left you some hot water, you wiry little bastard.'

'Ah, the terms of endearment only a brother can bestow,' said Danny.

The corners of Clay's mouth curled into a wry smile. 'So, who are we going to upset this morning?'

'Not sure, but the day is still young. Maybe we can up the game and roll a couple of drug lords over at Little Havana?'

Clay laughed. 'Sounds like fun, if a little stereotypical.'

Danny shook his head as he entered the bathroom, closing the door behind him. Moments later Clay heard the sound of jetting water. Nodding to himself, Clay was silently relieved to see Danny behaving a little more like himself. While he fully understood the sombre mood of his younger brother, it pained him to see it. Clay picked up the baseball bat from the table. The wooden shaft felt cool and comfortable in his grip. He rolled the bat in an overhand arc several times. Replacing the bat, Clay looked at the disposable pen that Danny had used to write his note. Reaching into his pocket, Clay pulled out his cell phone and scrolled through the contact list. He clicked on one of the highlighted names. The call took less than three minutes.

'What are you looking so pleased about?' asked Danny as he stepped from the bathroom. He was already dressed again in his jeans.

'While you've been in there soaping up and tugging your Johnson, I've been thinking.'

'Lord preserve us,' said Danny. 'I guess there's a first time for everything.'

'I phoned a friend. We're meeting him for breakfast. I should have thought about him earlier, might have saved us some leg work.'

'Who's the friend?'

'Terry Penn.'

'Where do I know that name from?'

'I worked with Terry a few years back when I was down here working as an extra and stuntman.'

'Aye, Terry Penn, the actor, big guy. I know who you mean now.'

'We're meeting him at the Raleigh Hotel on Collins,' said Clay. 'So, get your ass in gear.'

'Give me a couple of minutes and I'll be ready to rock 'n' roll.'

The drive to Collins Avenue was circuitous as Clay drove back to the Sunset Inn and swapped back to the rental. The Chevy was a mess, crumpled and missing the rear fender, and the last thing they needed was attention from a traffic cop. The Dodge Nitro was parked just where he had left it. There were no signs of the rental vehicle being tampered with. Regardless, Clay dropped to one knee, peering into the wheel arches and then fully underneath the chassis.

'I don't think the SU boys are quick enough to wire your car with a bomb,' said Danny.

'Better safe than sorry,' said Clay as he used the side of the Dodge, to lever himself upright.

'True dat,' said Danny.

Chapter 31

Terry Penn had starred in over forty movies and guested on at least as many television shows. Despite being neither of Italian descent or a native New Yorker he had carved out a lucrative career playing the stereotypical big city-wise guy. As he sat opposite, Danny took in his rounded features and dyed hair. No one had hair that black, especially considering that Clay had told him too that Penn had passed his sixtieth birthday nearly five years hence.

'Still a handsome bastard I see,' said Penn as Clay returned the actor's enthusiastic hug before sitting at the table. The diner opposite the Raleigh Hotel on Collins Avenue was filled with a wonderful aroma, the smell of strong coffee and griddled breakfasts.

'Still, downing cannoli like it's a health supplement?' punted Clay.

'They'll have to prise my last cannoli from my cold dead fingers.'

'Nice imagery,' said Clay. 'Thanks for meeting us on short notice. I know you're a busy guy.'

'Can't complain, but I miss our time together. Any time you want to log some more screen time, just give me a call.'

'Thanks, Terry, I appreciate the offer. Maybe when things quiet back down. What're you working on?'

Terry Penn flashed a smile befitting the Cheshire cat. 'I thought I'd expand my portfolio, so I'm playing a priest.'

'Really? That's great.'

'Yeah, a priest who used to be a hitman for one of the New York families. Now he's hiding out in Miami, trying to help people out of jams.'

'Sounds great,' offered Danny.

'Sounds a lot like Sun Burned, the show we worked on together,' said Clay.

'Hey, whaddya gonna do? It's a living. They offer the job, I take it. Badda bing. Badda boom.'

'A man's, got to work,' said Danny.

'You got that right. I have four ex-wives that still have their teeth in my ass, so I take the jobs as they come. Would you believe I got asked to double for Steven Seagal last month? Just a few distance shots, but hey. Like I look anything like that big palooka.'

'What did you tell them?' asked Clay.

'I start in three-weeks' time. I'll be doing some of the second unit stuff, you know, back shots getting in and out of cars and things.'

Danny smiled. 'I met him quite a few years back. He was teaching at a martial arts seminar in Prague. He's a big guy.'

Terry swivelled in his seat, the vinyl covering emitting a rodent-like squeak. 'You into that Kung Fu game too? I remember Clay showing some stuff when we worked together.'

'I dabble. I tried Aikido for a little while, hence the Seagal seminar, but it didn't suit my temperament,' said Danny.

Terry nodded then turned to Clay. 'D'you remember when you karate kicked the hat off Bruce Campbell's head?'

Clay gave a low chuckle. 'Yeah, I do. That could have spelt the end of my screen career before it started.'

'Bruce thought it was great. He's still got it on film you know. Showed it to me a while back. Great guy.'

'He is,' agreed Clay.

Terry cocked his head to one side. 'So, I looked into the name you gave me. It didn't ring any bells at first, then I saw a photo of the guy on Google. I knew the guy in passing, this Delacroix. He was always down here trying to bang the extras; you know the young ones looking for a break. He picked up a bit of work taking the cameras out to sea and stuff. Good with a boat.'

'Aye, that sounds like our man,' said Danny.

'Why the big interest in a dead man?' asked Terry, leaning back as a young waiter arrived at their table carrying three plates. The contents of both Terry and Clay's plates were considerably larger than Danny's spinach and tofu breakfast burrito. Between bites of the wrap, Danny brought Terry up to speed.

'And you think that your girlfriend was murdered because of something Delacroix did?'

Danny nodded. 'More like something that he had, maybe hidden in the house, or at least the fuckers thought that it was in the house.'

'Uh Huh,' Terry steepled his fingers. 'Well, I know a guy who knows a guy and he told me some interesting shit about Erik Delacroix.'

Danny felt a stirring in his chest. Maybe they weren't chasing the wild goose after all.

'Delacroix ran with a wild bunch and didn't let the law stop him doing anything once he had set his mind to it. I don't think he was a bad guy just a bit crazy when it came to the gold.'

'Gold?' asked Danny.

'Not just gold, any treasure he could find. He and his guys were treasure hunters of the rogue variety. Word on the street is that Delacroix and his boys found something big, so big that he couldn't sell it on the open market. The US government has some very strict rules when it comes to hauling gold out of the sea.'

'What did they find?' asked Clay.

Terry Penn scooped up a fork full of griddled ham and pushed it into his mouth. 'Did you ever hear of a guy called Mel Fisher?'

'Aye,' answered Danny. 'He was a famous treasure hunter too. Found a mega haul in the eighties.'

'The one, and the same.' Terry plucked a sheet of paper from the inside of his tan linen jacket. After slipping on a pair of spectacles, he began to read. 'Mel Fisher and his crew found the wreck of a legendary Spanish galleon, the Nuestra Senora de Atocha. The galleon was heading back to Spain laden with gold, silver, and jewels when it was caught in a hurricane off the coast of Key West. It was lost for over four hundred years. Mel Fisher's haul was worth something like *four hundred million dollars* and that was in the eighties.'

'That's a hell of a lot of money,' said Danny.

'Damn right. Mel had to fight the state of Florida to keep them from taking the lion's share. It took years in and out of courtrooms.'

Danny wiped his mouth as he finished his breakfast. 'Was Delacroix part of Fisher's crew?'

'No. Delacroix was his own man. He and his guys used to run a boat out of the keys called the Mariana Meg.'

'Yeah, we tracked the Meg down in Fort Lauderdale,' said Clay.

'The thing with the shipwreck that Fisher found is that despite him turning up one of the biggest hauls in history, the main treasure store of the ship is still missing.' Terry gave a suggestive nod.

'You think Delacroix found it?' asked Danny.

'That's what the whisperers say,' answered Terry.

Danny leaned back in his seat. He ran the palm of his hand across his chin. A couple of seconds passed. 'But he knew what Fisher had gone through, so didn't go public. He and his guys squirrelled the treasure bit by bit.'

Terry Penn gave his trademark wise-guy smile. 'Maybe this guy with the balls the size of coconuts decided to bring it ashore and hide it. Then he could sell it piece by piece over the years. It's what I would do. Did you know that four of his crew died at the same time when their plane went down over Belize? Delacroix had changed his plans at the last minute, he was the only one left alive from his original crew.'

'So, if they had looted the treasure from the

ship, Delacroix would have been the only one left that knew where it was hidden,' said Clay.

'Badda bing. Badda boom.' Penn chased the last of his ham around his plate.

'Any ideas where he might have hidden the loot?' asked Danny, the hint of a smile showing.

'Now, if I knew that, do you think I'd be sweating my cojones on set every day?'

'I think you would, the camera loves you.' Danny gave what he hoped was a sincere nod.

'Thanks for taking time out to meet us, Terry.' said Clay. 'You're a stand-up guy,' said Clay.

'Made a career out of it,' laughed Penn.

Chapter 32

Quantrill felt a familiar tingle in the pit of his stomach. The men had found no less than nine crates, more than he had expected, each marked with a distinctive red 'Q', a stamp used by the original storage depot. The break-in at the warehouse had gone without a hitch. No heroic security guards had come calling, no shootout in the middle of the night, good business.

The garage attached to Quantrill's house was neat and tidy. A hand-painted sign on the wall declared *'A place for everything and everything in its place'*, a creed he tried to live by. Above his workbench, a Cannibal surfboard was fastened to a wire rack with two bungee cords. The design of the board consisted of a sunset and a deckchair in Rastafarian colours. A set of crossed machetes adorned the wall next to the surfboard.

The team examined the various boxes, crates and containers pilfered from within the fenced holding area. Sticks looked up from the open trunk, his hands roving over its contents. 'You know, you should have been a detective man. You're frontin' some serious Sherlock Holmes skills finding that place.'

Quantrill gave a dismissive shrug. 'Not really.

We've been after this score for nearly five years now and the most we've turned up is a family-sized bucket of scuttlebutt. I just keep working the information. Tenacity is the name of the game.'

'Yeah, but we're getting closer, I can feel it,' said Gato. There was a low murmur of agreement from the others. 'And there was that bag of gold coins last year.'

'I know, but that's a drop in the ocean, literally, to the rest of the haul Delacroix stashed,' said Curtis. 'Let's take our time going through this stuff. I want everything examined. Every slip of paper read, every box opened, no matter how small. Delacroix was a smart son of a bitch and he knew what he was doing when he hid the stash. It won't be as obvious as a map with an X marked on it.'

'Or a Q,' said Blaine as he scattered a pile of buff folders across the workbench. Papers spilt from the folders. 'This is boring. We've been at this for over two hours and all I've got is a crick in the neck. I'm getting tired of chasing the Delacroix legacy. Come on man, why don't we head out to South Beach and go out on the jet skis? We can do this later.'

Quantrill paused, looking up from the pile of handwritten invoices he was holding. 'Do you want a cut of the treasure when we find it?'

'Yeah, but...'

'Then get your head back in the game and start reading.'

Blaine shook his head as he glanced at a folder at the top of the pile. He pushed the paper around for a few seconds. 'This is bullshit, we should be out checking real scores. I told you about that pawnshop over in Silver Lakes. It's an easy mark. The guy that owns it smokes enough pot to get us all high. The last time I was in the shop he wandered into the back room and didn't come out for about ten minutes.'

Fish spoke without looking up from the cigar box he was examining. 'If it was so easy why didn't you do it there and then?'

Quantrill watched Blaine's colour subtly darken.

'There were stiffs in the shop, some couple trying to find an engagement ring or something. The store stays open late. I scoped it out for cameras. There's only one behind the main counter. If we went in fast with our heads down, we could clean out the whole store and be out and drinking margaritas in two minutes. I'm telling you it's an easy score. We just have to hit it before someone else does.'

Quantrill noticed Fish raising one eyebrow and recognised the look on his face. 'Forget the pawnshop for now. Why are you sniffing around chump change when there's a chance of the biggest payday in history...if you can keep your minds on the job for more than ten minutes.'

Sticks slapped his hand down on the papers spread out before him. 'I think I've got something.'

Quantrill peered at Sticks, his black hair slicked back from his face and tied with a red bandana. 'What is it?'

Sticks held up a plastic bag the size of a paperback book. The clear polythene was wrapped tight and secured with a strip of silver duct tape.

Gato clicked his fingers in rapid succession. 'Come, man, open it. Don't keep us in suspenders.'

Fish laughed. 'Who you kiddin' Gato? We've all seen the photos.'

Gato flipped the bird. Fish responded by doubling the gesture, his tongue poking from his mouth like a deranged Maori.

Sticks produced a Balisong from his hip pocket. The outer handles of the butterfly knife made their distinctive *flack-flack-flack* as he exposed the blade.

'Careful,' warned Quantrill needlessly. He knew Sticks was an artisan, both with the blade and the ironwood cudgels that had gained him his moniker. Sticks opened the outer skin with two deft swipes of the knife. The plastic opened like a flower in bloom. The corners of Quantrill's mouth turned up into a smile. He recognised the exposed object.

'Great,' said Fish. 'You found the remote for Delacroix's broke-assed hi-fi.'

Quantrill picked up the rectangular device, turning it over in his hands. The smile dropped from his face. A smaller rectangular gap seemed to mock him, a gap that made all the difference in the world.

'What is it, an old phone?' asked Junk.

Quantrill huffed through his nose. 'Not a phone. It's an old GPS tracker unit, but the battery's missing.'

Fish nodded in understanding. 'So, we're looking for a battery now as well.'

'Yeah, keep looking,' said Curtis.

Chapter 33

'You sure you're okay doing this?' asked Clay. 'Going back and looking around Chrissie's house again?'

'We need to come at this from a different angle. I was full of fire yesterday, but all I've done is run us around in a big circle and upset the locals.'

'You do have a talent for that.' Clay motioned with the end of his half-eaten churro for Danny to continue. The other customers in the internet café paid the brothers little notice. A super-sized coffee sat either side of the sleek black desktop PC that Danny tapped at.

'We need to look at this like cops, follow the evidence.'

Clay washed down churro with a gulp of coffee. 'But we're not cops. We don't think like cops and certainly don't behave like them. There's a pesky rulebook they follow and it seems they expect others to follow as well. Uh, I think it's referred to as the law.'

'I didn't say we needed to be cops, just follow their example, their methodology.'

'Okay, it's new, but never let it be said that

I'm unwilling to embrace change.'

'Well, aren't you just the progressive Texan?' Danny too took a sip of coffee then pointed to his cell phone. 'While you were getting the coffee, I uploaded a picture of the drawing of that arsehole with the tattoos.'

'Okay.' Clay leaned closer to the screen. 'And?'

Danny pointed at the famous logo at the top of the screen. 'This is a reverse image search. Instead of searching using a web address or keywords you search by image.'

'And you think that…' Clay read the logo. 'This Silver-Mirror might recognize his face, even from a hand-drawn picture?'

'Let's find out.' Danny hit the enter key. Images began to fill the screen. Many of the pictures showed faces with similar facial tattoos as the drawing. Faces from every race were shown, each with ink work.

'Can you narrow the search to only include white men?' asked Clay.

'I don't know how to. I only found this site because I was thinking about this bald fucker again. I guess it'll be a trawl through these results. I'll click on each one that looks promising and then look for information that links him to Miami.'

Clay puffed out his cheeks. 'I think we may be here for some time. Okay. Let's have at it.'

The faces on the screen ranged from handsome to hideous. Most of the images were of men yet there were occasional women shown too, most with a facial tattoo. Several pictures of Bruce Willis and Jason Statham were scattered among the results. 'They must be in there because of the bald thing. I think we can rule out those two.'

'Aye, I think we can.'

'And I don't think Mike Tyson is our man, either.'

Danny glanced at the boxer but added nothing.

'Click on that one,' said Clay. The picture showed a thickset man, clean-shaven with a tribal tattoo curving down the left side of his face. The next page provided a link to the source webpage. After a few seconds, a new page opened and identified the man as John Stamper, a mechanic from Detroit. 'Maybe not. Try the next one.'

After watching Danny clicking two dozen or so pictures, Clay shifted in his seat. Glancing at the clock in the bottom right of the screen Clay declared, 'I'm starting to get a numb ass.'

'Go and stretch your legs. I'll keep at this.'

'Okay, I won't be long, I was never built for sitting at a desk.'

'Better suited for climbing the Empire State Building, sure enough.'

Clay stood and rolled first his shoulder then his neck. The muscle in his chest gave a sight tug. He huffed through his nose.

Danny looked up from the screen. 'How you doing?'

'I'm on the mend,' replied Clay. It was something his mother used to say. He still missed her. She had been a strong and stubborn woman. Her thick Scottish accent and piercing eyes he saw in Danny.

Danny smiled, recognising the term. 'Remember what she used to sing us, back when we were kids together, her rhyme about farting?'

'Remind me.'

'Hold yer arse to the chair, try an' stop the leakin' air. Shift yer arse from cheek to cheek…'

'And pray to God it does'nae reek,' finished Clay. 'She had a line for every occasion.'

'Aye, she did.' Danny pointed to the door. 'Now git yersel' oot fer a walk, yer face is botherin' me.'

Clay found himself chuckling as he stepped out into the unrelenting sunlight.

Chapter 34

Danny stared at the face on the screen. The background noise from the café faded away to a little more than a low murmur to his ear. The tattoo on the man's face matched the drawing exactly. The young Hispanic kid, Paco, had a gift. The face on the screen carried a certain quality that Danny had seen a thousand times before. The guy was big, bald, and tough and he knew it. The slight sneer, that air of arrogance captured by the camera was probably not an unfamiliar look on his face.

Danny clicked on the image which expanded to fill most of the screen. A series of buttons were now displayed below the picture. Danny clicked on the first social media link. The man's Facebook profile picture was the same as the picture he had just found. Danny stared at the name below the sneer. Caleb Blaine. Looking to the left of the screen he scanned the details displayed. *Lives in Miami. Works at Shock City Guns.* After searching for the gun store, he jotted down the address and numbers listed. He went back to Facebook. Danny scrolled down the page. The timeline showed entries on a fairly regular basis, the most recent picture and a status update was dated six days earlier. Caleb Blaine stared back from the screen, a set of free weights in each hand. Beads of sweat dotted his bald head. Veins were visibly raised on his arms, forming something akin to a road map. The background of the picture was slightly out of focus, but not so much that Danny couldn't read the logo on the wall behind. BodyTrick Gym. It was the same gym that Chrissie had worked at.

Danny scrolled down to the next picture. Blaine straddled a motorcycle, not a road bike; but what Danny called a 'scrambler', an off-road dirt bike. Blaine was covered in dust and a full-face helmet was perched on the handlebars of the bike. He cast the same sneer as in his profile picture. Danny scrolled again. The next picture showed Blaine holding a stein of beer aloft. Five men flanked him each with their beers raised. The bar looked to be an open-air venue. A neon sign shone brightly above the bar. *Bambu Daddy*. Danny moved the cursor over the various faces in the picture. No names appeared over the images.

Danny clicked on several of the pictures and then hit the print option. A printer behind the main counter whirred to life. Opening another tab on the screen, Danny typed '*Bambu daddy bar Miami*'. The results showed the bar had an official website. Clicking on the link, Danny wrote down the address of the bar. The blurb on the homepage showed the bar looking out across Morningside Park.

Danny closed the displayed pages then logged

out. He paid the server for the pictures he had printed. The young woman behind the counter smiled as she handed over the prints. 'You know you can do most of this on your phone, right? And for free.'

Danny rested his elbows on the countertop. 'How's that?'

'Your smartphone can do just about everything that a PC can, just faster.'

Danny raised one eyebrow. 'What makes you think I've got a smartphone?'

'Why wouldn't you?' The young woman raised an eyebrow of her own. 'My mom's ancient, nearly fifty, and she's got one.'

'Two things, yes I do have a smartphone; but I find it a pain in the jacksie to use,' Danny wiggled his fingers. 'Shrek hands.'

The young woman showed the stirrings of a smile. 'And the second thing?'

'Nearly fifty is by no means ancient.'

'If you say so.'

'I do.'

'You married?'

Danny tapped the prints on the counter. 'Why, you looking for a date?'

'No, but my mom may be interested.'

'Does she know her daughter is out here trying to line her up with strange men?'

'Are you? Strange, I mean?'

'Only in a good way.' Danny straightened. 'Maybe some other time. Tell your mom I said hello though.'

'I'll tell her it was an Irish guy and he was full of charm.'

'Scots,' corrected Danny.

'Huh…'

As he stepped from the cool interior of the internet café Danny smiled despite himself. He had been called Irish many times in America. There were worse things to be called so he let it slide. Rolling the prints into a loose paper tube, he looked both ways up and down the street. Clay was nowhere to be seen. Knowing he could reach him on the phone within seconds, Danny instead sat on a bench outside an empty storefront. Ragged posters filled the window of the store. *Final sale. Closing down.*

Pulling the phone from his pocket he tapped in the number he had found for Shock City Guns.

'Hello?'

'Hi, welcome to Shock City Guns. How may I help you today?'

'I'm trying to reach Caleb.'

'Caleb Blaine?'

'Yeah, Caleb Blaine, is he in today?'

'Sorry man, he doesn't work here anymore.'

'That's interesting. He applied for a position with my company and used you guys as a reference on his résumé. Why did he leave?'

The voice on the phone dropped in tone. 'Let's just say his safety protocols with firearms did not meet our standards.'

'Oh.'

'Yeah, you only need to get it wrong once and you've got a dead customer on your floor.'

'Have you got a home address on file for him?' asked Danny.

'I'm sorry but we can't give out any personal details, data protection. You must have his address on his résumé, right?'

'Yeah, just double-checking details before we make an offer of employment.'

'I'd think twice before doing that buddy, just saying.'

'Thanks for the heads up.' Danny killed the call. It was worth a shot. Leaning back against the brickwork, he enjoyed the sun on his face. The temperature was climbing steadily but a cooling breeze seemed determined to find its way into the city streets. He closed his eyes and let the sounds of the city filter in. He had found that many cities had their distinctive sound, as unique as the architecture. Miami was no exception. The sound of traffic seemed less intrusive to his ear in Miami. Certainly, there was no shortage of vehicles but there was less of the shouting and blaring of horns than in most large cities. Music too drifted to his ear; not Latin, but a relaxed reggae beat. Miami. The city Chrissie Haims had called home.

Chapter 35

*C*hrissie is laughing a soft and gentle sound. The corners of her eyes crinkle, something she does not care for but Danny finds immensely attractive. She pushes the plate away, the silverware crossed over the remnants of her meal. Danny is still eating, trying not to make a mess in front of her. The spears of grilled asparagus are perfectly cooked in the battered tofu fried tempura style. Tiny dishes of soy sauce seem to stare at him like the button eyes of a cartoon character. Chrissie is urging him to try some of the jasmine rice. Chrissie is sipping from her glass. The bottle of wine is nearly empty, another finished already. The Chenin blanc suits Japanese food perfectly.

Chrissie is looking across the table at him, her gaze steady and unaffected by the alcohol. She is saying something but Danny can't quite hear the words, maybe the wine is kicking in after all.

'What?' His voice is small, distant.

The sound of reggae drifts across the Japanese restaurant. The other diners are falling silent one by one. Heaviness like a rain cloud darkens the dining room. Somewhere, just out of his vision, a light incessantly flickers.

'What?' he is asking again, aware of heads tilting in their direction.

'I said, I think I'm falling in love with you, Daniel

Gunn.'

Danny feels the warmth creep up his neck into his face. He is trying to tell her he loves her too but the words won't come. A low keening is the only thing he hears. A low disparaging sound like a faulty machine, something that once had a purpose but is now obsolete.

Danny is looking behind Chrissie now. He hears a low hissing. The smell of spoiled food fills his nose. He recoils. Something dark is forming behind her. Turning like ink in water, something dark and putrid and dangerous. The dark thing, the cloud of putrescence, is taking on a shape. Arms and legs are forming from the languid maelstrom. Twin spots of red are shining now from a misshapen lump that must be the thing's head.

Danny is struggling to move. His arms and legs feel like they are bolted to the chair. His voice is now that of a child, pitched and confused. He tries to shout a warning.

The shadow man is moving behind Chrissie now. Why can't Chrissie see him? Why can't Chrissie hear Danny's warning? Why is she smiling and talking? Run Chrissie…RUN!

He is fighting against his invisible bonds now with all his strength. Old wounds become new once more. The skin across his ribs is on fire, flames burning through his shirt. A bullet tears a wedge of skin from his arm, then another. His mouth is filled with blood, teeth loose and painful. He is smashing through the windscreen of a van, tumbling through the air anticipating the wrenching impact to follow. A knife stabs deep into his thigh. Old wounds. He is still in his seat. Frozen.

The shadow man coils an arm around Chrissie's neck. Why can't she see him? Then another arm.

Run Chrissie!

But she doesn't run.

Chrissie is standing up, moving slowly as if beginning a romantic dance. Slowly, so slowly, then she is up on her tiptoes, so high there is no way she can be supporting her weight. Her teeth first clamp together then open wide. Danny can see the uneaten food in her mouth. Chrissie's eyes widen, the white visible all around her iris. The shadow man emits an extended hiss; a reptilian sound. Chrissie's feet are no longer touching the ground. They kick back, lost in the black smoke that is the thing behind her.

Danny strains to stand until he feels something tear in his lower spine. He feels warm liquid running from his ears, nose, and mouth. He knows what it is, he has tasted his blood many times before.

Chrissie's bulging eyes find him across the table. The look is abject fear.

An icy claw seems to grip Danny's heart and squeeze.

Chrissie is pulled inside the smoking mass inch by inch, absorbed, devoured. He forces against his seat, the skin ripping away from his muscles, the pain immeasurable. The smoking mass turns in on itself, folding and swirling and Chrissie is gone.

'NO!'

The shadow man looks dismissively at Danny, now half standing but still a million miles from saving her. The voice the creature speaks in is unmistakable. Chrissie.

'You said you would keep me safe…'

Chapter 36

Clay snapped his head to one side as Danny erupted from the bench. The hand that slammed into the side of his jaw felt like an iron weight. Clay rolled with the blow but still was sent staggering back across the sidewalk.

'Danny! It's me!'

Danny stood gasping, his feet planted wide, fists curled close to his face. Printed pictures lay scattered at his feet.

'Danny,' repeated Clay. 'Stand down! It's me.'

Clay held up both palms and took a slow step closer to his younger brother. Beads of moisture ran down Danny's face. Clay wasn't sure if it was sweat or tears. Danny dropped his hands and moved out of the fighting crouch.

'Jesus, Clay, I'm sorry. I don't know what happened there.'

Clay rubbed his jaw. 'You were snoozing in the sunshine. I didn't expect to get my clock cleaned just for giving you the wake-up call.'

'I'm so sorry Clay.'

'I forgot how hard you can hit, you wiry little

bastard.'

'I must have dozed off. I didn't even realise I had started to drift,' said Danny.

'Maybe we should get separate rooms when we get back to the hotel. I don't want the alarm going off and you spin-kicking me into the bathroom.'

Danny dropped to one knee and scooped up the pictures. When he stood again, his expression was composed and controlled: *Danny Gunn*. He cocked his head to one side.

'I'll be fine,' offered Clay. 'If a crack in the jaw is the worst thing that happens today, I'll mark it down as a good day.'

Danny gave a single nod which Clay took and accepted as an apology. He pointed to the papers. 'Did you join an online dating agency while I was gone?'

'Dumb ass,' said Danny. 'They're pictures of the guy with the tattoos. I've got a name and a couple of leads too.'

Clay smiled, the numbness in his jaw abating. 'We've got leads now? You're talking to the cop thing, aren't you?'

'Double dumb ass,' said Danny.

'Double dumb ass?' laughed Clay. 'Who said that? Socrates?'

'Jim Carey.'

'Alrighty then.'

'So, we've got a name for this asshole, huh? Caleb Blaine.' Clay held out his hand then flicked through the pictures. The corners of his mouth curled into the barest of smiles. 'You sure this is the guy?'

'He's a strong possibility. He's got the look.'

'Okay.'

'It's a lot more than we had this morning,' said Danny. 'I called the gun store but he doesn't work there anymore. I couldn't get anything more out of the guy there. Data protection and all that.'

'Well done for trying, little brother. You're not as dumb as you look. Where do you want to try next, the gym or the bar?'

Danny pointed to the picture of Blaine in the gym. 'We'll go there first, then check out the bar later. That's the same place where Chrissie worked, the BodyTrick Gym. I trained there a couple of times too. It's where I first met Chrissie. I took in some of her kettlebell classes.'

Clay rested his hands on his hips. 'If Blaine is a regular at the gym, they might have an address for him.'

'My thoughts exactly,' said Danny.

'Who are the other guys with him in the bar picture?' asked Clay.

'I'm not sure. They weren't tagged in the Facebook picture. I scrolled through his friends' list, but couldn't match any of them up either.'

'Not everyone in the world uses Facebook. I don't.' Clay rolled his shoulders. 'Until we know otherwise, we'll just presume they're his back up and that they're armed and dangerous. Plan for the worst and hope for the best.'

'Always,' said Danny.

'You okay driving again?'

'Of course,' said Danny. 'I thought I was going to have to argue the toss again.'

Clay smiled. 'Nah, I'm kind of enjoying being the passenger for now. You notice a lot more when you're not driving.'

'You do,' said Danny flicking the print out. 'Those other guys in the picture, they've got the look too, same as Blaine.'

Clay knew exactly what Danny meant without elaboration. Each of the five men surrounding Blaine had hard eyes. The flint in their expressions was not eroded by the wide smiles offered. Clay too could see what they were; bad men. Men of dark virtue. The corners of his mouth twitched once more. He knew that they would not go easy. That didn't upset his sensibilities.

Chapter 37

Clay was no stranger to the inside of a gym. He could hear the tell-tale sounds as he stood at the reception counter. High energy music competed from several rooms. Trainers yelled encouraging words, the clang of weights being dropped, metal on metal. Someone was pounding the life out of a heavy bag.

The young man behind the counter held up one finger as he spat rapid-fire English into a headpiece microphone. The man's hands moved as fast as his mouth as he gesticulated wildly. Clay made a show of studying the range of activities available at the BodyTrick Gym. He gave a wry smile as the young man ended the call and looked up.

'Those guys giving you a hard time?'

'Can you believe it?' asked the receptionist. 'You miss three months on your car loan and they want to repossess it.'

Clay leaned his forearms on the countertop. 'I hear you, man. Don't these pencil pushers know how hard it is out here in the real world? You gotta give a guy some slack. Am I right?'

'Damn right.'

'What kind of car you got?' asked Clay.

'Prius. It's not like I'm driving around in a Porsche or something. I need the car to get to work. If I can't work, how the hell am I supposed to make the payments on the car?'

'Exactly.' Clay glanced at the man's polo shirt. A name was embroidered below the gym logo. 'Hey Bruce, I'm supposed to be meeting a buddy of mine here but I can't reach him on the phone. I'm wondering if I got the day wrong?'

Bruce tilted his head to one side. 'Who you supposed to be meeting?'

'Blaine, Caleb Blaine.'

Bruce looked back with a blank expression.

'You know Blaine, right? Big guy, bald, tribal tattoo.' Clay ran a finger down the side of his face.

'Yeah, yeah, I know who you mean now.'

'Has he booked in today?' asked Clay.

'He is a member,' Bruce tapped at his keyboard for a few seconds. 'But not today.'

'Damn it, I'm sure it was today.' Clay pulled his phone. 'I'll try him again.'

After listening to dead air for ten seconds Clay shook his head in the negative. 'What number have you got for him on your system?'

Bruce relayed the number from the screen and Clay added it to his contacts. 'Yeah, that's the same one I've got.'

Bruce ran a hand through his spiky brown hair.

'What address you got on file for Caleb?' asked Clay.

'One-seven-six Flagler Street.'

'Yeah,' said Clay. 'That's the same as I've got already. I'll try texting the big dope again.'

Bruce looked like he was about to say something more, but was interrupted by four young women as they entered the lobby.

'Four for Zumba.' The first woman spoke as if Clay was not there. He let it go. 'And I'll take four smartwaters.'

Bruce took the dollars from the woman's hand. Giving the four young women the once over, Clay knew he was unlikely to wring any more details from the beleaguered receptionist. Clay gave a quick wave as he exited the gym. As he returned to his parked car, he knocked first on the hood then continued to rap his knuckles on the windows and roof. The vehicle seemed to groan as he climbed into the passenger seat.

'What's that all about?' asked Danny.

'Oh, you know, just in case you'd dozed off

again. I didn't want another ninja death punch in the side of the head.'

'How about a ninja boot, right up main street?'

'Nah, I'll give that a miss too if it's all the same to you.'

'Any luck in there?'

'I've got a cell number and an address for Blaine. Eliot Ness at your service.' Clay waggled his eyebrows. 'What say we go and take a look-see at Chez-asshole. See what we can see.'

Clay watched Danny's hands slowly curl into fists. 'Sounds like a plan.'

Chapter 38

Curtis Quantrill let the sheaf of papers he was inspecting drop to the tabletop as Junk shouted his name.

'Is this what we're looking for?'

Quantrill crossed the room in four rapid steps. 'Let me see.'

Taking the item from Junk he pressed the rectangular battery into the open port. The battery slid home with a satisfactory click. Despite proving a perfect fit, the display on the tracker unit remained dark. A power cord no thicker than garden twine dangled from the base of the battery unit, a two-prong plug swinging free. Quantrill found the nearest power socket and pushed the plug home. He glanced up at the men who gathered around him.

'Is it working?' asked Fish.

As if in answer, a red light began to blink a steady rhythm. Quantrill took a deep breath. His thumb found the main power button. His words were whispered, more to himself than to the men that surrounded him. 'Come on, come on.'

The screen remained dark.

'That thing has been lying in storage for years. It's gonna take a while to charge back up. Why don't we go get a drink or two, an' when we get back, we can see what the magic box has in store for us.' Gato licked his lips. 'I could sink a sud or three right now.'

'You guys go. I'm staying here.' Quantrill stared at the tracker unit, the pulsing red light holding his attention rapt. 'I'll call you as soon as I get a reading on this.'

'Do you want the Bambu Daddy or Mad Dog's?' asked Fish. He straightened his t-shirt. The acronym TEOTWAWKI stretched tight over his chest.

'I owe money at Mad Dog's…a lot of money,' said Sticks. 'I vote for the Bambu.'

Blaine rolled his shoulders as he regarded his friends with a sour expression. 'Don't know why you bother with Mad Dogs anyway. It's full of doped up, skinny-assed skanks.'

Fish drummed his open hands on the table. 'That's exactly why we go, my friend. You're way too picky about your women.'

'No, I just don't want my prized parts to turn green and fall off,' said Blaine.

The banter between the men washed over Quantrill with little effect. He'd heard it a thousand times before. His attention was held by the blinking red light. *One, two, three: blink*. He barely moved, only the twitching of his right index finger betraying the sense of anticipation he carried. His mouth creased into a narrow line. The other men had never fully grasped the possible enormity of the prize.

'You sure you're not coming, boss-man?' asked Gato.

Quantrill gave a brief shake of his head.

'Call us, if you get anything from that there, doo-hickey,' said Fish.

'Uh-huh.' Quantrill felt a slow burn, low in his stomach. The red light continued to blink. 'Have fun but try not to get yourselves arrested, with good luck and a tailwind, it'll soon be all hands to the pumps.'

Quantrill glanced up as the men left the premises, laughing and jostling each other as they went. The garage lapsed into silence. A single bead of sweat traced the contours of his face as Curtis Quantrill studied the blinking crimson dot. *One. Two. Three. Blink*.

How long would it take to charge? What if it failed after sitting in a crate for all this time? Would it lead him to the ultimate payoff?

One. Two. Three. Blink.

What if Delacroix had gone to his grave while playing them all for fools? He was known for being a devious bastard. Only one way to find out.

One. Two. Three. Blink.

Chapter 39

Danny pulled the shim set from the inside lining of his belt. After a cursory glance at the locked door, he selected a narrow tension bar and a hook pick. Dropping to one knee, he inserted the two picks into the lock. He didn't't need to ask; he knew Clay would be watching his six. A knock on the front door had brought no response from inside. The house had no visible alarm system. No window sensors, no intruder alarm. Maybe, thought Danny, Blaine considered himself too far up the food chain to ever be burgled. A silver Ford Fusion sat outside the house to the left of the front door. The car looked fresh from the showroom. The bodywork gleamed and was well cared for.

The door opened with a subdued squeak. Danny moved into the house like a wraith. Pausing, he rested the back of his hand on the closest wall, listening and inhaling the residue of stale cigar smoke and old food. A small kitchen sat off to his left. Dirty dishes and empty food cartons were dotted around the room. A machete lay unsheathed on the kitchen table. A pair of dirty sneakers sat on the countertop next to the sink. Danny huffed air through his nose. The vehicle outside was pristine yet the house needed a blitz by domestic service.

Ahead of the kitchen, a wide hallway showed four doorways. Two of the doors were flung open. Placing his feet slowly with each step, heel to toe, he moved silently along the hall. Taking nothing for granted, he listened for any signs of life. The house was silent. The first open door revealed a bathroom, tiled white. The mirror over the sink was streaked with grime. Using the edge of one knuckle Danny levered open the mirror. The small cabinet behind contained a razor, shaving brush, and soap dish. A toothbrush and paste lay alongside. No medication bottles. No feminine products of any kind. Blaine lived alone. That helped explain the mess.

Danny moved from the bathroom to the second open door. The living room was spartan. A two-seater couch sat against one wall, a widescreen TV on the other, a wooden coffee table sat in between. Opening the first of the closed doors, he peered into a spacious closet space. The room reminded Danny of a junkshop. Blaine's possessions included what looked like at least a dozen fishing rods, baseball bats, an oversized golf bag filled with irons and woods. An old wooden chest sat on the floor. The lock of the chest was open. Inside, Danny recognised the steel face-grid of a Kendo mask. A full set of armour, keikogi and hakama; the uniform of the Kendo fighter, lay below. Looking again at the bats, he could see that a bamboo sword, a *shinai*, sat alongside the baseball equipment. Danny first closed the chest and then the closet door.

The last door opened into Blaine's bedroom. A queen-sized bed lay on the far side of the room. A drop-leaf desk provided a home to a laptop. The lid was closed.

The doors of a double louvred closet stood open. The clothes hanging there filled less than half of the available space. The lower section of the closet was separated into a set of six drawers. Lifting the clothes, Danny carefully traced the bottom of each drawer in turn. *Nothing.* The corner of one eye twitched. *Was he wrong about Blaine?* It was his experience that the kind of man that could strangle a beautiful young woman to death usually manifested their sociopathic habits in their living space. The few he had seen were either meticulously tidy or complete crap-holes. Blaine's home just looked…ordinary; the living space of a single man, a mess but nothing remarkable. A look beneath the bed revealed only dust bunnies and a scattering of porno mags.

Danny opened the lid of the laptop, the screen black. A quick tap, on the enter button, stirred the machine awake. The security bar prompting a password came as no surprise. Danny typed the word 'password'.

'No. I guess that would have been too easy.' He tried several more variations, caps on caps off.

1,2,3,4,5,6. None of the lazy password combinations proved fruitful. Danny closed the lid with a muttered curse. As he moved back through the small house, an urge built inside him to leave a parting gift. It would be so easy to burn the house to the ground, leave behind only ashes. The knobs on the cooker seemed to invite him. It would be child's play: turn the gas on full, stick a magazine into the slot of the toaster and walk away.

Danny drummed his fingers on the kitchen door.

Chapter 40

The first beer went down quick and easy and Fish raised the empty bottle. The Corona was hardly the strongest of beers, but it certainly hit the spot when the sun seemed determined to peel the skin from your back.

'You want another?' asked the server behind the bar.

'Keep them coming,' answered Fish. He had seen the server on several previous visits to the bar. Marie was lithe, moving with a feline grace that he appreciated. The detailed inkwork she displayed on her upper arms only added to her allure. Her black hair was cut short and spiked. Yeah, Marie had it going on. Fish offered a smile as she removed the cap from the bottle and pushed it across the bar. Marie returned his smile with a curt bob of her head.

Fish swivelled on the bar stool as Blaine called to him from the booth now filled with his friends. 'Stop messin' with single bottles Fish, just get us a couple of pitchers.'

'They haven't got Corona on tap,' answered Fish.

'Never said it needed to be a specific cerveza!

Just bring the damned beer.' Blaine held his hands in the air.

Fish gave Blaine the finger but placed the order with Marie.

'I'll bring them over,' said Marie. 'You guys want any food to go with the beers?'

Fish looked again at his friends. He knew to get the money back from these assholes was always a struggle, but he nodded in affirmation. 'Yeah, we'll take a cheeseburger and fries apiece.'

Marie scribbled the order on a compact notepad and pushed it through the service hatch behind the bar. Fish tried another smile, hoping for a warmer response than the previous. *Nada...*

'I'll bring the beer over in a minute.'

Fish ambled to the booth. The four faces that stared back would not have looked out of place on a wanted poster.

'You luck out again, Fish?' asked Junk.

'I'm growing on her,' answered Fish, rubbing the back of his neck.

'Like a fungus,' added Gato.

Fish pulled a face. 'This from the guy whose favourite food is asshole casserole.'

The corners of Gato's mouth crept upwards.

'Bitch, sit your ass down. You're like Mondays; nobody likes you.'

Fish extended his middle finger once more as he sat at the table with his friends. 'Beer and burgers are on the way.'

'I take it back,' said Gato. 'You're not a complete dead weight on this crew after all.'

'Yeah, while I can't run up walls like some spider-man freak, I have my talents.'

Junk clicked his fingers. 'Yeah man, it's a real talent ordering beer and getting the brush off from every chick you meet.'

Fish made a show of looking at his watch. 'What day is it? Let's give Fish crap-day?'

Marie interrupted the banter as she placed the two pitchers of beer on the table. Moments later she was back with five frost-covered glasses. 'Enjoy guys. The food will be out soon.'

'Thanks, Marie,' said Fish. 'Why don't you join us?'

Marie flashed a curious smile. 'Way too much testosterone and manliness at this table for this little lady.'

Before Fish could offer another gambit, she was heading back behind the bar. He shrugged than filled his glass with the amber-coloured beer.

'As this beer fills my glass,' Sticks held up his drink. 'You'se ugly spuds may kiss my ass.'

'Bottom's up,' offered Junk.

'Are we back to Fish's sex life?' asked Gato.

Fish shook his head in mock sadness. Downing most of his glass in one long gulp he asked, 'You think Quantrill is right this time?'

'I hope so,' said Sticks. 'I'm getting tired of chasing dreams when we could be pulling real scores, and putting some green in our pockets.'

Blaine gulped beer. 'The pawn shop is still on the cards. I still vote to hit it before someone else beats us to the punch. The money that would bring would help tide us over while Quantrill figures out where the ark of the friggin' covenant is hidden.'

Fish looked at Blaine. He knew the big man was not one for idle boasts and he knew the risks of the job. If he said the pawnshop was real, it was real. 'Quantrill told us to hold off on that until we figured out Delacroix.'

Blaine's eyes were barely visible below his brow. 'I work *with* Curtis, not *for* Curtis. I do what the hell I want when I want. I say we drink these beers, eat our food then go and put some silver in the pouch.'

'What about Curtis?' Fish knew every man at the table was dangerous in his way but both Blaine and

Quantrill could kill with impunity. He had witnessed both in action. 'He'll be pissed.'

Blaine scowled. 'This is an easy mark. We'll be back singing kumbaya before he even notices we've been gone.'

The money *would* be good right now. Fish raised his glass with the other men. 'I'm in.'

Chapter 41

Clay pressed his hand against his left shoulder. The nipping pain inside the muscle seemed determined to remind him that he was not yet fully healed. Getting impaled by a crossbow bolt was not something he ever wanted to experience again.

'You alright?' asked Danny.

'Yeah man, I'm okay.' Clay nodded at the road ahead. 'Let's hope we get lucky at the next place.'

'We're getting closer to this prick; I can feel it.'

'What if he's not at the bar? Miami is a big city, he could be anywhere,' said Clay.

'People are creatures of habit. They tend to eat at the same restaurants, drink at the same bars, shop at the same stores.'

'I guess so.'

Danny pursed his lips. 'If he's not there, I'm going to stake out his house until he gets back. Then we'll have words.'

'We,' corrected Clay. '*We,* are going to stake out his house. Remember, we're in this together, wee one.'

'Aye, I know that,' said Danny. He thumped the steering wheel with the edge of his fist. 'I nearly set his house to burn down you know.'

'What stopped you?'

'Two things.'

'Which were?'

'Number one, I didn't want to chance, the fire spreading to his neighbours' houses.'

'Okay,' said Clay. 'I get that.'

'And number two: I want to look that arsehole in the eyes. I'll know in a second if he killed Chrissie, then it's payback time.'

'Yeah, you need to be double sure before torching the house.' Clay nodded. 'But payback time doesn't upset me none.'

Danny braked as a van emblazoned with a pizza delivery logo cut around him in a rapid slalom.

'Holy pepperoni,' said Clay, a lazy smile spreading across his face. He slapped a palm to his thigh. 'Hey, what does an aardvark like on his pizza?'

Danny dead-panned his brother. 'I'm sure you're gonna tell me.'

'Ant-chovies.'

'Dumb ass!'

Clay chuckled. 'Thank you, thank you very

much. I'm here all week.'

'You may not be if the rest of your jokes are as bad as that one.'

'Hyuk hyuk.'

West Flagler Street was long and straight, heavy with traffic. Yellow construction barriers forced Danny to make a right turn that took them through the middle of Little Havana. Danny pumped the brakes then inched forward. 'This is slow going.'

'At least the scenery is worth a second look,' said Clay.

Danny nodded. 'There's a lot of colour on these streets.'

'The coffee down here is great too. Can't beat the Cubans for coffee.'

'Aye, it's good. I came down here with Chrissie. She loved all the little cafés. I showed her how to play dominoes. It was a good day.'

'I like that it isn't the big-name fast foods on every corner.'

'Aye,' said Danny absently. *Chrissie's smile…*

The car in front made sharp left and Danny followed.

'So, what's the plan of action if Blaine is at the bar?'

Danny looked across at Clay. 'I'm not in the mood for subtleties.'

'Me neither, but getting into a pitched bar fight may well bring the boys in blue. It'll do neither of us any good if we end the day in the lock-up.'

Danny grunted but gave a slow nod.

'Danny, I can see murder in your eyes, but like I said the other day I don't want to see the inside of a jail cell.'

'We won't. I've put plenty in the ground, and so far, none have come back to haunt me.'

'Alrighty then. If he's there, chances are he won't be alone.'

'Well, God knows I didn't bring you along for your sparkling personality.' Danny watched the scars on Clay's face bunch as a smile crept across his face. 'You up for some arse-kickery?'

'I am.'

'How's your shoulder?'

'I'm fine. The day I can't drop the hammer on a handful of Miami ass-wipes will be a sad day indeed.'

'Blaine's mine. I'll know if it was him as soon as I look him in the eyes,' said Danny.

Clay returned a curt nod, 'No problem.'

Chapter 42

Caleb Blaine pushed away his empty plate. The cheeseburger had hit the spot. As he swirled beer around the inside of his mouth to dislodge the more stubborn threads of cheese, he glowered at the five young men at the bar.

'Sup?' asked Gato.

'It's assholes like that that give Miami a bad name.' Blaine did not attempt subtlety. 'This town used to be a town worth living in.'

Fish filled Blaine's beer mug. 'Just ignore them, man. They're just scooter boys.'

'What the hell is a scooter boy?' asked Gato.

Blaine curled his lip. 'I think it's another way of saying freak-assed loser.'

'I've seen them around. They all zip around town on those new Segway scooters.'

'Why are they all dressed the same? Those blue satin jackets?' asked Junk. 'Do they do that for a job?'

Fish pushed the beer to Blaine. 'Nah, it's just their thing, like skateboarding.'

'Disco jackets and Segways? Bunch of slack-jawed faggots if you ask me.' Blaine downed the full glass of beer in one long chug. One of the young men looked over from the bar. Four of the five had dark brown hair, all cut short with tram lines above their ears. The last had long strands of floppy blond hair. All looked to be in their mid-twenties. 'Yeah, I'm talking about you, limp dick.'

The young man looked back at Blaine with a sour expression. He turned back to the other scooter boys. A low ripple of laughter spread between them.

Fish barely caught the empty beer mug as Blaine sent it skidding across the table. 'What're you laughing at, pecker wood?'

The five men turned as one unit as Blaine marched from the table. The tallest of the scooter boys held up a placatory hand. 'Hey man, chill.'

Blaine grabbed the young man's extended fingers, locking them back at an angle they were never designed to bend. 'What's your name, ass-wipe?'

The young man emitted a high-pitched yelp as he was forced to his knees. The other scooter boys looked on aghast.

'Pierre!'

'Pierre? What kind of name is that for an American?' Blaine increased the pressure on Pierre's fingers and waited for what he knew would come next. 'You are American, aren't you?'

As Pierre opened his mouth wide in a silent scream Blaine rammed his knee into the young man with all his strength. The sound of his jaws snapping together resembled a pistol shot. Pierre went to the ground in a loosening of limbs. Blaine snapped the captured fingers to one side until he felt them dislocate within his grip.

The blond scooter boy, his face full of fear, barrelled into Blaine. 'Get away from him.'

The interloper was stronger than he looked and Blaine was momentarily thrown off balance. The young man was already turning to Pierre, his hands reaching out to offer succour to his friend.

Blaine caught his balance by gripping the side of the bar and levered himself upright. Heat crept across his face. *Nearly put on my ass by some prissy little dick-wad in a satin jacket? No way!* Blaine brought his right hand to play in a vicious hook punch, pivoting at the waist, his legs driving forward into the strike. The young blond man had both his hands grasping Pierre's shoulders as the punch slammed into the side of his unprotected face. Blaine felt the shock of impact deep within his fist and knew he wasn't getting up in a hurry. Blaine turned his wrath on the remaining three scooter boys. Three more punches ripped through the air in as many seconds.

'Blaine!' Fish's voice carried an edge that made Blaine pause, mid-action. His raised boot heel was directly over Pierre's bloodied face. 'Jesus, Blaine, that's enough.'

'Pencil-necked little pussies asked for it,' Blaine turned to see the thirty or so faces staring back. He shouted to make himself heard over the tropical music that usually added to the ambience of the bar. 'What?'

Blaine stared down at the five young men. Three had smears of blood wiped across their faces. The blond one looked devoid of life. *Yeah, it was a good shot.* Pierre had curled into a ball, his hands cupping his face.

'Stop that damn crying or I'll kick you so hard your boyfriend won't recognise you.' Blaine threw off the hands that sought to guide him from the bar.

'Come on man,' said Gato. 'We gotta go. I see most of these fools on their phones. Two things are sure, one; you can bet this will be on YouTube before we make it back to the car, and two, that the Po-po will soon be on their way.'

'Yeah?' Blaine took his time draining the last of the beer from the pitcher before following his friends from the bar. 'Well, fuck them too.'

Chapter 43

Danny glanced at the road signs overhead before taking a right turn. The neon lights styled in faux art deco lettering told him they had reached their destination. The entrance to the Bambu Daddy bar was framed by a pair of leaning palms decorated with strings of coloured lanterns. The thing that caught his attention was the squad car parked to one side of the open doors. The corners of his mouth turned downward. 'Cops.'

'I see them,' said Clay.

'Just what I need,' grouched Danny. 'I'm still going in. I just need to find a parking space.'

'Pull up there,' said Clay pointing to the next corner. 'You go on in and I'll take the car and park up.'

Danny brought the car to a stop and was on the sidewalk in a second. Clay walked around the rear of the vehicle and took the driver's seat. He pointed a finger at Danny. 'Don't you be starting anything before I get back, y' hear.'

Danny gave little more than a curt nod. The music from the bar was lively and up-tempo. He realised why the cops were here in an instant. Five young men were propped against the bar in various states of distress. All wore the same style of a jacket; blue satin windbreakers. The two cops were busy talking, one to the group of injured men, the other to the female server behind the bar. Moving close enough to eavesdrop without making it obvious, Danny leaned an elbow on the bar top. A second server approached.

'Modelo beer please,' said Danny.

The male server raised a finger in acquiescence. 'You need a glass?'

'Nah, the bottle's fine.' Danny took a long pull on the golden beer. He nodded at the young men. 'They disagree on how to split the bill?'

The server shook his head. 'Poor saps never knew what hit them. Some muscle head went all UFC on their asses. I thought he was gonna kill them for real. The look in his eyes was something else.'

Frowning, Danny took another sip of beer. 'One guy did this to all of them?'

'Yeah man, it was brutal. Two guys were down by the time I realised what was happening. The guy is an asshole but he has some serious skills.'

Danny raised an eyebrow. 'The cops get him?'

'No chance. His buddies had enough sense to get him out of here.'

'I thought this place was party land, you know like Margaritaville, but with better drinks. Looks more like a wild west saloon.'

The server rubbed the back of his hand across what looked like two-day's worth of stubble. He wore no name tag on his shirt. 'It's rare we have any trouble. That guy is bad news, it's written all over his face. Those tattoos on his face speak volumes, y' know what I'm saying? He looks like a shaved gorilla.'

Danny forced himself to take another slow sip of the beer. 'Tattoos on his face? I'm guessing they weren't declarations of his love for mankind?'

'You guessed right,' said the server. 'Tribal lines like Mike Tyson. Punches like him too.'

'Is he a regular? I don't want to walk in tomorrow and end up like those poor sods.'

'I've seen him and his buddies a couple of times, but no, they're not what I would call regulars.'

'That's alright then. I like beer and Key Lime pie, but I don't want my head getting used as a punchbag on any account.'

'I hear that,' agreed the server. The man moved to the far end of the bar as another customer waved to him.

Danny finished the beer and wedged a ten-dollar note under the empty bottle. Two EMT's, both young women, entered the bar and immediately began their administration. Danny skirted the medics and the two police officers. He had no desire to get in the way of any uniforms. Most were good people. They were here to do a job. The two cops looked like they would stand no-nonsense.

Looking down at one of the injured men Danny could see that his jaw was swollen, his eye blackened with an unsightly ballooning of skin. They were injuries he had seen, received, and delivered countless times before. These guys weren't fighters, little more than kids out for a good time. It was plain to see that Blaine had scuppered that game plan. Blaine, big with tribal ink on his face. Too much of a coincidence for it not to be him. Danny took another look at the five beaten men. Five more reasons to punch a hole through Blaine when they met.

Danny was back at the front doors as Clay strode towards him.

'What's the menu like in here?'

'Forget the menu, we've missed Blaine and his buddies.' Danny shook his head.

'So, what's going on in there?' asked Clay.

'Blaine knocked the living daylights out of five young lads.'

'For any reason in particular?'

Danny shrugged. 'He's a class-A arsehole. I don't think he knew them or had any beef. There's not one of them that weighs more than a hundred and forty pounds. He's just headhunting. Arseholes do what arseholes do.'

Clay rolled his shoulders. 'When we catch up with him, I'm sure we can find him, someone, to have a real fight with.'

'I'm not planning on fighting him. If he killed, Chrissie I plan on snapping his neck and leaving him in the glades for the gators to snack on. It won't be a fight.'

'Ay-men to that.' Clay peered into the bar.

'I'm sick of chasing Blaine and coming up empty. I need to bring him to us.'

'You still thinking of burning down his house?'

'Maybe later, but that would bring firemen and probably cops, neither of whom I want to be caught in the crossfire.'

'So, what then?'

Danny pushed out his upper lip with his tongue. 'Time for a little game of bumper cars.'

Chapter 44

Clay shook a Snickers bar in Danny's direction. 'You want one?'

'Nah, I'm good.'

'Thanks for stopping at that grocery store. I was starving.'

Danny gave his older sibling a sidelong glance. 'Aye, you're fading away before my very eyes.'

Clay made the chocolate bar disappear in three bites.

'You okay with this?' asked Danny. 'I plan to give it a decent hit.'

'Go for it wee one,' Clay emitted a soft chuckle. 'I took out full collision protection when I rented it. I'm not planning to drive this jalopy back to Texas when we're done and dusted.'

'Okay then.' Danny manoeuvred the vehicle to an angle, some thirty feet past the driveway of Blaine's house. 'Hang on to your lug nuts.'

Clay braced his feet in each corner of the footwell. Vibrations shook the car as Danny set it into reverse. A high-pitched whine grew in volume as he stamped down on the gas pedal. Clay forced himself to relax, knowing that the seat would absorb and nullify most of the force of impact. The sound of the collision still caused him to pull his chin low into his chest. A pain like a sliver of glass lanced through his shoulder. The rending of metal on metal filled the vehicle. The rear end of the speeding car momentarily left the ground then came down with a crunch.

Clay's shoulders shook as he began to laugh. 'You know, sometimes your blatant disregard for the possessions of others makes me consider your moral turpitude.'

Danny switched the car to drive and parked at the curb. 'Whoops. Did I do that? It must have been in my blind spot.'

Clay opened his door and climbed out of the damaged vehicle. 'There goes his no claims bonus.'

'Aye, my heart bleeds.'

Clay tilted his chin. 'There are the faces at the window you were hoping for.'

'Uh-huh.'

Clay placed a hand over his forehead and began a slow walk towards the neighbour's house. 'I'll get this.'

Danny looked like he might object but moved to knock at Blaine's door.

The front door of the house opposite Blaine's

opened while Clay was halfway along the path. The man that stood in the doorway was dressed in matching grey sweat pants and vest. What little hair he had was a curious shade of red. He had no moustache but sported a full beard. The word *Leprechaun* sprang to mind. 'You okay there, buddy?'

'Jeez Louise, I don't know what in tarnation just happened. We don't drive very often and must have put it into reverse by accident.'

'Man, of all the cars in Miami you could have run into, you probably just picked the worse one.'

Clay made a show of rubbing his face. 'Don't worry I'll make it right. I've got good insurance cover.'

'You better have good health insurance as well, 'cos Caleb is gonna be out for blood when he sees his car all ripped up like that. That's his pride and joy right there. It's less than a year old. He waxes it more than he drives it.'

'Oh man,' groaned Clay. He looked over as Danny approached. His expression was one of consternation. 'No answer?'

'No luck. Can't we just leave our contact details on the windshield?' said Danny.

'I don't want to leave it like this. I'd rather talk to…what did you say his name was?'

'Caleb,' said the neighbour. 'Caleb Blaine.'

'Do you know where he works? Maybe I can get in touch and square this away.' Clay pulled a wad of cash from his back pocket. 'Money's no problem.'

Clay tried not to smile as the lucky leprechaun stared at the roll of twenties with overt longing. Adding what he hoped might sound like trepidation, Clay leaned a little closer to the red-haired man. 'Do *you* know how to get in touch with this Caleb guy?'

A sly grin began to form above the red bristles of the man's beard. 'I may have his cell number... but there would be a, hell, let's call it a finder's fee.'

Danny interjected. 'Or we could just high tail it out of here.'

'You don't want to do that,' said the neighbour. He held up his cell phone. 'Not now that I've got a picture of your licence plate.'

'Okay, okay,' said Clay thumbing two twenties from the roll. 'Here man, we just want to do the right thing.'

'One more,' said the neighbour, shifting from foot to foot.

Clay gave an exaggerated huff then handed over the extra banknote. 'Now, can I have this guy Caleb's number so we can fix this snafu?'

The red-haired man took his time scrolling on his phone. Clay visualised reaching over and squeezing the man's head until his face turned blue. Instead, he gave what he hoped was a convincing smile as he copied the number from the phone. 'Thanks, buddy, I'll give him a call and tell him the good news.'

Rubbing his red bristles between his thumb and forefinger the neighbour replied, 'Rather you than me. Don't say I didn't warn you. Caleb is likely to want more than just money in the way of compensation.'

Danny took a step closer. 'Oh, don't worry. We'll make sure he gets what he's due.'

Chapter 45

Caleb Blaine gave his right hand a cursory glance. There was little more than a scuff of skin, slightly reddened, over his knuckles. Under his left arm, he clutched a twenty-four pack of Heineken. The other four men each carried beer packs of various brands. Looking to the table at the centre of the room, he could see Curtis Quantrill clutching the tracker unit in both hands. Blaine pushed the beer pack onto the kitchen counter. 'You got that thing working yet?'

Letting the tracker rest for a moment, Quantrill rubbed both hands through his hair. 'The damn thing keeps switching itself on and off. I thought that this was going to be it. I thought that I was back on the trail.'

Blaine ripped through the outer cardboard sleeve and pulled a beer from the pack. Pulling a second can, he handed it to Quantrill. 'Hey man, it's not the end of the world. There are real scores, real jobs we could be pulling.'

Quantrill took a long chug of the beer before talking again. 'I've told you before, I don't want you guys doing nickel and dime jobs and winding up in orange jumpsuits.'

'God damn it, Curtis, you're not the only one that can plan a job, you know. If you weren't so knuckle-head obsessed with this Delacroix bullshit we could be making some real money. Not just scraping by, but bringing it in regularly. We don't have a gilt-edged trust fund to fall back on like you. The rest of us came up the hard way.'

'This shit again?'

Blaine watched Quantrill slowly stand, his eyes like chips of flint. His right hand hovered close to his hip pocket like a gunfighter of old. All too aware that Curtis carried a set of brass knuckles and had busted more than one face with them, Blaine subtly shifted his weight. It only took one good shot with the knuckle dusters and that could spell the end of the fight.

Gato stepped between the two men. 'Come on guys, we're all friends here, right?'

Blaine angled his body, right foot creeping back. Quantrill mirrored his posture. Fish joined Gato in the space between the two men. 'Jesus Blaine, isn't one brawl a night enough for you?'

'You got into a fight?' Quantrill talked through tight lips. 'What the hell did I tell you? What was the last friggin' thing I said before you all trooped out of here?'

'Pull my mama's nightdress down when you're finished?' A vein is pulsed in the side of Blaine's face.

Quantrill's hand-dipped in and out of his pocket in one smooth motion. Blaine sneered. 'You think they would make a difference?'

The room became loud with voices, all four of their friends calling for the men to relax. Quantrill slammed the brass knuckles down on the table. 'You think I need these to beat the likes of you. I don't! I'm sick to the back teeth with your shit. Come on Blaine, let's do this once and for all.'

Blaine shouldered Fish out of his path, knocking him to the floor.

'Hey!' yelled Fish as he landed in an ungainly heap. Despite his protestations, Quantrill again scooped up the brass knuckles.

Blaine stared at the ageing surf-dog, a heat spreading across his face. He knew Curtis was the real deal, not to be trifled with. One of them would be spending the night in the ER. He was determined that it would not be him. Blaine lowered his weight and prepared to barrel into his friend. A shrill yelling made him pause. The ringtone of his phone was a looped version of the *Wilhelm scream*, a sound effect used in hundreds of movies. Played in a rapid loop it sounded absurd.

Fish picked himself up from the floor. 'You not gonna answer that? You might have won the Florida lottery.'

Red-faced, Blaine snatched the cell phone from his pocket. 'Yeah?'

A voice he did not recognise started to tell him things he did not want to hear. After the brief diatribe, he told the caller to shut his mouth. 'I'll be right over. You better still be waiting when I get there.'

Fish held out his hands, palms up. 'And?'

'Some pencil-necked jerk-off just ran into my car and wrecked it.'

Sticks raised his chin. 'What you gonna do, man?'

Blaine directed a crooked smile at Curtis. 'I'm going to find out if this asshole can write a cheque with two broken arms.'

'I'll come with,' said Fish. 'I'd like to see someone else on the brunt end for a change.'

Gato gave a lop-sided grin. 'I'm coming.'

Quantrill tucked the brass knuckles back into his pocket. 'You all going back out?'

'Nah,' answered Junk. 'I'm gonna chill.'

Sticks too waved away the idea. 'I've been thinking. Maybe I should take a proper look at that tracker unit, maybe get it working again?'

Blaine snorted a bovine breath through his nose. 'Pussies!'

Quantrill shook his head. 'Stay out of prison.'

'I'll see what I can do.' Fish raised both hands in an exaggerated shrug.

Blaine gave Quantrill a sour look. The day was turning to shit. He had wanted to hit the pawnshop but had been sidelined by the prissy scooter boys. Now some jerk had driven into his car. What else was going to happen? Some chick come out of the woodwork with a bambino and a court order for alimony?

Chapter 46

Danny accepted the candy bar from Clay. The red-haired neighbour had retreated inside his house but Danny noted the occasional twitch of the curtains. Aye, the lucky leprechaun was waiting for the fireworks show to start.

'Where do you want me?'

Danny took a bite of the Twix. 'Maybe you should hang back, stay out of sight, just in case we need a wee bit of shock value.'

'Sounds like a plan,' said Clay as he devoured his candy bar. The Butterfinger was gone in two gulps. Clay slowly turned a full circle. 'Although there's nowhere to go.'

'You take the car. Park far enough away that Blaine won't notice you.'

'Okay. I'll patch up that busted rear window. A grocery bag and some scotch tape will do wonders. Leave your phone on so I can hear everything.'

'No problem,' said Danny.

'Be careful,' said Clay.

Danny gave the briefest of nods.

'You still carrying?'

Danny tapped the front of his shirt with two fingers. The weight of the pistol in his waistband was a familiar sensation. Clay preferred revolvers so had taken possession of the Rossi five-shot. Danny had no preference, seeing firearms simply as tools to get the job done. The Smith and Wesson Shield was chambered for 9mm. Hardly a hand cannon but it would get the job done. 'You better get scootin', this guy sounded like he was coming with his arse on fire.'

Clay tipped an imaginary hat and within thirty seconds was parked at the far end of the block. Danny flexed and relaxed his hands, a faint tingle in his fingers. Leaning against Blaine's vehicle he looked at the damage incurred. The front grill was a crumpled mess, the fender hanging down onto the ground at a sad angle. The headlight too was smashed beyond repair. *Aye, he would be pissed.*

It took Blaine twenty minutes to show, but Danny knew it was him by the speed and sound of the vehicle as it tore down the street. A Hyundai Santa Fe. If a vehicle could exude promised violence it had arrived. Forcing himself to relax, Danny watched his quarry as he sprang from the passenger seat of the vehicle. The tattoos on the side of his face matched the kid's drawing perfectly.

Caleb Blaine.

He was big. He looked to be the same size and shape as Clay. Thick and corded, Danny estimated that Blaine's arms were on par with his thighs. The faded denim, boots and muscle vest lent Blaine a vague biker look.

'What kind of asshole do you have to be to crash into a parked car in a driveway?'

It only took Danny a second or two to appraise Blaine, then his attention flicked momentarily to the other two men as they climbed from the vehicle. He knew Clay was both watching and listening so allowed his gaze to snap back to the big man. 'A special kind to be sure.'

Recognising the barely contained fury in the big man, Danny centred his weight, ready to move.

'How the hell did you do it, anyhow?' Blaine's voice was growing louder with each word. Danny recognised all the signs of impending violence. The shortening of both breath and words. He hadn't even realised that there was no other vehicle parked in front of his house.

'I did it on purpose,' said Danny. He stared hard into the big man's eyes.

'You scrawny little shit, I'll stomp you into the ground like the maggot you are.' Blaine postured up, chest expanded, and arms were thrown back. A vein was pulsed in his neck.

'Don't you want to know why?' Danny took a step closer.

Blaine faltered for the briefest of moments. 'What?'

'I crashed into your car deliberately. I wanted to see for myself, look you in the eyes when I asked you.'

Danny gave the other two men, now flanking Blaine a contemptuous glare. The chords on Blaine's neck stood out as he hissed. 'Ask me what?'

'Why did you kill Chrissie Haims?'

'What?'

'Chrissie Haims. Why did you kill her?'

'You're crazy man, I didn't kill nobody.'

'Here's what I know,' said Danny. 'Your mouth is saying one thing, but your face is telling me everything I need to know.'

A redness swept over Blaine's face as he thrust out his chin. 'You a cop?'

Danny rolled his shoulders. 'Do I look like a cop?'

'You look like a piece of crap.'

Danny knew the time for words was over. Blaine's face was less than eighteen inches from his own. Danny considered pulling his pistol but decided to open Blaine up first. Pushing off the ground with a coordinated kick of his legs, Danny sprang into the air, his forehead slamming into the tattooed face. It was a solid shot, catching Blaine flush on the bridge of his nose. The big man staggered back, his face contorting. But he didn't go down. With a bestial grunt, Blaine returned a head butt of his own. Spots of light danced across Danny's vision. Something as hot as lava surged through his core. Even as Danny's right hand streaked to his pistol, he froze mid-action. A police cruiser was approaching at speed. A quick blare of the siren and the flashing of lights caused the two combatants to back away from each other. A trickle of blood slowly traced a path down Baine's chin.

Two uniformed officers stepped from the police cruiser. Both cops were tall and rangy, one black and the other white. The voice of the black officer was loud and full of authority. 'Is there a problem here?'

Danny shook his head in the negative. 'No problem. We were just messing around. I was trying to show my friend here a few martial art moves, but I messed up and hit him for real. Don't worry he's a tough guy. He can take it.'

The cops took their time as if committing each face to memory. The white cop stood back, his hand resting on the butt of his service pistol. The black cop gave the group of men the flat eye. 'Quit your shit and clear the street. If we have to come back here, you'll see a very different side of me.'

Danny monitored Blaine's friends, noticed the hands urging him to leave. 'You won't get any trouble from us officer. Just hi-jinks gone wrong. No hassle intended.'

The two cops exchanged a look. The white cop took his turn to speak. 'I want no more of this UFC kung fu bullshit in the street, y'all hear?'

Knowing that being searched by these cops would end in charges that he certainly did not want; Danny held his hands up in capitulation. 'Like I said guys, we were just messing around.'

'No more,' said the black cop. 'You, Irish, you go that way. The rest of you start headin' in the other direction.'

Blaine's eyes were burning orbs as he locked gazes with Danny. 'Be seeing ya real soon, buddy.'

'Oh, you can bet your back teeth that you will,' said Danny. A dull throbbing pain began to spread across his cheek. Blaine had caught him a solid shot. The bald bastard was no easy mark, but that didn't matter. He would die just the same. Nodding to the cops, Danny offered a parting shot. 'Scots not Irish, but not a million miles away.'

'Whatever, Braveheart, keep moving,' replied the cop.

A nerve ticked in the side of his face as Danny forced himself to walk away; away from the man he now knew in his heart to be Chrissie's killer. Clenching and flexing his fingers, Danny forced the beast of adrenalin rush back into its cage.

Chapter 47

Clay watched the situation unfold with grim resolve. Danny and the big guy that had to be Blaine had just traded blows; well, headbutts to be precise, and now two cops were in the middle of the mix. He gripped the steering wheel as he inched the car closer to the scene. He could hear every word; Danny had left the cell phone he carried on an open call. Clay ran the back of his hand across his mouth. If the cops searched Danny, they would discover the pistol he had taken from the SU skinheads. Carrying an unlicensed and concealed firearm in Florida was a felony and could earn you five years in prison, not a good career move.

Clay breathed a sigh of relief as he heard one of the cops declare in a gruff tone, 'No more. You, Irish, you go that way. The rest of you start walkin' in the other direction.'

Watching as Danny turned towards his car Clay strained to hear his parting words to Blaine and his two buddies. Danny turned back to the cop, a big black guy, 'Scots not Irish, but not a million miles away.'

'Whatever, Braveheart, keep moving,' replied

the cop. His voice sounded husky via the cell phone.

Blaine and the two others climbed back into the vehicle they had arrived in. The vehicle span in a tight three-point turn and left the street only slightly slower than it had arrived. Clay guided his vehicle around the first corner in front of Danny. He waited only moments before his younger brother slipped into the car. 'That could have gone south, real quick.'

The muscles in the side of Danny's jaw bunched as he spoke. 'It was him, Clay. I knew it would be. I could see it in his eyes when I asked him, when I said Chrissie's name. The bastard almost smirked at me, as if to say, *'what you gonna do about it?'*.'

'If those cops had shown up a couple of seconds later, they would have had you standing over three dead guys with a gun in your hand.' Clay rested his hand on Danny's shoulder. 'They have the death penalty here; you need to be careful. And the lucky leprechaun over there has our licence plate.'

'Aye, okay,' said Danny. 'Put your foot down and let's see if we can stay on that fucker's trail. I don't want to lose them and have to start all over again.'

Clay accelerated, taking another left. 'What were they driving? I couldn't make it out from back there.'

'Hyundai Santa Fe, dark blue.' Danny recited the number from the plates. 'It's got a roof box on top.

Red stickers on the side.'

Clay powered the Chevy Cruze through the narrow streets, his gaze flicking from vehicle to vehicle ahead. 'You see them?'

'No.' Danny craned his neck, head thrust forward as if that would somehow increase his chances of locating the vehicle. 'Where the hell did, they go as quick?'

'They can't be that far ahead of us.'

Clay said nothing as Danny let loose a string of expletives, each one thick with his Scottish brogue. Instead, he took a sharp left, the tyres scraping the curb. 'There!'

A dark blue SUV was three blocks ahead. 'Is that it?' asked Danny. 'I can hardly see it in this light.'

'I think so,' answered Clay. 'It's got a roof box.'

'Get after it then.' A taxi cut in ahead of them then a second cab swung in ahead. 'Come on Clay, Miss Daisy isn't in the friggin' car.'

'Just you tend to yer own knitting,' Clay rankled. 'These streets are narrow assed corridors. I've driven on wider tightropes.'

'Move it. We're gonna lose them at those lights,' barked Danny.

A cross-section marked the first of the wider

streets. A short bridge over the Miami River would lead them to easy access points of the highway. 'Unless we've got a flying car and I didn't get the memo there's not a lot I can do, Danny.'

The younger Gunn brother slammed his fist into the dashboard. 'If they get onto the I-ninety-five we've lost them.'

'I know!'

Clay watched the Hyundai breeze through the intersection, the lights green. One of the cabs followed. The lights turned orange.

'Keep moving, you bastard!'

The second taxi slowed. There were no pedestrians at the crosswalk. Setting his jaw, Clay slalomed around the cab, mounting the curb momentarily. There was a harsh *snap* and Clay watched the offside wing mirror clatter across the pavement. Keeping his foot pressed hard on the gas pedal, the Cruze shot across the intersection. Lights bore towards him, lights that belonged to a semi-truck. Clay gritted his teeth until he felt them grind. If they collided, he knew the truck would roll right over them. Grey smoke flew from the truck's tyres as hastily applied brakes fought to slow the juggernaut. The Cruze nipped past the truck with only inches to spare. The frantic blaring of an air horn filled the street.

'That's one way to get your ass shaved,'

laughed Clay. Despite his quip, he could feel his heart hammering in his chest. 'Mother trucker.'

'I can't see them,' said Danny. 'Where the hell did, they go?'

Clay swivelled in his seat, searching the side streets for a glimpse of their quarry.

'We've lost them.'

Chapter 48

Fish powered through the crosswalk; his eyes fixed on the rear-view mirror. 'Told you if I timed that just right, they would get stuck on the red. Frickin' amateurs. You sure they aren't undercover cops?'

'They're not the law. This guy wanted me dead, I could see it in his eyes.' Blaine looked back over his shoulder. 'I want that piece of crap choking under my boot heel. I need to know who he is and where they're coming from.'

'I could lead them out to the yard at Brickell Flatts.' Fish swung the vehicle around the next corner.

'Yeah,' said Blaine as he gazed over his shoulder. 'But make them work for it. If they tail us too easy, they might figure we're leading them into a trap. I want them breezing in with their dicks swinging.'

Gato reached a hand to his belt. 'Crap. I'm not carrying.'

'Worry not, mi amigo, I've got something in the trunk for that wiry little bastard.' Fish tapped the side of his nose.

'Maybe your prepping obsession isn't such a

dumb idea after all,' offered Gato.

Fish hooked a thumb at his shirt. 'TEOTWAWKI. The end of the world as we know it, man. It's only a matter of time. Corona didn't get us but the next one might.'

Blaine emitted a low growl. 'I can't see who's driving, but there's at least two of them in the car.'

'Who is the other guy? Did you get a look at him?' asked Fish. He received a negative shrug from Gato.

'I don't care if there's a battalion of marines in there, I want them crushed.' Fish flinched as Blaine slapped the palm of his hand onto his shoulder. 'Let's get moving. I like your plan, Fish-man. Take them out to Brickell Flatts.'

Fish pressed down again on the gas pedal. The traffic on South Miami Avenue was light and Fish was able to overtake several vehicles with ease. Glancing in the rearview he gave a brief smile. A dozen vehicles back, the car was again on their tail. 'They're persistent if nothing else.'

Another quick turn onto Seventh Street and Fish accelerated once more. 'Once we get into the yard at Brickell, we'll only have a few seconds to get ready. They're coming up fast.'

'Let them come,' said Blaine touching his cheekbone. 'I'm gonna squeeze the life out of that little fucker.'

'Listen, as soon as I stop the car I'll bear left, Gato you go right.' Fish cast another glance in the rearview. 'Blaine, you stay right in front of the car. We'll flank the bastards and put them down.'

Caleb Blaine's response was little more than an extended grunt. Fish took this as a sign of agreement. The big guy would have argued an alternative if he had one in mind. Another look in the rearview mirror showed now only five vehicles separated them from their pursuers. He had no doubt it was them. The car had burned rubber from one block away from Blaine's house. Fish whipped the car into a sharp left turn without signalling. A horn blared from behind. 'Get ready. It's a straight run from here to the yard. About three minutes.'

Gato fidgeted in his seat, his hands flexing and curling. Fish had no doubts about Gato freezing up when it hit the fan. He was lean and wiry but a born fighter. He had lived up to his moniker many times over the years. *Gato* was Portuguese for a cat, a nickname his Brazilian cousins had dubbed him within his early teens. A natural Parkour gymnast, he had a real affinity with the Capoeira fighting art of his homeland.

The chain-link gates of Brickell Flatts' yard stood open. Fish steered the car through the open portal at speed. The corrugated tin sheets that formed the perimeter of the yard would shield them from view, if only for a few moments, but still long enough to position themselves.

Fish stamped on the brakes. 'Here we go, mofos!'

Chapter 49

'Stay on them,' said Danny.

'I see them now, I've got them.'

'Put your foot down Clay, I don't want to lose sight of them again.'

'Don't worry wee one, this ain't my first rodeo,' said Clay as he accelerated, overtaking an open-backed pickup truck. The vehicle had only been lost from sight for twenty or thirty seconds. The lights had changed at the crosswalk. Now they were back on the trail.

'They're going left. And stop calling me wee one,' grouched Danny. 'That shit sticks.'

The panel van immediately in front of them slowed without indicating, then at the last moment moved over to the right, allowing Clay to speed into the left turn.

'Keep moving!' Danny ignored the semi-irritated face that Clay had on display. There was no way Blaine was slipping away from him if he could help it. 'Watch out for that motorbike.'

Despite nearly unseating the biker, Clay pressed forward, gaining some ground on the vehicle which held Blaine and his buddies. The street was long and straight, the houses and storefronts dropping away to a more industrial area. Danny watched the car steer through a set of chain link gates, some one hundred and fifty yards ahead. A series of graffiti daubed tin sheets formed a barrier fence either side of the gates. The corrugated sheets stretched off a hundred or so yards, each separated by a grey concrete stanchion. A line of thick shrubs with wide spiked leaves sat in front of the fence at varying heights. Danny stabbed a finger in the air. 'There! They're going through those gates.'

'I see them.'

Danny's hand moved to his pistol, Blaine's face filling his red-tinged psyche. As Clay rapidly followed the vehicle into the enclosed yard, Danny could see numerous rectangular stacks of timber. The wooden spars, cut and shaped into railway sleepers, each piled higher than six feet. The wooden stacks cast long shadows. Drawing the pistol, he readied himself. *Where were Blaine and the others?* Swivelling in his seat Danny scanned left and right as they passed each block of timber.

Where the hell was Blaine?

There!

Off to his left, the SUV was stationary, its doors and tailgate flung wide open. Blaine stood at the rear of the vehicle, with what looked like a tire iron in his hand. Clay needed no prompting and steered the Chevy at speed towards the tattooed man.

Danny was out of the car, pistol thrust forward before it had come to a full stop. 'You killed Chrissie, now I'm gonna do the same to you.'

'What? Like some limp-dicked faggot with a pop-gun? I thought you were going to be some kind of a challenge; how wrong can a guy be?' The smirk on Blaine's face almost made Danny pull the trigger. At the last moment, he realised that the other two men from the vehicle were not in view. A blur of motion above his eye-line made him snap to his right. Someone was on top of the stacked timber. As he sought cover, Danny snapped off a hasty shot aiming for the centre of Blaine's chest. Chrissie's killer first dodged to one side then combat rolled in the opposite direction.

Danny stayed in a half-crouch as he rounded the wall of timber. Knowing better than to remain in one place, he sprinted to the next rectangle of sleepers then doubled back in the direction that Blaine had moved.

The sound of protesting metal filled his ears.

What the hell?

Then three things happened in as many heartbeats:

Beat one:

To his right; Clay's Chevy passed him by, hoisted into the air on the prongs of a massive fork-lift truck.

Beat two:

To his left; a man sprang into view, a shotgun held tight to his shoulder.

Beat three:

The shotgun roared.

Danny's world turned to pain. An unbearable explosion of agony erupted in his abdomen. Suddenly he was looking up at the sky, his vision blurring. The taste of metal filled his mouth. It was a taste he had experienced many times; the taste of his blood. Despite the crippling pain in his chest, Danny brought his pistol to bear. The shotgun roared again and a new spear of pain cut through his body. The pistol barked once in defiance. Then the bulk of a man was on top of him. Danny felt his weapon hand pinned to the ground.

Can't breathe…

An elbow slammed into his face. Then again, and again. Danny felt his head ricochet from the hard-packed gravel below. Miniature explosions erupted behind his eyes. His vision swam. Felt the pistol wrenched from his grasp. He gasped for breath, but his lungs only spasmed in response. Danny fought against the darkness.

Blaine's face loomed inches from his own, the sneer sickening. Danny watched the tire iron descend through rapidly dimming vision. Danny heard the impact as he slipped into blackness.

Chapter 50

Clay knew that Danny was deadly efficient but sensed there was something wrong even as his younger brother sprang from the vehicle. Blaine was framed in view, positioned like bait on a bear trap. Danny was striding towards his quarry, pistol thrust before him. Unease swept through Clay like a riptide. His warning shout went unheeded. A new sound too reached his ears. An engine of some sort, not a car. Then, too late, he registered the source of the sound. The forklift truck rounded the closest pallet of stacked timber, its forks low to the ground as it sped closer. The truck was designed to transport and reposition the huge rectangles of timber around the yard. A vehicle the size of the Chevy Cruze would pose no problem. The forks of the truck squealed against the chassis of the Cruze as it rammed hard into the driver's side. Clay, acting on instinct, scooted half over into the passenger seat. The sound of protesting metal filled his ears. The already damaged car was hoisted high into the air. Clay reached for the revolver but no target presented itself. All he could see was the lifting mechanism and the upright base, of the forks.

'Where's the ejector seat when you need one?' Clay reached for the passenger door. *Too late.* The outer shell of the vehicle shrieked like a wounded animal as the thin metal contested with the weathered timber sidings. The pallet of heavy wooden sleepers barely moved as the car slammed into it. The windscreen spiderwebbed but held. With a curse that he would never utter in church, Clay tried to squeeze between the two front seats. The rear window had been smashed out earlier during the scuffle with the Southern Unification and now offered a chance of escape. He managed to insert his right arm, twisting in his seat, and pushing down with his legs before another jolting impact upset his balance. The forklift truck quickly reversed before slamming the car once more into the timber stanchions. Clay found himself wedged; his abdomen pinioned between the two seats. Using the revolver as a brace, he pushed against the rear footwell with little success. A lightning strike of pain tore through his shoulder, the wound from the crossbow protesting vehemently.

The Chevy took a third shuddering impact and Clay felt the bones in his right wrist turn at an angle they were ill-suited to. The revolver slipped from his grasp. There was a shift of inertia and Clay capitalised on the change to scoot back into the front seats, his head bumping hard against the roof. Then the car was rising. There was little mystery to this, the driver of the forklift was in control. Both side doors were buckled inward, their metal frames misshapen. The whole vehicle bumped and vibrated as the forklift truck bore it at speed in a new direction.

'Oh, shit on a shovel!' Struggling to turn in the confines of the front seats, Clay kicked at the passenger door to little effect. Realising the door was not succumbing he then brought his right foot up hard against the windscreen. The third kick loosened the glass and an elongated crack appeared down the centre of the window. The car lurched higher, skidding on the twin forks with another screech of metal on metal. The forklift truck came to a sudden stop and Clay felt the battered vehicle slide forward twelve inches. Clay peered first at the thick mechanism of the truck's lifting gear, then with dismay at the scene beneath him. They had reached the far side of the lumber yard, only a cinder block wall separating them from a wide concrete channel below. The base of the concrete gully was awash, the fast-moving water dark and foreboding.

Then the car was tilting. The forklift lurched forward, clattering the cinder block barrier. A moment of weightlessness, then Clay felt his world spin as the Chevrolet Cruze plunged into the swirling water below. Grunting as his face slammed against the glass, Clay felt an involuntary shudder as water began to rush in through the rear window space. *Too fast.* Clay took one deep breath before the chill water swept over his head.

Chapter 51

Fish watched as Blaine dragged the unconscious body behind him like a garbage sack. The man below him was a rangy little bastard with wide shoulders but Blaine managed him easily. The shotgun that had been in Fish's trunk was loaded with non-lethal riot rounds; the rubber bullets ready for use on any transgressor that didn't warrant a lethal response. Fish had readied the shotgun in preparation for the pawnshop heist, a heist, now forgotten. Gato had bagged his target with little problem.

The two rounds he had taken had done their job perfectly. The wiry little scrapper was down and out. Fish had no qualms about putting a body in the ground but knew dead bodies were bad for business. Not something to be done without good reason. These two guys, however, deserved their promised dirt nap, big time. The guy had balls, going after Blaine, but they would only add to his agony before he took his last breath. The other one, the driver of the car, had kicked and slammed but had gone over the wall into the water anyway. They only needed one of them to answer questions. Using the forklift as a platform, Fish leaned out to peer over the cinder block wall. Only the battered rear fender of the car was now visible. One sleeper jutted vertically from the water. A continuous stream of bubbles traced the path of the sinking vehicle. A large expulsion of air seemed somehow prophetic as it broke the surface with a vigorous *bloop*. 'Say hello to Davy Jones while you're down there, dick wad.'

Fish rotated the steering wheel of the forklift truck and headed back to his friends. Blaine hauled the unconscious challenger to the front of the vehicle, framing him in the headlights. Fish hopped from the forklift as Blaine searched the limp body. 'Anything?'

'Some loose bills but no wallet, no ID.' He pulled the cell phone from his front pocket. Blaine rapped the side of the man's face with the phone then threw it overhand into the darkness.

'So how sure are we that he isn't a cop of some description, undercover? Is he wired for sound?'

Blaine's head snapped in Fish's direction then back to his captive. Dropping to one knee Blaine hoisted up the man's shirt. A second later he rolled the captive face down and again peered at his bare skin. 'Nothing there.'

'But he knew you offed the woman,' said Fish. 'We need to know exactly who this yahoo is. I don't want SWAT kicking down my door in the middle of the night because we didn't bother to get a straight answer from this asshole.'

'He's no cop. Look at him. And he isn't even American. He told that cop he was Scottish. He came here to put a cap in my ass, not arrest me,' stated Blaine. 'I say I stamp his face in and throw him over that fence with the other guy.'

'Uh-huh, but what if he's got an insurance policy like if he doesn't come back, an envelope with details of how he found you, goes to the Miami PD?' Fish held out his hand and received his shotgun back from Gato.

Blaine's fist hovered above the man's face as if to deliver another blow. 'You watch too many cheap-assed, cop shows on tv. This cherry bomb isn't smart enough to build a safety net. He came rolling in all hot and heavy, ready to put a bullet in me and got suckered instead.'

'Are you willing to bet your life on it?' asked Fish. 'And ours? Because, if the law comes for you, they're coming for all of us. We'll all swing for this if it goes sideways.'

Blaine stood to his full imposing height. 'Fine, we'll take him back with us, but after I've beaten the truth out of him, I'm still packing him in a barrel.'

'I've got no problem with that, big guy, but let's be sure.'

Blaine gave a grunt which Fish took to be agreement. 'I've got some duct tape in the back.'

Gato pulled the man's arms behind his back as Fish picked at the end of the tape. After nine revolutions of the man's wrists Fish slice the tape with his pocket knife. He repeated the process, securing the man's ankles. A final strip of tape covered his mouth. 'You wanna do the honours?'

Blaine hoisted the man by the belt, dragging him carelessly to the rear of the Hyundai and tossed him in the rear open trunk space. The side of his face slapped against the floor as he landed. Fish exchanged a nod with Gato as he closed the tailgate.

Gato rolled his shoulders. 'Today just got a whole lot more interesting.'

Fish cradled the shotgun. 'That it did my friend, that it did. You drive, I'll watch the man of mystery back here.'

Chapter 52

The hair blows across Chrissie's face as she reaches for another plump strawberry. Danny sits on the edge of the picnic blanket, happy. The shadows are getting longer as the sun dips closer to the horizon. The smile Chrissie flashes send butterflies through his stomach. Danny pulls the cork from the bottle and pours a generous measure of red wine into each of their glasses. Chrissie gives that same beautiful smile as she takes the glass from him. Music drifts slow and easy on the air like a summer scent. Danny leans closer, enjoying the intimacy of the moment. He tries for a kiss. His lips touch the corner of her mouth. Chrissie brushes a strand of hair from her face then returns the kiss, this one finding Danny's lips fully. Chrissie Haims tastes like strawberries; a good taste. Leaning back, he offers a wide smile in return. The smile fades as an unwelcome aroma catches in the back of his nose. A carrion smell. Where the hell is that coming from?

Danny looks down at the blanket, surprised to see the corner is turning black. Charring of the cloth causes him to snatch his hand away from the rapidly spreading heat. Something as bright as the sun explodes, searing across the left side of his body. As his shirt bursts into a sheet of fire, he tries to beat the flames away with his bare hands. He opens his mouth to shout a warning to Chrissie. He wants to tell her to run. Get away from the fire. No words will come. A harsh buzz of static *fills his ears. Another voice that does not belong here is screaming for help. No, not help; air support. As Danny drops and rolls to quell the spreading flames, the park begins to explode around them. Flashes of black and orange fill his vision. The pain from his searing flesh begins to make itself known. The deep bass of the explosions is so loud they reverberate in his chest. Plumes of black smoke fill the air, roiling, expanding into writhing tentacles.*

Something is coming. The anamorphic smoke opens like the uncurling of a fist and a figure steps into view. The shape is that of a man but much too large to be human. Slowly, ever so slowly the thing moves closer. Step...pause. Step...pause. Danny bites down against the searing pain and tries to warn Chrissie.

Run!

But no words escape his mouth. Retching, thick gelatinous sludge pours from his throat into his blistered hands. The thing looms over Chrissie, its hands reaching for her neck.

RUN!

Incorporeal tentacles wrap themselves around Danny like an anaconda, pinning him to the ground.

RUN!

But Chrissie doesn't run. The huge figure reaches down, hands circling her neck, fingers interlacing. Danny feels unbridled hatred welling through every fibre of his body. Ribbons of fire drip down the giant's face forming some sort of tribal insignia. He has seen this before. Orange and red flames spike around the giant's head forming a jagged crown.

'No. You're not him. I don't believe that. You're nothing. Get away from Chrissie.' Danny's words are expelled with more black sludge. The smoke around the thing dissipates, revealing human features. The giant cants his hairless skull to one side, a sick smile crossing his face as he lifts Chrissie from the ground. Chrissie's arms and legs begin to shudder.

'NO! Let her go.' Danny vomits the warning. 'I'm going to kill you. Rip out your heart.'

The giant begins to squeeze. Chrissie's eyes bulge, staring into Danny's very core. Every fibre in his body strains against the burning pain yet he is pinned, helpless to the ground.

Chrissie!

The sound of snapping bones comes to him like a whiplash.

Chrissie...

The giant laughs, dismissive and cruel as he turns. He tucks Chrissie Haim's limp body under one arm and strolls back into the swirling darkness.

'No, you can't have her!' the words finally rip from Danny's throat.

The giant turns. A sickening smirk marring his face. 'I can...any time I choose.'

Danny feels the bones in his hands' fracture as he

clenches his fists with immeasurable fury. The giant steps back into the smoke and is gone.

Chapter 53

'Junk! Sticks!' Curtis expelled a whoop as the screen held its image. 'I've got it.'

'The clap?' laughed Junk.

'Oh no, my mentally retarded friend, not the clap. I've got a lock on. This tracker decided to start working.'

Sticks ambled over to the table, peering over Curtis' shoulder. 'A lock on or a hard-on?'

'If it keeps on working, I'll be saying hello to mister stiffie, that's for sure.' Curtis Quantrill drummed his open hands on his thighs.

'Do you know how to read that thing?' Junk pointed to the tracking unit. 'It looks like one of those baby scan photos before you can tell it's a baby.'

'You know what separates the two of us, amigo?' Quantrill shot Junk a grin. 'About two hundred IQ points.'

Sticks held out his hand. 'Let me see it. I used to work at NASA.'

Junk cocked his head to one side. 'You shittin' me?'

'Hey, it wasn't rocket science.'

'Dick head,' said Junk.

'Nom nom,' replied Sticks.

'What the hell does that even mean?'

'Go ask your momma, she'll tell you, I'm sure.'

Quantrill wagged his finger in front of the screen. 'I'm telling you guys; I'm laying odds on that this will lead us to Delacroix's main stash.'

Junk raised his eyebrows.

'Erik Delacroix went to his grave because he was a stubborn, defiant prick who didn't have the good sense to know that Blaine wasn't letting go of that chokehold, short of holy intervention.'

'Deus ex machina,' offered Sticks.

Junk shook his head. 'Call a priest, this asshole is speaking in tongues.'

Quantrill ignored the game of verbal softball the two friends seemed determined to play. 'Delacroix's last words as he choked were 'you'll never find it'. That told me that there was something to find.'

Sticks took the seat next to Quantrill. 'So…this isn't just a pipe dream.'

'Jesus Christ! How many times have I told you guys about this?'

'I know, but I always thought...'

Quantrill slammed his palm hard onto the table. 'What? That I was blowing smoke out my ass? You think I would have spent so much of my time effort and money chasing this if it wasn't kosher? What the hell do you take me for?'

Sticks held up his hands in supplication. 'Okay boss man, you've got my undivided attention. Tell me again.'

Quantrill felt a muscle jump in the side of his jaw. He took a deep breath before speaking again. 'In the sixteen-hundreds, a Spanish galleon went down somewhere off the coast of South Florida. The Nuestra Senora de Atocha was heading back to mother Spain with one of the largest bounties ever taken from the Americas. It was lost to history for hundreds of years, the thing of myths, then Mel Fisher discovered part of the ship's hull. That was the mid-eighties. His haul was valued in the region of five hundred million dollars. But there was still a lot more to be found.'

'And that's what you think Delacroix found?'

'Yeah, like I've been telling you for the last three years. The captain's manifest from the ship shows there was a lot more than even Fisher managed to find.'

'Yeah?'

'Jesus, have I been talking to the walking dead

for the last few years? I've told you all of this before. There's more than a hundred thousand gold coins, chests of emeralds and nearly twenty tons of silver bars. But that's not the best of it, there was still over thirty chests full of golden idols and jewellery, the chest themselves were even laid in gold.'

Both Junk and Sticks took up position either side of the table. Curtis looked at both in turn. 'In one of the chests of gold, there was a skull, cast from solid gold and encrusted with so many gems they were too many to count. I knew Delacroix, even worked with him a few times way back, and he changed in the last couple of years.'

Sticks raised one pencil-thin eyebrow. 'Changed, how?'

'He used to be a typical saltwater dickhead, full of his crap about the tail he'd pulled and the whisky he'd sunk. Then the old cock-knot got all reclusive, started going out on the water only at night. He had an old army truck that he used to use, the sides were always covered in with a tarp. He'd disappear into the 'glades for days at a time. No one knew what the hell he was up to. That's how it went, he'd go out on the Meg then no one would see him for weeks. Then he'd show back up in that old truck.'

'He was stashing the find...' Junk tapped his knuckles against the side of his head. 'That's what you think that their doo-hickey tracker is signifying.'

Quantrill leaned back in his seat. 'Well now, if the fifth grade is ever in need of a critical mind.'

Sticks chuckled and cuffed Junk on the shoulder. 'Yeah man, this year's Captain Obvious award goes to….'

'Your momma. It's obvious she shoulda drowned you in a creek at birth.' Junk gave his friend the middle finger.

Quantrill ignored the barbs; they were nothing out of the ordinary. 'Sticks, get the others on the phone. We're heading out ASAP. Junk, load some lamps and shovels into the back of my truck, I've a feeling we're going to be digging deep.'

This was the pay-off he had been praying for, he was sure of it. The smile on Quantrill's face dropped away as the door to the room flew open, clattering against the brickwork. Blaine stepped into the room with what looked like a dead body draped over his shoulder.

Quantrill glowered. 'What the fuck!'

Chapter 54

Something smacked hard against the side of Clay Gunn's chin as he pressed his face against the car roof. The rear window was gone but there was no way he was squeezing back there, between the gap in the seats. Sucking in a desperate breath, he ducked his head beneath the water once more. Tucking himself into a ball Clay managed to wedge his feet onto the seats. With his back to the windscreen, he straightened with all his strength. A pounding in his temples hammered a beat as he strained against the tempered glass. *Danny was alone up there.* There was a sudden release of pressure as one half of the glass succumbed to his efforts. His shoulders rammed through the open portal, something sharp biting into the skin across the back of his neck. The remaining air that had been trapped in the car's interior swept over his face in a myriad of frantic bubbles. Mud and silt darkened the already murky water as Clay twisted, using the steering wheel as a leverage point. Pulling down with his left, he then fed his right arm out of the window. His head and upper torso followed. The windshield clung stubbornly to its rubber fixings, preventing a clean exit. Numerous pinpoints of glass sought his skin as he hammered the glass away with his forearm. Kicking again with his legs, he managed to haul himself towards the hood. The turbulent water that swirled over him battered his face. With no other option, Clay knew he was trying to exit the car against the flow. The current pushed hard against his bulk, forcing him back into the vehicle. He felt his fingers slip and strain as he sought a solid grip on the vehicle's bodywork. With no way of judging the depth of the water in the channel, Clay doubled his efforts. Ignoring the numbness rapidly spreading through his limbs, he forced himself to slow down. Placing his feet on the backrests of the seats he began to push slow and steady.

It was working.

Inch by inch he felt his body pass through the window space. He was nearly free. Just a few more seconds and he could strike out for the surface. His last breath was starting to burn in his lungs, numbingly cold water forcing itself into his nose, his ears, his eyes. His forward motion halted once more. Clay tried scooting to one side with little effect. Something was cinching him at the waist. Reaching back, he pulled with savage focus. He felt fabric tear and release its hold, then he was again scrambling. Bending his knee, he succeeded in feeding his right leg too onto the metal hood. He would be free in a second. The brief sense of elation was swept away as something impossibly hard and heavy slammed into the vehicle inches from his head. Only his hastily crossed arms saved his face from being smashed into the vehicle. The swirling current pushed back against him, impeding his efforts to guard his head. Repeated impacts sent violent shudders through the already ruined vehicle. Clay emitted an agonised roar into the water as his back was pounded hard into the metal hood. Dark rectangular objects rained down around him like thunderbolts. The car bucked as another severe impact caused the vehicle to lurch away from the bottom of the silt-filled channel. Clay fought against the water that sped into his open mouth, gagged, and choked.

Jesus, is this how it ends?

Then he was free from the vehicle. Kicking against the car, his right ankle slammed against one of the plummeting wooden missiles. New sparks of pain lanced up his leg. Choking, desperate for air, Clay struck out following the direction of the air bubbles that swept over his face. He barely had time to clench his teeth in horror as the iron-hard wooden stanchion struck him like a torpedo. His limbs twisted loosely as the current seized him mercilessly and carried him in its icy grip. Clay felt his breath escape as the darkness began to take hold.

Chapter 55

Brockovich ran a hand through her raven hair, sweeping it back from her face. The CSI techs were nearly done. They'd been at it for over two hours, collecting evidence, bagging, and cataloguing various items. The crime scene photographer, having completed his task, was in the process of loading his kit back into the hard clamshell case he always carried. The two bodies in the apartment had been photographed from every angle. The photographer, a stick-thin man with a 'Zorro' style moustache, gave Brockovich a slow nod of understanding. It had been a long day. Brockovich returned the nod then cast a sideways look at her partner. Anderson was still jabbering into his phone. He'd been yapping double-time for the last twenty minutes or so. Something about incorrect pension funding on his account. Gina turned back to the scene. The older of the two corpses was a big man, a wide and bushy beard framing his square face. The cause of death was sure to be confirmed as the kitchen knife that protruded from his neck, just below the beard. At the far side of the neat apartment lay a woman, her features smashed and swollen into a grotesque mask.

Brockovich had seen this scenario several times in her career. The property had been visited by officers several times in the past year. The man, Gerald Banner, had a history of domestic abuse. The woman, Gloria Silver, his long-time partner too had a long history of walking into doors and falling down stairs. Each time she had returned to Banner. Back to the eventual fate that lay before her. Sad that she had been proved correct in her prediction, Brockovich took a deep breath. What a waste of life. Both Brockovich and Anderson had been called to the property less than a month earlier along with the uniforms. Gloria had been battered and bruised but had refused to press charges against Banner, the big bearded idiot blubbering like a child that he would never again lift a hand to her. *Yeah, right.*

Brockovich tapped her wrist, catching Anderson's attention. She received a look of frustration and annoyance in way of return. Pursing her lips, she again caught the attention of her partner. She pointed first to her chest then in the direction of the front door. Anderson gave her the briefest indication of a thumbs up and continued his relentless monologue.

Thankful for the cooling evening air, Gina Brockovich walked back to their vehicle and rested her butt against the hood. Her feet ached and despite Anderson's mistaken belief that she never perspired, she felt in desperate need of a long shower. She lifted her hair from her collar, enjoying the cooling effect. Closing her eyes, she allowed the sounds of the city to drift in on the breeze.

An image, cryptic and distorted, crept into her mind like a sneak thief. *Two men, one hulking, one small and mean, both men running...a sheet of fire behind them like a curtain in a theatre. Bodies lay on the ground. A car mangled and spewing fire to one side. Anderson reaching out to her. His blood-spattered face set grim.* Brockovich snapped back, her focus once more on the crime scene. An involuntary shudder racked her body. A drop of cold sweat traced its way down her face.

What the hell? Had she drifted into momentarily into sleep?

Standing straight, Brockovich took several deep breaths.

What in hell was that about?

Brockovich shook her head and sat back against the hood of the car. Puffing out her cheeks she allowed her eyes to close once more. After several minutes had passed, she heard a familiar sound. Anderson dragged his right leg ever so slightly when he walked, a result of his old football injury. Brockovich spoke without opening her eyes.

'You, done reading them the riot act?'

Anderson's voice carried more frustration than anger. 'That's the fourth time I've had to explain the same facts to these idiots. Don't they realise that they are dealing with people's livelihoods?'

'It's just numbers on a sheet to them, partner.'

'They're telling me some yak-yak about domestic bond performance not returning the expected yield values,' Anderson huffed. 'Like any of that will mean two scoops of shit when I tell my better half that my pension has just dropped a third in real-world value. If that's not a shit-frosted cupcake, I don't know what is.'

Brockovich opened her eyes. 'At least you have a pension. By the time I get there, I reckon I'll be in a shared house and living on food stamps and goodwill.'

Anderson cursed under his breath. 'Some kinda day, huh.'

'You got that right.'

'What were you doing out here, meditating?'

'Why the hell would I be meditating?'

A slow smile crept across Anderson's face. 'I thought that kind of thing was in your genes.'

'Again, with the genes?' Brockovich shook her head. 'You know I grew up right here in the big M, went to college in Jacksonville and not a Buddhist temple, right?'

'I hear Jacksonville is a very spiritual place,' Anderson chuckled. 'At least compared to Miami.'

'Hey, it's a great city but it's hardly the Shaolin Temple.'

'Uh-huh.'

Brockovich nodded at the crime scene. 'I think we've done all we can here.'

'Yeah, I'm ready to roll if you are.'

Brockovich pushed off the vehicle, stretching her legs. 'I've been thinking about the Haims case.'

Anderson nodded and held out his hands expectantly. 'And?'

'It's something that old gnarly dude told us.'

'Corky Collins?'

'Yeah, him. He told us that those two, the Gunn brothers, were in the Haims house for a couple of hours, you remember?'

'Of course, Alzheimer's hasn't got me yet.'

'He said that they never took anything in or out of the house.'

'Uh-huh.'

'But they were in there for quite some time.'

'Uh-huh.'

'So, what were they doing in there all that time?'

Anderson shrugged. 'Daniel Gunn was involved with Chrissie Haims; he could have been in there crying and thinking over old times.'

'Maybe, but I don't think he's the crying kind.'

'Some guys will surprise you.'

Brockovich continued, 'I think they were searching the house, playing amateur detectives. Remember the state of that place? There wasn't a floor or wall left without a big hole in it. '

'Uh-huh.'

'And we know they roughed up those couple of skinheads.'

'Uh-huh.'

'I want to take another look at the Gunn brothers. I think they might have found something out that we missed. It's been bothering me why they would go and pick a fight half the way across the city without a good reason.'

Anderson rubbed his hand across his chin. 'They hardly looked like altar boys. I don't think either of them needs much of a reason to get into a fight.'

'Hmmm, maybe,' said Brockovich. *Two men, one hulking, one small and mean… a sheet of fire behind them.* 'If we have any time tomorrow, I want to track them down and have a little dialogue with those two; a little tete-a-tete, see what they know.'

'What do think that might be?'

'I think that they may have found something that we missed,' repeated Brockovich. There was something about the brothers; *one hulking, one small and mean.* An itch in the back of her mind she couldn't quite scratch. 'Or maybe they talked to the locals, you know, the ones that would rather cut off their toes rather than talk to a cop.'

'Uh-huh.'

Brockovich tapped her watch. 'But right now, I'm going home, having the world's longest shower, a glass or two of vino and then it's pyjama time.'

'You better slow your role, with that rock 'n' roll lifestyle partner.'

Chapter 56

The skin on Clay's hands scraped along the concrete channel as he was swept along by the surging water. Despite forming his rapidly numbing fingers into claws he was unable to gain any purchase on the slick barrier. Kicking his legs, he felt himself slipping below the surface once again. Sucking in a desperate lung full of air Clay forced himself to be calm. The water that invaded his throat burned in the back of his nose like battery acid. Coughing and retching, Clay felt a new pressure building behind his eyes. The lights across the bay seemed to mock him in their elusiveness. The estuary that poured from Brickell Flatts emptied into Biscayne Bay, the water swirling into vigorous eddies, each pulling him in a new direction. As his face broke the surface, he abandoned all attempts at grabbing at the channel wall, instead began to swim with the current. Remembering an old training exercise from his days as a Ranger he partially rolled onto his side, the new angle of his body aiding his efforts. Despite the tugging of the undertow, each stroke of his arms and kick of his legs guided him slowly back towards the shoreline, inch by desperate inch. Then he was below the surface again. Water invaded his nose, ears and stung his eyes. The burning in his throat caused him to cough violently. Water and the contents of his stomach belched free from his mouth. His body turned and tumbled as another eddy caught him in its grasp. This time, again going with the current Clay ducked a little deeper into the water. Snapping down with his arms and legs in a coordinated effort allowed his head to break the surface once more. He sucked in another desperate breath, filling his lungs. The current seemed to ease its pull on his limbs and he again rolled onto his side, suddenly bone-tired. There; the shore or what passed as a shoreline at Brickell was almost within reach. A dark line, darker than the water that pulled at his limbs was now only twenty yards away.

Clay struck out toward land, his limbs now feeling like they were filled with ice water and sand, sluggish and tired. He looked up at the barrier wall as he again neared the water's edge. His brother was up there; alone.

Danny.

Lurching through the shallows Clay felt his lower legs sink into the muddy silt. His balance began to tilt, he thrust out his arms but too late. Pitching face down Clay again found himself underwater. His arms now too were deep in the silt. Arching his back, he forced his face above the surface. With infuriating lack of speed, he angled his chest to one side and slowly withdrew his right arm. Allowing his knees to fold beneath him he then freed his other arm.

'Come on you son of a bitch,' Clay spat out grimy water as he forced his legs to move in the mire. His feet pedalled in the thickness of the mud and silt. Then his left foot found a solid purchase and his weight plunged forward. Another faltering step and his upper torso broke clear of the water. He forced onward, each step raising him higher from the water level. Clay emitted a simian grunt as his hands found the lower edge of the barrier fence. The fence stretched at least twelve feet above his head. The shoreline was framed by a thick layer of corrugated metal and rocks. There looked to be no clear footholds in the barrier. Reaching above his head Clay hooked his fingers into an exposed section of the chain-link fence. The muscles in his arms, chest and shoulder protested as he drew himself slowly from the last vestiges of the mud and silt. Hand over hand he climbed the fence, the chain link buckling precariously under his weight.

A dagger of pain sliced through his left shoulder as he forced himself on. His feet finally found purchase and he went up and over the last few feet of fence in a lizard-like motion. Water ran in rivulets from his sodden clothes as he reached dry ground. He fought against the shivers that racked his frame. The waning heat of the day helped only a little.

He was back in the yard. The rectangular wooden pilings lent a maze-like effect to the industrial ground. Glancing at the closest stack of wooden stanchions he realised that the dick-wad in the forklift must have tipped one of the stacks onto his sinking car right after he'd dumped Clay over the edge.

Wasting no time, Clay ran back to the centre of the yard.

It was empty.

Danny was nowhere in sight.

Both vehicles were gone.

'Shit on a shovel,' cursed Clay. Danny had talked about thinking like a cop, but he needed little power of deduction to know that the three men had taken Danny.

The three had taken his brother.

They would die for that.

Chapter 57

Curtis Quantrill felt a sense of dread quickly replace the optimism he had experienced only moments before. Blaine stepped into the room with what looked like a dead body draped over his shoulder. Quantrill lurched from his seated position. 'Who the hell is that?'

Blaine dumped his payload on the floor with a look of disdain. Quantrill stared down at the captive. The man's wrists and ankles were duct-taped. His mouth too was secured by a strip of silver tape.

'Again, who, in Buddha's butt-crack is that?'

Blaine stared down at the man with unbridled aggression on his face, his chest rising and falling rapidly.

Quantrill added a scowl of his own. Blaine was again proving to be a class-A asshole. 'Fish? Who the fuck is that?'

'This is the ass-wipe that called Blaine earlier, the one that ran into his car. Made a real mess of it too.'

Quantrill spread his hands, waiting for more.

'This yahoo squared up to Blaine in the street. Things were starting to catch fire when a couple of street cops showed up.'

'You're friggin' kiddin' me, right? What did I say about cops?'

Fish continued, 'Don't worry they were a couple of Krispy Kreme eatin' assholes. They just shooed us on our way. I don't think they wanted the hassle, or the paperwork.'

'So how did that end up with a hog-tied body on my floor?' asked Curtis.

A wry smile spread across Fish's face. He braced his fingers like a pianist, cracking his knuckles before continuing. 'After the cops told us to get lost, this dumb shit and his ugly-assed boyfriend decided to follow us. We played a little cat and mouse then took them down to Brickell Flatts, you know the old timber storage yard, and served them a six-pack of whup-ass apiece.'

Gato struck a pose, his hands extended in a fighting guard. 'With a chaser of fuck you, and goodnight!'

Quantrill felt a raw heat radiating through his face. 'That still doesn't explain why in hell you brought one of them back with you. All you've done is involve me in your shit. Shit that I don't need to be involved in.'

'You're already involved,' Blaine tapped the toe of his boot hard against the captive's chin. 'This broke-assed boy scout was asking about the woman.'

Taking two quick steps Quantrill stood close to Blaine, their faces only inches apart. 'Woman?'

'Yeah,' answered Blaine. 'The woman. The one that got in the way.'

'That should never have happened. I swear to god; you fuckers are going to be the death of me.' Quantrill could smell Blaine, his sweat, old cigar smoke and beer breath. 'So, who the hell is he? I presume you bothered to find out before going all fast and furious on his ass?'

Fish moved closer. Quantrill shrugged away his hand from his shoulder. 'That's what I'm telling you, this is the guy that ran into Blaine's car. That was just a set up to get him back to his house, a lure. He fronted up to Blaine as soon as we got there, made no bones about it either, wiry little bastard, asking if Blaine killed the Haims woman.'

Quantrill continued to dead eye Blaine, the heat in his face continuing to rise. This was the last thing he needed. They were getting closer to Delacroix's legacy, so close. 'Tell me you didn't bring a cop to my house.'

'Nah man, he's no cop. I think he's the woman's family or maybe he was banging her or sumpin'.' Fish gyrated his hips in a dubious rhythm. 'We brought him here on account I reckoned you'd want to speak to him yourself. Find out what he knows, who else he's workin' with, that kind of thing.'

Quantrill ran a hand through his hair. He stared at the tracker unit on his table. He took a slow breath before speaking again. 'You shouldn't have brought him here, to my goddamned home. We could have done this out in the glades where small matters like forensic evidence wouldn't be such an issue.'

'For once I agree,' said Blaine. 'I would have been happy to stamp his face into the dirt then throw him into Biscayne like the other one. It was Fish that thought that we should bring him back to you.'

'Other one?' A muscle twitched in Quantrill's jaw. 'What happened to the other one that was with him?'

Gato nodded at Fish, a look of exaggerated respect on his face. 'Fish played it like Maverick, scooped the whole car up with a forklift truck and dumped his ass in the ocean. Then he dropped a pallet load of railway sleepers on him for good measure.'

'So, no one is following?' asked Quantrill.

'Nah man, as we said, we dropped the other guy in the bay and left the car they followed us in, down at the bottom of Brickell,' answered Fish. He smiled, giving two sharp claps then showing his open palms like a dealer in a casino.

'Not too shabby for a dickless wonder,' said

Gato.

Fish sneered at Gato. 'Ask your momma if I'm dickless, she might tell a different tale.'

'Cut the shit,' said Quantrill. 'This is serious.'

All six men now stood over the captive.

'What's your play, boss man?' asked Sticks.

Curtis Quantrill stared down at the transgressor. 'Get him back into your car, Fish. We'll find out what he knows then sink him so deep no one will ever find him.'

'So, my plan was a good plan after all,' said Fish.

'Yes, but we're not doing it in my friggin' house, you dimwit.'

'Where then?'

'Just get his carcass in the car and follow me,' said Quantrill. 'And please, do nothing else to attract the attention of Miami PD, for Christ's sake.'

Fish and Gato each grabbed the captive by his shoulders and dragged him back into the garage. Curtis Quantrill nodded to the rest of the men to follow. Albeit with a sneer, Blaine turned on his heel and strode after them. Quantrill picked up the tracker unit from his table and followed. This was all Blaine's fault.

Chapter 58

Clay Gunn forced his limbs to move. Involuntary shivers racked his frame as he slowly picked up speed. The stacks of timber stood to each side like ancient monoliths in the rapidly darkening night. Only the vestiges of the sun remained; a faint strip of orange on the horizon, visible as he dodged between the stacks. His clothes stuck like a second skin, heavy with the water that dripped at a steady rate. Every nerve in his body protested as he forced himself on. The yard gates were still open and he wasted no time gaining the service road that had led them there. A kid on a motor scooter whizzed away in the opposite direction, paying him no heed.

Bile rose in the back of his throat as he increased his efforts. His limbs, cold and numb seemed to conspire against him as he traversed the gravel road. His feet slipped from beneath him. His out-flung hands absorbed most of the fall, but not enough to prevent his face digging a shallow furrow in the shale. Spitting out dust he managed first onto all-fours. He stayed down as he vomited, the bile and seawater again burning his throat. He wiped his mouth with the back of his hand, chest heaving and stood to full height.

Danny.

Spitting the remains from his mouth as he ran, Clay reached the asphalt within minutes. He leaned forward, hands on thighs, as he sucked in huge breaths. He silently berated himself for letting his fitness slip. Time was he could have run ten times the distance without puffing out a candle.

Looking left and right Clay was for a moment undecided. Where the hell would they have taken Danny?

The truth was they could have spirited him to anywhere in the whole goddamned state. Clay thrust a hand into a pocket and stared at his cell phone. He knew what the odds were but tried keying it anyway. The phone was dead.

'Yeah, a ten-minute dip in the ocean will do that.' Clay swore under his breath. He again looked both ways along the road. 'If in doubt, go left.'

Clay began again his loping run, his feet slapping heavily on the asphalt, each step sounding like lazy applause. The distant lights of the city seemed to mock him. What would he do when he reached them? Call the cops, and say what? *'Hello there, my brother and I failed in an attempted murder and got our asses handed to us...can you help us out please, mister officer, sir?'*

No, that wasn't going to wash.

Clay kept running, his legs and lungs at last beginning to find some coordination. It looked about a quarter mile to the first main road.

Clay kept running.

The shivering in his limbs had abated but his face, hands and feet still felt numb. As he approached the junction, he could see sparse but regular traffic zipping by. Maybe he could flag one down and head back into Miami proper?

'And then what?' Clay chided aloud. These guys were in the wind and they had Danny, had his little brother. His top lip curled back over his teeth as he considered his brother's predicament. Thoughts of brutality were paused as a set of headlights turned onto the service road.

Clay squinted against the approaching lights, raising one hand to shield his eyes. The vehicle looked big and boxy. Had Blaine and his gang returned to ascertain his fate? As the vehicle drew closer, Clay moved to the centre of the road and held up a hand. The vehicle, instead of slowing increased its speed, heading straight for him. With a vile curse Clay dodged left, then a rapid tuck and roll carried him off to the right of the speeding vehicle. Clay felt the front fender clip the sole of his left boot.

The vehicle, Clay could now see was a van screeched to a halt.

'Shit on a shovel,' swore Clay. He recognised the van. It was the same one Danny had hijacked the first Southern Unification boys into.

Six men sprang from the van with an angry urgency.

'Don't do this. I haven't got the time to spare,' warned Clay.

There were no threats called, no verbal exchange.

They just attacked.

Chapter 59

Syrus Sanderson grinned without humour. A phrase an old friend had often used sprang to mind; *'Softly softly, catchee monkey.'* And here he was, at least one of them. He was one big-assed monkey, but this time the men of the SU were ready. Syrus had set one of the youngest members of the clan the task of shadowing the two roughnecks until an opportunity arose to even the score. Young Brent had proved his worth, following unseen on his Suzuki; a real Southern Unification trooper in the making. The phone call saying that the two men had gotten themselves into another fight and followed their quarry to Brickell Flatts was music to his ears. Only one of the roughnecks was in sight. The big one; Clay Gunn. One would do for now. They would track down the other one later. CJ was at the wheel and narrowly missed crushing the big cowboy beneath the wheels of his van. He slammed on the brakes.

Despite his earlier encounter with the brothers and subsequent warnings of violence, Syrus had no intention of letting them walk away. No way. 'Turn this motherfucker to paste.'

Sanderson and five of the remaining SU sprang from the van. Lyle leapt at Gunn, the length of rebar he wielded sweeping down at his head. But Gunn wasn't there, the big man had pivoted, snapping his head away from the weapon. Lyle was catapulted off his feet as Gunn kicked out with the side of his boot. The van rocked on its axle as Lyle slammed into the side panels.

Jesus H, the big guy moved as a man possessed. Instead of trying to escape the armed gang, he was among them like a whirlwind. Syrus; undaunted, sprang at Gunn and brought his weapon to bear. The spiked bat he hefted was lethal, the thick climber's pitons he had welded himself could crush a man's skull with one blow. Gunn had his back to him, slamming vicious punches into his men with abandon. CJ went down in a silent mess, his already damaged face now a bloody ruin. Syrus brought the spiked cudgel down with all of his strength, aiming for the base of Gunn's skull. One good hit there and the roughneck would be finished, it didn't matter how big or tough he thought he was.

Syrus heard an ungodly snap and realised that Gunn had shifted his weight at the last possible second. The big bastard caught Syrus by the wrist and locked his arm into a straight bar. The agony came a second later as he realised the snapping sound was his elbow hyper-extending past the breaking point.

Syrus went to his knees and could do little more than grit his teeth as Gunn brought up his boot.

A firework went off inside his head. Then a merciful blackness swept over him.

Blackness…

When Syrus stirred again, his arm refused to move. His shirt felt like a tourniquet around the grossly swollen limb. Looking around, his breath caught in his throat. Five of his oldest and closest friends lay broken around him. CJ stared into the sky, his face devoid of life, his lower jaw hanging open in a way it was never designed to. Lyle lay to his left with Syrus' spiked club embedded deep into the top of his skull.

'No, no, no,' Syrus' voice was a winter wind. The nightmare continued as he looked past Lyle. Bradley was spread-eagle on the ground, chest down, but his empty eyes stared into the night sky. Gunn had snapped his neck to an impossible angle. His right leg too was twisted in a way that was horrendous to even look at. Chuck and Julius lay on top of each other like tragic lovers. Julius still had his hunting knife but now it protruded from between his shoulders. Chuck was the only one moving, his fingers slowly waving as if strumming a guitar. Red bubbles popped each time he opened his mouth.

The van was gone.

Syrus inched his good hand to his pocket. He had to get medics on the scene or they were all for the pine box. He moved his hand to his side. Something sharp was poking out of his shirt. His mind reeled as he realised the sharp edge was one of his ribs. He coughed into his hand. His hand came away, sticky and dark. Syrus Sanderson lay back and stared up into the night sky.

So many stars up there...

Chapter 60

Gina Brockovich held the wine glass against her cheek. Closing her eyes, she inhaled the aroma. The wine was bordering expensive, but she loved the subtle after taste of the Sauvignon Blanc. The porcupine on the label too made her smile. As she lay back on her couch, she took a sip. Nice. Glad to be finished for the day, she had taken a long shower, scrubbing away the detritus of the day. Dressed now in over-sized pyjamas, she curled her legs beneath her and took another sip of wine. She glanced at the timer on her steamer. The kitchen gadget had ten minutes left in its cooking cycle. Ten minutes then she would tuck into her noodles and steamed vegetables. The asparagus, bok choi and broccoli were favourites, especially when slathered in nuoc cham gung ginger sauce.

Another sip of wine.

The Gunn brothers. *Why did they bother her so?*

Leaving the tv off, Brockovich instead used the remote to select a playlist on her media system. A tower stood to the left of the speakers. Several dozen CDs were arranged into neat rows within the tower, CDs she never listened to, but there they stayed. She set the playlist to random selection. Moments later Phil Collins began to sing about something in the air tonight. Brockovich took another sip of wine then realised the glass was nearly empty. Echoes of a dream, half-remembered, tugged at her memory. *Danny Gunn. Clay Gunn. Flames. A wall of flames.*

Shaking off the malady, she stood.

'Have another?' she asked herself as she drained her glass. 'Why, I do believe I will.'

Her hand was on the door of the refrigerator when her cell phone began to warble. Glancing at the screen her head drooped forward, her cheeks puffing out. She picked up the phone.

'I'm off the clock.'

'I'm sorry but Adams called in sick, and Liebowitz is on the scene at a shooting, over on Collins Avenue. You're the next name on the call list.'

Brockovich looked wistfully at the steamer. Callie had worked as a dispatcher for six years and Gina counted her as a personal friend. She cut her some slack. 'Okay, Callie, what you got?'

'An altercation at Brickell Flatts. Six men down, it's early days but it sounds like four of the six were DOA and the other two are bound for the ER.'

'Roger that,' said Brockovich, her fatigue suddenly evaporating. 'Do we know anything about the victims?'

Callie sniffed audibly down the line. 'It seems likely that all six are members of the Southern Unification.'

A tingle traced its way down the length of Brockovich's spine. 'Anyone in custody?'

'Not at the moment,' said Callie. Her next words were delivered in a slightly hushed tone. 'Maybe they met someone that didn't subscribe to their Nazi racist bullshit?'

'Yeah, a crying shame,' replied Brockovich. She knew Callie's own family, originally from Dominica, had suffered abuse and threats from the SU.

'Yeah, shame that there's still two of them drawing breath.'

'I hear that,' said Brockovich. She changed her tone back to the professional. 'Right then, I'm back on the clock. Send the details to my phone.'

'Doing it as we speak.'

'Have you called Anderson yet?'

'Not yet, you want me to do that next?'

'No,' said Brockovich. 'I'll give him the good news myself. He'll be overjoyed to miss his meatloaf supper.'

Callie laughed a good sound. 'I'm sure he

will.'

'Who's on the scene at the moment?'

'Four uniforms, Martinez and Williams, Magson and Gray.'

Brockovich recognised all four names. 'Let them know I'll be there in twenty.'

'Will do.'

'Maybe they met someone that didn't subscribe to their Nazi racist bullshit?' That's what Callie had said. Maybe they had met two men? The Gunn brothers had already knocked heads with the SU assholes. Had they escalated head knocking into murder? She thought back to the look in Daniel Gunn's eyes, the look behind the civilised façade. Damn it, there was a good chance the two roughnecks had done just that. Then again maybe not. The SU wasn't exactly renowned for their good neighbour reputation. She would keep her mind open until after she'd interviewed the two survivors. *An itch she couldn't quite scratch. Flames...*

Gina Brockovich walked back to her bedroom and picked a fresh two-piece suit from her closet. Dark blue jacket and straight-legged trousers. A lighter blue blouse and her usual low-heeled boots came next. She used a band to pull her hair back into a ponytail. The finer details of her dream proved elusive.

Flames...

She quickly dressed then called Anderson.

Chapter 61

As the body lying in the trunk space of the vehicle began to stir Blaine leaned over the back of the seat. 'You awake, pretty boy?'

A faint murmur sounded from behind the duct tape gag. Blaine drove his fist into the face below the tape. The man again fell silent.

'Where are we taking him anyway?' asked Fish as he steered the Hyundai away from Quantrill's house. They had loaded the unconscious body back into the vehicle in the privacy of the double garage.

Blaine thumbed the captive's eyelid open with little care. The man's iris was large and unfocused. With a low curse, he shoved the unresponsive face away.

'I've got an old thirty-footer to scupper down at Cutler. It's an off the books insurance job, so sleeping beauty is going in the hold with about twenty kegs of chemical waste,' said Curtis. 'We'll find out everything we want from him, then he goes down with the ship. There's enough benzine in there to turn him to sludge, so no worries about him washing up on the shore.'

'A scupper job?' Blaine looked at the ageing surf dog. 'When did this gig come in?'

Quantrill answered without turning to look back at Blaine. 'Two weeks ago. You were sitting right there at my table when I told you.'

'I don't remember.'

'That's probably because you were brim-full of Tequila,' replied Quantrill.

Blaine raised one eyebrow. 'You'll have to be more specific than that.'

Quantrill continued, 'I wish you'd all pay more attention. I shouldn't have to repeat myself like I'm training interns. The stakes are getting higher and higher. Now we've got dead bodies on our tab. You all need to be more careful, think before you go slinging your fists. The last thing we need...'

'Is the law poking into our business,' Blaine interrupted, his voice sharp. 'You've said that already.'

Blaine watched Curtis Quantrill slowly turn to lock eyes. He had the same expression as earlier and Blaine half expected him to reach again for his brass knuckles. 'If we put a body in the ground it should be for good reason. That shit can come back to haunt you twenty years later.'

'Screw them all,' said Blaine. 'Anyone gets in my way and I'm putting them down.'

'For god's sake!'

'Put your face back in its box, Curtis. The

woman showed up out of the blue while we were searching in her house on your errand, remember. We were in there because of the major hard on you've got for Erik friggin' Delacroix. What was I supposed to do, huh? She walked in and saw our faces. If I hadn't have grabbed her, she would have been screaming off down the street like the Kentucky derby. I'm more than certain that the very same cops you are desperate to avoid would have been crawling all over us in minutes.'

'Jesus Christ, Blaine, can you ever admit you fucked up?'

'I would if I had,' countered Blaine. The desire to reach out and crush Curtis' trachea was growing. 'When I grabbed her, I put my hand over her mouth, warned her to stay quiet. You saw that, right, Fish? Gato?'

'You did,' agreed Fish. Gato gave a nod.

'But oh no, the dim bitch had to go all Krav Maga instead of doing what she was told. She nearly crushed my balls. I wasn't about to let her stick her fingernails in my eyes, so I yanked her 'til she was quiet.'

'You choked her to death, Blaine,' said Quantrill.

'And what would you have done?' Blaine locked his right wrist back just out of Curtis' line of sight. 'And don't give me any shit about tying her up.

She'd seen our faces remember. We'd still be on the bulletin boards of every precinct in the city.'

Quantrill turned back to stare out of the windshield. The corners of Blaine's mouth twitched. It was a small victory but he'd take it.

Fish lightened the mood by loudly breaking wind. 'That's for you guys in the back. Don't say I never give you anything.'

'Jeez man, your insides are rotten. You need a colonic or something,' said Gato.

Sticks rolled down his window, the night air whipping inside the vehicle. 'He needs a Febreze infusion up his ass.'

'How long do we have to be in here with this guy's obnoxious fumes?' asked Junk.

'Just until we get our guest of honour onto the boat,' said Quantrill.

'I want first go at him,' declared Blaine. There was no way he was being done out of that. 'That little shit will be spilling his guts in five minutes.'

'For once we agree on something,' said Quantrill.

'Look at that, all one big bunch of happy campers again,' said Fish. 'Does anyone know the words to kumbaya? I'll give you the opening note.'

Blaine scowled as Fish broke wind once

again.

Chapter 62

Vibrations. Rattling through his face. His head bouncing against the floor. Hard to breathe. His arms and legs secured.

Danny kept his eyes closed and listened. There was music playing, the radio turned loud. Voices. They were talking, laughing like they were on a road trip. Beers and babes. The fact that they had a man hogtied in their trunk didn't bother them at all. No nervous chatter, no jitters. Danny allowed his head to roll to one side, his eyes opening a fraction.

He was in the back of the trunk space. The vehicle bounced and jostled and Danny figured they were on a back road, unpaved. Not good. But then again, if they had wanted him dead, they could have easily ended him while he was unconscious, or just used lethal rounds in the shotgun. As if in tribute a wave of pain washed through his torso. The muscles in the back of Danny's neck tensed. He felt sure he knew what was next on the agenda. He had shown his hand against Blaine, spoken Chrissie's name. They knew Danny's motivation but would want to make sure he wasn't part of a bigger group. They would not be asking their questions gently.

It would not be the first time Danny had been on the receiving end of the interrogator's fist. It was going to be a hard night ahead. With his mouth taped shut and blood in his nose, Danny realised that he was slowly asphyxiating. He forced himself to breath slowly. He timed his breath. Inhale; *one, two, three, four, five*. Exhale; *one, two, three, four, five*.

The vehicle slowed. Someone up front turned off the music. A faint buzzing took up residence in his ears. The vehicle rolled to a stop. The voices that followed sounded slightly distorted. Different voices. How many men were in the vehicle?

'Is that it?'

'Yeah, that's it.'

'How do you want to do this, boss man?'

'We'll take him aboard. Then we'll find out where he's from, if he's got any more friends that will come looking for him.'

'You mean apart from Captain Ahab?' A ripple of laughter. 'Because I don't think he's coming back anytime soon.'

'Yeah man, Fish did him real good.'

Danny scowled beneath the tape. Two names now: *Blaine and Fish*. He risked a glance through barely open eyes. Someone killed the lights. Danny next heard doors being opened then felt the vehicle rock as the men clambered out. The tailgate swung open like a predator's maw. Hands tightened around his legs and he was yanked bodily from the trunk space.

Air blasted from his nose as he was dropped onto his back. Sparks flared behind his eyes as his head met the unyielding ground.

'Whoops,' laughed one of the men. Not Blaine.

'Hey watch it, Fish, you break it, you bought it!'

Blaine's face loomed into view. 'I'm going to do the breaking, and this asshole is going to buy it.'

Another of the men laughed. 'Hey, Blaine is waxing lyrical. That's a first.'

Danny looked at the darkened forms that surrounded him. Six silhouettes. Six against one. Nasty odds, even in an open running battle.

'Get him onto the boat.'

'Is he awake?'

Danny's head snapped to one side as Blaine slapped him hard across the face. 'He's awake, playing possum is all.'

A moment of weightlessness assailed him as he was lifted bodily from the ground. More rough hands seized him, hoisting him to waist height. Danny looked into the encroaching darkness. No landmarks, no lights, no chance of help. Tall, elongated shapes towered into the night sky. Trees. That didn't help him much. He could be anywhere in the state of Florida.

'I can't see shit.'

'Hold on a minute.'

Different voices again.

Someone turned on a light on their phone. A shallow cone of light now led the way. Danny angled his head to see a wooden pier stretching out into black water. At the end of the pier, a boat was tethered.

Shite!

Danny drew his legs up as fast as possible and stamped out with his heels. One of the men caught the unexpected blow in the ribs and tumbled away. Danny again landed hard on the ground as he slipped from the men's grip.

'You asshole!' cried the downed man.

Danny could do little but curl into a ball against the kicks that slammed into his body from every angle. The blows against his spine were the worst, blasting precious air from his lungs. Deep throbs of pain converged with roving splinters of agony as the assault slowly abated. The men above him spat vile curses.

Blaine's face loomed close to his. 'You just made it even worse for yourself, dick wad.'

Danny too cursed into the tape over his mouth.

The men scooped him up once more, conveying him along the wooden planks of the narrow pier.

'Give me a minute, I'll get the gangway so you don't end up in the bay.'

Someone laughed. 'That's why you're the boss man, Curtis.'

Danny scowled. Three names; *Blaine, Fish and Curtis.*

A muted clanging rang out, then metal scraping on metal. Danny was manhandled onto the boat then propped unceremoniously against a narrow stanchion. The metal was cold against his spine. A hand closed tight around his throat. Blaine. 'You try anything and you're going into the water and you won't come back up. Got it?'

Danny could smell stale cigar smoke on Blaine's breath. He gave nothing in way of reply.

'Get him below,' said Curtis. *The boss man.*

The smell of old fuel and a thousand cargoes filled his senses as he was conveyed down a short series of steps. Footsteps echoed slightly in the confines of the vessel. Danny gritted his teeth beneath the duct tape. He knew what was coming next. They would torture him, beat him to within an inch of his life to satisfy themselves that he was not part of some law enforcement agency or at least that he wasn't part of a larger team. Then the final hammer would fall. Danny was again dropped to the floor. His arms, still pinioned behind him, folded painfully into the small of his back.

A single bulb, set inside a wire protector, cast a weak orange light over the room. It looked like an old galley kitchen, longer than it was wide. The floor was encrusted with grime and several of the cupboards were missing their doors. A dead bird, its wings spread like a fallen angel, regarded him with empty eye sockets.

Curtis placed the heel of his boot on Danny's chest. 'Sticks.'

Another of the men stepped closer, his black hair tinted orange by the overhead light. 'Yeah, man?'

Curtis spoke again. 'Strip him. Everything off.'

The one called Sticks produced a knife from his pocket with a grin. *Snik, snik, snik.* The butterfly knife rolled fluidly within his grasp. The man pulled at Danny's shirt, inserting the narrow blade. The steel grazed the skin of his abdomen. Seconds later the shredded garment was cast aside.

Four names; *Blaine, Fish, Curtis, and Sticks.*

As he prepared himself for more pain, Danny

huffed. They sounded like members of the world's worst boy band.

Chapter 63

'Well this night's just going to hell in a handbasket,' said Clay as he steered the stolen van through the suburban Miami streets. With no trail to follow he decided in an instant to navigate back to Blaine's house. Danny had talked about torching it but had erred on the side of caution. That time was past. Something dark and brooding swirled behind his eyes. They had taken Danny. Now he would take everything from them.

Ignoring the various pains that aggressively vied for his attention, he forced himself to drive within the speed limits. Getting pulled over by a cop while driving a stolen vehicle wouldn't serve his purpose. The encounter with the Southern Unification had taken its toll, adding new pains to his already aching body. His hand moved to the egg-sized lump on the back of his head. Rebar and craniums were never meant for intercourse. A shallow wound along his left forearm oozed blood. Nothing critical but it stung like a hornet's jamboree. His clothes clung to his body, the cold of the water finally abating as the cloying Miami night slowly dried him out.

Cursing under his breath, Clay stopped at a crossroads. All the streets looked the damned same to him. Blaine's house was on Flagler Street, he remembered that much, but where the hell *was* Flagler? Clay rolled down the window as a young woman on a scooter pulled up alongside the van. 'Excuse me, can you tell me how to get to…'

'Sesame Street?' The woman on the scooter smiled up at Clay, enjoying her joke. A stack of four pizza boxes was secured to a parcel shelf behind her seat.

'Flagler Street?' said Clay, a brief smile of his own.

'I'm just yanking your chain. You're only ten minutes away. Take the next left and follow the road until you see a painted mural on the side of a building. It's painted up like a giant dollar bill, take a right there and keep going. You'll get to Flagler sooner or later.'

Clay tipped an imaginary hat. 'Appreciated.'

'Welcome, big fella.' The moped sped off as the light turned green.

Clay followed the instructions which held. A smile devoid of humour tightened his lips as he spotted Blaine's damaged car. Yeah, Danny had certainly put his stamp on that jalopy.

The front wheels of the van mounted the curb as Clay sprang from the vehicle, almost before it stopped moving. The front door of the house was locked. Clay stamped out with his right heel just below the door handle. The door clattered against the wall as it was catapulted open. Moving directly into the kitchen, Clay spotted several bottles of spirits to the left of the sink. Grabbing up a bottle of whisky he twisted off the cap and began scattering the liquid like a fervent exorcist. A bottle of tequila came next, soaking into the fabric of the couch in the living room. Clay spotted what he required next, a magazine, which he rolled into a loose tube. Moving back to the kitchen he ignited one of the gas rings on the stove. Seconds later he had a burning torch in his hands. He bared his teeth as the flame snaked from the torch to the whisky covered countertops. Moving back to the living room, he tossed the burning magazine onto the couch. The material seemed to defy the flames for a few seconds then began to succumb to the heat. Clay scooped up another couple of magazines from the coffee table and added them to the burgeoning pyre. Smoke began to fill the house even before Clay marched back out of the front door.

Leaving Blaine's house to its certain fate, Clay made his way over to the neighbour's house. The red-haired man appeared at the front door. He pointed to the smoke streaming from Blaine's house.

'What the hell is going on?' asked the leprechaun. 'Hey, I know you. You're one of the guys that ran into Caleb's car earlier. I saw the tussle after that too.'

Clay's hand around his throat cut off his next words. The red-haired man gagged as he was propelled back inside his house. Clay kicked the front door closed with his heel.

'You call Blaine. You tell him that his house is going up like a Roman candle. Understand?'

The leprechaun's eyes bulged as Clay gave him a shake, bringing his face close to his own. 'Understand?'

The man nodded, coughing as Clay released his choke. 'Jeez man, take a chill pill, I'll call him.'

Clay watched as he stabbed at the cell phone with his finger. The man's eyes flicked between the phone and Clay. 'Did Blaine try to stiff you because of his car?'

Clay grunted a monosyllabic reply.

'I mean, am I getting this right? You just set his house on fire? Man, you guys must be getting into it. No offence but you look like a bear ate you and shit you out.'

'You got his number yet?' asked Clay. 'Or do I need to shit *you* out?'

'Here man, take it. It's ringing.'

Clay took the cell phone and pointed to the living room. 'Park your ass and stay quiet.'

The red-haired man did as he was told.

Clay pressed the phone to his ear. A muscle at the side of his eye twitched. Each ring seemed to take a minute. His grip tightened on the handset.

'Yeah?'

'Blaine. You've got my brother.'

The phone went silent for long seconds. Then Blaine spoke again. 'Is this the fucker we dropped in the bay? I thought you were fish food.'

'You thought wrong,' said Clay. 'I want my brother back.'

Blaine laughed; the contempt clear in his voice. 'I want to screw Wonder Woman, but we can't all get what we want.'

'Have you got anything you're attached to in your house? Because I've just set the thing ablaze.'

'Yeah right.'

Clay held the phone towards the red-haired man.

'Blaine, it's Rudy from across the road. It's true. He just torched your crib, man. There's smoke like I've never seen.'

Clay spoke again. 'Before I did that, I hacked your computer. I know everything about you. Everything. Those websites you visit, oh man, friggin' disgusting even for a class-A asshole like you. I haven't been through it all, but everything you've viewed or saved in a file is now mine. It's surprising how much you can fit on a couple of flash-drives these days.'

A smile crept across Clay's face as Blaine exploded into a string of vehement curses. 'Yeah, yeah, tough guy on a phone. Now that I've got your attention, here's what's going to happen.'

Chapter 64

Brockovich slowly turned a full circle as Anderson loomed over the ruined bodies. The CSP had just finished photographing the scene. The uniforms had done their job well, the two survivors had been whisked away under emergency medical supervision. One of the beat cops waved to Brockovich. She tapped Anderson's shoulder then pointed to the trooper. 'I'll be over there if you need me.'

Anderson grunted, understandably not happy about being called back out on duty.

'Hey Martinez, what you got for us?' asked Brockovich.

'A couple of witnesses if that helps.' Martinez smiled, showing perfect white teeth.

Brockovich tilted her head to one side. *Damn, he's cute.* 'It does, where are they?'

'On the other side of the squad car with my partner, you remember Williams?'

'Yeah, sure.'

Martinez continued, 'Two kids, both fifteen. They were down here messing around on their bikes.'

'In the dark?' asked Brockovich.

'Kids.' Martinez shrugged. 'They were trickin', you know, doing jumps and bunny hops and stuff on their bikes. They were the ones that called 9-1-1.'

'Really?' Brockovich cast a glance at the squad car. 'Nice to know that there are decent kids still growing up in this city.'

'Amen to that,' said Martinez.

'So, what are they saying happened?' asked Brockovich. She knew that the kids would tell her in their own words, but standing next to Martinez didn't upset her sensibilities any. He was single, handsome, and straight; what was not to like?

Martinez crossed his arms across his chest. 'A dark coloured panel truck nearly ran some big guy down on the road. Six guys jumped out of the truck and attempted to assault the unknown male.'

'Attempted?'

Martinez nodded to the broken bodies. 'They didn't do that to themselves.'

Brockovich again looked at the closest body. A spiked club was embedded in the man's skull. 'That's some medieval shit right there.'

'Uh-huh.'

'Which one of the bodies is the one they tried

to run down?'

Martinez gave a small laugh. 'Oh, that's the best part. After this little shits and giggles show was done, the kids say the big guy jumped in their van and drove off.'

'Wait, you're telling me that one man put the finishers to six men, on his own, and was still able to drive away from the scene?' Brockovich looked towards the squad car then back again at the grotesque corpses. 'Have we got an ID on any of the dead?'

'The one with the club in his head is Lyle Miller. That one,' Martinez pointed to another twisted body. 'Is Nelson Bradley. The others aren't carrying ID, but I'm sure there's a good chance they're in the system. One of the survivors is a guy called Syrus Sanderson.'

Brockovich exhaled slowly, realisation creeping through her. *Syrus Sanderson of the Southern Unification.* Callie from dispatch had said as much.

'You know him?'

'Yeah, Sanderson is a chapter leader with the SU. They run out of that old red church building.'

'Yeah, Williams pegged them as SU.'

'Callie from dispatch said as much.' Brockovich plucked at lint that wasn't there. 'You know, my father used to say if you go around with your chin sticking out someone will knock it back in place for you, sure as the sun comes up.'

'Oh no,' Martinez adopted an exaggerated expression of sadness. 'Did the great white supremo society pick on the wrong guy? What a bummer. I'll be sure to send flowers. White ones, of course.'

Stifling a laugh, Brockovich waved, catching Anderson's attention. 'We better go talk to the kids.'

'Okay,' said Martinez. 'Enjoy.'

'Stay safe,' said Brockovich.

'Always.' Martinez reached out, his fingers brushing the arm of her jacket. 'Hey, a few of the guys are going down to Key Largo next week, just for the day. You know, a day on the beach. If you weren't busy...'

The corners of Brockovich's mouth curled upwards. 'What day?'

'Thursday.'

'Give me your number,' said Brockovich. 'I'll call you.'

Martinez scribbled his cell number on a scrap of paper; old school and handed it over.

Brockovich deadpanned him. 'Now, officer Martinez, go protect and serve.'

'I aim to.'

Gina Brockovich again stifled her smile as Anderson joined her. 'Let's go talk to the witnesses.'

'I'm missing dinner for this,' said Anderson.

'You could stand to miss a dinner or two Carl.'

'Harsh.'

Brockovich looked at the two kids as they leaned against their bikes. She had a good idea what they would tell her about the guy that stole the SU van: *Big and mean-looking, well over six foot, scars down one side of his face.*

Chapter 65

Chrissie smiles at Danny. Her mouth is moving but he can't make out the words. He leans closer. Sees her face now. Chrissie looks different, like an actor playing someone else, subtle darkness upon her features.

Chrissie?

The smile is frozen on her face as she begins to pluck the hair from her head. Slowly at first, then faster and faster, pulling huge unruly clumps from her scalp.

Chrissie?

Her features begin to swell, her once beautiful face expanding, widening out of proportion. A blight mars the skin on the left side, ragged lines etched into her skin like wounds from an animal. A tribal tattoo.

Now a different face stares back at Danny. A face he detests.

***

Danny Gunn snapped fully awake as the bucket of water was cast over him. The water was cold. He first spat the brine from his mouth then shook his head, rapidly blinking to alleviate the stinging in his eyes.

The stinging persisted. He lay on his back, his limbs still secured with duct tape. His mouth was now free of the gag.

Blaine dropped to his knees, straddling him. Danny tensed his neck as Blaine's grip again found his throat. His fingers felt like meat hooks on his skin. Danny could do little more than tense his jaw, keeping his teeth clenched tight together. Blaine slammed his fist into the side of his face. Pain flared both in his jaw and the back of his skull as it rebounded from the floor. Blaine followed with a second punch then a third, his fist falling like a blacksmith's hammer. Danny had suffered concussion several times in the past and knew he was beginning to succumb to the blows. He'd already blacked out at least once again since they had hauled him inside the boat.

'Wait,' said Danny.

Blaine wiped a contemptuous backhand blow across Danny's jaw in way of response.

A disembodied voice; 'Blaine. Ease up a minute.'

'Just let me do my thing, Quantrill,' huffed Blaine.

Quantrill. *Curtis Quantrill. The boss man.*

Danny turned his gaze to Quantrill as he squatted close to his pinioned shoulders. The man looked like an ageing surfer. He was ropy and weather-beaten. A man that spent a lot of time outdoors. His face carried deep lines, his eyes intelligent and dangerous.

'You must know how bad this is looking for you, right?' asked Quantrill.

'This wasn't how it looked in the Miami tourist brochure, that's for sure,' replied Danny, his voice thick with his natural Scottish brogue. 'I feel swizzled.'

'You came at Blaine, head-on, that makes you very brave or very dumb.' Quantrill nodded at the focus of Danny's planned retribution. 'I don't think you're dumb, but I do think there's more to you than meets the eye.'

'Oh, there is.' Danny spat blood from his mouth. 'I like pina coladas and getting caught in the rain.'

'Funny guy, huh?' Blaine's fist snapped Danny's head to one side as it again cracked against his jaw. 'How's that, funny guy? I'm going to enjoy beating you to death one punch at a time.'

Danny fought to keep his face straight against the pain. 'Is your arse jealous of the shite that just came out of your mouth? You hit like a monkey pulling on its pecker. At this rate, my grandkids will be growing beards, do your worst, ya melon domed fuck nut.'

Quantrill stalled Blaine's raised fist. 'Who was

the other guy with you, the one in the car that went into the sea?'

An icy ripple spread across Danny's chest. *Clay.* 'What did you do to him?'

'Rolled his ass up like a sandwich wrapper and dropped him in the bay.'

Danny looked now at the one they called Fish.

'Oh, I know what you're thinking,' mocked Fish. 'But my man is such a tough hombre and can swim like a champion. That's why I dropped a pallet load of railroad sleepers on his sorry ass for good measure. He's gone for good, fish food if you will. If he was your boyfriend, you've ridden that buckaroo for the last time.'

Danny spat more blood and brine from his mouth.

Quantrill dead-eyed Danny. 'You have one chance to make this right. You know you're not leaving this boat alive, don't you? The big difference is how you spend your last minutes. Blaine here is not joshing when he tells you that he will punch you to death, he's a man of his word if nothing else.'

'So am I,' said Danny. 'I give you my word that I will kill every last one of you fuckers if you had a hand in Chrissie Haims' murder.'

'I'm sure you'd like to try.' Quantrill gave a small laugh. 'You don't know how much trouble that woman has caused me. She was nothing, collateral damage. She walked into something that she was never meant to see.'

'Aye, let me guess, she walked into her own home and seen you bunch of bastards pulling her house apart.'

'Something like that.'

'Were you all there?' asked Danny. A red mist began to creep at the edges of his vision.

'Cut the shit,' barked Blaine. 'I did her. The bitch was never meant to be there, but she showed up out of the blue. She took one look at us and set off like shit off a hot tin roof. I only caught her because she slipped on a broken floorboard. I warned to stay quiet but she fought me, wouldn't stop.'

Danny couldn't begin to imagine the horror Chrissie must have felt. Home invasions often ended in rape and murder. *She fought me, wouldn't stop.* He hadn't been there to keep her safe, but he would take revenge in her name. Danny repeated his question; 'Were you all there?'

'Yeah, they were all there, front and centre for the big show,' spat Blaine. 'But it was me that killed her.'

'I'm going to kill you last.'

Blaine raised his chin, a sneer creeping over his face. His grip again tightened on Danny's neck. 'And how are you planning on that?'

'Because Quantrill here is going to let me up any moment now,' said Danny. Desperate thoughts pin-wheeled around in his mind. Stall them, keep them talking, wait for your chance.

'And why would I do that?' asked Quantrill.

Danny rolled the dice; 'Because I know all about Erik Delacroix.'

Chapter 66

Caleb Blaine raised his fist, ready to slam it into Danny's face once more. Danny forced himself to breathe slowly, ready to exhale as he accepted the strike.

'Wait,' said Quantrill.

Blaine stayed his hand.

'How do you know about Delacroix?'

'Get this shaved gorilla off me and we can talk.'

'Really? You think I'm the soft touch in this posse? You think you can drop a name and waltz up and out of here? It's not that easy.' Drops of spittle flew as Quantrill barked the words. 'Get him up.'

Danny felt himself be yanked to his feet in one severe action. Blaine squeezed his throat with increased vigour. Jesus, he was strong.

'You mistake my intent I think,' said Quantrill. 'You will tell me everything you know, I can assure you that, and just so you know I'm not just blowing smoke, these good old boys are going to take turns in working you like a piñata. Gato, kick this fucker into next week.'

Five names; *Gato*.

Gato appeared in Danny's line of sight. The man looked dark and menacing, his body long and lean. Blaine released his hold and stepped back. Danny teetered for balance; his legs pinioned together with the duct tape. Gato span in a rapid circle, his right leg whipping around into Danny's chest. The impact was devastating, like being hit by a car. Danny was catapulted off his feet, his lungs going into spasm. Well versed in martial arts, Danny had thrown the same spinning back kick countless times, but never as fast and brutal as this guy.

'One shot each, then I'll ask him a question,' said Quantrill.

As Danny fought to take a breath, an unexpected sound cut through the room. A ridiculous scream looped over and over. The ring tone of the phone rang harsh in the confines of the room.

Blaine pulled the phone from his pocket. 'Yeah?'

Still gasping for breath, Danny was again hauled to his feet, this time by Fish and the one man he didn't yet have a name for. The man was squat and ugly, his nose flattened like an old-time boxer. The expression he sported betrayed the obvious joy he would take, beating on Danny.

Fish got up in Danny's face, a hand pressed

hard against his chin. Danny fumed, that ruled out a sneaky headbutt to keep him occupied. 'My turn next tough guy, then you're at the mercy of the Junk Yard Dog. Junk, my man, you mind if I go next?'

Junk. Six men. Six names. All targets marked.

'Light him up, Fish,' said Junk.

Blaine was swearing, each curse delivered louder than the previous.

Fish turned at the sudden outburst, his hand slipping from Danny's face. Seizing the moment, the wiry Scotsman snapped his upper body forward, his forehead smashing into the side of Fish's cheekbone. While the bridge of the nose was the optimum target for the vicious streetfighter's blow, it took a toll where ever it landed. Fish emitted a strangled cry as he dropped ass first to the floor. Scowling, Junk pulled his right hand back to his shoulder, his fist held high. Severely hampered by his bonds Danny only had one viable option. Junk's right hand ripped through the air as Danny dropped to the ground, tucking his knees to his abdomen. Stamping out with both feet, his heels found Junk's left leg. Junk was pitched off balance and landed face down, his hands slamming hard into the floor. Danny allowed himself the briefest of smiles. He knew he was about to go through the grinder, but even the grinder carries a cost. He would not go easy.

Turning, Blaine planted the toe of his boot hard into Danny's stomach. 'That other fucker's still in the game. He just set fire to my goddammed house!'

Between pained ragged breaths, Danny emitted a barking laugh. *Clay was still alive. Making friends and influencing people as usual.*

Fish and Junk were back on their feet, both glaring down with undisguised hatred. Grasping a handful of his hair, Quantrill pulled Danny into a sitting position. 'Who's out there? Who else have you got in your crew?'

Danny dead-eyed Curtis. 'Your worst nightmare...on steroids.'

Blaine's face contorted as he stuffed the phone back into his pocket. 'It's the other one. The one we dumped in the bay. He says he hacked my computer before he set the fire. Says he's going to give everything to two of his friends; two fucking detectives, Brockovich and Anderson.'

Danny's stomach muscles ached as he sucked invaluable oxygen. Quantrill tightened his grip on his hair. 'What did you have on your computer Blaine? Nothing to do with business, right?'

Chrissie's killer shifted uncomfortably, his face taking in a new expression. His voice carried none of the usual bravadoes. 'I kept the video of me choking Delacroix to death.'

All six men in the room fell silent. Danny allowed himself the briefest of smiles.

Chapter 67

A sense of foreboding washed over Curtis Quantrill like a tidal surge. Everything he had tirelessly worked towards could be lost. Months…no, *years* of work, sifting through scraps, chasing leads however tentative, to find Erik Delacroix's legacy. A painful pressure began to spread behind his eyes. He stood to his full height. 'Jesus H, Blaine. I told you to get rid of that footage. The only reason we filmed that was in case Delacroix gave something up, we could replay it if we needed to. Why the hell did you save it on your computer?'

'I haven't got time for this shit,' said Blaine.

'Answer me, goddammit!'

The dismissive sneer that Blaine gave in way of an answer was too much. Quantrill slammed his fist into the side of the big man's face. Blaine, caught off guard, was staggering as he followed with a second punch. Blaine tumbled over the captive sending Fish sprawling again.

Curtis' throat was raw as his words exploded in a torrent. 'They have the fucking death penalty in the state of Florida! Jesus H, Blaine, how could you be so stupid? What were you doing with the film, jacking off to it on a Saturday night? You're going to get us all the lethal injection, you fucking imbecile. If we have to kill, we make it look like something else, a home invasion went wrong, a mugging. What we don't do is keep the footage for our self-gratification.'

Blaine rose as a man possessed. Curtis Quantrill knew that Blaine was dangerous, very dangerous. Quantrill raised his hands into a fighting guard, peering over his knuckles. The punch Blaine threw crashed into his raised forearms like a sledgehammer. Letting his legs absorb the heavy punch, Quantrill swayed with the force. The next two punches slammed into his guard with the same ferocity. The third caught him by surprise, a vicious uppercut that ripped up between his arms finding his jaw. An explosion of sparks flared inside his head as he fought to stay on his feet. *Jesus H, Blaine hits hard.*

Then the other four men were crowding them. Two on each combatant. Fish and Junk on Blaine, Gato and Sticks pulling back on Curtis' arms. Quantrill visualised putting a bullet in the back of Blaine's head, dumping the body at the same time as the captive.

Fish's voice was high and shrill. 'What the hell are you doing? The last thing we should be doing right now is turning on each other. We need to stop and think.'

Quantrill held up his hands in capitulation.

His eyes never left Blaine, ready for more. The big man wiped a hand across his mouth. He sneered again as his hand came away stained with blood. *That fucking sneer.* Quantrill knew they weren't finished yet. They would knock heads again soon and next time it might not be mere punches that were traded. One of them would end as gator food. Quantrill was determined that it would not be him.

Fish crowded between them his palms held out to either side. 'Blaine, what did the guy on the phone say?'

Blaine took a step back, his head sweeping from side to side like a caged animal. 'He said that he set fire to my house, that he hacked my computer and knew everything about me. He said if we don't bring his brother back, he'll give everything he has to the detectives.'

Quantrill thought about the tracker unit. They were so damn close. Now that would have to wait. Or would it? Could he ditch his five friends and go for the legacy himself?

Blaine spat blood as he continued to glare menacingly.

'Brother?' asked Quantrill. He looked down at the captive. 'That right tough guy, that's your brother out there, stirring up a shitstorm?'

'More like a duo; we're a double act. We go

by the name of Norfolk and Good.'

'That certainly describes your lame ass jokes,' said Gato.

The captive stared back at Curtis; his face devoid of fear. An after pain rippled through his jaw where Blaine had caught him. It would ache for days yet. 'What's your deal funny guy? What do you want?'

Blaine's voice cut through the lull. 'I haven't got time for this shit. The other guy said if we don't bring him his brother in an hour we're toast.'

Quantrill forced himself not to again attack Blaine. 'Did he say where he wanted to meet?'

'Yeah, in the parking lot at the American Airlines Arena,' said Blaine.

'The Heat is on,' said Fish. No one laughed at his joke.

'You wanna go check on your crib?' asked Gato.

'No,' snapped Blaine. 'If it's burning now, it'll be ashes by the time I get there. Fuck it, the insurance can pay the fuck up.'

'The American Airlines Arena? No. We're not doing that. Get him back on the phone. If he wants his brother back, we need everything back from him. This ends tonight.' Quantrill looked down at the captive. 'What's your name so he knows we've got you and that you're still sucking air.'

The captive stared back at Quantrill for long seconds, his gaze unsettling, before answering. 'Danny Gunn.'

'Okay, Danny Gunn, what's your brother called?'

Again, Gunn stared back impassively. *Didn't this asshole know the mortal danger he was in?*

'His name is Clay. I better warn you, Clay's not calm and considerate like me. He gets that from my father's side. You may want to do as he says, he can take mighty umbrage when he gets a mind to.'

Mighty umbrage? Quantrill almost smiled. *Crazy fucker.* They would deal with Clay. There would be a time in between to find out more on Delacroix, find out exactly what Danny knew. 'Get him back on the phone. This is what's gonna happen.'

Chapter 68

Red and blue lights danced to the backdrop of flames reflected from the surrounding houses. Blaine's home was way past saving but the fire service was busy unrolling their hoses regardless. Clay felt a slight twinge for the neighbours. They would be fearful of the flames spreading to their properties. A single patrol car was parked behind the two fire engines. The cops looked to be two different officers from the earlier altercation. A dozen or so of the locals had congregated on the street. Some of the older residents looked dismayed at the orange flames that hungrily consumed the house. Clay could smell the smoke even from inside Rudy the leprechaun's house. Glancing at the wall clock, Clay tuned back to Rudy who seemed transfixed by the blaze. 'You got a car, Rudy?'

'Yeah, a Jeep Cherokee, it's parked out back.' The red-haired man continued to stare at the proceedings. 'Why?'

'I'm going to need to borrow it for a few hours.'

'Jeez man, you're a real number, you know that? First, you wreck Blaine's car, then you torch his crib, now you're carjacking me in the comfort of my own home.'

'Quit yer whining, lucky charms. I'll pay for the Jeep, rent or buy, it's your choice.'

Rudy rubbed the bristles of his beard between his thumb and forefinger. 'I was thinking of trading it anyhow, let's call it a straight thousand and it's yours, how does that grab you?'

Clay looked him up and down. 'Let's call it seven hundred and I won't have to knock you out and leave you hogtied in your bathroom. How does that grab you?'

Rudy huffed but pointed to the rear of the house. 'She's outback. There are a few dings on the body but she drives straight and true.'

'That's all that matters.'

Rudy flicked a finger to the street. 'What about the van you arrived in?'

'Let's just say that might be a little hot, and I don't mean because it's parked next to a burning house.'

Rudy began chuckling, a sound like water glugging from a bottle. 'Hey man, I like your style. You're a rule-breaker, I like that. I like you…despite you rolling up in my crib and kung fu-ing my throat, I didn't care for that much. Come on out back and take a look at your new set of wheels.'

Clay followed Rudy through the kitchen and out of a side door. The garage was cluttered with boxes, tools, and old garden furniture. The Jeep Cherokee had certainly seen better days. A long strip of duct tape was losing its battle to keep a tear in the fabric of the roof together.

'Keys?' asked Clay.

'Oh sure, man.' Rudy bobbed back to the kitchen then handed Clay a key fob. 'Start her up, you won't be disappointed. She still runs well for an older gal. You can drive stick, right?'

'I can.' Clay inserted the key into the ignition barrel. The engine sprang to life on the first turn. The tone of the engine sounded correct and true to Clay's ear.

'These babies are built to take a knock. There're two new tyres on the back and a winch on the front. I had that fitted myself. That's the control for it just to the left of the gear stick.'

Clay climbed out of the Jeep and reached for his wallet. The leather was wet and clammy in his hand. Flipping open the billfold he looked at Rudy. The notes inside were stuck together. The corners from several fifties came away in his hand. 'Crap. My money is ruined.'

Rudy looked at the mulched bills then up at Clay. 'So, what's the plan?'

'I haven't got the time to go to an ATM, so you can let me take it and if I'm not back in the next two days, report it stolen to the police, or…'

'Or?' asked Rudy, slightly pulling his chin into his neck. 'Or what?'

'I can hogtie you in the bathroom.'

'Yeah, let's not do that.'

'I'll need your phone too.'

Wincing, Rudy handed him the cell phone. 'Jeez man, d'you want to rifle my underwear drawer too?'

'That won't be necessary,' said Clay. 'I will come back and pay you what I owe you, you have my word as a Texan.'

Rudy gave that same watery chuckle. 'Okay man, I believe you. You've brightened up my day anyhow with all this drama. It's better than the crap on the TV.'

'I better get going.' Clay cocked his head to one side, his eyes roving around the garage walls. 'D'you own a gun, Rudy?'

'Sorry man, I'm probably the only guy on the block that doesn't.'

'Worth a shot,' said Clay. With what he had planned, a heavy-duty shotgun would have been useful.

'I've got an old bow if that's any good? I was into bow hunting for a little while, I call it my Rambo phase, I just wasn't very good at it.'

'Have you got arrows as well,' asked Clay.

'Yeah man, there's a quiver with twelve. Give me a minute.' Rudy moved to the far side of the garage and began tossing garden furniture to one side.

Clay glanced at his watch. He needed to get going.

'Here they are,' said Rudy. He handed Clay a black bow and a quiver of arrows. 'The arrows are broadheads, and the bow is laminated fibreglass so it doesn't matter if it gets wet. Have you used one before?'

Clay thought back to his teenage years, to the long summers of target shooting with bows very similar to this. 'Once or twice.'

Rudy rested his hands on the roof of the Jeep. 'I know it's none of my business but if you're going after Caleb and his crew, I don't think a bow will cut it. Those guys aren't the kind to mess with, but I guess you've figured that already.'

Clay gave a wry smile. 'I'll step lively.'

'Good hunting,' Rudy extended his hand.

'I'll be back to pay you what I owe you.'

'I believe you, man.'

Clay shook his hand and placed the bow and arrows on the back seat.

'I'll open the door for you.' Rudy pulled on a length of knotted rope and the garage door swung up and over. Clay gave the man a curt nod as he guided the Jeep into the street. The firefighters directed powerful streams of water at the ravaged house. The night air was thick with smoke and flying embers. He had barely passed the fire engines when the phone in his pocket began to warble.

A gruff voice demanded without preamble, 'Rudy, is that asshole still with you?'

Clay gave a tight smile then imitated Rudy's slightly nasal voice as best he could. 'Even better than that, We're BFF's. I've asked him to move in, you know like roomies for the summer season.'

'Rudy?'

'It's no fun when you have to explain it,' said Clay. 'It's the asshole speaking. I hope you're heading to the arena at Bayside or the cops are going to have a field day with the shit I've got on you.'

'We're not doing this at the arena. Change of plans.'

'Oh really, then I hope you like prison food, dipshit,' said Clay.

Blaine's voice carried no sense of idle threats. 'If you ever want to see your ugly-assed brother in one piece you'll shut your friggin' mouth and listen up.'

'Go on.'

'There's an abandoned railway station just south-east of Naranja. It's near the Air Force base. You, be there in one hour. No cops or the funny guy gets an extra hole in his head.'

'Wait, let me speak to Danny.'

'One hour, or that's it for mister personality.'

Blaine killed the call.

'Crap.'

Chapter 69

As Danny Gunn regained consciousness sour acid rose in the back of his throat. With no option of vomiting, it out, he swallowed the bitter fluid. The thick duct tape that held his mouth closed felt like the same tape that secured both his arms and legs to the metal chair. They'd gagged him again. Blood trickled from a laceration at the corner of his left eye. A layer of grimy sweat coated his skin; the smell sour, but hardly noticeable against the heady fumes in the room. Glancing down, he remembered he was naked.

The last thing he could remember was Gato again kicking him, his foot whipping into his face like a battering ram. He'd been hit so many times recently, he feared brain damage would come calling.

Looking at the barrels that surrounded him, he grunted with dismay. The contents of any one of the fifty-gallon drums, if ignited, were more than enough to kill him. He could count at least twenty barrels. A low rumbling sent a constant vibration through the steel panels of the floor and walls. Was the boat moving? He couldn't be sure.

A single wire enclosed bulb flickered

overhead. He tried pulling against the tape on his limbs. Tensing every muscle in his body, he attempted to stand up. The pressure behind his eyes was almost unbearable as he strained. A gnawing pain spread across his ribs. They had worked him over pretty damn well. Every muscle and bone in his body seemed to ache. Succeeding in lifting his hips only an inch or so from the seat, he flopped back in place. The chair felt welded to the floor. The men that had secured him had again done a thorough job.

Who was on the boat? he wondered. Blaine and two of the others had stormed out of view. He remembered raised voices, a one-sided conversation, Blaine shouting, giving Clay a final ultimatum. More punishment and questions about Delacroix had followed. Then Gato had given him the boot.

The duct tape now covered his forearms from his elbows to the back of his hands, only his dirt-encrusted fingers were free. He felt sure his lower legs had received the same level of attention.

At the opposite side of the room; just out of reach even if his arms were free, a simple yet ominous mechanism had been rigged to one of the fuel barrels. A fist-sized block of what looked at first glance to be putty sat at the centre of a clear plastic tub. Danny felt confident that this putty was not the kind used to secure window panes.

Shite on a shovel…

Fixed to the side of the explosive block was a basic model cell phone, its display screen unlit. Danny forced himself to breath, his racing heartbeat pounding heavy inside his chest. He had made a serious error in underestimating the men that had done this to him. Against all his experience he had allowed himself to be bated, controlled, his desire for revenge overriding any caution. Blaine had murdered the woman he loved. The other five had been party to the killing.

As he looked around the room Danny realised that his feet were wet. The cold steel plate of the floor too was covered in what he presumed to be gasoline or its maritime equivalent. Was one of the barrels leaking? The smell of the fuel did little to ease the cold spider of dread that traced a path down his spine. Whatever the liquid was it stung his eyes.

A single door faced him. A spine work of metal divided the door into six equal sections. A rusted metal lever formed a handle. Locked, he was sure.

For the first time in his life, Danny felt completely helpless.

Where the hell was Clay?

Knowing that simply straining against his taped bonds would do little but fatigue him, Danny instead began to concentrate only on his right arm. First tensing the muscles of his forearm and pulling against the tape, then relaxing and pushing the opposite direction. He began to count his exertions.

Each time he moved against the tape he recounted their names.

Blaine. Push against the tape.
Quantrill. Pull against the tape.
Gato. Push.
Fish. Pull.
Junk. Push.
Sticks. Pull.

At first, he could feel little in way of results, his skin pulling back and forth over his muscles, then after his twenty-seventh motion, he felt the edge of the tape lift away from the skin of his arm. A gap of a quarter-inch or so now showed between the duct tape and the crease of his elbow. Sweat trickled down his face, adding to the stinging of his eyes. A shake of his head sent a spattering of sweat and semi-congealed blood onto his thighs.

'I will not die in the hold of a rust bucket ship,' thought Danny. He started to work at the tape again, repeating the six names in his mind like a mantra.

After another ten minutes of repetition he could roll his lower arm in a circle, the gap between skin and tape widening. The constricted smile that spread across Danny Gunn's face was wiped away as the cell phone illuminated. A second later the lyrics

'Boom, shake, shake the room' filled the air. His captors had a jet-black sense of humour.

Danny winced as he waited for the explosion.

Seconds ticked by.

No explosion came. No: *'tick, tick, tick, tick, boom'.*

Was this some elaborate ruse, designed to scare him? No, that wasn't how this crew operated.

The ringtone sounded again. *'Boom, shake, shake the room.'*

A groan escapes Danny's throat.

A digital display next to the cell phone sprang to life, its numerals glowing bright red.

A countdown had begun.

'Tick, tick, tick, tick, boom'...

Sixty seconds....

Fifty-nine.

Fifty-eight.

Fifty-seven.

Danny punched his arms back and forth with a desperate effort. His right arm slipped from the confines of the tape, his elbow cracking against the metal chair frame.

Thirty-five.

Thirty-four.

Thirty-three.

Danny ripped at the coverings on his left arm with little effect, his fingernails sliding in vain across the layers of duct tape.

Twenty-three.

Twenty-two.

Twenty-one.

Is this how it was all going to end? Blown into bloody mulch with no one to ever know his fate?

Ten.

Nine.

Eight.

Danny screamed into the tape that covered his mouth, not in fear but unadulterated fury!

Seven.

Six.

Five.

The metal door swung open and Quantrill stepped into the room. He pressed a button on the phone he held. The countdown on the explosive block froze. *FOUR.*

'Looks like your brother did what he was told. This isn't over 'til it's over. I just want you to know if this goes south, if he tries any hero bullshit, you go back in that chair, that countdown starts again, and you know how that ends.'

Fish appeared at Quantrill's side. The look he gave Danny was scathing. 'Ew, I can see your old man wrinkly balls from here. That's just nasty.'

Chapter 70

'All I need you to do is watch my six. These guys are slippery fuckers and I can't trust them to honour their word and not try to shoot me dead as soon as I get there. I think they'll try to off both Danny and me, as soon as they figure out I've got nothing on them,' said Clay.

'Fuhgeddaboudit,' said Terry Penn. Beads of sweat dotted his forehead. The big guy cradled a matt black Colt 1911. 'I've got something for these assholes right here in my lap, an' I don't mean my king-sized Johnson.'

'I mean it, Terry, I just need you to stay with the car, no heroics. I just need a second pair of eyes. If I do wave you down, I need you to play the detective. Keep your radio in your hand, like you're taking to SWAT or something.'

'No problem, I've done this in the movies a hundred times.'

'Yeah, but if this goes shit shaped there ain't no do-overs, no take-twos.'

'I know that Clay,' said Penn. 'I owe you big time. We both know I would probably be in the morgue or the state pen if it wasn't for you. That debt collector was going to shoot me. If you hadn't dropped the hammer on him that day, well, you know.'

'Fuhgeddaboudit,' reciprocated Clay.

'Hey, you're too ugly to be a paisan, best leave the panache and Peroni to the professionals.'

'Jokes aside, I appreciate you doing this on such short notice. I feel bad dragging you into this crap, but my ass is against the wall on this one.'

Penn nodded, lips pursed, his chin bouncing as if on a spring. 'This crew, they the ones that killed the girl?'

'Yeah, there's a big bald fucker with a tattooed face. Blaine. Danny's pretty damn sure it was him that killed Chrissie.'

'Chrissie, yeah,' said Penn. 'Fuggin' animals.'

'And now they've got Danny.'

Clay gave a single curt nod.

Terry tapped the Colt 1911 on the top of his thigh.

Clay steered the Jeep along a narrow street, there were a few parked cars, but little else of note. The radio display console showed the time. It had been fifty minutes since Blaine's call. Calling and meeting up with Penn had eaten up the time. Clay pressed down on the gas pedal. 'I'm gonna be cutting it close. Have you been to Naranja before?'

'I haven't, sorry man.'

'I hate going in blind, but there's no other option.' Clay glanced over at his old friend. New beads of sweat had formed on his face. Penn's fingers fluttered on the grips of his pistol; a nervous rhythm.

'Blaine said there's a deserted railway station there. That's where the meet is.'

'You know where it is?'

'Kind of, the asshole said it's close to the Air Force base.'

'Google maps.' Penn clucked his tongue against the roof of his mouth. 'What century are you living in?'

Clay huffed air through his nose. 'I feel like a dinosaur regularly.'

Penn's thumbs twitched like an insect's antennae. Seconds later he turned the cell phone towards Clay. 'Got it. Take the next left.'

'Well done, Penn. I pan-handled a phone from a leprechaun but it's little more than a burner, not a smartphone by any stretch.'

Terry Penny raised one eyebrow high. 'Leprechaun?'

'I'll explain later.'

'So, what's the plan of action when we get there?'

'That's the crappy part of this escapade, I haven't got a plan. If they've got Danny with them, I need to deep-six them all as fast as possible.'

'As plans go that's pretty slim.'

'Slim?' said Clay. 'It's a friggin' anorexic. I'm hoping I can create enough ruckus when the time is right, so Danny can do some of his Houdini shit and lend a hand.'

'What are you supposed to be giving them in exchange for Danny?' asked Penn. He wiped the palm of his hand first over his face, then on his trouser leg.

'I spun them a tale about hacking Blaine's computer. It's bullshit though. I've got nada.' Clay kept his foot heavy on the gas pedal. Indistinct shapes that might have been trees seemed to whiz past the windows like phantoms in the night. 'I rolled the dice and struck lucky. At least it bought some time. I thought an asshole like Blaine might have something in his browser history or saved as a file, that he wouldn't want out there for public consumption.'

'Hmm,' Penn again drummed his fingers on the pistol. 'What happens when they realise you've got nothing?'

'Hopefully, by then I'll be finding out if those dick wads can tap dance with a broken spine.'

Penn lifted his phone. 'Turn here. This road will take us past the base, then it's one more left turn and on to the railway station.'

'Once more down the left-hand path,' said Clay.

Penn fidgeted in his seat, wiping fresh beads of sweat from his face. 'Is that a good thing?'

Clay touched the scars on his face. 'It's seldom turned out that way for me.'

The chain-link fence surrounding the Air Force base was dotted with yellow signs, warning that it was a government facility. The concrete support posts whizzed past as Clay pushed the Jeep to its limit.

Penn stabbed the air with his finger. 'That's it. Take that turn.'

Clay's lips tightened as he caught sight of the abandoned structure. Two vehicles were parked at the far side of the single-storey building. He exchanged a glance with Penn. 'Here we go.'

Chapter 71

Blaine watched the two dots of light trace their way down the narrow road. It had to be him. *Clay Gunn.* They had the other one, Danny Gunn, naked in the hold of the ship, just a minute away. The Gunn brothers; what a fucking joke. Even their name was lame-assed. He rolled his shoulders, anticipating the violence to come. As soon as he had the flash-drive back from this buckaroo he would end it for both brothers; no way was either of these sacks of shit walking away tonight. How they died would be dictated by the circumstance. If they were lucky, they would both be on the old scrapper ship when it went down into the big blue. If they tried to fuck him over, they would die choking on their blood, his arms tight around their throats. Either way was good by him.

Blaine held his cell phone to the side of his face. Quantrill answered after a single ring. Blaine's voice was a winter frost; 'They're here.'

The approaching vehicle stopped at the far side of the old platform station. There wasn't much to the building, a low single-storey affair no more than fifty feet long. Every inch of the building looked to be daubed with graffiti. The disused train tracks were overgrown with high spiky grass and sorry-looking bushes. Blaine moved to the abandoned platform. A trash can lay on its side. He sent it spinning away with a kick.

'Look alive,' said Blaine as a solitary figure climbed from the vehicle. An anticipatory tingle ran the length of his spine as the man walked closer.

'I want to see Danny out here, right now!'

'The balls on this guy.' Blaine sneered. He needed to look this jerk-off in the eyes, see what he was about. 'You got the flash-drive with you?'

'I got it. Get Danny up here, then we can talk.'

Blaine felt his blood rising, who was this jerk-off to demand anything? 'Why don't I just rip out your heart and toss you and your little runt of a brother into the sea for the sharks?'

As he marched closer, Blaine gave him the once over. He was big, shoulders like a goddamned gorilla. No matter, he had put the ruin to bigger guys than Clay Gunn. He slipped his fingers into the brass-knuckles he had tucked in his hip pocket. 'Step into the light so I can see you properly.'

Clay Gunn paused; his face still obscured by shadows. 'Before I do that, I want you to know three things.'

'You're starting to piss me off and that's not good, I know that. Burned my house down? You prick.' Blaine visualised slamming the brass-knuckles into the side of Clay's head, smashing the temporal and sphenoid bones into his brain. *Let's see what he knew then.*

'Let me tell you those three things, Einstein. One: if I don't return to a prearranged location within two hours, a copy of those drives will be delivered to the two detectives I mentioned earlier.'

Blaine moved closer.

'Two; if Danny isn't standing in front of me in the next minute, a copy of those drives will be delivered to the said detectives.'

Blaine smiled; his lips tight as Clay too moved closer. The big guy's face, at least the left side was road-mapped with scars. No worries, Blaine was sure he would be adding to them very soon.

'And three; if Danny can't walk out of here on his own two feet, I'll kill every last one of you.'

'I'm sick of listening to your yak-yak, big shot. You need to shut your mouth and slow your roll.' Blaine looked to his right, to the single-track road that leads down to the waterside. A car slowly approached. 'He's coming.'

Clay took another couple of steps closer. Blaine continued to stare at his challenger, their eyes locked. Blaine would not look away. He would end it for the Gunn brothers; both of them, if not tonight then very soon. No way were they shaking him down, threatening him. Burning his goddamned house down. The smaller one would be no problem; he would snap Danny's neck like a twig. This one though, Clay, he might take a bit more effort, but he would get put down all the same.

The car rolled to a stop. The headlights flicked to full beam casting a myriad of elongated shadows. The abandoned station was little more than two rectangular cinderblock buildings connected by a corrugated sheet roof. Blaine had positioned himself on the old platform. The concrete area sat a couple of feet above the overgrown tracks. Blaine's gaze never left Clay as he listened to the car doors open. He raised the cell phone. 'Bring him up.'

Chapter 72

Danny showed no emotion as rough hands dragged him from the car. His hands were again bound with duct tape, this time in front. His feet were free. Fish had his fingers clamped tight around his left elbow. Danny was acutely aware of the knife pressing into his ribs. Junk seemed all too willing to push the blade home.

'Bring him up.'

Danny recognised Blaine's gruff voice instantly. Beneath the tape that still covered his mouth, Danny swore. There, twenty feet ahead, Blaine. In front of Chrissie's killer stood a squat building. A thousand graffiti tags decorated its walls. Danny scanned the vista, desperate for any advantage. Only four of the six-man team were in view. Where the hell was Sticks and Gato?

To the far right of the building, a hulking figure stepped into view. 'Bring Danny into the light so I can see him!'

Clay.

Fish pulled on Danny's arm. The cold steel of Junk's blade too prodded him forward. He looked at his captors again, they had made an error. The explosives on the boat, while probably real, had never been intended to detonate at that point. Quantrill and the others had still been on board. They were playing cruel power games; mind-fuckery, with him after all, showing him who's boss. The boat too was moored at the end of a narrow wooden pier less than a quarter-mile away.

Just ahead, Quantrill and Blaine exchanged words. Quantrill raised a hand, his finger pointing to Clay. 'You've got one chance to make this right or Danny boy gets to see what his liver looks like.'

'Take it easy big man, I've brought the flash-drives as promised.' Clay's voice seemed amplified by the building. 'Walk Danny forward and we'll exchange in the middle.'

Flash-drives?

'I won't ask again,' said Clay. 'You okay, Daniel?'

Danny tugged back on his elbow hiking his thumbs to his face. Fish spared a glance at Quantrill then tore away the duct tape. Danny forced himself not to grimace as the hairs ripped from his face. Both his face and naked body ached from the earlier beatings. He knew if he survived the night, he would be black and blue for a couple of weeks. *So, what was new?* 'I'm okay, Clay.'

'Bring him closer,' demanded Clay. As Danny was moved closer, Clay held his hand out in front of him. 'That's it, keep him coming. Hey, Daniel, I guess these assholes are sorry they tangled with one of the best hackers in the country. I've got everything from Blaine's computer right here.'

Danny felt a cold sensation ripple through his stomach. He never used Danny's given name. *Clay had nothing.* His IT skills were average at best. There was no way he could hack anyone's computer. Danny rolled his hands slow and easy, working against the duct tape. It was all gathered at his wrists. As he increased the pressure in his arms, he felt the tape wrinkle.

Clay stepped fully into view.

Danny began to wretch, coughing loudly. He bent at the waist. 'I'm gonna puke.'

Fish and Junk moved away from him, one either side. Danny gave a loud choking cough as he raised his hands above his head. In one motion Danny drove his elbows down past his ribs, the palms of his hands smacking into his lower stomach. The duct tape split under the sudden pressure, his arms free. The stiffened edge of his left hand slammed into Junk's face driving the brawler's head back. Danny felt Fish's fist crack against the side of his jaw but he was already moving, negating the force. As Fish followed with another heavy punch Danny batted it away with the palm of his hand. Surging away from Junk and his knife, Danny snapped a rapid two-count into Fish. Danny's open palms both found their mark, smashing his nose into his face. Fish went down in the dirt, cursing.

Danny launched his whole weight back into Junk, his heel slamming sideways into the man's hip.

Then the night was split by gunfire.

Chapter 73

Terry Penn watched Clay march past the deserted railway office. Headlights at the far side of the building lent a surreal look to the structure. As he wiped the beads of sweat from his face with his sleeve, Penn climbed from the Jeep. Raised voices drifted on the night air. His fingers tightened on the chequered grip of his pistol. The Colt 1911 felt heavy in his hand. He had shot dead countless cops, gangsters, and soldiers but always on-screen; *blanks and blood squibs*. Something fluttered wildly in his chest. He looked down at the weapon, suddenly feeling foolish. What the hell was he going to do with it anyway? He was no killer. Taking a deep breath, he crossed his arms over his chest, the pistol tucked under his left armpit, suddenly chilled despite the cloying humidity. The lights beyond the station seemed to contort, shimmering like an old-time magic lantern show. A truck's horn blared from somewhere in the distance.

A voice whispered to him from the dark. 'Don't move fat boy or I'll open your throat from ear to ear.'

Penn felt a little liquid seep into his underwear. A man-shaped shadow seemed to materialise at his left side. Something very sharp pressed into the skin of Penn's neck. Struggling to swallow, he forced himself to speak slowly. 'Take it easy.'

'Shut it, Mister Stay Puft. Keep your arms right where they are. That's it, now, slowly does it. Start walking.'

Penn turned his head just enough to get a look at the knifeman. His black hair and dark eyes afforded him a look every bit as sinister as the blade he wielded. A second man jogged into view. Instead of a knife, this one carried a length of steel pipe in each hand. The lump in Penn's throat felt like a sour apple.

'Nicely done, compadre,' said the man with the steel pipes.

'Hardly a great achievement, stealing upon grandpa here.'

Penn rankled. Clay and Danny needed his help, and here he was, fallen at the first hurdle. 'Who the hell are you calling grandpa?'

'Keep moving or I'll give you a new hole big enough to push a doughnut through.'

'You know who I am?' asked Penn.

'A soon to be very dead fat guy with a bad wig and halitosis?' The knifeman brought his face close. 'Last warning chubs, move.'

His heart hammered a heavy and ragged beat in his chest. Terry Penn's eyes closed involuntarily as he pulled the trigger. The pistol, tucked under his armpit sounded like a cannon. The knifeman yelled in surprise, leaping bodily away from the discharge. Had he shot him? Penn wasn't sure. Uncoiling his arms and dropping into a more stable shooter's stance, Penn rapidly snapped off two shots. The man with the knife was moving fast and low. In a second, he tucked his head and rolled away from the gunfire. A brief flame from the muzzle flash gave a strobe effect against the side of the Jeep. Penn pivoted and snapped off another two shots, this time aiming for the guy with the steel pipes. The man listed to one side but continued sprinting away from the Jeep. One of the steel weapons dropped from his grip. Penn turned again, his eyes struggling to focus. His breathing was now a series of short gasping inhalations. A pain like a tightening cable passed down the length of his left arm. Panting as he moved, Penn angled away from the body of the Jeep, circling the vehicle. Where the hell was the knifeman? *Was he down? Was he dead?*

Something heavy and ragged sailed through the air, catching Penn in the side of his face. Staggering, Penn felt a flash of pain sear across his skull. The ground seemed to tilt and gravity conspired to take him butt first into the ground. Penn snapped off another shot. The guy had clocked him with a fist-sized piece of concrete. His face burned with a strange heat.

Rolling first onto his knees, Penn struggled to get his feet under him. The pistol was still tight in his grip. Coughing and dizzy, Terry Penn lurched from the ground like a drunkard. His left hand came away from his face sticky and dark.

The man with the knife moved faster than anyone Penn had ever seen. A new pain erupted in his left arm. The horrid words; *heart attack,* flashed through his mind. He found himself falling once more, the knifeman on top of him. Penn stared aghast at the knife that was wedged through his upper arm. Both men went down into the dirt. The knifeman tugged on the blade sending unbelievable tremors through his arm. Gasping uncontrollably, Penn clamped his damaged limb tight to his chest. The knifeman's free hand closed around his wrist. *No!*

Penn bared his teeth and snapped at the man's face like a wild animal. As the knifeman lurched his head away from the biting, Penn bucked to one side, rolling the man from his dominant position. Brief flashes of light erupted between the two bodies. Gasping shorter and shorter breaths, Penn squeezed down on the trigger until the pistol fell silent. The knifeman lay on his side, curled like a sleeping child. There was nothing theatrical about his death. No screams, no explosions of blood; he just crumpled. Penn again staggered to his feet. Holding the pistol in his right hand he waved the weapon awkwardly in the air. Where was the other man, the one with the steel pipe?

With hands that had begun to violently tremble, Penn struggled to change the magazine. After several fumbles, he heard the magazine click into place. As he worked the top slide another bolt of pain lanced through his left arm. The knife hilt protruding from his bicep looked unreal. With tears in his eyes, he pulled the knife free, letting it fall to the ground.

A stream of vomit escaped from his throat and he bent at the waist until the heaves had subsided. Casting another panicked glance at the man he had just killed; Penn clambered into the Jeep and started the engine. He wanted to be a million miles away from this nightmare.

Chapter 74

Clay raced at the men holding his brother. Gunshots sounded from behind him. *Penn!* With little choice, he continued forward. Terry Penn was armed with his Colt pistol. He would be okay. Clay knew that Terry was tougher than he gave himself credit for.

Clay vaulted from the raised platform, his bent knees absorbing the fall. Ahead, Danny was already moving. Two of the men were reeling, clutching at their bodies. Another two, one unmistakably Blaine; his tattooed bull-head leaving little doubt, were mid-way between Clay and Danny. Tucking his head low, Clay pushed off with his legs. His right foot cut the air on a direct path to Blaine's head. Clay felt the impact in the lower part of his leg but it was not the clean shot he had hoped for. Blaine had hunched over, his forearms taking the brunt of the kick. Clay exhaled as Blaine surged into him at speed, his arms scooping him up at the knees. Instead of contesting the grappler's gambit, Clay too dropped his weight back, carrying Blaine up and over his head. Both men went down in the dirt. Something hard and unforgiving slapped into the side of Clay's face. Spots of light danced across his vision. Latching onto the first thing he found, Clay's fingers dug deep into Blaine's pectoral. With his fingers deep in the man's armpit, Clay twisted and ripped at the thick slab of muscle. Blaine reared back, emitting a low howl. Clay followed, swiping his knuckles backhand across the side of his face. Blaine's bald head rocked back from the force of the blow, the big man staggering.

As Clay cocked back his rigid open hand, Blaine's exposed throat his target, another body crashed into his. Someone had leapt from the raised platform. Caught off balance, Clay could do little more than tuck his head as he tumbled away from the assault. A length of steel pipe missed his face by a mere inch.

As he came up onto his feet Clay caught a brief glimpse of Danny. Fists slapped against flesh. A body was thrown headlong through the air.

Danny was naked?

Then the two men were on him. Blaine launched a vicious kick at his groin which Clay barely dodged. Again, the steel pipe whistled at his head. Pain flared through his injured muscles as he twisted away from the cudgel. The breath caught in his throat as he felt his right foot twist against something immovable. His weight canted to one side as Blaine swung a wild overhand punch into his face. Clay again tumbled into the dirt, his head ringing. A flash of red behind his eyes and he rose to his feet with a bestial growl. *These fuckers were for it now!*

The dirt around his feet erupted in a sudden cloud as a new weapon roared.

Shotgun!

An intense burning began in his left leg. He knew some of the buckshot had found its mark.

Move!

Banking on the chance that the man would not fire directly at his friends, Clay closed on the man swinging the steel pipe. Forming a triangle with his bladed hands, Clay speared into the man as he brought the pipe around in a diagonal slash. Stepping inside the storm, Clay wrapped up the man's arm tight under his armpit. He felt the joint constrict in his grip. Turning against the locked elbow, Clay used the man as a shield. The shotgun remained silent.

Chapter 75

Curtis Quantrill groaned in disbelief. The frigging ball busting Gunn brothers were turning his life to shit. All of the team were capable men, but these two, goddamn it, making them look like rank amateurs. His men had been caught napping. Gunshots had lit up the night from the far side of the building. Who the hell was up there? To his left, Clay was pumping out blows, twisting back and forth like a bull terrier. To his right Danny, buck naked, dropped both Fish and Junk with some Bruce Lee speed Kung Fu bullshit.

Quantrill snatched at the brass-knuckles in his pocket. He had threatened Blaine with the same weapon but had hesitated. He felt no moral ambiguity when it came to smashing in the faces of the Gunn brothers.

Racing into the fray Quantrill aimed for the centre of Danny's face. The blow he unleashed was perfect, full shoulder rotation, hip twist, and weight transfer. Yet the brass knuckles barely skimmed the side of Danny's face as he snapped his head away from the punch. Quantrill felt his balance tilt as he overextended his blow. A lightning bolt of pain shot through his torso. The wiry little bastard had not only dodged the headshot but had replied with a liver shot of his own. Only the tracker unit in his jacket pocket had saved him from a crippling blow.

As Quantrill again closed on the smaller of the two Gunn brothers, he swung a loose left punch at his head. As expected, Danny ducked under the bait punch. Quantrill was ready, ripping a vicious uppercut at his lowered head. It was a move he had used several times in the past; each time to devastating effect. *Set them up, knock them down.* But Danny wasn't there. Again, he had drifted just away from the path of attack. Snarling, Quantrill ripped out another punch, hitting nothing but air.

A harsh boom lit up the night. Fish had broken from the group and retrieved his shotgun from the trunk. On Curtis' say so he had reloaded the weapon with lead shot cartridges, the earlier rubber bullet rounds now discarded. Quantrill risked a glance at Fish's target. The ground around the big guy, Clay, seemed to come alive as dust and shale leapt into the air. Clay's hand flew to his legs. *One point to the home team.*

Quantrill span on his heels, his right hand again whipping through the air. He felt the breath catch in his throat as Danny's arms closed tightly around his waist. The little bastard was behind him. He struck back with an elbow as his feet were lifted from the ground. The solid impact he delivered was a short-lived victory as he was upended. Twisting, his hands sought something to break his fall, but there was nothing. Arms milling, his face slammed into the dirt. The impact across the side of his head was numbing but not enough to keep him down. Cursing, Quantrill turned onto his hands and knees. The barefoot that rocketed into his face snapped his jaws together. Sent sprawling, furious curses filled the air. Voices coming from every direction, all of the vile language promising serious harm.

The edges of his vision seemed to dim, narrow, and darken. Something hard and unforgiving cracked against the back of his skull. As Quantrill rolled onto his back, his arms tightening around his head, his legs tucking up at the knees, he caught sight of Danny. Dirt covered most of his naked body, his face streaked with a thick red line from his eyebrow. Danny's expression was something from a horror movie. The whites of his eyes were visible all the way around, his lips pulled back into an animalistic snarl, teeth bared.

A fresh wave of emotion swept over Quantrill as he realised what Danny had just hit him with. The tracker unit was held fast inside his dirt-encrusted right hand.

The tracker!

Delacroix's legacy.

No!

As he lurched to his knees, desperately reaching for the tracker, Danny's foot lashed out once more, catching him in the centre of his chest. The breath exploded from his lungs as he collapsed to the ground. Groaning, he again felt his vision transform to a darkening kaleidoscope. Then impossibly bright lights seared his eyeballs. Too late, he identified the roaring sound and blinding lights. Unable to breathe or gather his feet beneath him, a stab of abject fear pinned him to the ground. The vehicle that raced toward him was only seconds away.

Chapter 76

The other men in Danny's peripheral vision moved like wraiths. Blaine. There he was, just forty or fifty feet away. A ripple of elation spread through his body as he watched Clay drop one of Blaine's buddies.

Good to know Clay was very much alive and kicking.

The roar of Fish's shotgun instantly dropped the curtain on the elation. The ground erupted around Clay's feet, dust, and shale peppering into the night air. Danny watched Clay latch onto one of Quantrill's gang; using him as a shield. Danny had no such protection.

Curtis Quantrill was on his knees, his arm reaching for the hardware that Danny had pulled from his pocket, an impromptu weapon. With a sharp exhalation, Danny twisted his hips, adding as much weight to the kick as he could. The ball of his barefoot slammed into the target. Danny felt the impact in his ankle and knew it was a good shot. Quantrill went backwards into the dirt once more.

The pains that echoed in his head were forced away as Danny's attention strobed between Blaine and Fish. The thought of snapping Blaine's neck was his intent but there was a lot of open ground to cover. Fish would get him with the shotgun to be sure.

As if on cue Fish pivoted, the shotgun high on his shoulder seeking a target. Danny dropped to the ground close to Quantrill; knowing that this would only buy him a second or two. Fish only had to move a little closer to be able to fire on Danny while avoiding catching his friend in the spread of the shotgun blast.

The roaring of an engine seemed to grow exponentially. Twin spots of light too increased in intensity. Danny swore under his breath. *'What new flavour of crap is this?'*

Fish turned the shotgun away from Danny and blasted the oncoming vehicle. One of the lights exploded but the vehicle kept coming. Tucking his feet beneath him, Danny readied himself. Moments from knocking him flat the vehicle slewed in a tight arc, casting a shower of dust and pebbles over his naked body. The passenger door flew open.

'Get in!'

Danny accepted the invite and dove bodily into the vehicle. The driver stomped on the gas pedal even before Danny had righted himself in the seat. The shotgun blasted again and the rear end of the vehicle bucked against the impact.

'Penn?' shouted Danny. 'What the hell are you doing here?'

Penn only managed one word as he wrenched the steering wheel in a tight circle. 'Clay.'

Another blast from the shotgun rocked the rear of the vehicle. 'He's there. Get him.'

Danny watched Clay grow larger in his view as the vehicle shot towards him. Penn let out a yelp as the vehicle sideswiped the corner of the deserted station building. Sparks flew as Penn angled-away the vehicle. One of Curtis' men leapt from the path of the speeding Jeep, tumbling from view. A second later the breath caught in Danny's throat, momentarily weightless as the vehicle soared through the air. With barely enough time to clench his teeth together, Danny was slammed sideways into the dashboard. Something sharp raked his ribs, his head bouncing against the windshield. The vehicle continued to bounce as it settled back onto four wheels.

Finding himself wedged arse first in the footwell Danny uncoiled and levered himself back into the seat. A loud buzzing filled his ears. He yelled something intelligible. Penn was hunched over the steering wheel. Strands of black hair were plastered to his blood-dappled forehead. His face was a mask of effort as he yanked on the steering wheel, turning the vehicle in another tight arc.

The shotgun boomed again, a tongue of a flame brief in the encroaching darkness. The hood of the vehicle rang like a bell. Danny stared back over his shoulder. They had driven clean off the edge of the low platform in a wild slalom and were now at the far side of the building.

'Clay's still back there,' yelled Danny as he watched a body tumble from the raised platform, briefly illuminated from the headlights at the far side of the building. He was sure it was not Clay.

'I'm on it!' sputtered Penn. He powered the vehicle back up the sharp incline, again reaching the ground level with the old station.

There!

Clay was running full tilt, head down and arms pumping. Penn again yanked hard on the steering wheel sending the vehicle into a short drift. The rear door was wrenched open and Clay entered like an Olympic diver. Penn stamped on the gas pedal as Clay landed in a heap across the back seats.

Behind them, the shotgun boomed.

A cold rage flooded over Danny as he stared at Blaine. Chrissie's killer was shouting something at the escaping vehicle. His face was contorted to match Danny's sentiment.

'You okay?' Danny reached for the back seats.

Clay levered himself into a sitting position as Penn raced the vehicle around the old station building. 'Well that was hardly military precision, but I got you back at least.'

Danny reached over to Clay's legs. 'You're bleeding.'

'Story of my frigging life.'

'You're bleeding too.' Staring at Clay, Danny pointed at the driver. 'What the hell is Penn doing here?'

The ageing actor's head snapped towards Danny. 'Hey, I owed Clay a favour, fuhgeddaboudit.'

Chapter 77

'Where the hell are your clothes?'

Danny shrugged in response to his brother's question. 'Those numb nuts probably figured that it would help intimidate me while they kicked the shit out of me.'

'Did it work?' asked Clay.

'Well now, they may have loosened some shit with their kicking, right enough, but intimidated, no, not really.'

Clay gave a low chuckle. 'Are they following?'

'I can't see any lights. Why aren't they following us?'

'Maybe we got lucky for once.'

'I don't like it,' said Danny.

'Let's just be thankful for the break. We need to regroup and come at them from a new angle.'

'This is my fault.' Danny shook his head. 'I ran at them with my head down like a dumb arsed billy goat. I let my temper get the better of me. Won't happen again.'

'Don't beat yourself up, Danny. We underestimated those shit heels, as you say, it won't happen again.' Clay touched the side of his mouth. His fingers came away flecked with red.

'I wanted to kill every one of them. All I succeeded in doing was getting my arse shot with rubber bullets and my head used as a football for an hour or so.'

'You're still breathing so it's not all bad,' said Clay. 'Lumps and bumps we can live with.'

Danny looked back at his older brother. The compassion in his eyes was a stark contrast to the scars that marred his features. 'When they had me, I heard them say that they dropped you into the bay, that right?'

'Damned right they did. Scooped me up on a goddamned forklift and dropped my ass in the drink. Then dropped a whole bunch of railway sleepers on me for good measure.'

Danny nodded, the corners of his mouth curling at Clay's resilience. 'And then you made it back to Blaine's house and set it on fire?'

'Eventually yeah, it's been quite the night.'

'And it's not finished yet,' said Danny. 'We need some new weapons and kit then I'm going back out for these fuckers.'

'You gonna get some clothes on or is that one of the weapons you'll be swinging?' asked Clay.

Penn waved a hand in a loose arc. 'Yeah, put a hat over that thing, I'm startin' to feel inadequate.'

Danny gave a wry smile. 'I hear going native is all the rage with the kids these days. Clothing is optional.'

'Thanks for that, king ding-a-ling, we'll get you some duds at the next store,' said Clay.

'You can bet the next time we tangle with these lug nuts they'll be fully tooled up. We need to bring the boom to them.' Danny tapped Penn's shoulder. 'You have any contacts that could get us some hardware?'

'Depends on what you want. I could probably lay hands on a couple of pistols, if you want anything higher grade, I would need to make a few calls. That might take some time, maybe tomorrow.'

Danny shook his head. 'I don't want to wait that long. I need to keep these arseholes on the back foot. I don't want to give them time to roll us again.'

'Walmart sells shotguns,' said Penn. 'And rifles come to that.'

'No good, they'll want state ID. I don't want our names in any firearms database with what I'm planning to do.' Danny expanded his chest. The sensation in his sternum alternated between a dull ache and splinters of glass.

'If you wanted to buy some hardcore drugs, where would you go?' asked Clay.

Penn raised his eyebrows almost to his hairline. 'Why is ya asking me? I'm a law-abiding citizen.'

'Who knows just about everybody in this city,' said Clay. 'Let me put it another way. Where would you never be seen dead buying contraband?'

'Ah, I see where you're going now.' Penn tapped a finger to the side of his head. 'There's a place, twenty minutes from here. They'll have what you're looking for.'

'Okay then. Let's get Danny some clothes first then that's our next stop.'

'Aye, sounds like a plan,' agreed Danny.

Chapter 78

Clay looked at his brother and smiled. He was now dressed all in black; boots, black denim, sweatshirt, and a lightweight hunting vest. Clay too had bought new dry clothes and redressed. Both now carried knives. The sporting goods section of the supermarket proved fruitful. Clay had looked longingly at the hunting section, the shotguns, and rifles there exactly what they wanted. Yet Danny was right, they wanted no paper trail linking them to weapons. They had taken time to dress any wounds with Bactine and band-aids. Clay's legs had been peppered with shot, undeniably painful, but thankfully none of the wounds was much more than superficial.

'How do you want to do this?'

'In and out. Quick and quiet,' said Danny.

'Let's hope it goes that way,' said Clay.

'You sure this is the place?' Danny looked to Penn.

'Yeah man, see that truck sitting under the overpass. The one with the three guys at the side. That's the one you need.'

'You're sure there's just the three amigos?'

'Yeah, just the three. Cousins, I think,' answered Penn. 'They sell their junk out of that back of the van. They'll be armed.'

'I'm counting on it.' Danny nodded at Clay. 'Give me about ten seconds with them then flip the switch.'

Clay nodded in understanding.

Danny moved away from the parked Jeep on a direct path to the van. Clay watched Danny hunch over, rounding his shoulders, his gait suddenly slightly off-kilter. The three men at the van perked up like meerkats as Danny drew closer. Clay huffed as the tallest of the three men challenged Danny.

Danny's right hand lifted in an open greeting. His head bobbed side to side. Clay couldn't hear the verbal exchange. One of the men beckoned Danny closer.

Clay flipped the switch. The remaining headlight and roof-mounted spotlights burned away the night. As quickly as he had illuminated the area, he turned them off again.

The sound of rapid-fire impacts carried where the words had not. *Six sharp cracks almost without pause.*

Clay pointed to the van. 'Drive.'

Penn powered from the curb to the van in less than five seconds. Clay was out of the Jeep even before it had stopped moving. Three bodies lay on the ground. Two of the men were unconscious; star-fished on the sidewalk. The third lay groaning, a thick stream of blood running from his nose. All three men had stared into the halogen lights of the Jeep, momentarily blinded. That's all the wiry Scotsman had needed. Danny moved from man to man taking the items they had come for. A streak of red marred the knuckles of his right hand.

'He's fast,' said Penn, his wide face framed in the driver's window.

'That he is,' agreed Clay. 'Faster hands than most pro boxers.'

'I'm inclined to agree.'

Clay allowed a brief smile as Danny pulled two pistols from inside the shirts of the downed men. Clay accepted the weapons. One Glock 17 and a smaller Kimber Micro 9. A quick inspection revealed that both pistols held full mags. The Glock seemed well cared for. The Kimber looked like a Colt 1911 that had shrunk in the wash.

'Anything in the van?'

Danny moved first to the front seats but returned moments later empty-handed. 'Nothing in there. I'll try the back.'

Clay looked down at the man who was cupping his face in his hands. He considered giving him a punt with his boot but he posed no threat. Danny closed the back doors.

'Nothing in there either.'

'Slim pickings, but these are better than nothing.'

Penn leaned, from the driver's window. 'We better hit the highway fellas. I know they're only mid-level dope dealers, but I don't want to get caught up with the rest of the family if they happen by to check on those three.'

The corners of Clay's mouth curled as he noticed the hidden weapon. Stooping, he picked the MAC 10 from the rear wheel arch of the van. Clay pushed the pistols into his waistband. He ejected the MAC's box magazine. The compact machine pistol too was fully loaded, the magazine filled with .45 ACP rounds. 'This is more like it. Even bottom feeders can afford big boy toys.'

Danny joined him at the side of the van.

'Guys?' Penn's voice carried obvious concern.

Clay gave his old friend a quick nod then climbed back into the Jeep. Danny hopped into the back seats. Penn steered away from the van. 'That's it for you, Penn, old buddy. I owe you big time. You need to get your shoulder looked at properly. I can see it's still bleeding. I don't want to drag you into this crap any further than I already have.'

'Clay, I…'

'No argument. We'll drop you at the next hospital,' said Clay.

'It's not that,' said Penn, his head hanging. A short sob shuddered in his chest. 'The guy that stabbed me in the shoulder…I think I killed him. We both went down to the ground together. I didn't mean to kill him but…'

'It was him or you.' Clay ran a hand across the scars on his face. 'I'm so sorry old buddy. I never meant for you to get hurt.'

A whisper; 'Fuhgeddaboudit.'

Clay struggled to swallow as a thick tear ran down Penn's face.

Chapter 79

Curtis Quantrill looked down at his friend's body. Gato lay curled on his side. He looked so young; all tension, gone from his handsome face. A dark patch the size of a dinner plate stained the front of his shirt. Thoughts span around his mind in a maelstrom yet no solutions presented themselves.

Blaine and the others were berserk with rage.

'What the hell are we going to do about Gato?' asked Fish. His knuckles were as white as his face as he gripped his shotgun. 'We can't call the cops and I'm sure as hell not leaving him here for someone else to find. Pele didn't deserve to go out like that.'

Quantrill forced himself to breathe slowly. The night was going from bad to worse to unbearable. They'd lost any advantage over the Gunn brothers. Gato was down. The rest were hurting. 'Put him in the back of your truck, Fish. I'll figure something out.'

'Gato was like my brother and now we're going to wrap him in a tarp, like some camping gear. The man was a fucking warrior, an athlete. He was the best of us.'

Quantrill placed a hand on Fish's shoulder. A slight tremor shook through his muscles. 'We'll get them back for this. They'll die for this. I give you my word.'

Sticks shook his head, his gaze downcast. 'When the fat guy started shooting, I told Gato to run for it. I thought he was right behind me. Didn't realise he'd caught a bullet.'

'We'll end it for all of them, that's a fucking promise.' Quantrill rolled his shoulders. The bones of his chest hurt like a sonofabitch.

'They're in the wind,' said Sticks. 'They could be halfway to Atlanta by now.'

'I don't think so,' said Quantrill. 'This all started with Blaine. They came to kill you, Caleb, I think they'll want another run at that.'

'Good! Let them come. I'll bury both of those assholes next time I see them.' Blaine stared at Curtis; his face full of defiance.

'No argument from me,' said Quantrill. 'I want these douche bags as much as you do, but I need them to talk before we off them for good. I need my tracker back.'

'No more talking. Look where that got us. We know they were on my tail because of the Haims woman. I need to end this crap show now,' said Blaine.

Quantrill stared into the night. 'That little Scottish fucker took my tracker, smacked me upside the head with it as well.'

'I don't give a rat's ass about the tracker,' said Blaine. 'The big one still has the film from my computer.'

'Well I do give a rat's ass,' said Quantrill. 'I need the tracker back before we kill these butt monkeys. I got it working just before the shit hit the fan, now Danny's got it. If I'm right, that beacon will give us the location of Delacroix's legacy. This is the payday of a lifetime.'

'I don't give a rat's ass about fuck face Delacroix's treasure trove, either. I want those two full of holes by midnight.'

'Three,' said Sticks. 'Remember there's three of them now. There was the big dude with the black hair, the driver. He was the one that did Gato. He's mine when we catch up with them again.'

Junk spat into the dirt. 'How? It's like Sticks said already; they're in the wind. We know next to nothing about them. All we know is that they're slippery mofos and tough as a commando's boots. We had them and they rolled us. The smaller guy was tied up, buck naked and kicked shitless and he still managed to go all Jason Bourne on our asses. If we're going after them, we all need to be loaded for bear. And do it *before* the cops come looking for us.'

'Fuck the cops!' spat Blaine.

Quantrill looked around at his team, studying each face in turn. The eyes that stared back all carried the same capacity and need. Revenge. 'All right, we meet back at my place in an hour. I want you all strapped and ready. If you see any cops, we'll meet at that basketball court on Miller Street. We'll put these yahoos so far underground it'll take an archaeologist to find them again.'

'How we gonna find them?' asked Fish.

Blaine's phone warbled. Cursing, he pulled it from his pocket. 'Yeah?'

'Sucks, when they fight back, doesn't it?'

Quantrill bobbed his head. 'Put it on speaker.'

Blaine pressed a button. The unmistakable Scottish voice filled the air. 'You want your tracker back and I want your heads on spikes, so here's where I'm going to be in exactly one hour from now…'

'No more tricks, let's finish this tonight,' said Blaine.

'Fine by me. Here are the coordinates. I'm guessing the location on the tracker is important to you.' Danny Gunn recited the string of numbers. Quantrill quickly entered them into his phone. 'I'll be wearing a fedora hat and a pink carnation.'

'Always trying to be the comedian ain't ya? It'll be funnier when I'm pulling your spine out through your mouth,' said Blaine.

'Just be there and we'll see what we see.' The call ended.

Quantrill gestured to his men. 'Let's move. We need to arm up and get to the meet before they do. Bring everything you've got. Vests too.'

'I get to kill the mac daddy,' demanded Blaine. 'I need some kit from you guys.'

'I've got you covered,' said Fish. 'I've got something real for these gummy bear eating motherfuckers in my lock up.'

'Like what?' asked Junk.

Fish gave a lop-sided smile. 'I've been prepping big time for a couple of years now, you know, for the event; the *SHTF*, it's bound to happen, only a matter of when. Big boys' toys.'

'Let's move,' said Quantrill. 'Maybe we can salvage something from this shit show after all.'

Chapter 80

The new clothes stuck to his body like a second skin. The smell of rotting vegetation filled his nose. Insects, invisible in the darkness buzzed around his face and neck. Danny ignored them. They had reached the location after a hectic twenty-minute drive. Penn had bid an emotional farewell before being dropped at a walk-in medical centre in Princeton. The sat nav on Clay's new phone took them south-west through Florida City then onto Ingraham Highway. A smaller spur road had routed them from the last of the street lights out into the oppressive darkness of the everglades.

Clay backed the Jeep off the narrow road onto a switchback, its rear fender butting up tight against the curving bole of a tree. The vehicle would not be easy to see from the road. The time they had taken to reconnoitre the road ahead had paid dividends. The path continued for less than another quarter mile, terminating at the boundary fence for some kind of Everglades wildlife attraction. Danny knew that there were some small family-run parks dotted around the state. Caged bears and penned alligators did little for Danny, the fence with its padlocked double gate and the circular turning space, however, served his purpose. Then a short but furious spate of activity followed.

'You good?' asked Danny. Sweat dripped from his face as he finished his preparations. He tossed the now-empty jerry can into the back of the Jeep.

'Better when we put these yahoos down for good,' replied Clay.

'Aye,' said Danny as he studied the tracker, its screen a muted green. It was an older model but one he was familiar with. He had used similar hardware as part of his duties with the PMC outfit, Odin Corp. At the centre of the screen, a darker green light pulsed. They were almost on top of the coordinate points. Danny thumbed one of the buttons on the side of the unit and the display blurred. After a few seconds, the screen zoomed in, showing slightly more topography detail of the area. Another press of the button and the coordinates were displayed in numeric sequence. Satisfied that they were where they need to be, he pocketed the unit and checked his weapons. The Kimber Micro 9 was compact but deadly up close; just where Danny liked to work. He pushed the pistol into a front pocket of his hunting vest. The blade that hung at his right hip was a Boker hunting knife with a drop point blade, thick and sturdy. The quiver of arrows dangled on his opposite hip. Clay hadn't used the bow earlier, but Danny knew the ability to kill silently would be an advantage.

'Better get a step on, wee one,' said Clay.

'I'm going,' said Danny as he nocked an arrow to the bowstring. He pulled back on the string, testing the action. The bow felt good in his grip. A wry smile crept across his face moments before Clay killed the lights on the Jeep. 'And stop calling me wee one, that shit sticks.'

The dense foliage seemed all too eager to swallow Danny, to snag his limbs and arrest his progress. Moving in a simian crouch, keeping his chin tucked low, Danny moved away from the single-track road. He knew Clay would be busy with his preparations. Pausing, he allowed the smells and sounds of the everglades to permeate his senses. A low insectoid buzzing filled the air. Danny forced himself to ignore the tiny creatures that flitted around his face, creatures that seemed very interested in his eyes, ears, and mouth. Tracing a wide arc around the clearing, he allowed his eyes to become more accustomed to the darkness. Reaching out with his left hand, he allowed himself the briefest of smiles. 'This'll do nicely.'

Chapter 81

Carl Anderson slowly shook his head. He'd missed dinner for this shits and giggles show. Brockovich was a great cop, but way too eager to please for his liking. She could have told dispatch where to get off. Instead, they had spent hours standing around with their thumbs up their ass. The bodies at the Brickell Flatts yard had been tagged and bagged. Once satisfied that the crime scene had been fully preserved, Brockovich had made a beeline to the ER where the two survivors had been taken. Neither had been in any state to talk let alone give a coherent statement.

'Those guys are a dead loss. It'll be days before they speak any sense. They both look like they've been run over by a semi-truck.' A sudden wave of fatigue swept over Anderson. He rubbed his eyes then pinched the bridge of his nose with thumb and forefinger.

'This isn't finished,' said Brockovich. 'I can feel it in my bones.'

Anderson rolled his shoulders. His shirt felt tighter than usual across the expanse of his chest. 'What do you mean?'

'This,' said Brockovich spreading her arms.

'Those guys in there breathing through tubes and on IV drips. I don't think these are the last bodies we'll be scraping up before we're done.'

'I just wanted my dinner,' said Anderson. 'Vending coffee and twinkies just don't do it for me.'

Brockovich slowly walked to a row of plastic seats arranged along the outside wall of the ward. She flopped into one of the seats. Anderson too took a seat, leaving one place between them as was his habit.

'You okay partner?' he asked. He looked at Gina's face and not for the first time wondered why in hell would someone who looked as good as Brockovich waste her talents being a cop. Gina was beyond just pretty, she was beautiful. But it went beyond that, she moved with the grace of a dancer and could talk effortlessly to street kids one minute then schmooze with the mayor the next. To top it all off she was tough as nails when she needed to put the hammer down. A frown spread over Anderson's face as Brockovich began to talk, her voice barely above a whisper.

'When I was a kid, probably about five or six, some men came to my father's house. They'd hassled him before, but never at home. It was night time. I was reading one of my books; one fish, two fish, red fish, blue fish.'

Anderson canted his head to one side.

'Okay…'

'I remember they came in two pickup trucks. My bedroom lit up like the boardwalk from their lights. My father and grandpa went outside to see what was going on. The men set on both of them, beating them. They all had bamboo poles. My father tried to reason with them, but they kept knocking them down, kicking them, hitting them over and over with their canes. The men kept shouting 'go home gooks' over and over. I thought they were going to die. I was so scared. My mom was screaming. I still remember the looks of hatred on the faces of the men. They were all white. I kept thinking, why are they yelling go home? *We were at home*. My father was born in Miami. He was as white as they were. One of the men stamped on my father's arm. I heard the snap inside the house. They dragged my grandfather out into the middle of the street. His face was covered in blood.'

'Hell, Gina, why have you never told me this before?'

Brockovich continued. 'They held my grandfather down and poured gasoline all over him.'

'Jesus.' Anderson reached out, his hand resting on his partner's shoulder. He found it hard to swallow.

'The men that did it looked a lot like the men we've seen tonight. Same ethos, same twisted code. I remember the look in my grandfather's eyes as one of the men sparked a lighter. He looked at us and held up his hand as if to tell us to stay back, no fear; just a sad acceptance.'

'Gina…'

'Then a man appeared from the darkness and grabbed the asshole with the lighter. He knocked the living crap out of that guy in five seconds flat, I mean messed him up good. He chased off the others with one of their poles. He beat their asses something serious, one man, he saved my grandpa from a horrible death.'

'Who was he?'

'Just some guy who lived down our street. He wasn't very big. His name was Eddie Farmiga. He worked construction. Such a quiet fella, a nice guy, an old-fashioned gentleman.'

'Not all heroes need to look like Dwayne Johnson,' said Anderson. 'He still around?'

'No. Eddie died about four years back. Pancreatic cancer.'

'Jeez.'

Gina Brockovich straightened in her seat. 'These two roughnecks, the Gunn brothers, I see a lot of Eddie Farmiga in them.'

Anderson jutted his chin before he spoke. 'They're still on the wrong side of the line on this.

There're still bodies on the slab to be accounted for. They don't get a free pass, even if they're knocking down bad guys. That's not their job.'

'That's not what I meant,' said Brockovich. 'But I'm not shedding any tears for the assholes that got their tickets punched tonight.'

Anderson made a show of dabbing his fingers to his face. 'No tears here either, partner.'

Chapter 82

Clay spat out the insect that seemed intent on burrowing into the corner of his mouth with aplomb. With the vehicle lights now extinguished, the darkness of the everglades seemed to push down on him like a shroud. The Jeep was just another patch of black in a hundred other angular pockets of shadow. Thick clouds scudded in front of a crescent moon. He knew Danny would be able to see him from whichever vantage point he had decided upon. The boxy weapon he sported was warm in his hands. The MAC-10 was chambered for .45 ACP. Capable of delivering its full magazine in less than two seconds, it was a brutal but short-lived beast.

Dropping to one knee, Clay rested the machine pistol on his thigh. Working by touch he drew the Glock 17 and ejected the magazine from the pistol grip. Angling the magazine to what little light was afforded by the moon, he tapped the cylinder twice on the side of his head. He huffed as he inserted the magazine back into the pistol, giving the assembly a sharp tap with the heel of his hand. He worked the top slide and tucked the sidearm into his waistband. Moving into deeper shadow Clay held the MAC-10 close to his chest. The sounds of the night drifted into his senses. Something vigorously splashed in nearby water. Further away a bird hooted in a strangely morose pitch. Then came a slow two-tone whistle; *Danny.*

They were coming.

The unmistakable sounds of a vehicle engine stuttered through the surrounding trees. Clay tilted his head to one side, his mouth open to allow his hearing as much range as possible. The engine sounded odd to his ear; the tone strangely metallic. Staying low, he moved a few steps closer to the twin rutted track that served as a road. The first dots of light sparkled through the proliferation of trees. Letting his vision drift away from the lights, he stared into the various shades of shadow. He knew that the men they were about to again face were not stupid. They would not make the same mistake Danny had by charging in with a scowl.

Clay's lip curled as he identified two separate engine pitches; one a heavy vehicle sound, the other sounded like some kind of motorcycle. Daggers of light strobed through the closer trees. They were almost upon them. Pressing himself low against a curving tree trunk, Clay watched the rear set of lights slow. The larger vehicle continued uninterrupted on its path. A few seconds later not one but two bikes sped past his position. Ignoring the vehicles, he angled the MAC-10 into the darkness. The growling of the engines diminished as they reached the clearing at the end of the track. A brief revving from the bikes then they fell into a more languid pitch. Voices, quiet and angry blended with the chittering of insects.

Clay slowed his breathing as he registered the first indication of movement. Twenty yards out, an indistinct shadow detached itself from one tree and blended with another. The muzzle of the MAC-10 tracked ahead of the shadow. The stubby weapon felt like a child's toy in his hands as Clay moved his index finger from its resting position onto the trigger. The shadow which now displayed arms and legs flitted again from tree to tree. A few more steps would bring the interloper directly into the kill zone.

The breath caught in Clay's throat as a second shadow lurched into view. This shadow carried a wide circular pipe on its shoulder. As he launched himself bodily away from his resting position the tree exploded in mind-numbing gout of fire.

Chapter 83

Danny turned his head, protecting his night vision as the headlights illuminated the wide circular turning area. Seconds later, two off-road bikes followed the minivan into the clearing, casting plumes of dirt behind them. The riders wore leather jackets and full-face helmets, obscuring their identities. Danny scowled as he drew the bow to its full capacity, the nock of the arrow touching his bottom lip. He sighted on the rider furthest from his position. The corner of his left eye twitched as he counted down the seconds. Clay knew what to do.

Any second now...

The curse caught in his throat as the night was lit by an unholy explosion. Danny squatted, holding the bow in position as a fist-sized chunk of tree whizzed past his head. From his braced position he dropped to one knee and let the arrow loose. The projectile hit straight and true. Danny was already moving to a new position as the rider toppled to one side, his bike spinning out from beneath him.

A bullet storm shredded the tree where he had knelt only a second earlier. In a half-crouch, he traced a rapid skirmish line through the trees. A second arrow lodged deep in the front grille of the minivan. A third impaled the fuel tank on one of the bikes. As he again evaded the bullets that sought his flesh, he cast a sideways glance at Clay's position. What remained of the trees there was now blazing. As he nocked another arrow, another sheet of flame flared across the narrow road. These flames were however expected. Before Blaine and his asshole brigade had arrived, the brothers had found a fallen tree trunk and with much effort, levered it up into position then doused it with gasoline from the Jeep's jerrycan. The tree had toppled as planned, forming a burning barrier across the rutted track. They weren't taking the vehicle back out of the clearing any time soon. Clay had been ready to set the tree alight then kick it down into position. The unexpected explosion looked to have performed that task for them.

Danny doubled back to his first position. *What the hell were those guys shooting?* The explosion looked like a grenade or even a LAWS rocket. These fuckers had come loaded for bear. Air huffed through his nose as he watched the fallen biker climb to his feet, the arrow standing out from his chest at a right angle. The man swiped down with his arm, snapping the arrow free. Orange flames danced, reflected in the visor of his crash helmet.

'Every arsehole is wearing Kevlar these days.' Three men huddled at the side of the minivan. Danny fitted another arrow to the bowstring. The fibreglass bow creaked under the tension as the wiry Scotsman drew it to its full capability. He sighted on a new target.

One of the men pointed a hand cannon at the burning barrier. The arrow struck his arm just above the elbow. Danny heard the sickening impact even over the crackling of the burning trees. The man; the second of two the bikers, disappeared silently behind the side of the minivan.

Bullets cut through the night air in retaliation.

Danny was already moving.

Chapter 84

Fish leapt from the back of Blaine's bike; his grip latched tight to the first of three LAWS rockets he had brought to the fight. No way were these boy scouts getting away with any more shit. He would leave smoking craters where the Gunn brothers used to stand. He owed them for Gato and he would collect big time. He would piss on their corpse. Quantrill was still squirrelly about killing the brothers before retrieving his all so frigging important tracker unit. Fish could give a flying fuck about Delacroix's legacy right now. He was here for blood. He had armed his friends too with a deadly assortment of weapons from his *'Doomsday Stash'*.

Two of the LAWS were snug against his back, fixed with bungee cords. The third was in his hands. As the vehicles sped forward to the designated meeting point Fish pulled at each end of the single-use rocket launcher. The lightweight tube extended to its full length with a muted pop. Shouldering the weapon, he crept forward; seeking a target. Using the trees which stood at seemingly abstract angles, as cover, Fish flitted from one point of cover to the next. The LAWS on his shoulder caught momentarily on an overhanging branch. With a silent curse, he tugged the weapon free.

As Fish repositioned the deadly canister on top of his shoulder his eyes snapped to the left. *Someone there?* A patch of shadow, slightly lighter than the surrounding shades of black. Moving ever more cautiously, he altered his speed and gait between each tree. He felt sure the Gunn brothers would be armed and dangerous. Knowing enough not to make himself an easy target by moving at a predictable pace, Fish raced behind one of the wider trees available then immediately doubled back. No bullets ripped through his body. He allowed himself a smile, his grip slightly tightening on the trigger mechanism. The weapon was a beast. The single-use rocket launcher was built for idiots to use. Once armed, just squeeze down on the trigger plate housed on the top of the tube.

Fish wasn't even sure if one of the brothers lay hidden in the shadow he fixated on. That wasn't going to stop him.

Let's get this party started.

Fish squeezed down on the tube. The trees in front of him exploded in a concussive whoosh of smoke and flame. Pieces of shattered timber flew in every direction. A spinning branch walloped into Fish's chest, bouncing off the lightweight body armour he wore. His voice was loud, 'That's what I'm talking about. Take that, bitches.'

A column of fire engulfed the trunk of a tree a yard to the left of the explosion. Slowly at first then with an alarming suddenness, the burning tree dropped across the width of the road. A shower of sparks flew into the air as the bole came to rest at a diagonal, its upper branches crackling as the fire rapidly spread. Fish cast aside the empty tube. His right hand drew the pistol from his hip. The Desert Eagle was one of his favourite weapons. The pistol felt reassuringly heavy. The hand cannon was chambered for .50 calibre, with a seven-round magazine. Only seven shots, but it just took one hit from the Eagle and they tended to stay down. Each of his Eagles was a prized item in his prepper stash. Fish moved closer to the burning trees, his left hand securely cupping the butt of the pistol grip.

Thick grey smoke stung his eyes as he marched forward, intent on finding a definite target, or even better the dead body of one. A staccato rattle of gunfire sounded through the surrounding trees. He had armed his four friends well, each man taking his fill from his prepper armoury. Fish angled his weapon as the sound of something splashing in nearby water caught his attention. A shadow moved way over to his right. The pistol boomed, bucking in his hand. A second shot followed in less than a second. If the LAWS hadn't got the bastards, then the Eagle would.

'How you like a fifty in your ass, you piece of shit?'

The retort of more gunfire rattled through the

trees. Fish moved rapidly towards his right; his vision hyper for any sign of movement. *Clok.* Something clunked against, wood. Fish thrust his pistol in the direction of the sound.

Too late he realised his mistake. An intense ribbon of fire sprang from the base of a tree to his left. He knew the cause of the pain in his chest; one of the fucking Gunn brothers had shot him. As he pitched back his skull slammed against something hard and immovable. Sparks danced behind his eyes. Tepid mud and water sloshed over his face as he tumbled to one side. The pain in his torso was like nothing he'd ever known.

Another firecracker rattle of gunfire echoed around him. Fish managed to lift his face from the foul-smelling mud, rolling onto his side. He couldn't breathe. The bastard had drilled him with some kind of machine gun, two seconds of full-auto rapid fire.

'Bastard!' Darkness swept over Fish Wyszogrodski.

Chapter 85

The tongue of fire that leapt from the muzzle of the MAC-10 was brief and furious. Less than two seconds on full auto and the machine pistol was spent. Clay grabbed at the ruined stump of a tree and levered himself upright. The pain in his left pectoral radiated into his shoulder with a new intensity. Letting the spent weapon fall into the mire, his hand streaked to his waistband and drew the Glock 17. Clay crab-walked towards the fallen man. He'd caught the full load centre mass. There was no way he was shooting any more rockets tonight. Clay's head ticked once as a dark thought blossomed. *'Body armour?'*

A parabellum round through the face would lay any uncertainty to rest.

'Fish?'

The voice was little more than a cold whisper. Somewhere over to his right.

'Fish? You get the fucker?'

Another gunman close by.

Turning slowly, Clay placed each step with care, wary of any snapping twigs. The mud that dripped from both his limbs and torso smelled putrescent. Clay silently pushed slime from his mouth with his tongue, fighting the urge to vomit. Only his headlong dive away from the explosion had kept his body in one piece. The landing in the swamp water had been far from graceful. The trees to his right were ablaze, the heat building exponentially. Branches and hanging moss crackled as the flames devoured them. The tree that he'd planned to kick over into the road had fallen, the gasoline igniting from the explosion.

Crack!

A bullet walloped into the tree inches from Clay's head. Dodging to one side he snapped off a shot of his own.

The voice was loud now. 'Fish!'

Clay ducked low and as soon as his feet found dry ground he ran, tracing a wide arc through the myriad of cypress trees. A sharp pain flared in his left shin as he barked it against one of the hundreds of cypress knees, stubby pointed spears of wood linked to the root system of the trees. Each 'knee' tapered to a point like a living wooden stalagmite.

Crack. Crack. Crack.

Chips of bark flew from a tree less than a yard to his right. Veering first left then rapidly to his right Clay pressed his back against a wider tangle of trees; one wide enough to shield him on two sides. His lips curled as the last of the swamp water dribbled from his mouth. He'd need med shots when they got back to

Miami.

'Fish? Where are you?'

Clay peered through a gap in the vertical cypress trunks. A shadow bobbed from view. Wiping the stubborn black mud from his mouth he silently rolled his back against the wooden support. With a push-off, he moved in the same direction as the other shooter. He was calling for someone called Fish. Was that the asshole with the rocket launcher? Clay guessed so.

Go Fish.

The spreading flames caused shadows to undulate before his eyes. Something he was sure was a shotgun boomed twice. Furious voices followed the shots. Clay almost smiled. It sounded like Danny was leading the others a merry dance. His attention snapped back as he detected motion in his peripheral vision. The pale smudge moved again. The man was dressed in dark clothing, only his face registering in the less intense patches of shadow. Ignoring his many pains and the ringing in his ears, Clay set off in pursuit.

Chapter 86

The surrounding flames reflected in the paintwork of the minivan danced as if animated. Danny sprinted headlong from tree to tree, first leaping over a fallen log then ducking low beneath a hanging branch. The men in the clearing were using the minivan to cover their backs. It was a mistake they would pay dearly for. His primary target was Blaine, but every man out here tonight was on his kill list; each culpable in Chrissie's murder. The two bikers had removed their helmets and Danny could see that the first man he had hit with the chest shot was Blaine. The inkwork on the side of his face seemed almost alive as he turned, no doubt seeking a target of his own.

Blaine!

Danny had killed many men but had ended it for most with a cold and clinical detachment. Blaine was different. He had taken Chrissie's life needlessly. He would pay the ultimate toll. Yet there would be no more charging in. No more reckless mistakes. This time he would dissect them piece by piece. Taking care to place himself between two interwoven tree trunks, he took several seconds, satisfying himself that there was no silent assassin creeping behind him. What sounded like several pistol shots reverberated through the trees. *Clay.* Lowering his weight, Danny peered through a V-shaped gap in the trees. The other man he had tagged in the arm was obscuring Blaine for a clear shot. Danny recalled that the man had been called Sticks. The arrow still protruded from his arm. It would be a real bitch to pull out. 'Quantrill!'

The ageing surf-dog held out his hand. Blaine spun on his heel, the shotgun he toted tucked to his shoulder. The gun boomed. Danny grimaced. Blaine's shot hit nothing but hanging moss. 'You want your tracker unit back, Quantrill?'

'I'll take it from your cold dead fingers, you ass wipe,' yelled Blaine.

Danny drew the bowstring almost to breaking point, slowing his breathing. Shooting between the two trees severely hampered his view but the shot was a good one. The arrow cut through the night air, invisible in the darkness. Sticks collapsed to the ground. The scream he let loose caused a brief chuckle to escape Danny's clenched teeth. The second arrow jutted from Sticks' shoulder six inches above the first.

'You know there's no way you and your jolly boys are driving out of here, right?' Danny repositioned behind another cypress tree. Slowly he drew another arrow. Behind him, an exchange of staccato pistol shots rattled the night. 'I told you I was going to end it for you tonight.'

Danny watched Quantrill turn a tight circle. The AR15 semi-auto rifle that he brandished was all business. 'What will it take to get my property back?'

'You could shoot Blaine in the legs, leave him for me and then you and the human pin cushion there could walk on by. I'll give you the tracker and you can come back another day and do your geo-caching thing.' Danny almost smiled as Quantrill and Blaine dead-eyed each other. The moment was broken as Sticks let out another gut-wrenching howl. He was half-lying against the side of the minivan, his free hand grasping the space between the two arrows. The parlay had served its purpose, buying him enough time to re-engage.

Danny let his gaze drift slightly out of focus then tilted his chin to the optimum angle. The bow creaked again as he drew his right hand back to his cheek. The timing was everything. He leaned out from his position of cover and released the arrow. The AR15 in Quantrill's grasp dangled, swinging momentarily like a pendulum as he slapped his right hand to his ear.

Danny cursed under his breath. The arrow had missed its true target, scoring a gash across the side of his face. Quantrill stared down at his crimson-stained hand for a moment then levelled his weapon. The combined barrage from Blaine and Quantrill was fearsome. The tree he hunkered behind vibrated, bark and chips of wood flying in every direction.

In the momentary lull that followed, Blaine's

baritone voice carried across the clearing. 'You want me, Gunn? Come and get me.'

Danny lurched from the shredded tree trunk as both Quantrill and Blaine sprinted away from the minivan. Sticks lay mewling, huddled by the rear wheel. He wasn't going anywhere soon. *He would get it last.* Slinging the bow across his back, Danny drew his pistol and gave chase.

Chapter 87

All notions of sleep were forgotten by Gina Brockovich. There was no way she was settling after seeing the crime scene. The seat gave a soft squeak as she settled her weight. Anderson sat in the passenger seat; his arms crossed over his chest. 'What the hell are we doing, Gina?'

Brockovich looked into his eyes. He hardly ever used her first name. 'Waiting.'

'That's not our job and you know it.' Anderson shifted in his seat. 'You need to back off this partner. You think this is going to end well? If what you're waiting for happens at all, there's SWAT for that kind of shit. I've no desire to get caught in the middle of some testosterone-fuelled dick-swinging contest between those two roughnecks and the SU nut-crackers. Let them all kill each other I say. I'll happily scrape up what's left and write the report.'

Brockovich tapped a key on the in-car data-screen. 'I can drop you at home.'

'God damn it, Brockovich! This is not the way we do things and you know it.'

'Ten more minutes.' Brockovich's voice was flat. 'I can't shake the feeling that something big is happening tonight.'

'That's what I'm afraid of,' said Anderson. 'You know I'd walk through fire for you, but that doesn't mean I want you to light the fuse.'

'Anderson…'

'There's no reason to go rogue on this, Brockovich. If this thing blows up like you think it will, we need to go in with back up.'

'I can't explain it, Carl, there's just something about those two brothers. It's like an itch in my mind that I can't scratch.'

'Look, I get it, the Gunn brothers remind you of Eddie Farmiga, the guy that saved your grandfather. We talked about this. That doesn't make what they're doing right.'

Brockovich stared at her features reflected in the car window. 'It's not just that. I dreamed about them.'

'What?'

'I dreamed about them a week or so back. Two brothers, one big as a house, the other smaller and mean as a rattlesnake. I can't explain it, but I feel like I'm supposed to meet these two, that it's important.'

'You dreamed about them? What is this crap, Gina, you some kind of psychic detective now? Dreamed about them. Jesus, give me a break. You need to shake this shit off.'

Gina Brockovich touched the service weapon on her hip. It was an itch she couldn't scratch. *The Gunn brothers.*

Her phone warbled. She answered before the end of the first sequence. Callie's voice was calm and methodical as ever. Brockovich thanked the dispatcher. The call lasted less than a minute.

Anderson gave a protracted sigh. 'So? Where the hell're we headed?'

'Possible shots fired out near Reptilicus Park. The park has a night watchman. He just called it in. I asked Callie to send me any calls like this.'

'So now you're touting for extra work.'

Brockovich canted her head to one side, her lips pursed.

'Reptilicus park? That's way out in the boonies. Jesus, Brockovich, we're not dressed for that shit.'

'I can drop you off.'

'Oh, can it, sister. I hate it when you get fixated, you're like a damn Pitbull.'

'I'll take that as a compliment.'

'It wasn't meant to be one,' huffed Anderson as he checked his weapon. 'You think that this is the Gunn brothers again?'

'There's a damn good chance.'

'On what basis?'

Brockovich canted her head to one side and tapped her chest with her fingers.

'You just feel it, right?'

Brockovich nodded once.

'And you dreamed about these two?' Anderson shook his head, puffing out his cheeks. 'I don't see the connection. But okay. I'll back you; you know I will. You've got a shotgun in the trunk, right?'

'Two.'

'Okay. You win. Let's go and see what we can see.'

Gina Brockovich pressed her foot heavy on the gas.

Chapter 88

The sweat that Junk excreted clung to his skin like an oily residue. Where the hell was Fish? He had come loaded for bear. After years of jibes about his friend's prepper obsession, Junk had to admit that he had some great kit. But where the hell was, he? He had let loose with one of his LAWS rockets, turning the trees to matchwood. Then there had been another exchange of gunfire. Had he missed his target with the rocket? How could you miss with one of those?

'Fish?'

The Desert Eagle felt heavy in his grip as he moved rapidly from one tree to the next. Fish had sworn by this pistol. It was a beast to be sure. Junk stooped, his bull neck brushing under a branch that blocked his path. As he straightened, the blur of motion ticked in his peripheral vision. Something moved. Something big. Something fast.

Junk's voice rasped between clenched teeth. 'Fish?'

A protracted scream cut through the trees. The anguished howl was drowned by a rattle and boom of gunfire. Rifle and shotgun.

Another blur of motion. The hint of light-coloured hair. It wasn't Fish. The Desert Eagle released its round with a furious bark. Another three followed in rapid succession. Junk squinted into the darkness; his vision compromised by the brief strobe effect of the shots.

A branding iron lancet of pain seared across his chest as two retorts sounded in return. His left hand flew as if possessed to the source of his pain. A bullet had cut a furrow across his chest just below his collarbone. The burning sensation was like nothing he'd ever felt before. Punctuating each shot with a vile curse, he let loose another battery of frenzied rounds into the trees. *Jesus H, getting shot hurt like a sonofabitch!*

The slide locked back on the handgun. 'Shit!'

Junk fumbled with the pistol's mechanism. Fish had made it look so easy, ejecting the magazine and slapping home a fresh one within seconds. Feeling suddenly exposed Junk scuttled on his heels, pressing his back hard against one of the surrounding trees. Smoke stung his eyes as the fire crackled with a new intensity. His hand stabbed into his back pocket, pulling a second magazine free. He closed his teeth around the metal carrier. *Damn!* The spent mag was still in the pistol. Titling the handgun to one side his thumb found the release and the empty dropped free. He pulled the replacement from his mouth and pushed it into the pistol grip. A slap with his palm drove it home.

'Locked and loaded!'

Junk's moment of relief was cut short as another pistol was jammed against the base of his skull. The voice that accompanied the weapon was inches from his ear. 'I'll take that if you don't mind. Slow and easy slick or you get your eggs scrambled real good. That's it, pass it back.'

Junk's gaze darted left and right. Where the hell was Fish? A ripple of uncertainty passed the length of his spine as he passed the Desert Eagle back over his shoulder. A mud smeared hand plucked it from his grip. Sour bile rose in the back of his throat. Where the hell was Fish? Dead already?

'How many of you are out here?'

Junk swallowed the acid in his mouth. 'Enough.'

'Fine, don't play, your choice. I'll find out my way.'

Junk turned his head a couple of inches. The face that stared back was etched by a lattice of scars. *Crap*.

'Do you know what the medulla oblongata is, slick?'

'What?' Junk shook his head, the muscles bunching in his jaw. *Where the hell was Fish?* 'What's this pop quiz crap?'

'Were you one of the fuckers that dropped me in the bay earlier?'

'Thought that would be the end of you, to be fair,' said Junk.

'Thought wrong.'

'Figured that for, myself.'

'Anyhoo, the medulla oblongata is part of your brain stem, a rather crucial part too. You any idea what a parabellum round will do to your noggin at this proximity?'

'Wait…'

'I'd love to, but I've got an uncertain number of assholes to deal with.'

A harsh slap sounded inside Junk's skull. A brief kaleidoscope of fire exploded behind his eyes then he was falling. There was an intense burning then no more.

Chapter 89

Danny ducked his head at the last possible moment, the clawed branch skimming the top of his head. Blaine and Quantrill had sprinted away from the clearing, abandoning their vehicles. There was no way they were driving out of here in the minivan until the burning log that had dropped across the road had been reduced to ash. The bikes were a different matter. They could scramble a new path through the glades, but they had abandoned those too.

Every racing step he took could prove to be his last. Danny accepted this as he gave chase, knowing that he was being led into a trap. There was no other reason for the two heavily armed men to flee. They weren't afraid. They would try to flank him, catch him unawares or lure him into a bottleneck and drop him.

That wouldn't stop him following.

The Kimber Micro 9 pistol was a snug fit in his hand, the bow now slung tight across his back. The pistol held only seven shots. Every 9mm round would need to count. Quantrill was toting an AR15 and Blaine had lit up the night with an assault shotgun. Both men too could easily have sidearms in addition to their long weapons; a safe bet they would.

That wouldn't stop him following and killing them both.

Danny's left hand brushed the tracker unit that he had taken from Quantrill. The corner of his mouth twitched as he considered putting one of the seven shots through the screen. But no, it might still have value.

The two men reached the chain-link fence at the far side of the clearing, both running side by side. Danny dodged left using a tree as cover. The Kimber was not suited for long-range shots. He would need to be within spitting distance to put these fuckers down. Blaine was wearing body armour which had saved him from the arrow in his chest. It was a safe bet that Quantrill would be protected to the same level.

'Headshots it is then, boys!' hissed Danny.

Blaine's shotgun boomed. Quantrill dropped to one knee, his rifle sweeping the clearing, searching for a target. Danny could feel his heart hammering in his chest as he held his position.

Blaine kicked the now ruined lock free, then pulled at the chain, the links rattling loud in the night. The gates swung open on rusty sounding hinges as both men ran into the darkness beyond.

Avoiding the direct path to the gate, Danny sprinted in a shallow arc, his pistol clutched close to his chest. As he reached the open gate he dropped and rolled. The gate was a natural choke point, a good place for a turkey shoot. No bullet storm erupted, and Danny exhaled as he came to his feet. The path beyond the gate was almost identical to the one that had led them through the glades. A pair of ruts carved into the dirt, a scattering of worn gravel here and there. Thick bushes loomed either side of the track. Each outcrop of shrubs would provide adequate cover for a shooter. Cursing under his breath Danny slowed his pace. One mistake would likely prove to be his last. A sound from up ahead caught his attention. A raised voice.

Danny silently slipped between two of the burgeoning plants, pushing branches from his path. He turned his head as a sharp twig raked his chin.

The raised voice cut through the darkness. 'You can't be in here!'

The next sound that came was not a raised voice but a plea for help.

Chapter 90

Sonny Chen turned off the lights, plunging his office into darkness, a pattern of strobing flashes again catching his attention. Moments later the tell-tale sounds followed. Rattles and booms. It was gunfire; he was sure of it. He had heard it many times in his past. His legs protested fiercely as he jogged up the set of stairs to the manager's office. Kenny, the owner, left it unlocked during Chen's shift as a night watchman. The cabinets and desk were locked for safekeeping but Chen was free to use the coffee machine at any time. But all thoughts of the Saeco and its delicious brews were forgotten.

Sonny Chen had been a watchman at Reptilicus Park for nine years, joining just after it had opened. The balmy Floridian weather suited him just fine after a lifetime of Baltimore winters. The security at the park was so low key it was hardly a real job. He spent most nights slumbering through the shift, half-watching Netflix on his iPad.

But not tonight.

He had called the police moments before climbing the stairs. How long would it take them to get out here? He didn't know. He had no police training.

His former life had consisted of repairing vending machines in the greater Baltimore region. No police training, no military service. He carried no firearms. The job had never required it. A few years back some college kids had broken in, trying to mess with the animals. Not a good idea. Some of the residents of Reptilicus Park had more teeth than the kids had IQ points. A firearm had not been necessary to shoo the drunken pranksters off the grounds.

Another boom echoed through the night. It sounded much louder and closer.

'Shit!' Chen pulled his Maglite from his belt, hefting the aluminium alloy tube with white knuckles. There was no way anyone was coming in to injure or kill any of the animals, not on his watch. Maybe if he switched on the outside lights that would be enough to send the intruders scuttling into the night? He hoped so. The trip back down the stairs was easier on his knees. Chen pulled open the metal cover of the circuit breaker box. His hand hovered over the set of twelve nubby switches. Then in one motion he swiped the edge of his hand down. The halogen spotlights lit up the park in incandescent splendour.

Gripping the Maglite like a billy club, he stepped outside. He glanced over to his left. The door to the 'gator house was closed. That was the last place he wanted any trespasser breaking into.

The breath caught in Chen's throat as two men

raced directly at him. Both carried weapons that looked terrifying. One of the men span on his heel and let loose a rapid set of three shots. With no idea of what the man was shooting at Chen too turned and made for the door, he had just used. If he could get back inside and drop the deadbolt...

'You can't be in here!' Then the bigger of the two men was on him. The man's hand clamped onto Chen's collar, dragging him off his feet. Bared teeth loomed inches from Chen's ear. Twisting in the iron grip, the ageing watchman stared into an intricate tattoo that marred one side of his captor's face.

'Who else is inside?'

Chen shook his head in the negative. His voice was little more than a croak, his mouth dryer than he ever thought possible. 'No one. I'm here on my own.'

Chen found himself crashing to the ground, his head bouncing against the bottom step of the access platform. The business end of the shotgun was now pointed directly at his face. 'Wait! Don't!'

The tattooed man cast a hurried glance at his accomplice. 'Quantrill, in here!'

The man with the rifle faltered, his weapon bobbing as if seeking an uncertain target.

Chen pressed his spine into the concrete. 'I...I called the cops. You better run while you have the chance.'

'Cops, huh?' The big man stared down with undisguised contempt. 'Let them come. I'll end it for them too.'

Chen screwed his eyes shut as his tormentor reversed the shotgun in his grip and brought the stock down into the side of his face. The impact was sickening, and Chen lay as still as a corpse. The sounds of rapid steps passed close by him as he tried not to vomit over himself. He kept his eyes closed long after the men passed by. Sweat beaded on his face, clung to the small of his back as he lay motionless. He could feel his face beginning to swell and tighten.

Chapter 91

The flames from the downed tree quickly spread, devouring the Spanish moss that hung from surrounding trees in profusion. The moss crackled as hungry tendrils of fire spread from branch to branch. Clay moved away from the burning curtain. The resulting smoke carried an acrid smell. Taking care to protect his vision Clay squinted, his eyes barely open. A rapid scuttling run took him into the wider turning area. The minivan sat at an oblique angle as if mid-way through a turn, then abandoned. The shaft of an arrow protruded from the front grille. Two motorbikes lay on their sides. The fuel tank on the nearest bike too was punctured by a single arrow shaft.

The twin gates lay open at the far side of the clearing. They had been locked earlier. It was a safe bet that Danny and his quarry were down there somewhere. Clay had taken just three steps when the ear-pounding blast sent him tumbling to the ground. The pain in his right shoulder was a devil's firebrand. The Glock 17 slipped from his grasp as he struck the hard-packed dirt. Another boom sounded from behind him. Forcing against the pain Clay rolled over one of the downed bikes. Something unyielding dug hard against his ribs as he sought what little cover the bike could offer.

A series of sparks cascaded into the air as more shots followed. Clay recognised the burning pain in his shoulder. He had taken bullets before. He forced the pain to the back of his mind as his left hand found the grip of the Desert Eagle he had taken. He wrenched the weapon free from his waistband. Angling his body alongside the bike's engine, he canted his head to one side, scouring the darkness for the shooter's position.

Boom! A tell-tale flash flared from the far side of the minivan. Using the bike's engine for support, Clay snapped off two shots of his own. The man-shaped shadow ducked back behind the vehicle. Keeping the large pistol aimed at the minivan Clay rolled onto his knees. The pain in his right arm flared as he attempted to lever himself to his feet. He swore under his breath. Glancing down he could see his hand was stained a deep red.

Boom! Another shot erupted from the far side of the vehicle. Clay lurched to his feet as he felt the bullet sear the skin of his cheekbone. The minivan rocked as he slammed bodily into the side-panel. A roman candle of agony flared again in his shoulder. The bullet he felt sure had struck bone. The surrounding muscles coiled, constricting even as he sucked in a huge lung full of smoke-infused air.

Move! Clay pivoted away from the vehicle, his finger squeezing the trigger. The Desert Eagle bucked in his hand, the side windows of the vehicle exploding. Moving parallel to the minivan a roar escaped his throat as ribbons of fire filled the night air. His target moved on a path mirroring his own. Each shot from their pistols punched through the vehicle body as if it were paper.

Then the two men were facing each other. Clay didn't hesitate. He pulled the trigger. Nothing. The other shooter stared back at Clay; his weapon now silent. Both men had emptied their weapons in the furious exchange.

'Well, this is a fine how do you do,' growled Clay as he flipped the pistol in his hand. 'There's never enough bullets.'

'Don't need bullets for a shit kicker like you. I'm gonna chop off your fucking head and mount it on my wall.'

Clay noticed the two shafts protruding from the man's upper arm. Broken arrows. 'That's gotta sting, slick.'

Scowling, the man threw down his pistol and his hand streaked to his back. The machete he drew was long and straight. The silver blade glinted as he raised it to his shoulder.

'I hope you can use that,' said Clay as he too cast aside his spent pistol.

'My father was a blade master, second-generation Filipino Moro warrior. I've trained with weapons since I was a kid.'

'Colour me impressed,' huffed Clay. 'Don't tell me, your friends call you Machete?'

'Sticks.'

'Never mind, maybe when you grow a pair, they might let you upgrade.' Clay drew his Bowie knife with his left hand. Every inch of his body was pained. The day's events had hammered him thin.

'I'm gonna split you open,' said Sticks.

'Quit your yackin' and let's get hackin'.'

Both men started forward.

Chapter 92

Gina Brockovich steered the unmarked cruiser into the main entrance. The sign to the left of the gates was the size of her windshield, the golden letters standing bold against the green background. Reptilicus Park.

'This the place?' asked Anderson. 'I've never been here before. You?'

Brockovich gave a single nod to the negative.

Anderson rolled down his window and poked out his head. 'Over thirty animal exhibits. Gators, crocodiles, turtles, wildcats and exotic birds.'

'Well, you just proved you can read the sign,' said Brockovich.

Anderson pointed to the gate. 'Looks like it's locked up for the night.'

'The call said that there was what sounded like gunshots from behind the park. We've no way of knowing how to get there so we need to go through the main gate and speak to the watchman.'

'He the one that you said called in?'

'Uh-huh.'

Anderson opened the door and shrugged himself from the seat. 'Keep an eye out. I'll go ring the bell.'

Brockovich climbed from the car and opened the trunk. Two Remington 870 shotguns lay snug within their spring clamps. Brockovich pulled the first shotgun from its resting place. She knew both weapons were loaded to capacity. Six shells in the pipe, ready to rock and roll. The twelve-gauge solution. 'Anything?'

'No answer on the intercom,' said Anderson.

'Try again.'

Anderson held his finger to the buzzer. 'Nada.'

Brockovich joined him at the gate. She passed him one of the shotguns. 'You smell that?'

'Sorry, I had chilli tacos for lunch.'

'Dumb ass,' said Brockovich. 'You smell smoke?'

Anderson lifted his chin high. 'Yeah, now you mention it, I can.'

'And where there's smoke there's fire.' Moving back to the intercom unit, Brockovich pressed a finger on the call button. The green metallic box emitted a buzz like an angry wasp. Another two extended presses brought no response.

Anderson tapped his middle. 'Vests?'

'Just mine.' Brockovich shook her head. 'Sorry Carl, my head is all over the place. I should have told you to bring yours when I picked you up.'

'What now?' asked Anderson. 'We shoot out the lock and go in?'

Brockovich pulled a slimline flashlight from her jacket and directed the beam over the centre of the gate. She lay the shotgun on the ground. A quick tap with her foot nudged the stock below the gate. 'I don't think it's padlocked. Give me a boost.'

'You sure?'

'Well, I'm sure as shit not lifting your saggy ass over the fence.'

Anderson huffed but after leaning his Remington against the enclosure, cupped his hands. Brockovich placed her foot in the impromptu vantage point and levered up and over the fence. Landing silently in a crouch she scooped up the shotgun. Turning in a slow half-circle Brockovich shouldered the Remington. No immediate danger. The gate latch resisted her first attempt but opened with a slight squeal as she bumped the gate with her shoulder.

Anderson joined her, shotgun in hand. 'So, what are we looking at here?'

Brockovich canted the shotgun to a safe angle and nodded at the angular silhouette. 'You see that orange glow behind those buildings.'

'Uh-huh.' Anderson opened the second gate and dropped the bolt into a hole in the concrete. 'Looks like the barbeque got out of hand.'

'Yeah,' said Brockovich. An image from her dream strobed through her mind; *one of the brothers running toward her, behind him, a wall of flames.* 'And then some.'

Anderson moved to Brockovich's car and drove it through the open gate. 'Come on partner, let's go take that look-see.'

Brockovich cast a sideways look at her partner. Another distorted image seared through her mind. *Anderson, lying on the ground, his face a mask of agony, his hands reaching for her. Fire.* The detective blinked the image away as she slipped into the passenger seat. 'Be careful, Carl.'

The silhouette of the building showed a series of squat rectangular structures. As Carl guided the car Brockovich peered at each one in turn. The buildings looked to be the size of maybe two shipping containers. Behind the buildings, the glow of flames seemed to undulate, casting irregular shadows. 'Slow and steady.'

Anderson gave a nod.

Brockovich took a deep breath, held it, then like a pressure release valve, exhaled. What the hell was she doing here? Why hadn't she followed Anderson's logic and brought proper backup?

The image from her dream assailed her once more: *a wall of flames.*

Chapter 93

Curtis Quantrill took the short flight of steps in a coordinated leap. Shouldering the door open hard on its hinges, he swept the room with his weapon. No other security guards tried to intercept him. The old guy that Blaine had just dropped was more than likely here on his own. The room was configured in a basic office layout. Two desks, each adorned with a computer screen stood to his left. To his right an older model copier machine, a printer, and a coffee station. At the far end of the office another door, its window frosted.

Blaine strode into the room, his shotgun canted across his chest. 'That dick wad is only five steps behind us.'

Quantrill showed a tight-lipped smile. 'Good. I want my tracker unit back.'

'I just want him dead,' said Blaine.

'That as well,' agreed, Quantrill. An image of Sticks peppered with arrows flashed through his mind, his friend bloodied and down. Gato, dead and wrapped in a tarp. A few rapid steps carried him to the opposite side of the room. The door opened easily. A narrow corridor turned a corner. A sign with a cartoon style hand pointed in the direction of the turn. Below the wide fingers, another sign: *Danger! Live Animals!*

'This is a good place to take this asshole down,' stated Blaine. 'You hunker down behind that desk and I'll go wide. No way he can get in here without us dropping him like a sack of shit.'

Quantrill glanced at Blaine, begrudging the fact that for the first time in a long time he had provided a viable idea. 'Go for his legs if you can. That way I can quiz him if he isn't carrying my tracker on him.'

'I'm gonna take his head off!' said Blaine.

'Blaine, for god's sake. There's a lot more going on here than the butting of heads.'

'That's your business Curtis, not mine. I owe this asshole the dirt nap and I aim to deliver.'

'He's got Delacroix's tracker and that means millions of dollars shared between us.'

'I could care less about dickhead Delacroix,' grunted Blaine.

'I'm warning you, Blaine!'

'And who the fuck do you think you are, to warn me about anything? I work with you, not for you.'

Curtis felt his rifle angle towards Blaine as if propelled by another's hand. His finger slipped back onto the trigger, adding pressure. A single burst would end the Blaine dilemma forever. A bead of cold sweat traced its way down the curve of his face. If he ended Blaine, the Gunn brothers would still be to deal with. Swearing under his breath Quantrill turned his weapon back to the door. Time seemed to elongate, seconds stretching into agonising slowness. *Where the hell was Gunn?*

Treasure worth many millions of dollars on the black market, so close Quantrill was sure he could feel an almost magnetic effect. Gunn had the tracker. The tracker showed the coordinates. The coordinates, he felt sure, marked the location of Delacroix's legacy, a legacy that would soon be his. *But where the hell was Gunn?*

Chapter 94

Danny fought the urge to sprint through the open doorway. The two men, Blaine and Quantrill had double-timed it across the gravelled road, racing from the access gate to the first of the squat buildings that stood as harsh angular shadows. Security lights burned bright above the doorway. A figure lay sprawled in the dirt. An older Asian man. The uniform he wore gave goods odds he was a night watchman. A purple welt marred the side of his face.

Danny's focus flicked between the downed man and the open door. He knew they were in there, waiting for him, hoping to catch him in a bottleneck. Emitting a vile curse, Danny made his choice. He could catch a bullet any second regardless of his actions. He sprinted to the downed guard, catching his left arm in a vice-like grip. Keeping his pistol trained on the doorway he dragged the old man to the side of the building. As he pressed two fingers to the side of the guard's neck the old man's eyes fluttered open.

'You okay old feller?'

The guard stared up at Danny.

'It's alright, I'm not with the arseholes that just

cold-cocked you.'

'I tried to stop them.'

'Don't worry about that now,' said Danny. 'Can you walk?'

'I think so.'

'Have you got a car?'

'Out front.'

'Good, get in the car and head for home.'

The guard shook his head. 'Keys are inside the office.'

'Shite. Then here's what I need you to do, start running. Head for the front gates. Keep your head down and keep moving. Don't look back, don't stop 'til you hit civilisation.' Danny helped the man to his feet.

The old man pressed a hand to the side of his face. 'What's your name?'

'Best if you don't know,' answered Danny. The sound of furniture crashing to the floor pulled his attention to the open door.

'My name's Chen. Sonny Chen. I want you to remember that. You saved an old man when you didn't have to. You're a good man, whatever your name is.'

'Go,' said Danny.

Chen shook his head. 'I figure that gunfire and

those flames are all part of whatever beef you've got with the men inside.'

'Uh-huh.'

'If you go in through that door, they'll kill you.'

'Any better ideas?' asked Danny. 'I can't let them get away.'

'This way.' Chen led Danny around the next corner. 'Up and over.'

Danny placed a hand on the metal rung. The service ladder curved over the parapet. He gave Chen a nod of approval.

Chen gripped Danny's shoulder. 'I called the cops. They can't be far away.'

'Duly noted, now go.' Danny watched Chen acquiesce, the older man breaking into an awkward approximation of a jog, one hand pressed to the side of his head.

The metal rung of the ladder was warm in his grip as Danny hauled himself up onto the flat roof.

Chapter 95

Clay snapped his head to one side, barely escaping the brutal slash of the machete. Ripping up with his weapon, he aimed for the heart. The Bowie knife cut the air as Sticks evaded the attack.

'You're gonna have to do better than that, old man.'

Clay chided as he circled left. 'Big words for a pencil-necked dip shit. Blade master my ass. I've seen better fighting skills in eighties action movies.'

Both men brandished their weapons left-handed. Clay's right arm was stained crimson, his shoulder on fire. Clay glanced down at the shallow slice Sticks had opened on the top of his wrist, another inch and Clay would have lost a hand. Despite his baiting, it was evident that the younger man did have keen skills with the blade. It was in his motion, never overextending his strikes, recovering each blow in a tight arc. His footwork too was elusive, constantly shifting, just out of range of Clay's Bowie knife.

Sticks faded back a step, his machete carried high. In one fluid motion, he whipped the blade down into the ground and up again. Clay closed his eyes as dirt and shale stung his face. Sticks barrelled forward, a bestial roar escaping his throat. Clay let his right leg fold, dropping to one knee. The machete whistled inches above his head. The Bowie sliced left to right. The impact barely registered in Clay's grip, but the blade struck home.

Blood darkened Stick's trousers above his right knee. The corners of Clay's mouth twitched as Sticks back-pedalled several steps. 'You said your granddaddy was a ninja or something? It seems that ninjas bleed just like that rest of us.'

Sticks' face was a mask of hatred as he renewed his attack. The machete slashed left and right in a deadly figure-eight pattern. Sparks flashed as the two blades met several times, Clay's Bowie batting the strikes away. A bolt of pain lanced through Clay's chest as he fought to match the speed of the younger man. The hilt of the Bowie knife turned in his grip as the machete slammed down again and again. Numbness spread through his fingers as he fought to retain his weapon.

Sticks gave a manic promise, 'I'm gonna kill you!'

Clay snapped out his right hand. The resulting flash of pain was horrible. Ignoring the sickening jolt through his arm, Clay delivered a second punch. Both jabs struck home, crunching hard into the younger man's face. As Sticks reeled back, blood jetting from his flattened nose, his weapon hovered close to his injury.

Ducking his head first to his left Clay launched his bulk in the opposite direction. The blade of his Bowie knife bit deep into the flesh under Sticks' left armpit. As the razor-sharp steel grated against bone Clay seized a handful of hair. Sticks gave out a keening wail as the blade edged deeper into his torso.

'You killed Danny's girl.' Clay twisted the blade, wrenching from side to side. Sticks came up onto his toes, his machete slipping from his grasp. A croaking inhalation escaped from the younger man's throat. Clay yanked back on his hair as he pushed the blade deeper. 'That was a big mistake.'

'Wait!'

Clay thrust the knife until his knuckles butted against the curve of Stick's blood-soaked ribs. The younger man dropped like a puppet devoid of strings as Clay ripped the Bowie knife free. The heel of his boot sent the younger man into a slow roll. Sticks raised one hand as he coughed dark liquid over the lower half of his face.

'That's the last hurrah for you, ninja boy.'

Clay held his Bowie angled across his chest. Incandescent tendrils of pain crackled through his upper body. The blood-soaked arm of his shirt clung like a second skin. Gravity seemed to exert an extra pull on his limbs. The gates that hung open at the far side of the clearing seemed to mock him.

Danny.

Body protesting, Clay headed for the gates.

Chapter 96

Fish stared into the night sky. Why was it red? Why were the stars hissing and popping? His breath was a series of shallow and ragged inhalations.

One of those fuckers had shot him.

His hands moved to his chest. The lightweight body armour was torn up something good. The very fact that he had regained consciousness was a good sign. It hurt like a son of a bitch, but he was still breathing. Shaking free the delirium, he realised what he was looking at. Wide tendrils of fire danced above him. Bright sparks crackled as the flames sought new purchase.

'Jesus Christ!' Fish clambered to his feet, batting at the length of burning wood that dropped onto his left forearm. The trees all around him were fully ablaze. The heat threatened to sear his skin as he lurched away from the approaching flames. Ducking low, he buried his nose and mouth tight in the crook of his elbow. The damp fabric of his shirt provided scant protection from the acrid smoke. The water that soaked his lower legs felt thick and grimy against his skin. Bent almost double, he pulled his feet free from the mire as he angled away from the blistering heat. He staggered, slipping face-first into the swamp. Eyes stinging, chest feeling like a mule had kicked him, Fish forced himself to keep moving. Staying still meant burning. That wasn't an option.

Something writhed in the black water close to his legs. Fish angled away from the swirling water. He knew there were gators out here. 'I'm not your barbeque, you son of a bitch.'

Clambering over the trunk of a fallen tree, his legs splashed into deeper water as he landed. Looking to his left he allowed himself a brief smile. There were no flames there. *Where were the other guys? No gunfire or screams filled the night. Just the crackling of burning wood.*

Knowing better than to shout and again betray his presence, Fish moved as rapidly as he could. As he reached the solid ground he sucked in cleaner air. His hand went to his hip. The holster was empty. The Desert Eagle was gone. He'd lost it when he'd caught a chest full of lead. *Thank God for Kevlar.* Reaching over his shoulder his fingers brushed against the two LAWS sitting tight in his webbing. He had more weapons too. *Still in the fight.*

Following the natural path between the trees, Fish managed an uneven jog. The two bikes lay on their side. Further across the clearing, the minivan stood dark and foreboding. An arrow jutted from the front grill. One of the bikes too looked like it had been peppered. Fish reached to the left of his belt buckle. The Walther P99 was half the size of the Eagle but still packed a punch. After he'd ejected the mag with a flick of his thumb, Fish gave both the pistol and magazine a vigorous shake. Drops of dark water gave a brief shower. Huffing, he slapped the mag home. *'Where the hell are the guys?'*

As he rounded the rear fender of the minivan the breath caught in Fish's throat.

Sticks lay motionless on the ground, his body curled and limp.

'Oh, no. No, man, no, no.' With hot tears stinging his eyes Fish dropped to one knee next to his friend. The skin on Stick's face was cool to the touch. The blood that stained his friend's body left little doubt. Fish pressed two fingers to the side of his neck anyway. The roar that ripped free from his throat echoed through the burning trees. The desire to put bullets in both of the Gunn brothers raged. A curse accompanied each step as Fish swept the clearing with his pistol. No target presented itself. To the rear of the minivan, chain-link gates stood open. Fish swept the clearing once more determined not to get shot in the back. He raced through the open gates.

The angular shadows vied for his attention as he jogged in a half-crouch. His pistol snapped to his left, his finger tightening on the trigger.

'Fu…' Fish chided himself as he dismissed the vaguely man-shaped bush. The last thing he wanted to do was begin shooting shadows.

A red pain flashed across his chest. He felt sure he had some broken ribs. Even wearing a vest; getting shot was a nightmare.

Twin lances of light cut through the night. Fish dropped to one knee. A car was slowly moving, tracing a path close to the buildings. Moments later raised voices echoed through the night. Fish crept forward. There he was. The big cowboy asshole. His wide back presented as a target. Was he the one that had killed Sticks?

A woman's voice rang loud. *'Stop right there! Drop your weapon! Do it now!'*

'Who the shit is this?' Fish chewed his bottom lip then decided. The Walther P99 silently slid back into its holster. Fish reached over his shoulder and pulled the LAWS rocket free.

Chapter 97

Twenty feet away, a skylight beckoned. Blaine and Quantrill were inside. Both were armed and dangerous, ready to send him to the afterlife. Bullets ripping up through the roof, shredding his flesh were a real possibility. Moving in a half-crouch Danny took each step with care. Heel to toe, Danny transferred his weight slow and easy. His jaw bunched as the roof below his feet creaked almost imperceptibly. The sound amounted to nothing more than a squeak, yet the breath caught in his throat. The slightest sound may end the game.

No bullet storm interrupted his path. Shadows moved below like primal spectres. Shadows he had to deal with. The glass of the skylight was caked with grime. Danny lowered his weight, moving slowly to one knee. As he edged closer to the glass, he adjusted the bow tight across his back. The skylight stood twelve inches above the roof, formed by two panes of glass set at a right angle. It was a sealed unit. He could see no obvious way of opening the skylight. Inching lower still, Danny caught a blur of motion. Bodies moving below.

Knowing it would be a fatal mistake to try and break through the glass, Danny moved to the opposite end of the roof. A low wall some twelve inches high traced the edge of the roof. The flat roof of the office was linked to another rectangular structure. The second building was at least ten times larger than the office. Danny moved silently to the parapet wall. Glancing back the way he had come; he could see shades of vivid orange among the darkness of the trees. The flames were getting closer.

Had the old night watchman reached safety? He hoped so.

Rubbing a hand across his face Danny considered his options. He needed to get inside. If he smashed the skylight he would be shredded before he had a chance to drop into the room below. The side of his mouth pulled tight. A couple of hand grenades would be damned handy.

With no explosives to hand Danny instead peered over the side of the building. The Kimber Micro 9 felt like a child's toy in his grip, but a deadly toy none the less. He swept the area below with the handgun. No target presented. The wall dropped away to reveal two dumpsters and several fifty-gallon drums. An upturned wheelbarrow was propped against the brickwork, on the far side of the barrels.

Danny pushed the Kimber into the waistband of his trousers then swung his legs over the edge. Going in from the roof had proved a bust, maybe a back door would prove more fruitful. Bracing his feet against the wall Danny stretched his body like a cat, only the tips of his toes and his clawed hands holding purchase. The lid was down on the dumpster. Aiming for one corner Danny relinquished his grip on the brickwork. The dumpster shifted as it absorbed his weight. One of the oil drums emitted a single ponderous knell. Using his left hand for support, he vaulted to the ground. His pistol was secure in his grip before he landed.

Whoomph!

Something exploded on the far side of the building. It was the second such sound he had heard this evening. Those fuckers had brought some serious party favours. Clay was still back there somewhere. *Clay.*

Danny wrestled his focus back to the task. *Clay could look after himself and then some.* Ten feet away from the building a chain link fence stood dull in the meagre light of the moon. Going over the fence would take him further away from his target. Moving into a semi-crouch Danny pressed his back against the wall. Pain rippled through his chest, sour bile rising in the back of his throat. The beatings he had taken still demanded his attention. It would for many days to come. Inhaling through his nose, Danny forced the air deep into his lungs. His ribs protested. Another breath. The pain was still there, persistent.

Danny moved.

At one end of the path lay the main door to the office. He discounted that option with a vile curse. That would be his last choice. Looking past the dumpster and oil drums something caught his attention. He moved rapidly. The door looked to be a single sheet of wood. No windows. His fingers traced the outline of the lock. The rounded handle refused to turn in his grip.

'Well, that would have been too easy.' Danny pursed his lips. He had lost his shim kit when the gang had stripped and beat him. No lock picking today then. He was going back to the front of the building. Crap! He was going through the front door. Into the killing field. No more options. The percussive whump of another explosion filled the air. Jesus, what now?

Danny rounded the corner.

Chapter 98

Brockovich canted her head to one side as she stared at the spreading flames. A sense of déjà vu assailed her. Anderson moved to her left, his shotgun sweeping the area as he kept pace. Trees at the far side of the perimeter fence were ablaze. The acrid smell of smoke was unmistakable. A cold spider of dread traced its way up her spine.

'This is bad,' said Anderson. 'We need to call this in.'

'Do it,' agreed Brockovich. The night watchman had reported possible gunshots, but this was way beyond that. *What in hell had possessed her to chase ghosts out in the goddamned everglades?*

Her partner was right, she'd broken protocol on the strength of some half-lucid dreams. *Visions?* She shook her head. *Idiot.* Some real back up and a fire crew would help.

Anderson was barking the information in his staccato voice. Brockovich almost smiled. Carl had his angry bear face on. Something large entered her field of vision. There! Twenty or so yards away. A large man, moving in an awkward loping run. The over-sized blade he carried demanded her attention.

'Stop right there!' Brockovich raised her weapon; the stock of the shotgun tight against her shoulder. 'Drop your weapon! Do it now!'

Anderson angled to one side, several steps away from Brockovich, his shotgun too raised for business. 'Do it!'

'I won't ask again. Drop the goddamned pig sticker and get down on your knees.' Brockovich felt the familiar coldness in her stomach. She'd never drew down on anyone she wasn't prepared to shoot. Today was no exception. She'd put the guy in the ground if she had too. Better than her or Anderson, that was for sure.

The man's voice carried on the night air; the words thick with a southern accent. 'I can't do that. My brother is in there.'

'Drop the fucking knife,' shouted Anderson.

The big man continued forward, his left hand thrust out, the knife still in his grip. The big man's face and hands were streaked with dirt and blood.

'Clay Gunn,' said Brockovich as she confirmed what she already knew. 'This is your last warning. Drop the weapon. Now!'

She watched Clay's gaze turn towards the buildings.

Raising the shotgun high, she squeezed the

trigger. The retort from the weapon was fearsome. With deliberate care she realigned the shotgun, aiming for centre mass. 'The next one sends you back to the goddamned Alamo.'

Clay remained immobile for long seconds. Her finger again caressed the trigger. The knife dropped point first into the ground. Brockovich released the breath she hadn't realised she's been holding.

'Where is your brother?' asked Brockovich. She raised her voice. 'If you're there Daniel, step out where I can see you.'

'I told you,' said Clay. 'Danny's down here somewhere, probably in those buildings. We got separated. I need to catch up with him.'

Brockovich exchanged a glance with Anderson. Moving slow and steady he angled away from her and she knew without looking he would be scanning the terrain for any further threats. They'd cuff Clay then proceed. Carl was big and ungainly at times but was a hard ass when it came down to the wire. If either Gunn brother tried anything stupid, he would pay dearly.

'We found a stack of mangled bodies at Brickell Flatts earlier today. Members of the Southern Unification no less. There was a description of a single perpetrator. Big, wrestler big, face all scarred up.'

Brockovich's gaze never faltered as Clay locked

eyes with her. 'Wasn't me. I've been out here all day watchin' the gators do their thing.'

'That's bullshit, Gunn. You know it and I know it. I warned you and your brother not to kick the hornet's nest, but you couldn't let it go, could you?'

Brockovich never heard Clay's answer if he gave one. The world exploded around her.

Chapter 99

Fish felt his pulse pounding like a jack-hammer as he made the split-second decision. The two others, the man and the woman were almost certainly cops. He hated cops. The cops had shotguns levelled at Clay Gunn. They were barking commands at him in their cop voices. *Drop your weapon, hands up, blah-blah-blah!* No way was that fucker walking out here; even if it was in handcuffs.

The LAWS M72A6 was a fearsome weapon. The light anti-tank weapon was designed for punching through steel plate armour. Human flesh and bone weren't even a consideration. Fish never hesitated. His fingers found the top-mounted trigger. *Whoomph!*

A brief flash and then the car behind the two cops erupted into a monstrous fireball. Fish felt the resulting explosion of pressure deep in his chest. *Hot damn!* All three of the targets were sent tumbling through the air. He had been aiming for the centre of Gunn's spine, but the LAWS was hardly a precision weapon. No need for precision with this much badassery. Fish discarded the spent tube.

'Now that's what I'm talking about, bitches!' Fish pulled the Walther P99 free from its holster. The three bodies lay groaning on the ground. Clay; his main target was down, his head sandwiched between his hands. He would enjoy killing that asshole, big time.

One of the cops, the big guy, was reaching for his fallen shotgun. Striding forward Fish put a bullet in his back, centre mass. 'You sound like a virgin on prom night, lard ass. Here, have another one.'

Fish again squeezed the trigger. The big guy twisted, writhing, and turning on the ground. Fish levelled the pistol, slow and easy. He centred on the gap between the big cop's eyes. 'You still squirmin'?'

'Don't!' croaked the other cop. Fish cast a scathing glance at the woman. She too had lost her shotgun as the LAWS tore the car apart. What was she? Latino? Asian? Hard to tell with the ragged crimson ribbons that adorned her face.

'An' who's gonna stop me?' asked Fish. 'You?'

'He has a family,' croaked the female cop. 'He has a wife at home, waiting for him.'

'Huh,' Fish gave a sour grin. 'Then I'm doing him a favour.'

The woman's right hand crept towards her hip. Fish adjusted his Walther and put a round into her too. Her body jack-knifed on the ground as the bullet found its mark. He closed on her in seconds. Using one boot to pinion her hand to her body, Fish pulled the service pistol free from her hip holster. He now held a pistol in each hand. 'I'll take that, little lady.'

'Police!'

Fish pivoted away from the three prone bodies as the new voice demanded his attention. Shit...more cops! He should have known. Wolves tended to travel in packs.

Crack! Crack!

Two savage impacts set him ass first in the dirt. The big cop had shot him. Despite having eaten two lead slugs for supper, the fat fucker was up, on his knees. Red rage exploded his mind.

No way was he dying here tonight.

Fish rolled onto his side and unloaded both pistols into the bear of a cop. *Body shots*. The big man managed one more shot as Fish's onslaught ripped him to shreds. *Headshots*.

Again, the voice rang out, shrill and loud, 'Stop. Police!'

The big cop dropped, unmoving.

Fish threw down the woman's spent pistol. New pain radiated through his torso. Again, Fish's ballistic vest had saved his life. The vest was torn and ragged. His fingers sought out a fresh mag for the Walther. He still had to put an end to that shit-kicker of a Gunn brother before the other cops closed on him. First Gunn, then a final bullet for the woman if she needed it. Ripples of unadulterated excitement flooded through Fish as his actions weighed true. As he'd made his preparations over the years, he always thought his hour would come as the government collapsed or a mega-plague devoured America. Yet his moment of truth had arrived because of two storm-in-a-teacup brothers, two nobodies with a taste for trouble. SHTF? It had hit the fan big time and was still flying!

'Stop. Police!'

Fish began to laugh. Where the hell was that voice coming from? Fish slapped a full mag into the Walther. He turned, sighting on Clay.

But the big man was gone.

Chapter 100

Every atom in Clay Gunn's body seemed to scream in protest. His breath was blasted from his lungs as the car behind Brockovich and Anderson exploded. The fireball that lit up the night sky sent his senses reeling.

Can't breathe.

Darkness pushed hard at the edges of his vision. A high-pitched whine burrowed through his skull with ferocious intent. Flashes of light strobed across his dimming vision.

Get up!

The world was canted to one side.

Can't breathe.

The destroyed vehicle emitted a low keening moan as a secondary explosion rang out.

Clay fought against the darkness.

Is this where he was to die?

He managed the smallest of breaths. The desperate inhalation sent a new dagger of pain ripping through his chest. Clay tasted blood in his mouth as he demanded control of his limbs. With a grunt, he gathered one knee beneath him. Where the hell was his knife? To his far-right stood a man. The man that had just taken the three of them down in one shot. Was it the same fucker with the rocket launcher from earlier? Or maybe more of the gang had come, armed for bear?

Clay felt a pang of despair as the man, backlit by fire, put several rounds into the big cop. The big guy, Anderson, was still moving. The asshole shot him again. The gunshots sounded like bricks being thrown into water. Then the guy was standing over the woman; Brockovich.

Then Anderson was shooting back!

Blam-blam-blam. A furious pistol exchange.

Clay sucked in as much air as his body would allow then lurched to his feet. The world seemed to tilt first one way then the other. He dropped to his knees but again surged upright. The ground beneath his feet felt like a hooker's mattress. Back on his feet, he angled away from the shooter. He knew he would die if he went straight for him.

Then the burning car was between them. Clay spat blood and dirt from his mouth. He took another breath, this one deeper than the last. Glancing down Clay winced despite himself. What looked like a sliver of curved metal now protruded from his right hip. Cursing under his breath Clay pulled the object free. He tossed the door handle to the ground. 'Enough!'

Clay knew he was torn up, bleeding from God only knew where; that wasn't going to stop him. A wraith moved around the vehicle; its right arm extended. Death was assured from that right hand.

Clay dropped low, like a sprinter on the blocks. He would only have one chance. Running away wasn't an option, he was too ripped up for that, even if it was the prudent course of action. The man swept his pistol side to side, seeking a new target. Clay felt his feet slide in the dirt as he powered forward like a quarterback. His shoulder slammed into the shooter's body like an express train, pitching him clean off his feet.

As both men tumbled to the ground Clay seized the man by the wrist, wrenching it back against the joint. The pistol spun away, landing somewhere closer to the vehicular inferno.

A fist crashed into the side of Clay's face. Clay gave him one in return. A wild exchange of blows, fists and elbows ensued.

Both men rolled away from each other. Brockovich had been pinioned beneath them as they had torn at each other. The two men gained their feet in unison. Their eyes locked as they stood and faced each other.

Chapter 101

Danny pressed his back to the office wall as he rounded the corner. Flames leapt and crackled from the tree line. A hundred or so feet away what looked like the remnant of a car burned ferociously. Indistinct shadows danced within the flames. Danny stared into the fire from below a furrowed brow. The night watchman had escaped in that direction. *What the hell?*

At the side of the building, a bush the size of a trashcan crackled in flames. At the side of the bush lay a misshapen strip of indeterminable material. Something from the exploded car maybe?

Forcing his attention back to the doorway, he inched closer. A flight of five steps led to the doorway. Gripping his pistol close to his body Danny dropped to one knee. The door stood open as if in a mocking invitation.

'Come on in and die'…

Moving his head in a single fluid side to side motion Danny risked a look inside the office. No bullet found its mark. Two desks, both overturned, formed a makeshift barricade to the left of the door. He could not see the right side from his vantage point.

'Come on in and die'...

Danny vaulted down the steps and raced back to the dumpsters. He thrust the Kimber pistol back into his waistband. Wrenching open the lid he reached inside and swept his hand back and forth. His lip curled into the briefest of smiles as he found what he needed. He sprinted to the front of the building. Squatting at the burning foliage he thrust the crumpled cardboard boxes into the flames.

'Come on, light you bastards,' hissed Danny. Long precious seconds seemed to tick by before the boxes began to burn. Danny could feel the heat on his hands as he ran back to the doorway. He would only get one chance at this.

Three rapid steps carried him inside the office. Veering left he vaulted the overturned desks and landed in a low crouch. A shotgun blast peppered the wall inches above his head. Quantrill's face stared back at him; his eyes wide.

Danny brought his hands together either side of Quantrill's head. A kaleidoscope of orange sparks burst outward as he struck home. Bullets stitched a ragged line in the ceiling as Quantrill clamped down on the AR15, emptying the mag in two seconds. Danny butted forward with his shoulder. Quantrill went down on his back hollering, his hands now batting at the sides of his face. The rifle clattered across the floor as it flew from his grasp.

The top of one of the desks bucked, slivers of wood exploding as a shotgun boomed again.

Blaine!

Danny lobbed one of the burning boxes in the direction of the blast.

'Scum sucker!' Another shotgun blast bucked the desk a quarter turn.

Snarling, Quantrill grabbed at Danny, his hands like claws. Danny slammed his elbow into the side of Quantrill's face sending him reeling back. Across the room Blaine was fully upright, his shotgun tucked to his shoulder. The tribal ink on the side of his face looked almost mythical. Danny pitched the second burning box at the tribal tattoo. As he moved, vaulting the overturned table, Danny cracked Quantrill under the chin with the toe of his boot. The ageing surf dog twisted away, grunting as he rolled onto his back.

Knowing a contest between a shotgun and a Kimber was a losing battle, he held the pistol close. Danny rushed Blaine, driving in below the shotgun. The weapon discharged, booming inches from Danny's ear. Blaine's body felt like a brick wall as Danny crashed into him. Ducking to avoid the butt of the shotgun that was aimed at his face, Danny grabbed Blaine's belt. The Kimber spat fire. Two rapid shots. Crack-crack.

Blaine launched himself back as a red ribbon

tore a line across his thigh. As Danny brought the Kimber up, the barrel of the shotgun again sought a target. Both men moved, crashing into a table, sending a printer tumbling to the ground. Danny felt the edge of the table bite into his back as the two men wrestled to bring their weapons to bear. He snapped off another shot that punched a hole in the ceiling. How many shots left in the Kimber?

The shotgun roared once more, scattering papers from the table, the blast so close it hurt Danny's eyes. Blaine's arms were corded as Danny tried to leverage the shotgun from his grip. The dome of Blaine's head-butted into Danny knocking him away. Danny stumbled; the toppled printer a conspirator behind his knees. As his back slammed into the floor Danny squeezed hard on the trigger, one shot struck Blaine in the chest. The second cut a deep furrow across the side of his face. The Kimber was empty.

Danny stared down the barrel of Blaine's shotgun. There was nowhere to go.

Chapter 102

The scream that caught in Brockovich's throat felt like broken glass. Carl lay lifeless in front of her. His head and upper body ripped to shreds. His once handsome features were distorted, his mouth hanging open as if in final defiance. Carl Anderson had died because of her recklessness, her single-minded attitude. Why had she been so hell-bent on following the Gunn brothers? Where could have it led, apart from a scenario like this one?

Carl Anderson, her partner, had died at the hands of some nameless asshole. Tears streamed. An image of Carl's wife washed over her. Cindy, loveable, quiet Cindy, sat at home watching television, eating snacks, oblivious that her husband of twenty-three years had been gunned down without mercy. A crimson bubble first formed then popped from a hole in the side of Carl's throat.

Carl...Oh Jesus, Carl.

Brockovich forced herself up from the ground. To stay there would be to await death. The shooter was moving, the flames from the destroyed cruiser obscuring her vision. As she made it to her knees a searing pain flashed through her torso. Her hand flew to the pain. The shooter had put at least one round into her. Her palm came away thick with her blood. The bullet had caught her just below the vest on her left side. The muscles in her jaw bunched tightly as she willed herself upright. The shooter had taken her service pistol, something she would have to live with if she made it through the night. Her bullets would be found inside of Carl's body. Where was her shotgun? Her vision dimmed, ebbing like a light with a failing battery.

Anderson, lying on the ground, his face a mask of agony, his hands reaching for her. Fire all around them.

Her dreams had manifested, made real with terrible clarity and consequence. *Fire all around.* The cruiser was a blazing inferno, the tree line too at the far side of the buildings crackled with orange intensity.

Brockovich pressed her hand tight to her side as she scanned the ground for a weapon. She coughed and gave an involuntary shudder as blood spilt across her chin. Another flash of pain exploded in her torso. Her side was hot, branding iron hot. Staggering but refusing to go down, she fumbled at her waist. Damn it, her cell phone was not clipped in its usual place.

Gina was pitched off her feet as two writhing bodies slammed into her. Something impossibly hard crashed into her face. She was on the ground again. The two combatants fought over the top of her, crushing her, with savage abandon. The combined weight of the men and their violent thrashing was terrible to endure. Her attempts to extricate herself from the combat proved futile. A skull pelted her full in the face. A starburst of agony exploded, her nose the nucleus.

Striking blind, she joined the fray, her fists scything into unseen targets. Then the men rolled off her. Gina Brockovich sucked in an agony filled breath. She was still alive.

Chapter 103

Fish spat blood. He knew now that the big fucker had earned every line that marred his battle-scarred face. He'd survived not one but two blasts from the LAWS. The corners of his mouth twitched down. The man that stared back had murder in his eyes. Clay *motherfucking* Gunn. Fish raked his belt but found no pistols.

Reaching lower to his boot top, the hilt of the Recon Tanto knife fit his grip perfectly. The Japanese style fighting knife was designed to do one thing only; kill! Ten inches of razor-sharp high carbon steel, the perfect back up weapon. The big marauder was visibly damaged, ragged, and torn, blood dappling his body, hands and his face. The Tanto would end it.

Fish wasted no words, gave no warning. Aiming for the sweet spot an inch to the side of his trachea, Fish backed the strike with all the momentum he could muster. The blade cut the air but failed to score blood. The big guy faded back, his feet moving in short crab-like steps. Fish followed, slashing backhand, again targeting his throat. A bestial grunt accompanied the strike. Clay shifted his weight, his head bobbing out of danger, just far enough to make him miss. Fish huffed. For a man the size of a goddamned Kodiak, he moved like a ghost. Tricky bastard, but Fish had a few tricks of his own. Raising his weapon high he darted forward, his left hand scooping the ground. The cloud of dirt and shale peppered Clay's face. As the big man raised his hands Fish ripped his blade in a wide loop aiming for Clay's stomach. The tip of the blade snagged fabric, but Clay again had evaded the killing blow.

Fish cursed through clenched teeth. He should have pulled the last LAWS and ended this Brokeback Mountain asshole for good.

Fuck it!

Fish reached back over his shoulder.

The pain that exploded in his neck was horrific. Clay's left hand had whipped out, a blur in the undulating effect of the burning car. Biting down against the pain Fish slashed with the Tanto, his hips twisting in the direction of the strike. His wrist felt like it had hit a concrete stanchion. Clay had blocked the vicious attack with his forearm. The deadly Tanto knife spun away into the night like the blade from a helicopter. Still reeling from the spasming pain in his neck, Fish tried to retract his hand. But his hand was trapped, twisted, but not just his hand. His arm, his whole arm was now twisted, locked strangely, the muscles bound tight like a wet towel. A wail escaped his throat as something tore in his elbow.

Fish stamped down with the heel of his boot. It was a move he had used before. Done correctly it would shatter the opponent's knee cap, ripping it free from the joint. When the big man dropped, he would get another stamp, this one to the throat. He would choke to death on his blood. The kick found a target but raked down Clay's shin. Slamming forward with his forehead Fish again scored a glancing blow. A ripple of fear flashed down his spine as he found his feet losing contact with the ground. Clay had ducked his head beneath Fish's captured arm, stretching the already flexed joint tight across the back of his shoulders. A moment of weightlessness, then the joint snapped with a mind-numbing separation of tendon and bone.

Fish tried to claw himself free.

Tried to jam a thumb into his eyes.

Tried to…

Tried…

His legs whipped high into the air as Clay threw him away. The flames seemed to reach out in a terrible welcome as he slammed onto the hood of the burning car. There was no air to breath; only fire.

Limbs scrabbling against the unbelievable heat, he lurched up from the pyre. He was on fire. His hair, his clothes.

He needed to get clear from the car. Away from the flames. *Drop and roll, drop and roll.*

His throat constricted in protest, a desperate gulp of searing hot agony.

Something impossibly hard slammed into the side of his face sending him back, sprawled over the hood. Searing flames engulfed him.

Fish Wyszogrodski could not scream.

The pain would not allow it.

Chapter 104

Danny stared down the business end of Blaine's shotgun. There was nowhere to go. Blaine was beyond kicking range, no chance of tripping him down.

'Close,' Blaine leered down at him. 'But no cigar, sucker!'

'Wait!' Quantrill clambered over the table. Blood trickled from his blackened mouth. 'I want the tracker.'

'No.' Blaine pulled the trigger.

Click!

Empty!

The impotent click brought Danny up from the floor like a wild animal. Blaine raked the butt of the shotgun at his face. Danny rolled his head, absorbing the shock and replied with two-piston punches, aiming for the savage line his earlier bullet had scored.

Blaine staggered back, blood marring his left eye. 'Son of a bitch.'

Danny scowled, ignoring the many pains vying for attention. He adjusted the Kimber in his grip. 'You killed Chrissie.'

Blaine wiped the blood from his face.

Quantrill closed on Danny.

The edge of Danny's heel slammed into Quantrill's gut sending him again reeling. Then Blaine attacked.

Danny avoided another raking blow with the stock of the shotgun and whipped the Kimber across Blaine's knuckles. The shotgun remained tight in his grasp. Blaine tucked his head, rounding his shoulders and jammed the gun across Danny's chest. Knowing Blaine outweighed him by at least fifty pounds Danny did not try to match his strength. Letting the Kimber fall from his grasp, he too seized the shotgun.

Bait the hook.

Danny made a show of pushing against the weapon, his face straining. Blaine added even more pressure.

Reel him in.

Danny suddenly reversed his action now pulling Blaine on as he dropped to the ground. Blaine sailed through the air as Danny rolled onto his back, his stiffened leg wedged into the bigger man's stomach. An ungainly somersault and Blaine hit the floor with a sickening slap.

Kill the catch.

Danny again rose from the ground like a

vengeful spirit. 'You killed Chrissie.' He brought the shotgun around like a baseball bat. Blaine's head bounced off the floor.

Danny was mid-action of again raising the shotgun when Quantrill tackled him around the waist. Both men hit the floor, their faces inches apart. Quantrill's skin was seared red. Despite looking like a surf dude with far too many summers on his ticket, Quantrill was wiry and strong and very much alive. His hands tore at Danny's clothes. The bowstring pulled taut across his neck as he was wrenched off-balance, Quantrill seizing it in both hands. Danny shucked sideways and the bow tore loose. Quantrill cast it aside with derision. Closing, both men exchanged head butts. *Clok, clok.* Then Quantrill broke free, clambering to his feet. The look in his eyes was close to madness as he gripped his trophy. The tracker unit.

Danny surged up from the floor once more. Turning into the kick, Danny thrust his leg out sideways with everything he could muster. Quantrill was blasted across the room. He disappeared through the open doorway at the far side of the office with a strangled wail. *Fuck the tracker.*

Blaine was back on his feet. Blood now streaked down both sides of his face, merging with the tribal ink.

Danny rolled his shoulders. His voice was a winter wind. 'You killed Chrissie.'

'An' now I'm gonna kill you.'

Both men tore into the fight. Neither gave ground. Fists pounded into jaws. Knees sought testicles. Fingers sought eyes. Teeth sought flesh.

Showing skill, Blaine caught Danny around the neck with one arm and passed the other behind one of his knees. Danny could do little more than tuck his head as he was sent flying across the room. He crashed into a wall then the floor rushed up to meet him. The impact seemed to jar every bone in his body. Bright spots danced across his vision.

Blaine grinned; his teeth-stained red.

Danny used the edge of an overturned desk to lever himself from the floor. Blaine scooped up an old model printer like it weighed nothing, raising it above his head. Danny braced his arms knowing one shot from that impromptu missile would be the end.

Then the room exploded in flames and fury.

Chapter 105

Clay staggered back, sparks dancing across his eyes. The man on the hood of the car was going up like a Roman candle. His muted screams were a wet gargling monstrosity. *Good!*

Brockovich and her partner were both still down. The big cop, Anderson, wasn't moving. No way was he ever getting up. Clay cast a hasty glance at the building behind. Danny was sure to be in there.

Brockovich raised a blood-streaked hand.

Crap!

Dropping to one knee alongside, he rested a hand on her shoulder. Her face was streaked with blood, her nose misshapen. 'Where are you hit?'

Brockovich's voice came through clenched teeth. 'Left side. Ahh, Jesus.'

'I have to move you away from the fire,' Clay seized the back of her collar with his left hand. The ballistic vest she wore cinched up under her arms as he dragged her twenty or so yards away from the burning vehicle.

Brockovich raised her hand. 'Carl.'

'I'll get your partner,' said Clay. He exhaled

through his nose. The big guy was dead, ripped up. He wouldn't be easy to move. The muscles in his jaw bunched as he took hold of the murdered policeman.

A startled yelp caught in Clay's throat as the hood of the car seemed to belch fire. A streak of scalding hot air blasted close to his face, he found himself dropping, ass first next to Anderson. The building behind exploded. Slivers of wood and chunks of cinderblock rained down around them.

'Danny!' Clay lurched to his feet, his hands clutching the sides of his head. The pain in his ears was sending mind-numbing needles through his skull. Brockovich was shouting something but he could not discern the words. He would come back for her.

'Danny!'

The Kentucky fried asshole on the hood of the car must have had another rocket on his back. Jesus, how had he missed that?

Clay moved like an automaton on unsteady legs, each step sending new needles of pain through his body. The rocket had struck the building a direct hit in the doorway. A fiery claw with red and yellow talons ripped at the walls. The cinderblocks above the door first bowed then dropped, clattering to the ground. A great gout of black smoke billowed like a dragon's exhalation.

A pang coursed through his chest as Clay

reached the ruined doorway. 'Danny!'

The heat stopped Clay in his tracks. The interior of the building was ablaze. Wrapping his left forearm across his nose and mouth did little to negate the effects of heat and smoke. Managing only two steps inside Clay was forced back. What appeared to be a solid wall of flame barred his way. Casting a frantic glance in each direction only served to frustrate him more. To his left the downed cops and the burning vehicle, to his right the treeline crackled and snapped, the fire there too, expanding.

He looked over to Brockovich. There was a good chance she would live as long as she received medical attention, and soon. Anderson was gone. A hissing spark leapt from the doorway catching the side of Clay's face. He brushed away the cinder and took another step back. There had to be another way inside this damn building. Moving to his right he found a dumpster and a locked fire door. No good. Heading the opposite direction took him past the burning vehicle once more.

Brockovich raised her hand. 'Gunn, there's a couple of shotguns here somewhere.'

Clay jogged back to Brockovich; his gait uneven. 'I'll come back for you, but I've got to find my brother.'

'Do it.' Brockovich canted her chin. 'I think my

shotgun went that way.'

Clay stared in the direction indicated, but could see little other than flames dancing around the vehicle. 'Can you call for an EMT?'

'My damned cell is gone too.' The look in her eyes was unfathomable to Clay. 'Carl. Check Carl's belt. He should have one clipped on his left hip.'

Clay moved to the dead policeman. Taking hold of his wrist, Clay managed to drag him away from the burning frame of the car. Ripples of agony blossomed in his right arm. There was still a bullet in there. His left arm too was not yet fully operable, the pain in his damaged pectoral a constant nag. Getting shot with a crossbow hurt like a sonofabitch. Getting shot by *anything* hurt like a sonofabitch. Huffing, he dropped to one knee at Anderson's side. He pulled a cell phone free. After handing the phone to Brockovich he began a hasty search for the shotgun.

'More cops will come,' said Brockovich.

Clay gave a single nod in response.

'There will need to be a reckoning.'

'If that's the way it has to be,' said Clay. Fleeing the scene was out of the question. He would never abandon Danny.

There!

Clay scooped up the shotgun.

'Clay.' Brockovich had inched over to Anderson. 'That's fully loaded for bear. Make them count.'

Cop and marauder stared at each other. No more words. Clay again gave a curt nod then skirted the building's walls.

Chapter 106

The horrific ringing in Blaine's ears was beyond anything he could have imagined. The floor beneath him seemed to undulate, rocking wildly like a boat at sea. The doorway or what was left of it was a curtain of fire. Ceiling tiles dropped like incendiary flakes in a storm. Bare wires now protruded from the wall nearest the door, angry sparks flashing through the thickening smoke. Something in the roof gave a muted pop and yet more sparks began to cascade. Water too now sprayed the room, the fire sprinklers active.

Where the hell was Quantrill? Had he been caught in the unexpected blast? Blaine wasn't sure. Danny friggin' Gunn had been closer to the doorway than Quantrill. Blaine shook his head to regain some equilibrium. Using the edge of the overturned desk as the support he climbed to his feet like a wrestler preparing a mid-match comeback.

Danny Gunn was doing the same, hand over hand, using a filing cabinet as an impromptu mobility aid. This wasn't over.

Blaine locked his gaze with Gunn. The wiry little bastard was earning his stripes tonight. The look in the Scotsman's eyes carried the same flint edge as before. Getting blown out of his footprints hadn't dampened his urge for retribution.

Then Blaine realised Gunn had kicked Quantrill out of the room, side-kicked him like Bruce-shit-kicking-Lee.

Black smoke was filling the room at an alarming rate, catching deep at the back of his throat. With eyes stinging he made for the open doorway. A ceiling light flickered sporadically lending a strobe effect. Using the walls as support, Blaine scuttled on unsteady legs. Immolation was not a way he wanted to die. Gunn would follow and that suited him fine. The air was cleaner further along the passageway and he sucked in huge breaths. A door stood open at the far end of the corridor. A printed sign next to the door declared: DANGER LIVE ANIMALS.

'You killed Chrissie!'

Blaine cast a glance over his shoulder. Gunn was moving like a punch-drunk boxer, but he was still moving. Blaine clattered through the open door. Quantrill was nowhere in sight. He would settle things with Curtis later. The room looked like an industrial kitchen; stainless steel countertops and wide sink units. Mesh fronted cabinets held a myriad of plastic containers, each labelled in bold black print. At the far side of the room stood a pallet stacked with oversized bags, animal feed if he cared to hazard a guess. Space smelled of disinfectant and old straw. It was a better smell than smoke.

The door clattered again, and Danny Gunn burst into the room. 'Going somewhere, fucknuts?'

Blaine gave a short huff, the sides of his mouth curling for a second. He gave no verbal response instead put a little more distance between them. He wiped at the blood and water that dappled his face. Another huff. He spat out a red gobbet as he looked his adversary up and down. The little bastard was tough and wiry, but he was knocked to shit, that was plain to see. Blaine would end him.

'Keep coming asshole, I'll knock the Guinness out of you.'

'That's Irish,' replied Danny as he advanced. 'Arsehole!'

Blaine shrugged as he pulled something free from the wall. Another two knives rattled across the metal counter as they dropped from the magnetic bar. The cleaver that he held was a solid piece of steel and looked to be razor-sharp. The weight felt good in his hand. It would only take one good shot from this bad boy and it would be the end of Gunn.

The wiry little bastard kept advancing.

Blaine readied the cleaver, hefting it near his shoulder.

Gunn slowed, his hands reaching out to the countertop as if to steady himself. The sprinklers activated in a whoosh. Within seconds every surface on the room was water-laden.

'Come on little man.' Blaine allowed himself a wry smile. 'Chop, chop.'

Gunn angled sideways; his hands raised in a fighting guard. It wouldn't make a difference. He had no weapon. He had no room to duck or dodge. He was going down.

A brief whoosh of flames belched from the office behind Gunn.

Then the lights went out.

Chapter 107

The cleaver in Blaine's hand was big enough to split his head clean in half. Forcing himself to relax, Danny continued to advance. Steel countertops hemmed him into a narrow path. When facing an armed attacker there were only two viable options: evasion or pre-emptive attack. Evasion was pretty much out of the question. Blaine cocked the massive blade near his shoulder. The look in his eyes betrayed his intention. He was going to slam that cleaver down into Danny's face with all of his strength.

Danny took a step closer.

Breathe…

Danny moved his weight onto the balls of his feet ready to burst forward.

Then the air in the room turned to fire. A great whoosh of flames blasted searing heat across his back.

The lights went out.

Dropping to one knee; momentarily blinded, Danny rammed into Blaine. The big man folded at the waist. The cleaver smacked into a countertop, metal on metal. Wrapping his arms around the back of Blaine's knees, he straightened his legs in one violent snap. The tattooed brawler felt like solid oak as Danny snatched his feet from the floor. A staple move in the world of mixed martial arts, the double leg takedown is simple but effective. Danny rammed forward with his upper body, driving Blaine hard into the tiled floor. The harsh slapping sound of the fall told him it was a clean throw. Water flowed around them. Something sharp and heavy scoured across his back.

Blaine still had hold of the cleaver!

Gripping the bigger man with his knees, pinning him to the ground, Danny struck out with the heel of his hand. The first shot missed but the second, third and fourth struck home, each blow rocking the big man's head against the floor. Wrapping up Blaine's arm at the elbow Danny wrenched against the joint with a twist of his hips. Blaine emitted a pained yelp. Danny wrenched again. The cleaver rattled across the tiled floor as his grip failed. Danny wrenched again hoping to snap his elbow. He was rewarded with another pained outburst but no satisfying popping of bones and ligaments.

Blaine bucked his hips high, twisting to one side as he moved. Danny was pitched from his mounted position. Stacks of metal and plastic containers were sent flying as Danny tumbled through the gap beneath the countertop. Danny winced as the unyielding edge of a steel pan impacted the side of his head. Scrambling, casting more containers in all directions, Danny rattled his way out the opposite side of the counter.

A light in the ceiling began to rapidly blink. As he lurched to his feet Danny pitched a metal container at Blaine's scowling face. The big man snapped his head to one side avoiding the projectile.

'That all you got, maggot?'

The roar that built in Danny's throat was primal. 'You. Killed. Chrissie!'

Another explosion of flames erupted from the office. The air in the kitchen area was filling with smoke. Blaine moved to the far end of the room wrenching the door open. The light continued to rapidly flicker bathing the room in a blued strobe.

Danny followed.

Chapter 108

Gina Brockovich stared into the eyes of her dead partner. Carl Anderson. Big goofy, gentleman Carl. Dead. Murdered in cold blood by some psycho with military-grade weapons. She turned her attention to the cell phone Clay had passed her. The display illuminated, casting a blue glow over her blood-stained hands. A picture of Cindy Anderson stared back at her. The *widow* Cindy Anderson. Oh Jesus, how would she be able to ever face Cindy again?

The display on the cell changed to a dozen or so familiar icons. The display showed no signal. Brockovich shook the phone as if that would cause bars to appear. 'Fuck!'

She buried her face in the crook of her arm. Guilt assailed her. Why in hell had she followed her nose out here to the back of beyond? The dreams? The sense of *needing* to be there? What had that achieved? The death of her closest friend. Carl hadn't wanted to follow this thread. This was on her. He had followed because he was a good partner, a good friend, a good detective. He had followed his partner and she had led him to his death.

Brockovich rolled onto her knees. The red flash of agony erupted in her torso with the abruptness of an exploding firework. Gasping for breath, willing for the pain to subside, she lurched spasmodically to her feet. The pain did not subside, instead intensified, seeming to conspire against her intentions. Brockovich managed three steps then found herself staring into the sky once more. What little air she had taken in was knocked from her lungs as she landed flat on her back. A weakened cry escaped her lips as darkness threatened to take her.

No!

If she went to sleep that would be the end. Bled out in the parking lot of some two-bit animal park in the boonies. Clutching her left side as if to hold in her vitality, Brockovich again fought to her feet. Rolled onto her front. Right leg first. Get the foot flat on the ground. There. Now tuck the left knee.

'Ahhh.' Pain like broken glass in her side. The bullet, in below her vest.

There.

Left knee under.

Now straighten up, get your balance.

Brockovich shook her head realising she was talking out loud, vocalizing her instructions. A new whisper formed in her throat. 'Move. Move. Move.'

A hunched figure loomed up in front of her like a spectre. Brockovich raised her right arm in defiance and instantly regretted it. The burning in her side went from a flaming torch to a furnace. Staggering, she fought to stay on her feet.

'Hey take it easy. I'm here to help.'

Brockovich latched onto the man with a death grip. 'Who the hell are you?'

'My name's Chen, Sonny Chen. I'm the night watchman here.'

Brockovich stared into the face of an older man, his silver hair cropped close to his skull. His mouth looked slightly misshapen, his lips red and swollen. The hands that steadied her were surprisingly strong. A tear rolled down Brockovich's face. Chen looked a lot like her own grandfather.

'Are you real?'

'I'm real.' Chen gave a pained and nervous smile. 'I was making a run for it when you zipped past me in your car. I thought you might be one of those bad guys, so I hid at the side of the road.'

Brockovich allowed some of her weight to sag against Chen. 'Why did you come back?'

'One of the men who was fighting saved me. I was down in the dirt. Wiry little guy dragged me out of harm's way. He helped me. I help you. I tried to distract the shooter by shouting police.'

'That was you?'

'Yeah.'

'I've got to get to a phone. Need to call for assistance.'

Chen shook his head. 'There's hardly any cell coverage out here. You'll pick it up about six or seven miles back towards the city.'

'Have you got a car?' asked Brockovich.

'I've got a car, but the keys were inside the office.' Chen cast a pained look at what was left of the building.

'Get me to it,' said Brockovich through clenched teeth. 'I'll hotwire the fucker.'

Chen emitted a nervous chuckle. 'Drive it like you stole it, that's what the kids say, isn't it?'

Brockovich lifted her hand from her side. The blood there was a thick and gloopy red syrup. Shit. That was bad.

Chapter 109

Clay skirted the roughcast wall as he searched for another way into the building. The air was smoke-filled and caught at the back of his throat. Coughing, he moved in a half-crouch, every muscle protesting. He forced the myriad of pains to the back of his mind. Danny was in there somewhere. Had he been caught in that last explosion? Clay pushed that possibility to the same place as his pains. Glancing over his shoulder his thoughts flashed to Brockovich. She was badly hurt, bleeding profusely. Leaving her lying there didn't sit easily with him. Another thought flashed into his mind like a physical slap. His wife, dead now for so many years. Diana's mangled body trapped inside her car. Killed by a hit and run driver. No one had witnessed the accident. The other driver had fled the scene. No one had been there to save her. Diana had died alone at the side of a deserted highway. Was it to be for Brockovich?

Clay gave another glance over his shoulder.

Danny was like a mountain lion, wiry, resourceful, and tough. He would be raising hell inside no doubt.

'Crap!' Clay hurried back, retracing his steps.

He had cursed the world at large upon hearing of his wife's death. He wouldn't leave Brockovich to the same lonely fate. There must be something he could do for her.

An orange glow seemed to backlight the building. Clay was under no illusion of the source of the light. The building, vehicle and the surrounding trees were ablaze. The fierce popping and crackling of the spreading flames seemed to intensify with each step. The skin on his left forearm was seared red. When had that happened?

As he rounded the corner of the building his feet seemed determined to conspire against him. His right foot caught on some unseen obstacle and his balance shifted too rapidly to correct. With a pained grunt, Clay found himself lying face down, the taste of blood in his mouth. It was a familiar taste.

Everything hurt. His limbs were sluggish to respond despite the red flash of anger that coursed behind his eyes. A double tsunami of nausea and fatigue washed over him, keeping him scrabbling on the ground.

A voice like a winter wind whispered to him; *just stay down. Rest awhile. Just stay down...*

A bestial roar ripped free from his throat as he forced himself up from the ground. *Danny. Diana. Brockovich!*

He moved on unsteady legs, but he moved. Cradling the shotgun across his chest he laid one finger alongside the trigger, ready. With each step came a mental chiding. Twenty-five years ago, he could run six-minute miles with a full combat pack on his back. Heat, cold and pain had been of no consequence. He had been a Ranger. One of the best warriors in the world, one of the Iron Brotherhood. Clay again stumbled but refused to go down. Words, almost silent, broke free from his mouth. *'Rangers lead the way.'*

As he rounded the corner, a surprised laugh too escaped. A vehicle sped past him and for a moment he caught sight of Brockovich. Her face streaked with red. She wore a pained grimace on her face. If she was in pain, she was still alive. Clay gave no more than a moment's thought to the identity of the driver but again spun on his heel. A glance back to the burning car showed the flames were persistent, devouring the vehicle down to its frame. Yards to the left of the burning car a familiar sight caught his attention. The blade of his dropped Bowie knife seemed to glow as the flames were brightly reflected. A few loping steps and the knife slid home into its sheath.

Time to find his brother.

'Hold on Danny, I'm coming for you.'

Chapter 110

Danny fixated on Blaine's outline as a wave of nausea swept over him. He forced the air deep into his lungs, holding the breath for long seconds before releasing it through clenched teeth.

Blaine stood defiant, wearing a sneer. He showed no fear of Danny, but why would he? He had held his own each time they had clashed.

'Come on then, you gimp,' spat Blaine. 'You keep spouting hissy fits about Chrissie and how you're gonna do the same to me, but to tell the truth I'm kinda disappointed. I thought you'd be more of a challenge.'

'Keep talking fucknuts, it's coming.' Danny gave an inward smile as his equilibrium seemed to correct itself. The floor again felt solid underfoot, the walls vertical and straight. He rolled his shoulders, then his neck. The dull ache that had taken up residence at the base of his skull eased a little.

A glance showed the room was again very different to the office and food-prep areas; the walls painted various shades of green, the floor coated with thick vinyl tiles. The light and dark green tiles were arranged in a checkerboard pattern. The wall to the left held three items; a galvanised bucket hanging on a hook and two wooden poles. One of the poles ended in a loop of wire. Danny had seen animal handlers use them to safely capture dogs and the like. The second pole ended in a net.

There was no solid wall to the right, instead, a barrier of clear Plexiglass sheets topped a waist-high row of cinderblocks. The cinderblocks too were painted green. Each Perspex sheet looked to be about four feet square and attached to steel upright posts. On the other side of the barrier; a wide pool, dark and circular and still.

Blaine made a show of looking at the exit behind him. Then with exaggerated deliberation, he pulled one of the poles free from its retaining clips. Angling the pole against the wall Blaine stamped down with his heel, snapping off a third of the wooden shaft. The detached net skittered across the floor. Spinning the pole, Blaine hefted the wooden stave into a two-handed grip.

Danny pulled the second pole free from its moorings. The wooden shaft snapped cleanly over his raised knee. Holding a cudgel in each hand, Danny moved into a crossed guard, the staves forming an X in front of his chest.

Blaine shuffled closer, his face a mask of contempt. He emitted a low guttural growl.

Danny recalled the Kendo armour from Blaine's closet. Many Kendo fighters were a force to be reckoned with; fierce and determined. He could understand why Blaine had studied the art. Kendo was typified by lightning-fast attacks, rushing in to close the distance while striking down the opponent.

Danny barely had time to raise his crossed sticks as Blaine surged forward, his weapon crashing down in a vertical slash. The impact reverberated through Danny's wrists as he blocked the attack. Blaine's boot stamped into Danny's torso sending him flying off his feet.

Tuck and roll.

Danny allowed his legs to pass over his head as he absorbed the force of Blaine's kick. He was back on his feet even as the bigger man renewed his attack. Blaine again chopped down with savage speed. Danny shifted his weight, dodging to one side. Both of his shorter sticks whistled as he countered Blaine's surge with a rapid series of strikes. Although no expert, Danny was well versed in the art of Escrima. The deadly Filipino martial art was based on tried and tested sword and dagger combat. In demonstrations it resembled an intricate dance, but stripped to its basic form was brutally effective. Danny attacked with a continuous figure-eight pattern first aiming for Blaine's hands, wrists, and elbows.

Clack, clack, clack, clack.

Blaine swiped at his head with a horizontal cut but Danny moved below the danger and punched up with his right hand. The butt of his stick snapped Blaine's head back.

A second pounding blow struck home.

Blaine roared in defiance, slashing at Danny with a double diagonal cut. Danny dodged the first blow, the stave passing an inch from his face. Bright sparks flashed behind his eyes as the second attack rattled his skull.

Both men closed on each other. Blaine hammered down as Danny tucked his head low. One of Danny's sticks flew from his grasp as Blaine's weapon ripped across his forearm. Blaine's raised knee missed his groin by a mere inch slamming instead into his hip.

Twisting his body, Danny felt his elbow slam into the side of Blaine's face with a satisfying crack. The big guy shifted sideways, his wooden pole dipping erratically. Pressing the attack, Danny stomped down with his heel, buckling Blaine's left knee. The length of the wooden pole he held snapped in two as he whipped it across Blaine's forehead. A grunt befitting a dying cow echoed around the room as Danny slammed him again with the remnant of the stave. Blaine's cudgel rattled against the wall as it flew from his grasp.

Snarling, Blaine threw his arms around Danny

in a crushing bear hug. Both men wrenched side to side. Danny felt his feet momentarily lift from the floor. Hooking his head in a sharp flick, he butted Blaine in the side of his face. The plexiglass wall vibrated as they tore at each other. Both men repeatedly slammed into the barrier, each time with more force than the last. Releasing his full bearhug, Blaine's fist bludgeoned Danny, his head snapping back with each blow.

Then gravity seemed to fail. A section of the plexiglass gave way and both men cartwheeled in an ungainly tangle of limbs into a new environment. Dark water sloshed over Danny's head.

Chapter 111

Gina Brockovich tilted to one side as her stomach convulsed. An icy claw seemed to grip her spine, tugging violently. Cupping her hands in front of her face did nothing to contain the bitter liquid she vomited. Coughing, her throat burning, she struggled for breath. Beside her, Chen's voice seemed a million miles away. Dark shadows flitted outside the window.

'Worry…keep…help…hospital…pressure…' The disjointed words seemed to ricochet inside her skull as she fought against the darkness. The lights from the dashboard grew hazy and indistinct. Her hands were coated red.

Carl's face, once handsome, now shattered by a murderer's bullets loomed in front of her. She knew it wasn't real. Her mind firing thoughts and images like sparks from the burning trees.

'Carl.' Barely a whisper.

'Hang on in there,' said the man next to her. What did he say his name was? Chen? Yeah, Chen.

Brockovich inhaled, pushing the breath deep into her lungs. Something popped with a wet sickening splotch on her left side. Jesus, she was bleeding out.

Would she even make it to the city?

Her head lolled against the seat as she felt her eyes close. Eyelids, so heavy…just rest them for a minute. Darkness wrapped her like a mother's embrace.

The man's blood-spattered face was a mask of disbelief. Brockovich too was bleeding, a furrow in her scalp testament to how close his blade came to punching a hole into her brain.

'Drop it, Granger! Last warning!' Brockovich fought to control the tremble in her hands. Chasing down Granger had taken its toll. Only two months out of uniform, Detective Gina Brockovich had bumped into Granger, literally, by chance while making a follow-up house call on an unrelated domestic violence case. Granger was known and a wanted felon. Evil was an overused word but described Granger perfectly. Cruel, cold, evil. Alex Granger was a thrill killer; a rabid dog. Spending much of his life incarcerated for an ever-worsening list of crimes, his latest had left three children, orphans. Of the three he had left alive, two now required prosthetic limbs. He had butchered the Rhee family with a machete. His neighbours only infraction against him seemingly that of being Korean immigrants.

Her chest still heaving from the frantic foot chase, Brockovich had lost her cell phone in the initial scuffle. With no opportunity to call for back-up she had made a snap decision, let the killer escape, or pursue, solo. There was no choice.

Granger stood, dappled with blood, and sweat; his eyes

stark.

'Drop the knife. Do it now!' Brockovich's Ruger P94 was centred on his chest. 'There's nowhere to go. If you're dumb enough to run down a dead-end alley you've got to take your lumps.'

Granger made a show of hefting the hunting knife to his face. His tongue traced the length of steel from hilt to tip. 'Mmmm, sweet.'

'Drop it and get down on your knees!'

Grinning, Granger moved to one knee before casting the knife down the alley behind him.

'All the way, down. Place your hands on your head, fingers interlaced. Do it.'

Granger began to laugh, a sound abhorrent to her ears. 'You know what, cop-bitch? When I get out of the joint, and I will, I'm gonna visit you. You won't know where or when, but when I do come calling, I'm gonna peel the skin off your back while I'm deep inside you. I'm gonna take my knife and cut you so many times you'll beg me to...'

Boom!

The single-shot punched a neat hole in Granger's chest. The killer's mouth continued to move; his mocking laugh now a wet gurgle.

Brockovich looked on as Granger keeled to one side.

'Fuck.' Detective Brockovich watched the life drain from Granger's eyes. Two fingers on the side of his neck gave

no pulse. After long seconds she holstered her weapon. Looking back along the alley she was satisfied there were no witnesses. Looking up revealed no windows overlooking the narrow alleyway, no spectators with camera phones. It was a few seconds work to recover Granger's knife and place it by his side.

Justified…

The vigorous shaking woke her from her stupor. Chen's voice. 'Hey, you've got to stay awake. Hang on in there. We're getting closer. Five minutes more to the hospital.

The thumb she held up in affirmation was scarlet.

Chapter 112

A set of double doors barred Clay's progress. Locked. Both doors were solid wood, no windows to smash through, no easy access. To either side of the doors, a narrow strip of frosted glass, the same height as the doors less a few inches, but only six or eight inches wide. No good even if he could smash out the glass without cutting himself to ribbons. At the centre of the door, a brass lock sat solid. Shooting out a lock was often made to look simple in the movies, but in reality, was often a messy ineffective operation. Even with a shotgun, many doors resisted. Nothing else for it. Stepping to one side to avoid any ricochets, Clay levelled the shotgun. Aiming to one side of the lock; he squeezed the trigger.

Boom!

Clay raised his right foot, slamming his boot heel into the lock. The door remained solid. Another hard stamp of his heel shook the door in its moorings. Another blast from the shotgun ripped up the wood just below the lock.

Another kick. The door shook in the frame. Another kick. The door began to loosen. Clay raised the shotgun once more sighting this time an inch above the lock.

Boom!

Danny was in there somewhere.

It took another three stamping kicks, each one delivered with a curse before the door swung open. Clay rushed inside, the shotgun sweeping the room. No target presented itself. The room before him was a large empty rectangle. At the far end of the room, a sales counter, and a ticket booth. A series of dim lights, the glow afforded a wan yellow, dotted the walls just below the ceiling. Large posters, framed in a dark wood, told of the many animals beyond the turnstile. Pictures of turtles, exotic birds and multi coloured snakes furnished the left side of the room. Their eyes were dark buttons. The right side of the room carried a more threatening line up; alligators, crocodiles, even a shark tank. Teeth seemed to be the common denominator in these species. Clay gave the posters the barest of glances. The danger he was most concerned with was of the two-legged variety.

Traversing the room was no more complicated than choosing a straight path to the ticket booth. Clay paused as he reached the counter. Three doors; one to the right, one to the left and one more behind the counter itself.

Above the door to his right, a sign, *'This way to begin your Reptilicus adventure!'*. The font used in all of the posters and the signage bore more than a passing resemblance to that made famous by the Jurassic Park movies. Coincidence, he was sure.

To his right, EMPLOYEES ONLY.

The door behind the sales counter was unmarked but Clay could hazard a guess that it would lead to an admin office of some kind. Clay moved through the doors that promised a Reptilicus adventure. The room was deliciously cool, soft blue light emitted from twenty or so fish tanks spaced evenly around the walls. A soft bubbling lent a tranquillity to the setting. Fish of every imaginable colour bobbed and turned within the aquarium display tanks.

As Clay passed a vertical tube of glass, he brushed it with his fingertips. Cuttlefish. He'd always liked cuttlefish. But the enigmatic cephalopods could not hold his attention. If Danny was still alive, and he dared not consider the alternative, he would need his help.

The next set of doors swung open on greased hinges. Clay was silently thankful that the internal doors were unlocked. He had no problem kicking them open but knew that there was nothing worse than telegraphing the enemy your location. Smashing through wooden barriers tended to do this in spades. The external doors had left him with no alternative and had depleted the shotgun ammo to one remaining shell. The noise he had made was deafening, unmistakable. There could be an armed enemy waiting for him behind any of the doors or corners he rounded. He moved.

The next room was little more than a wide corridor. The walls were heavily textured. Various sea creatures were formed bas relief within the height of the walls. Starfish, squid, stingray, and turtle. On the opposite wall; crocodiles and sharks.

A series of sharp but muffled cracks echoed in the corridor. Not loud enough to be gunfire.

Clack, clack, clack.

But certainly, rapid enough.

Gripping the shotgun port arms, Clay headed toward the sound, one shot, remained.

As he pushed open the next door his breath caught momentarily. A whoosh of ice-cold water began to cascade from the ceiling. Not part of any marine entertainment, Clay knew that the sprinkler system had kicked in. Little wonder, the rear of the building had been torn asunder by the rocket-propelled grenade, now a flaming inferno. As the heat spread so too would the fire prevention measures. Cocking his head to one side he knew the sprinklers would do little to quell the worst of the flames.

Dank smelling water soaked into every inch of his clothes, already wet and ruined with swamp mud.

He paid the water no heed as he stalked onward.

Chapter 113

The impulse to scramble for the surface kicked in as soon as the tepid water engulfed him. The bulk of Blaine's body was on top of him, pressing down. Something impossibly hard rattled Danny's teeth, slamming his head deeper underwater. Fingers closed around his throat like a steel trap. The water burned the inside of his nose, a cascade of bubbles rolling over his face. Danny clamped his hands around Blaine's, levering against his thumbs. In a sterile and controlled self-defence class, students are taught that the thumb is the weakest point of the grip, pulling the digit and breaking the hold with relative ease. Danny knew that real fights were something else entirely. Digging his fingers deep and twisting had little effect on Blaine's grip. Danny's fingers slipped from Blaine's, the water doing little to help his efforts. Pulling his knees tight to his abdomen, he managed to wedge one foot against the bigger man. Straightening his leg as he arched his back provided Danny with greater leverage. He again tore at Blaine's chokehold.

As he sprang free of Blaine's grip Danny jackknifed his body, his feet seeking the bottom of the pool. With no solid foundation to be found he bore down with his arms. As his face broke the surface he sucked in a desperate breath, Blaine's fist glanced the side of Danny's head. In way of response, Danny thrust his stiffened fingers at his glaring eyes. As Blaine reeled back to save his sight, Danny followed with a straight left. Callused knuckles powered into Blaine's mouth, rewarding a satisfying crack. Danny dodged his counterpunch by a bob of his head. Danny rattled him again with a rapid series of piston punches. The water which reached his chin slowed the blows but five of the six forced Blaine back.

Danny spat foul-tasting water from his mouth as he again sucked in a sorely needed breath. They were in one of the massive aqua tanks, the plexiglass wall and now open gate stood several feet above. The base of the wall was about four feet above the surface of the water. It was going to be a bitch getting out in a hurry. Yet Danny had unfinished business at hand.

Blaine spat blood into the water. 'I'm gonna kill you now, you little prick.'

Circling left, Danny moved in a series of short bounces. After moving several feet his heels rested on the base of the pool, the water shallower there. Another few bounces and the surface reached his solar plexus. Only then did he answer, 'You killed Chrissie.'

'Mother fucker!'

Blaine surged forward and Danny timed his motion perfectly. The heel of his hand stiffened and locked back at the wrist, slammed into the target. Blaine's nose exploded in a welter of blood as the vicious blow struck home. As the bigger man reeled back, his hands bunched in front of his face, Danny Gunn surged after him. The water took away any option of kicking but Danny employed his legs in a powerful motion, pushing hard against the bottom of the pool. As he sprang high in the water his elbow was already winding in a loop. As he landed, the tip of Danny's elbow cut down in a ferocious swipe, mashing Blaine's fingers against his wide skull.

As Blaine again reeled back, his mouth hanging open in a pained grimace, Danny renewed his attack. A double snap with the left was immediately followed by an overhand right. All three punches landed on Blaine's jaw.

Danny ducked his head low to his shoulder as Blaine swung a big right hand. Danny was knocked sideways as the punch walloped like a cannonball into his shoulder.

Recovering from the clubbing blow, Danny fought again to keep his feet under him. *So tired!* Whipping out his right hand, the open edge caught Blaine just below the ear. The big man grunted but didn't go down.

The breath caught in the back of Danny Gunn's throat as something huge came bursting from below the surface of the water. Jaws impossibly wide snapped shut inches from his outstretched arm. 'Jesus Christ!'

Both men turned, their attention fixed on the open section of plexiglass. Blaine was closer. He too let out a surprised yelp as a second animal broke the surface closer to the wall. The second was between them and the only viable escape route. The two crocodiles closed in.

Chapter 114

Raised voices, muffled but delivered in rapid-fire bursts leached into the room as Clay swung open the door. Brushing water from his eyes he covered the narrow rectangular room in seconds. Rows of chairs faced a blank screen. A projector unit dangled from the ceiling. Racing to the door adjacent to the screen Clay found himself again muttering a curse as it proved to be locked. The internal door looked to open toward him so kicking it would be of little value, one shot, remaining…

Clay aimed an inch to the right of the lock. Boom. A fist-sized hole appeared in the wooden panel. The lock and handle tilted askew. Taking the handle in his grip it was a second's work to rip it free from its moorings. Smoke, thick and choking poured from the open portal. A glance to his right revealed angry flames pushing through the smoke and water.

A fearful yelp demanded his attention. The sound had emanated from the other end of the short passageway.

Clay charged forward…

Into a nightmare!

Two massive reptiles thrashed in a large

aquarium pool. Two of the largest crocodiles Clay had ever seen. Clay had encountered the creatures several times during his army days. He recognised the longer more tapered snout that set them apart from the American alligator.

'Danny!' The warning shout echoed in the room as one of the monstrous creatures surged at his brother. Jaws filled with flesh rending teeth snapped shut inches from Danny's right arm. The second reptile was closing on Blaine, its powerful tail thrashing the water.

Racing to the opening in the plexiglass wall Clay shouldered the shotgun, aiming for the croc closest to Danny. As he squeezed the trigger he was rewarded only with an impotent silence. The shotgun was empty.

Casting the firearm aside, he ripped the Bowie free from its sheath. Blaine's eyes were stark as he roared at Clay for help. The tattooed man was not Clay's concern. With no forethought, Clay launched himself in a headlong dive through the open barrier, past Blaine, and the closer crocodile.

The coolness of the water washed over him as he landed in the pool. The beast that threatened Danny's life turned momentarily as Clay hit the water. Countless teeth seemed to fill his vision as his head surged free of the surface. The monstrous reptile snapped its jaws shut as if in a warning then launched after Danny.

Clay punched down with his blade, the steel of the Bowie wedging into the thick reptilian hide. The massive crocodile hardly seemed to notice. With a single thrash of its tail Clay was sent reeling. Gritting his teeth, he powered after the reptile. The handle of the Bowie was locked tight in his grip.

Clay felt his feet slip and slide on the bottom of the pool as he tried to gain speed. Every muscle in his body screamed in protest as he lurched forward, wrapping his left arm around the tail of the powerful reptile. Flung bodily side to side as the creature moved, he brought the blade up from below. The knife struck home close to one of the crocodile's rear legs. Clay pushed the blade deeper, twisting the blade. The water around him turned red. The crocodile, contorting to an unbelievable angle, turned its focus and jaws to Clay. Immensely powerful jaws snapped shut like a bear trap an inch from Clay's head.

'Clay!' Danny's voice was broken glass to his ears.

Clay again punched into the ferocious predator with his Bowie knife. This time the blade went deeper, much deeper. Then the air was blasted from his lungs as he was slammed against the outer wall of the pool. The force from the crocodile's tail was unbelievable. A shower of red frothy bubbles, cascaded over him. Struggling to draw a breath Clay slashed with the knife, hitting nothing but water.

Then the crocodile, the biggest he'd ever seen, enveloped his right arm in one mind-numbing snap of its jaws.

So, this was how he was going to die…?

Chapter 115

Danny Gunn felt raw terror squirm as the monstrous reptile turned in the water, so unbelievably rapidly and clamped its jaws onto Clay. The sound was sickening. The crocodile had been hissing like a ruptured steam pipe. The water around Clay was already stained red. If the beast took Clay into a death roll his arm would be ripped off. Pushing hard against the bottom of the pool, Danny launched himself bodily. His arms barely met around the upper body of the monstrous reptile. The muscles and power beneath the armored hide were like nothing he'd ever experienced. The crocodile was a force of nature, a perfect eating machine. With the strongest bite in the animal kingdom; there were no second chances. Locking his legs around the croc's thrashing torso, he grabbed onto one of the stumpy forelegs with his left hand. Even the relatively short legs were like pistons on a machine. Pressing his forehead tight against the ridged back of the reptile he began to drive his fist into the beast's bulbous eye.

Clay was bellowing, blood and water erupting with each wrench of the croc's head.

Danny doubled his efforts, trying to drive his knuckles through the monstrously thick skull. The crocodile, hissing and thrashing, opened its jaws wide. A triangle of steel two inches high protruded from the upper side of its snout.

With a battle cry of a desperate man, Danny hauled back on the creature's neck. The curved point of the Bowie knife now stood a full six inches through the upper mandible of the apex predator. The pressure behind Danny's eyes clouded his vision as he hauled back against the crocodile's spine, his fingers perilously close to its jaws. The knife was ripped free. A second later Danny felt the savage impact as his older brother brought the thick blade down between the crocodile's eyes. The handguard of the knife butted against the top of the ridged skull. The great reptile shuddered in its final moments. The beast gave a protracted hiss as the tension left its body. With a scowl, Clay twisted the blade free from the croc's head.

'Jesus H Christ!' Danny's vision swam. 'Your arm!'

Clay looked down at his limb now dotted with several ragged tears. 'Looks worse than it feels, I managed to get the knife in before it took my damned arm off.'

Danny's chin bobbed once. They would both require serious medical treatment very shortly. The sound of frantic splashing snatched Danny's attention back. *Blaine!*

Danny cursed the vilest of curses as he watched the back of Blaine's tattooed skull disappear through the strands of a thick plastic safety curtain. Danny had missed the exit point earlier. Chrissie's killer had somehow evaded the other crocodile and fled out the far side of the pool.

The other crocodile!

The explosive force of nature erupted from the water. Danny Gunn's right fist whipped up like a piston, slamming into the underside of the beast's jaw. As the crocodile momentarily reeled from the blow Clay again brought the Bowie to bear. The edge of the steel blade left a gaping wound across the predator's hide. The crocodile cast a baleful look then submerged in a welter of red water.

'Move!' urged Danny as he grabbed onto his older brother's shoulder. 'That way.'

Danny felt the injured crocodile would clamp its jaws onto one of his limbs with every waterlogged step he managed. He allowed the smallest of breaths as they reached the heavy plastic curtain with all limbs attached. The curtain consisted of multiple ribbons of thick opaque plastic. Danny had seen many similar curtains in factories and warehouses. Pushing Clay ahead, the Gunn brothers stepped into another room.

Danny surged forward, a fierce pulse behind his eyes. 'Blaine!'

Chapter 116

Blaine feared no man, yet the terror that gripped his very soul was unbearable. It was no man that caused the bile to rise in his throat. The wiry Scotsman was tough and undeniably dangerous but crocodiles and alligators were something else entirely. He had barely escaped the jaws of the first croc, more by pure dumb luck than any skill factor. The beast had snapped at him several times but seemed undecided as to which target to fully pursue. The two brothers had caught its attention as they fought with the other reptile in the shallows. Blaine had wasted no time in wading to the far side of the pool. The thick ribbons of the curtain parted to show the continuation of the reptile habitat. This side of the pool proved much shallower than the previous. The water reached only Blaine's waist. The lower level of the water proved much easier to move in. The pool looked to be about forty or so feet wide, another plexiglass wall framed around its perimeter. Further past the plexiglass Blaine could see several rows of bleacher-style seats and three sets of doors. Exit signs glowed a dull red above each of the doors.

'Blaine!'

Turning on his heel Blaine watched both the

wiry Scotsman and his brother burst into the room. Both were dripping blood, the big guy more so. Blaine's gaze flicked from the two harbingers to the closest of the exit doors. About twenty feet of water, a vault over the plexiglass barrier and a quick sprint to the doors. They would be locked, but an emergency push bar glinted the invitation in the middle of the doors.

Blaine turned back to face the brothers. The bigger one, Clay, clutched a big assed pig-sticker of a knife in his left hand. Knives didn't scare Blaine. The Gunn brothers looked like hammered shit. He could take them. Both of them.

'You think that hunk o' steel scares me?' Blaine rolled his shoulders, the tension in his muscles palpable. He would take the big idiot down first, take his knife and end it for him. Then it would be Danny's turn. 'I'll take that away and open you both up from nut-sack to neckerchief.'

Blaine shook both of his hands, the numbness in his fingers abating. A grimacing smile spread slowly, his teeth baring. Yeah. He could take them.

Danny Gunn powered into the pool, his face a steely mask. 'Where ya going, arsehole? We're not finished yet.'

'My thoughts exactly, sucker.' Blaine raised his hands, his fists balled and ready.

Danny Gunn skidded to a halt.

'Come and get it, you little limey prick.' Blaine's voice echoed across the water. But Danny wasn't looking at him anymore. He was looking past him. Blaine turned his head, an involuntary yelp escaping from his mouth.

The reptile that stared back at him was the stuff of nightmares. It's head alone looked more than two feet long, most of it containing teeth. Its yellowed eyes, unblinking, fixed on him. The monstrous reptile was the colour of sour milk, its albino skin adding to its terrifying appearance. The predator was so close Blaine could reach out and touch it. He began to back away from the opening jaws.

'Jesus H…'

The crocodile streaked forward; its immense jaws snapping shut with mind-numbing force. Blaine stared in disbelief as the monster croc seized his left leg in its horrendous maw. A bomb seemed to explode in the muscle of his thigh as he was wrenched off his feet. The surrounding water turned a murky red.

Sour bile erupted from his mouth as the reptile shook its head side to side. Blaine hammered at the nearest of the albino eyes with his closed fist. A scream sprang free from his throat as the reptile, instead of releasing its hold bit even deeper into his leg. Muscle and sinew separated from bone as the croc thrashed its head once more.

'Jesus Christ, help me.' Waves of unadulterated terror washed over Blaine as he felt the predator drag him inch by inch under the water. 'Help me!'

A hand reached out and seized his wrist. The grip was like a steel band.

'Help me,' Blaine stared up, imploring. The eyes that regarded him burned with a cold intensity. Danny increased the pressure of his grip.

'You...'

Blaine screamed as the bones in his knee snapped with a sickening wrench. 'Help me!'

'Killed...'

Raw spears of agony tore through Blaine's entire frame as the crocodile dragged him into deeper water.

'Chrissie...'

Blaine managed a single vile curse as Danny released his grip. Dark water washed over his head as the ghostly white reptile again wrenched its head in a ferocious shake. Screaming in unbearable agony Blaine desperately punched at the crocodile even as the blood-stained water rushed down his throat. He tried to cough out the water. Another scream, then an involuntary breath.

Water.

Choking.

Fireworks searing his brain.

Darkness took him.

Chapter 117

Grasping one of the thick plastic strips, fatigue washed over Clay in a sudden wave. His limbs leaden, his throat dry and sore. The day was demanding its heavy toll. Every nerve in his body seemed to carry extra weight. A slow pounding rhythm took up residence behind his eyes. Yet he forced his limbs to move, staying close to his brother. 'We gotta get out of here. God knows what else is in here, and I sure as shit don't want to find out the hard way.'

The nightmare albino croc twisted in the pool, tail churning the water. One of Blaine's hands thrashed above the surface. Red stain surrounded the spasmodic limb. The wavering hand submerged in a single sudden burst of bubbles.

'Danny?'

'Aye,' replied his brother. 'I'm just pissed off that I didn't get to finish the fucker myself.'

Clay raised one scarred eyebrow. 'Getting eaten by that freaky Jurassic Park lookin' bastard seems a fitting end for him if you ask me.'

'Aye, fuck him. Dead is dead.'

Clay steered Danny to the nearest of the exit

doors. The massive tail, coloured like sour milk broke the surface once more with a powerful beat.

Clay rammed the emergency bar with his hip. The door sprang open and Clay continued to shepherd his sibling into the night air. 'We should double-time it back to the clearing. I hope our getaway vehicle is still there. I'm pretty sure I wouldn't make a walk back to Miami.'

'We'll make it, big brother. I'll carry your baggy arse if I have to.'

Clay slid the Bowie into its sheath. He flexed his fingers several times until the tremble had subsided. 'Just keep moving wee one. I'll be right behind you.'

Danny jolted to a sudden stop.

'What is it?' asked Clay, his bloodied hand streaking to the hilt of his knife once more.

'I think there's still one of those yahoos out here. The leader, Quantrill. I kicked his arse out of the office back there. Haven't seen the fucker since.'

'If he's still got a gun, we could run right into him, could be anywhere.' Clay studied the terrain, all shadows and flickering orange flames and smoke. 'No choice but to risk it, I guess.'

'Moving targets are harder to hit, so let's keep moving,' said Danny.

As both Gunn brothers rounded the building

Danny slowed momentarily. 'You do all this?'

Clay glanced at the burning building and then at what remained of the burning car. 'Shit escalated pretty damn quick out here. One of those fuckers had a gunnysack full of LAWS rockets.'

'That's what hit the office there? That makes sense now. I nearly shat a taco when that went up.'

A low rumbling laugh began deep in Clay's chest. 'Shat a taco...who said that? Shakespeare?'

'William Shitspear maybe,' replied Danny, the beginnings of a smile forming. 'Is this a crap filled chimichanga I see before me?'

'Profound.'

'Indeed.'

'Nice to hear you quoting the bard, it tells me a lot,' said Clay. He pressed his open palm to the series of bite wounds on his upper arm.

'You okay?' asked Danny.

'Yeah, I'm just glad my arm is still attached.'

'That's it, Clay, glass half full and all that.'

'Wouldn't mind a glass half full of bourbon right now,' added Clay.

'Drinks are on me,' said Danny. 'Just as soon as we get back to the world and patched up.'

Clay continued moving as he added his next

gambit, 'This is going to bring a shitstorm down on our heads. The two cops, Brockovich and Anderson showed up while you were inside.'

'Shite,' spat Danny. 'Where are they now?'

Clay laid it out for him.

Chapter 118

Clay ran his hands first over his face, then over his upper arms. Shaking his hands sent red droplets dancing from the ends of his fingertips. 'At least we made it back without Quantrill trying to put more holes in me, more than I've already got.'

Danny sat in the driver's seat; his brow furrowed. 'Quantrill was there when Blaine killed Chrissie. He's the last one on the list.'

'I hear you little brother, but he could be anywhere, no way to know. Fucker could be drawing a bead on us as we speak. I think he's a job for another day.'

'Aye, you're right,' said Danny. 'We need to get you patched up double quicksy.'

'Double quicksy?'

'Aye, that's twice as fast as normal quicksy.'

'No argument from me,' said Clay. Multiple pains lanced through both his limbs and torso, each vying for his attention. 'I think it would be easier to tell you what doesn't hurt at the moment. There will be questions from the medics.'

'We'll figure it out. We always do.' Danny's voice softened. 'I wonder how Brockovich is faring?'

Clay tried to ignore the feeling that crept behind his eyes as he contemplated the cop's fate. 'I hope she's okay, but I think we might be fucked, even so. She and Anderson seemed straight-up work-a-day cops, she'll be duty-bound to put out a BOLO on my sorry ass. You can bet your bottom dollar that your name will be number two on the list.'

Danny started the engine and flicked on the lights. Seconds later they were bouncing along the rutted track, the vehicle rattling loudly. 'I shouldn't have gotten you mixed up in this. I'm sorry Clay.'

'Bullshit!' spat Clay. 'You were right to call me. You think for one minute I would sit idle at home while you were risking your neck out here? Dream on, wee one.'

'But it's like you said, Clay, they have the death penalty down here.'

'Screw them all, that's what lawyers are for.'

'Aye, but your brief and his team are still up to their necks in all the shite we left in Mexico.'

Clay gave a single huffing laugh. 'And probably will be for the next few years. This'll just add a few more zeroes to his bill.'

'I'm sorry Clay. I don't want to bankrupt

you, I'll find my own defence lawyer, I don't want to be a burden.'

'Just keep driving and let me worry about the legalities. What else have I got to spend my money on, huh? It's only money. Truth is I've got way more than I would ever spend in three or four lifetimes. I've got everything I want at home.'

'More money than sense,' added Danny. 'Mind, that wouldn't take much for a shit-kickin' Texan.'

Clay began to laugh while clutching his chest. 'Couple of hundred bucks would cover that, I reckon.'

'Aye, with change for a burger and fries too.'

'Now why did you have to go and mention food? Damn it, my stomach thinks my throat's been cut. I'm so hungry I could eat a pizza with pineapple on it.'

'I like Hawaiian pizza,' said Danny. 'With extra pineapple, and barbeque sauce.'

'Jeez, no. Somethings are just plain wrong. Pineapple…pizza.' Clay knocked his knuckles together.

'Clay, I've seen you eat rattlesnake cooked in an old coffee can, quit grouching about the finer delicacies in life and give your jaws a rest.'

A sharp nipping pain cut Clay's laughter short. 'Crap, I think I've torn up my chest, real good. Ah well, if the cops do show up, they'll have to wait to arrest my sorry ass, until after I get out of surgery.'

'Aye, I know just what you mean. Welcome to the brotherhood of hammered shit.'

Clay slumped lower in his seat. As he slowly exhaled the muscles in his jaw bunched tight. *They have the death penalty down here…*

Chapter 119

Danny sat ill at ease in the moulded chair. The red plastic seat seemed to have been designed to dissuade anyone sitting on it for more than a minute or so, at least in anything resembling comfort. Nurses hustled past him as if he was invisible. Just another joe mishap, face dappled with bruises and decorated with sutures. In the upper corner of the room, a TV played a news channel in silence. There was no mention of last night's events on the ticker tape headlines that scrolled across the bottom of the screen. Rain dappled the windows, drumming ominous spots from the darkness outside.

A low grunt sounded from across the room. Danny stood and moved to the side of the bed.

'Déjà vu,' said Clay, his voice thick and raspy. 'Me waking up in a hospital bed, and you all up and at it already.'

'Here,' said Danny. He held a plastic water bottle fitted with a curved straw to Clay's mouth. 'It's smart water. Try to drink it down.'

'Smart water, huh?'

'Vitamin infused. And no, it won't do anything for your pitiful IQ, before you ask.'

'In that case, the next drink I get should include bourbon and coke. I always feel smarter after a few of those.'

'I think we can arrange that. Maybe a little while though,' said Danny. He again pushed the bottle toward Clay's mouth. This time he began sucking the water down.

'That's a bit better. I feel like I've been licking stamps for an hour or two.' Clay went to raise himself higher in his bed. He looked down at his arms. 'Crap.'

Danny blew out his cheeks, puffing before he again spoke. 'The doctors told me that you tore up your previous surgery, something chronic. The internal stitches in your chest had all opened and bled. They managed to redo the procedure but said your chest will be black and blue for a week or two. They picked a bullet out of your other shoulder too.'

Clay offered a wan smile. 'Could have been worse, I guess. At least I've still got all of my limbs.'

'Aye.'

'They say when I can leave?'

'No, but I didn't ask. You need to rest up,' said Danny. 'Seriously Clay, you need to chill. You lost a lot of blood and there is a threat of sepsis from both the bites on your arm and all of those pepper wounds on your legs. The doctors were hours picking pieces of gravel out of you.'

Clay gave a nod. 'Shotgun. Again, could have been worse.'

'And there was the threat of infection from swamp water. Turns out that stuff's full of virulent bacteria. They walloped us both with king-sized tetanus shots for good measure.'

'Christ Danny, you got any good news?'

'As you said, at least everything important is still attached to your body.'

Clay gave a low grunt then took another sip of water. 'You look like shit.'

Danny laughed. 'Aye, I've looked better.'

'You look like Rocky on one of his bad days.'

'Thanks for that.'

'Welcome.' Clay tipped an imaginary hat. 'Mind, you weren't much to look at before those fucknuts used you as a punchbag.'

'Quiet you, big lummox, or you won't need that morphine in your drip to help you sleep.'

Clay took another sip of water. 'The law been by yet?'

Danny shook his head in the negative. 'Early days though.'

Clay raised his chin to the TV. 'Any mention on the box?'

'No, but it seems the Kardashians are launching a new online channel where you can instantly buy whatever outfit they're wearing.' Danny clicked his fingers. 'Just like that. Isn't the internet just magic.'

'Saints preserve us,' said Clay.

Danny crossed the room and closed the door. 'I've been asking around, seeing if there's any word on Brockovich.'

'And?'

'She wasn't brought here to the Winchester Hospital. But that means nothing, there's quite a few ER's in south Miami to choose from.'

Clay gave a sullen look. 'Keep at it. Call other hospitals, I need to know if she made it.'

'I will. Try to get some sleep.'

'What about you?'

'I'm going to Chrissie's grave. Let her know what happened. Then I'm heading back to our hotel. I need some shut-eye too. I'll call around for Brockovich before I put my head down though.'

'Okay,' said Clay, his eyes beginning to close. 'Watch out for assholes with guns.'

Danny waited until he was sure Clay was asleep once more then left the room. *Assholes with guns.* So many of them around to contend with.

Chapter 120

Danny looked around the hotel room as he rubbed the sleep from his eyes. He awoke in the exact position he had fallen asleep in. Fully clothed, boots still on his feet. Every inch of his body ached. The skin on his face was tight and tender. The muscles in his jaw protested as he yawned. A quick look at the bedside clock-radio told him he had slept for eleven hours straight. Jeez, eleven hours.

A groan escaped him as he sat upright. Vertebra popped as he first stood upright, then stretched his arms above his head. Exhaling against the steel-tipped claws that seemed to be wedged in each of his muscles, Danny moved to the bathroom. He let the cold tap run for a few seconds to get the temperature down. After splashing his face with the icy water, he stared at his reflection in the mirror. Droplets traced their way over his angular features. The left side of his face was one big bruise, various shades of purple and blue, the right side wasn't much better. 'There's a face for radio, if I ever seen one.'

After pressing fingers to the side of his jaw, and instantly regretting it, he decided to forgo shaving for a day or two. Countless abrasions covered his arms, most shallow, but a few were deeper, wedges cut into his skin. He couldn't even start to identify the cause of each of the wounds. Scars: hazards of the job, he thought.

Every scar he accepted in the knowledge he'd earned them bringing down Chrissie's killer.

Chrissie. He had told her everything at her graveside.

Pushing down on the pain, Danny forced himself to move as close to normal as he could manage. He again pressed fingers to his face. Heat blossomed in his jaw. He pressed harder. With a snort of self-derision, he first vigorously brushed his teeth, then shaved to parade ground standard.

'If you're feeling pain it means you're alive, so stop belly achin' and get your arse in gear.' Danny's self-chiding voice was thick with his native Scottish brogue.

A few minutes later he retraced the route back to the hospital. The traffic was light and he made good time despite one planned detour. After finding an empty parking space in the hospital car park he gathered up the large brown paper bag and walked to Clay's room. The gold-standard private health insurance that Clay maintained afforded him a private room. That was probably best for all concerned. Danny had often likened Clay's snoring to a chainsaw with broken gears. He wouldn't wish that on the infirm.

Clay was sitting up in bed, laughing. At the far side of the room sat Terry Penn, his arm in a sling. Both men clutched food in their hands. Clay waved Danny in. 'Terry brought cannoli. Now that's what I call a real friend.'

Danny hoisted the paper bag high. 'I see your cannoli's and raise you a king-size burrito and a bottle of hot sauce and sodas.'

Penn eyed the bag with suspicion. 'How many did you bring?'

Danny laughed. 'There are eight bad boys in here. That's two each for me and you and Frankenstein's monster there can still fill his belly.'

Clay stuffed a six-inch strip of cannoli into his mouth, chewing voraciously on the fried dough and cream cheese filling. 'Today is getting better and better.'

'Wipe your face ya big lummox, it's covered in powdered sugar.' A wide smile spread across Danny's face. It was great to see Clay on the mend. A healthy appetite would only add to the rest and recuperation of his damaged body. Danny pulled a chair alongside Clay's bed. 'Have the doctors been in this morning?'

'Yeah, two doctors and about twenty medical students. They all took turns poking and prodding me,' said Clay.

'So, they recognise a medical curiosity when

they see one,' said Danny. He busied himself unpacking the bag, lining up the wrapped burritos on the bedside table.

'Don't poke the bear,' offered Penn with a waggle of his eyebrows.

Clay went to reach for a burrito but paused mid-action with a pained expression.

'Sit back, ya big ape,' said Danny. 'Let me help you.'

After partially unwrapping the savoury treat, Danny passed the burrito over.

'Gracias,' said Clay.

'De nada,' replied Danny.

Penn pointed to the remaining burritos; his eyebrows raised almost to his hairline. 'May I?'

'Of course, get it down ya,' said Danny. 'I owe you a lot more than Mexican take out.'

'Fuhgeddaboudit.'

'Seriously, Terry, if you ever need my help, I'll be there for you.' Danny reached out and squeezed the big guy's arm. 'How's your shoulder?'

'Hurts like a sonofabitch.'

'Join the club,' said Clay. 'We owe you, Terry. Both of us.'

Terry Penn bobbed his head in

acknowledgement. 'These burritos are damn good.'

Clay rolled the wrapper into a ball, coughing theatrically.

'You ready for another?' asked Danny.

'Yeah,' replied Clay. 'Not my fault if you eat as slow as you drive.'

Dany passed another burrito. 'Here. At least you're not spouting shite when you're eating.'

Chapter 121

Brockovich walked slowly, each step a challenge. The meds helped a little. Her breathing was forced and shallow, her whole torso wrapped tightly in bandages. Beads of sweat dappled her skin, her clothes clinging uncomfortably to her body. She paused at a water cooler, filling the paper cone several times. Pausing at a reception desk she exchanged a few words with the duty nurse in attendance. Seven minutes later she pushed open the door with her foot. Three men stared back at her.

'Shite!' A thick Scottish accent.

Brockovich fixed Danny Gunn with a look. Straightening as much as she could manage, Gina walked to the end of the bed, grasping the rail with both hands. She turned her attention to the third man in the room. 'You. Big guy...you need to leave...now.'

Clay lay bandaged in bed, looking like an industrial accident. 'Terry, this is Detective Brockovich. Better do as she says.'

The big guy gave a knowing nod then made the shape of a phone with his fingers. 'Let me know what's what.'

Gina Brockovich watched Terry head for the

door. 'Close it behind you.'

The door shut with an ominous click.

'Good to see you on your feet again detective. I mean that.' Clay's voice sounded raspy and dry. He tilted his head to one side, looking past her. 'Is there a SWAT team out there with our names on their hit list?'

'No, it's just me.' Brockovich shifted her weight, doing little to alleviate the burning in her side.

Danny Gunn moved a place, pushing a chair in her direction. 'Here.'

Brockovich let her attention rove back and forth between the brothers several times before lowering herself into the seat.

'So, what's next?' asked Clay.

Her hand pressed lightly to her side, her face contorting into a brief grimace. 'Well, I think I'm pretty much finished as a detective. I'll be lucky if I end up directing traffic outside an elementary school. I fucked up bigtime, plain and simple.'

'How so?' asked Danny.

'I got my partner killed, that's how so.' Brockovich stared at the forgotten food on the bedside table. Burritos. 'I failed to follow procedure and Carl's dead because of it. That's on me, something I'll have to live with for the rest of my life.'

'So why didn't you bring back up this time and

at least have a couple of arrests to even out the scales?'

Brockovich turned to Danny, studying the tiger-stripe bruising of his angular face before answering. 'I made a big mistake, pure and simple, and it got my best friend killed. I was following my bullshit reasoning, for my bullshit reasons. I watched Carl get shot full of holes. He died right in front of me. I would be dead too if it wasn't for Clay.'

Danny gave a single nod. Brockovich again studied the Scotsman's face. The absence of both fear and aggression in his eyes reaffirmed what she already knew in her heart.

'So, what's next?' asked Clay again. 'Where does that leave us? Do we need to lawyer up?'

'How long 'til you're out of here?' asked Brockovich.

'That depends on the doctors, but another two days in bed was mentioned,' answered Clay.

'I'll tell you what's gonna happen. As soon as you get signed out of here, both of you are getting on a plane, train or automobile and getting your asses out of my city. I never want to see either of your faces ever again. Are we one hundred per cent clear on that?'

'Yeah.'

'Aye.'

'I know what you did out there, both of you.

You tracked down Christine Haims' killers and you made them pay. I understand why you did it too, I've crossed lines that I shouldn't have, but at the end of the day, it still cost Carl his life. I would have gone that same way if it wasn't for you. That's the only reason you pair of roughnecks ain't wearing orange as we speak. Your names aren't linked to this as yet. If the CSI guys find forensic evidence, that's a different matter. But the link to you two won't come from me.'

Danny rolled his shoulders. 'Caleb Blaine, he was the one that killed Chrissie. He strangled her to death because she walked in on them when they were ransacking her house looking for clues to a hidden treasure hoard. Delacroix's treasure.'

'Hidden treasure, you shittin' me?'

'No,' said Danny. 'They killed Chrissie because the house she lived in was one of Delacroix's previous addresses. Chrissie stumbled into a bad situation and paid the ultimate price.'

'Delacroix?'

'Erik Delacroix, a treasure hunter. Reckon he found some mother lode. That's what Blaine and the others were after all along.'

'And the treasure?' asked Brockovich. 'Is it real?'

'Not a clue,' said Danny. 'Those fuckers believed in it enough to kill Chrissie and to die trying to end us too.'

'Uh-huh, did you get Blaine?' asked Brockovich trying to keep her face stoic despite the pain in her side.

'Aye, that fucker's gator food. Literally.'

'And the others?'

'All gone,' said Danny. 'Well, no, I'm not sure about one of them. The leader of the band, Curtis Quantrill. That slippery bastard might have gotten out.'

'Curtis Quantrill...' Brockovich made a mental note. 'Leave that with me.'

Brockovich stood. 'Remember what I told you. Gone. No more chances.'

'You'll never see us again, that's a promise,' said Clay.

Brockovich slowly exhaled. 'I mean it. No more chances.'

'You're a good cop,' said Danny. 'Like Clay says; you'll never see us again.'

'I'm not a good cop, I'm the worst kind. The kind that gets her partner killed when he should have been at home on the couch with his wife.'

'Blaine and his goons killed your partner, not you,' said Clay.

'He's still dead.'

'You gonna be okay?' asked Clay. He pointed a

finger to her torso.

'One bullet got through under my vest. Went clean through my abs. The doctor said it only missed vital organs due to the diagonal trajectory. She said I was lucky, one in a million chance.' A tear tracked its way down Brockovich's face. 'I don't feel lucky.'

Brockovich headed for the door. She had said her piece.

'How come this isn't all over the news?' asked Danny.

Brockovich half-turned. 'The department has lost a few too many officers lately. What with the massive fire out there and a meat wagon full of dead bodies, the guys upstairs are trying to figure out how to spin this as a win. The mayor's up for re-election in a few months, so it'll stay out of the news 'til it serves his purpose.'

Clay blinked slowly. 'Go easy, Detective.'

Brockovich pulled the door closed behind her. 'I'll see you both in hell because that's where we're all going.'

Chapter 122

Curtis Quantrill clutched the tracker unit tight in his left hand, a top of the range metal detector in his right. Three days had passed since the shit storm. All of his friends, his team, were gone. Gato, Sticks, Fish, Junk and Blaine. All missing, dead, or presumed dead. How in hell had that happened? A rhetorical question, because he knew all too well what had happened: *those rat bastard Gunn brothers!*

He had stayed away from his home address, fearful of police surveillance and his subsequent arrest. It was only a matter of time until they came knocking. Once the dead were identified, the cops would check for known associates. Quantrill's name was sure to flash up on a police database. He couldn't wait any longer. The cops must have tagged and bagged all of the crime scenes by now. If he spotted any uniforms, he would backpedal and lay low some more.

His friends were gone, but he still had the most important thing; the tracker unit. He could live with the trade. He could always find new friends.

The everglades had a distinctive smell, an aroma that seemed to leach, into his very pores. Placing his feet carefully with each step, he moved deeper into the swampland, past the burned trees. The ground underfoot was solid, hard-packed earth. The buzzing of insects seemed intent on providing him accompaniment as he doggedly followed the tracker unit. The older model displayed a solid dot in the one o'clock position. Quantrill turned and re-orientated himself, bringing the dot back to twelve. Dressed in high-quality woodland clothes, he carried several items on his back. The largest of these items was a fold-out holdall. The holdall was unusual in that it contained an alloy frame, complete with four lightweight wheels that locked into position forming a cart. An army style entrenching tool dangled from his belt. He paused again scouring the trees for any sign of police. Nothing.

He quickened his pace. The dot was now almost at the centre of the screen. He was close, closer to his objective than he had ever dared to hope.

Ping!

The marker dot was dead centre on the screen. Quantrill slipped the pack from his back and studied his surroundings. Trees, both straight and strangely bent surrounded him. Less than a half-mile from the scene of so much carnage. He stood in the centre of a small clearing, hard-packed dirt beneath his feet. To his left a tree was marked with three nails, with what looked to be red sheathed electrical wire wound around them, arranged in a triangular pattern. Quantrill allowed himself a smile; Delacroix had probably marked it as a secondary means of location. After placing the tracker unit to one side, Curtis Quantrill unfolded the entrenching tool and locked it ready for use. He swept the metal detector back and forth in slow considered sweeps. The detector sounded. He swept again. It sounded again in the same spot. Another smile, this one full and excited.

Turning a slow circle, he studied every inch of his immediate surroundings. Delacroix was a slippery bastard who had died rather than give up his secrets. His original team, the very men that had discovered the treasure from the lost Spanish galleon, had all died suspicious deaths in a plane crash. Quantrill would wager heavy odds that the downed plane was no accident. Erik Delacroix; *slippery bastard extraordinaire.* But not just cold-hearted, Delacroix had managed to keep his haul, his legacy secret from the world. The guy was both smart and cunning.

'Proceed with caution,' Quantrill told himself. He began to dig at the centre of the clearing. Almost immediately thick beads of sweat began to dapple his face. He scraped away the dirt, an inch at a time. An hour later, his body drenched, clothes sticking like a second skin, the blade of the shovel struck metal. The rectangular pit he had created was three feet deep. Moving now like a rabid beast, Quantrill dropped to his knees scooping at the remaining dirt with his hands. He traced the outline of a large metal container. The rectangular lid was at least six by nine feet.

'Jesus, this thing's massive.' He took several deep breaths to slow the hammering of his heart. 'Now then, Erik fucking Delacroix, what have you left for me?'

The lid of the container was sealed with four spring-loaded handles on each side. Quantrill worked the edge of his shovel under the closest of the handles. The handle sprang free with a sharp metallic screech. Moving like an automaton he repeated the action on the remaining handles. Placing the shovel to one side, he drew a thick-bladed knife from his belt and levered the lid open a fraction of an inch. No way would Delacroix leave this treasure unguarded without a booby trap. Quantrill next pulled a mini Maglite from a pocket. The bright beam from the torch illuminated swirling dust motes as he levered the lid another half-inch. He scrutinised the narrow void.

There!

Quantrill set aside his blade and fed his right hand into the gap, moving like melting ice. Sweat stung his eyes but he dared not shake his head an inch. Flexing his fingers to still their trembling, he tightened his grip on the object.

The deep breath that he sucked into his lungs held fast. With his left hand, he pulled the lid free. The hand grenade, its pin already removed, stayed locked tight in his fist.

'Got you, you bastard.' Holding the release lever tight to the grenade to prevent it exploding Quantrill moved to his backpack. Not wanting to throw it and cause an attention alerting explosion, he retrieved a roll of duct tape, its end neatly folded and ready for use. Using his teeth, he tore a long strip free. The tape held the grenade secure. Only when he satisfied himself that he was safe did he throw the grenade overhand into the surrounding swampland. A faint slash was his only reward.

Muttering with excitement, Quantrill dropped back into the hole he had cleared. Beneath the metal lid, he had removed, lay a thick tarpaulin sheet. Still wary of booby traps, he gingerly lifted one corner. Seconds later he pulled the tarp free. The breath caught in his throat. Thousands of gold coins, too many to count seemed to shimmer and undulate in the bright sunlight.

Quantrill's mouth hung agape. At the centre of the exposed container sat an object that surpassed beauty. A large golden disc, the size of a dinner plate, displayed the famous Mayan calendar. The outer edge of the sun disc was finished in a multitude of precious stones. This piece alone would be worth millions to the right buyer.

Quantrill dropped to his knees, his hands grasping the edge of the disc, lifting it free. Solid gold! *Jesus, it was heavy as hell.*

In a split-second, Quantrill's eyes flicked from the Mayan disc to the red light below. The vile curse caught in his throat. As he sprang back, the exposed Semtex charge exploded. Gasping, red liquid spilling from his mouth, Quantrill stared down, His legs were gone. Countless golden coins, cast as shrapnel decorated his torso. Clawing at the side of the pit proved fruitless as Quantrill toppled back onto the chest. The sparkling of the gold was now marred by his spurting blood. Water began to stream into the pit from two sides of the treasure trove. There would be nothing but a rectangular pool within minutes. *Fucking Delacroix.* Quantrill's hands closed on the Mayan sun disc; the gold so heavy in his grip. The red mess that used to be his legs mingled with the rapidly encroaching water. He clutched it tight to his chest as the world darkened.

Chapter 123

Clay had politely refused the offer of a lift from the airport. Sebastian Chavez was still orbiting around Celine, his returned daughter. No; he was happy to let them be. It was a simple matter to hire a car and Danny was more than willing to make the drive home.

'Five minutes out,' said Danny.

Clay nodded, taking in the familiar surroundings, Texas; his home turf. 'I'll be glad to be eating Salma's proper food again. I need to build myself back up.'

'Aye, 'cos you're wasting away before my very eyes,' said Danny.

'Is that sarcasm I detect, wee one?'

'Oh, no sarcasm from me,' said Danny. 'All you've done is eat, for the last four days. Miami's financial stability will have dropped since you left. The burrito and taco market will have dropped several points on Bloomberg, I'm not sure if they'll recover anytime soon.'

'Dumbass,' said Clay.

Danny shot him a grin. 'Hey, I think I can see

casa de fathead, dead ahead.'

'Yeah, there she is,' agreed Clay. 'Home sweet home.'

'You gonna have a shower when you get home? 'cos there's nothing sweet about your feet at the moment.'

'I'm gonna lie in the bathtub for an hour or two, I think. Chase away the last of these aches and pains, although the meds they gave me are pretty damn mellow. Yeah, soak away an hour.'

'Sounds like a plan,' said Danny.

'You can stay as long as you like, you know,' said Clay. 'Plenty of room if you feel like setting down roots here.'

'Thanks, Clay, I might take you up on that. Texas does agree with my sensibilities.'

'Damn right, the best place in the whole goddamn world.'

Danny slowed the rental as he steered onto Clay's driveway. 'Those yours?'

Clay stared at the three large SUVs parked in a row to the side of his house. All three vehicles were big and boxy, with blacked-out windows. 'No.'

In one fluid motion, eight men sprang from the vehicles, each man armed with an assault rifle. A fourth vehicle sped in behind, blocking the gate to his property.

An ice-cold spider of dread traced its way down Clay's spine.

'You know these fuckers?' growled Danny.

'Out!'

Clay and Danny climbed from the vehicle as ordered.

Clay stared at the tallest of the eight men. He shook his head. His voice was barely a whisper as he climbed out of the vehicle. 'Impossible.'

The tall man stepped forward. 'Surprised to see me?'

'You're dead. I watched you die,' said Clay.

'I told you I would pay you back one day. You think I was going to let a little thing like dying get in my way?' The tall man pulled back the bolt on his rifle. The seven men behind him replicated his action. 'Time to pay the piper.'

Clay followed Danny, diving for cover as the gunmen unleashed hell.

About the Author

James Hilton is the author of the electrifying Gunn Brothers Thriller series. His work has also appeared in anthologies both in print and as e-books. A lifelong martial artist and fitness enthusiast, James has studied various arts and is currently ranked as a 4th Dan Blackbelt in Jujitsu and Kempo Karate. He is a frequent visitor to the USA, being particularly fond of all things Floridian and Caribbean. James lives with his wife, Wendy, in the beautiful but rugged north of England. Blood and Silver is his fourth novel in the Gunn Brothers Thriller series.

www.ingramcontent.com/pod-product-compliance
Lightning Source LLC
LaVergne TN
LVHW091610070526
838199LV00044B/751